Centaurus Changeling—How could humans ever make Theta Centaurus IV their home, when the very act of creation was a death sentence for mother and child alike?

The Climbing Wave—Generations after their ancestors had fled to distant stars, they returned to Earth to find a world and people beyond their wildest dreams.

Bird of Prey—In the Dry Towns waited humanity's greatest danger and future destiny, a madman's key to the universe which only the mind of a child might hope to master. . . .

The Wind People—Abandoned on a world devoid of all human life, would they fall prey to their own imaginings . . . and the ever-present calling of the wind?

These are just a few of the action-packed planetfalls you will make as you rocket your way through far-flung starfields charted for you by that most daring of science fiction explorers—Marion Zimmer Bradley!

THE BEST OF
MARION ZIMMER BRADLEY

Marion Zimmer Bradley Titles
Available from DAW BOOKS:

THE DARKOVER SAGA

THE BEST OF MARION ZIMMER BRADLEY

EDITED BY
MARTIN H. GREENBERG

DAW BOOKS, INC.
DONALD A. WOLLHEIM, PUBLISHER

Contents

Introduction

I've told the story before; how, on a train journey from Watertown, New York, back to my family home in Rensselaer County, I changed trains in Utica, and, almost for the first time in my life, bought myself a box of chocolates and a magazine of my own free choice. It was literally the first time in my life that I had been in a newsstand with money from my summer job in my pocket; and I happened to have memory of reading a couple of issues of *Weird Tales* which I'd found in our attic before my mother, troubled by the lurid covers and the fear I'd have nightmares, took them away from me. I had intended to buy myself a copy of *Weird Tales*; but they didn't seem to have that magazine, so I looked around and bought myself a copy of *Startling Stories* containing the Kuttner novel THE DARK WORLD, which I later knew to have been written by Catherine Moore Kuttner instead.

Looking back over a long, not uneventful life, I can honestly say that no experience in my life has ever given me the same excited delight as riding through the twilight, reading Kuttner's wonderful mythic novel of a man who changed worlds. Perhaps it could compare only with the fascination of my first LSD trip, or the time I first walked through the British Museum of which I had read so much, or my first *Turandot* at Lincoln Center, or standing high atop the shrine at Delphi and looking down at the old Sacred Way. To this day, I can remember the shock of delight reading Tennyson's poem Tithonus where I discovered the quote which must have been used for the title:

"A soft wind blows the mists away: I feel
  A breath from that dark world where I was born."

When I finished the Kuttner novel, I read a couple of the short stories—I remember Jack Vance's "Planet of the Black Dust"—and then turned to the "fan letter columns" in the back. Shock of thrills: there were other people who loved this kind of story and were willing to talk about them—and even published fanzines to write about them.

By the time my journey was finished, I knew not only that I wanted to be a writer but that I wanted to write science fiction. Later that summer I typed a first draft of the novel I had written the year before, which ten years later was to see print under the name THE SWORD OF ALDONES, and submitted it to *Startling Stories*: it was kindly rejected by Sam Merwin, the editor at that time. Later, Leo Margulies, the editor of *Startling* and its sister magazine *Thrilling Wonder*, bought several of my short stories. At that time I also began writing to magazines and to fanzines, and that fall I started fan activity. After a desperately lonely childhood as a bookworm among kids interested only in throwing various shapes and sizes of balls, or dressing up in short skirts and jumping around yelling "Yay, yay, yay" *about* the ball-throwers (an activity which is still, I consider, the only activity sillier than throwing the balls themselves), I discovered congenial people, who would and could talk to me as if I were a person, not a little girl.

Three years later, still an active fan, I married (it was, and in some areas still is the only way for a young woman to get away from a bad home situation) and during fourteen years in Texas in small and smaller towns, following the fortunes of the Atchison, Topeka and Santa Fe Railroad for which my first husband worked as an Agent-telegrapher, I substituted fan activity for the football-and-church centered life of Texas. To this day the mail is the high point of the day, and an empty mailbox will make me sulk or fall into a depression. I published fanzines, wrote voluminously for them, wrote reams of letters (I still do), and tried to write for the pulp magazines I still passionately loved. (I couldn't afford to buy books, and it never would have occurred to me—then—to try writing them. That came later, with my first novel, SEVEN FROM THE STARS. "Falcons of Narabedla," and "Bird of Prey," which later became novels, were novelette length Kuttner pastiches; not because I was deliberately imitating but because I wanted to write stories like the ones I read in the magazines.

Nevertheless my first long published novelette was not a pastiche, but my first really original work; in this day of embryo transfers and test tube babies it seems almost prophetic. "Centaurus Changeling" reflected my love of reading medical books. "The Wind People" was, I think, a dream I had in Texas. Most of those early Texas stories were reflecting a drab daily life cooking and washing diapers and cleaning our small rented houses; and an extremely lively interior life based on the books I read and the people I knew only through fanzines. Big events in my life were a sandwich at the local hamburger cafe (a night out); there was nothing else to do except go to church or listen to football games, and I have kept a perfect record: I have never yet attended a football game. I was, on the other hand, a vigorous listener to the Metropolitan Opera radio broadcasts, and my first use of money, when I began having it, was to buy season tickets to the San Francisco Opera; my biggest indulgence now is for telecast video tapes and laser disc performances of real operas.

Well, a day came when I sold my first long novelette: "Bird of Prey," later to be DOOR THROUGH SPACE, a novel about the Dry Towns which would surface later in the Darkover novels. Then I began writing about Darkover. About the time I was beginning to write science fiction again after a long hiatus writing pseudonymous novels for a trashy publisher called Monarch Books, I left Texas and my first husband.

I have nothing bad to say about my first marriage: the enforced loneliness threw me on my own resources and gave me leisure to write. Brad thought I spent too much money on paper and postage, but if I was willing, as he put it, to have these things instead of fashionable clothes and possessions, it was OK with him; he was not ambitious. Also, if I was willing to live modestly on his salary instead of getting a job (I preferred not to raise our son in the care of someone whose market worth was even less than mine—i.e., leave him in the care of an uneducated woman who would otherwise be doing unskilled labor) he allowed me to do so. Eventually, the Monarch romances paid my tuition to a local small college—ostensibly so I could get a teaching certificate and support the family after Brad retired from the railroad. Instead I left Texas, moved to Berkeley, and married again; had two younger children by my second marriage, and once again discovered that writing was a way to stay home with my kids while working. This is why I have never believed the story that domesticity damages a woman's intellectual life; while the kids were small I wrote a few books every year.

Not easily. I remember training the kids that Mommy was never to be interrupted at the typewriter, and I bribed them shamelessly for letting me alone—they call it positive reinforcement, now.

But I had to learn to be sociable. I remember being afraid that with intellectual stimulation, libraries, music, free concerts and a loving husband who wished for my company instead of using me as a housekeeper, cook, laundress, I would lose the impulse to write. I still prefer to keep people at arm's length so that I can find the best company in the world; the characters who come out of my brain and mind.

Becoming an editor—when I had money enough, I published a fiction fanzine—helped me at long last to write more than the occasional short story. I never felt much at ease writing short stories: my "natural" feeling is to write novels, the longer the better. I learned painfully during the "Monarch years" to write novels to severe plot and deadline requirements, to cut my work to the bone: but only when I was freed of these length requirements by Don Wollheim's willingness to experiment with *long* novels like THE HERITAGE OF HASTUR (1975) did I really begin to write naturally.

Over a forty year writing career I have written forty odd novels (some of them, as I like to say, very odd indeed) and considerably fewer short stories, the great majority of them being impulses—I would wake up with an idea, juggle the plot a bit, and sit down and write it on a sustained impulse, not stopping till I finished it. Since I usually write novels "on contract," the short stories were seldom profitable. I write a short story only if I can't figure out a way to make the idea into a novel, or want to write a little known episode in the life of a character from one of my novels. "To Keep the Oath" is such a story; I was curious as to how Camilla met Kindra. Both characters were in THE SHATTERED CHAIN (1976).

I don't imitate Kuttner any more, or even Leigh Brackett. My current enthusiasms, besides opera, are Gay Rights and Women's Rights—I think Women's Liberation is the great event of the twentieth century, not Space Exploration. One is a great change in human consciousness; the latter is only predictable technology and I am bored by technology.

I write on a word processor, but prefer my typewriter. And I am still a fan at heart—because I am still looking for any reading matter which will arouse in me the old thrill of those early pulp magazines. FOR BETTER OR WORSE, A WRITER IS WHAT I AM, and I no longer bother to explain or excuse it. I prefer science fiction to any other reading or writing— and to people who ask why I don't read mainstream (or write it), I say I cannot imagine that the content of the mainstream—spy novels, corruption in the streets, adultery in the suburbs—can possibly compete with a fiction whose sole *raison d'etre* is to think about the future of the human race.

Centaurus Changeling

". . . the only exception to the aforesaid policy was made in the case of Megaera (Theta Centaurus IV) which was given full Dominion status as an independent planetary government; a departure almost without precedent in the history of the Terran Empire. There are many explanations for this variation from the usual practice, the most generally accepted being that which states that Megaera had been colonized from Terra only a few years before the outbreak of the Rigel-Procyon war, which knocked out communications in the entire Centaurus sector of the Galaxy and forced the abandonment of all the so-called Darkovan League colonies, including Megaera, Darkover, Samarra and Vialles. During these Lost Years, as they were called, a period embracing, in all, nearly 600 years . . . the factors of natural selection, and the phenomenon of genetic drift and survival mutation observed among isolated populations, permitted these 'lost' colonies to develop along scientific and social lines which made their reclamation by the Terran Empire an imperative political necessity. . . ."

From J. T. Bannerton: *A Comprehensive History of Galactic Politics*, Tape IX.

The Official Residence of the Terran Legate on Megaera was not equipped with a roofpost for landing the small, helicopter-like carioles. This oversight, a gesture of bureaucratic economy from the desk of some supervisor back on Terra, meant that whenever the Legate or his wife left the Residence, they must climb down four flights of stairs to the level of the rarely used streets, and climb again, up the endless twisting stairs, to the platform of the public skyport a quarter of a mile away.

Matt Ferguson swore irritably as his ankle turned in a rut—since no Centaurian citizen ever used the streets for walking if he could help it, they were not kept in condition for that purpose—and took his wife's arm, carefully guiding her steps on the uneven paving.

"Be careful, Beth," he warned. "You could break your neck without half trying!"

"And all those stairs!" The girl looked sulkily up at the black shadow of the skyport platform, stretched over them like a dark wing. The street lay deserted in the lurid light of early evening; red Centaurus, a hovering disk at the horizon, sent a slanting light, violently crimson, down into the black canyon of the street, and the top-heavy houses leaned down, somber and ominous. Wavering shadows gloomed down over them, and a hot wind blew down the length of the street, bearing that peculiar, pungent, all-pervasive smell which is Megaera's atmosphere. A curious blend, not altogether unpleasant, a resinous and musky smell which was a little sickish, like perfume worn too long. Beth Ferguson supposed that sooner or later she would get used to Megaera's air, that combination of stinks and chemical emanations. It was harmless, her husband assured her, to human chemistry. But it did not grow less noticeable with time; after more than a year, Terran Standard time, on Megaera, it was still freshly pungent to her nostrils. Beth wrinkled up her pretty, sullen mouth. "Do we have to go to this dinner, Matt?" she asked plaintively.

The man put his foot on the first step. "Of course, Beth. Don't be childish," he remonstrated gently, "I told you, before we came to Megaera, that my success at this post would depend mostly on my informal relations—"

"If you call a dinner at the Jeth-sans informal—" Beth began petulantly, but Matt went on, "—my informal relations with the Centaurian members of the government. Every diplomatic post in the Darkovan League is just the same, dear. Rai Jeth-san has gone out of his way to make things easy for both of us." He paused, and they climbed in silence for a few steps. "I know you don't like living here. But if I can do what I was sent here to do, we can have any diplomatic post in the Galaxy. I've got to sell the Centaurian Archons on the idea of building the big space station here. And, so far, I'm succeeding at a job no other man would take."

"I can't see why you took it," Beth sulked, snatching pettishly at her nylene scarf, which was flapping like an unruly bird in the hot, grit-laden wind.

Matt turned and tucked it into place. "Because it was better than working as the assistant to the assistant to the undersecretary of Terran affairs attached to the Proconsul of Vialles. Cheer up, Beth. If this space station gets built, I'll have a Proconsulship myself."

"And if it doesn't?"

Matt grinned. "It will. We're doing fine. Most Legates need years to find their way around a difficult post like Megaera." The grin melted abruptly. "Rai Jeth-san is responsible for that, too. I don't want to offend him."

Beth said, and her voice was not very steady, "I understand all that, Matt. But I've been feeling—ah, I hate to be always whining and complaining like this—"

They had reached the wide, flat platform of the skyport. Matt lighted the flare which would attract a cariole, and sank down on one of the benches. "You haven't whined," he told her tenderly. "I know this rotten planet is no place for a Terran girl." He slipped an arm around his wife's waist. "It's hard on you, with other Terran women half a continent away, and I know you haven't made many friends among the Centaurians. But Rai Jeth-san's wives have been very

17

kind to you. Nethle presented you to her Harp Circle—I don't suppose any Terran woman for a thousand years has even seen one, let alone been presented—and even Cassiana—"

"Cassiana!" said Beth with a catch of breath, picking at her bracelet. "Yes, Nethle's almost too sweet, but she's in seclusion, and until her baby is born, I won't see her. And Wilidh's just a child! But Cassiana—I can't *stand* her! That—that *freak*! I'm afraid of her!"

Her husband scowled. "And don't think she doesn't know it! She's telepathic, and a rhu'ad—"

"Whatever *that* is," Beth said crossly. "Some sort of mutant—"

"Still, she's been kind to you. If you were friends—"

"Ugh!" Beth shuddered. "I'd sooner be friends with—with a Sirian lizard-woman!"

Matt's arm dropped. He said coldly, "Well, please be polite to her, at least. Courtesy to the Archon includes all his wives—but particularly Cassiana." He rose from the bench. "Here comes our cariole."

The little skycab swooped down to the skyport. Matt helped Beth inside and gave the pilot the address of the Archonate. The cariole shot skyward again, wheeling toward the distant suburb where the Archon lived. Matt sat stiffly on the seat, not looking at his young wife. She leaned against the padding, her fair face sulky and rebellious. She looked ready to cry. "At least, in another month, by their own stupid customs, I'll have a good excuse to stay away from all these idiotic affairs!" she flung at him. "I'll be in seclusion by then!"

It hadn't been the way she'd wanted to tell him, but it served him right!

"Beth!" Matt started upright, not believing.

"Yes, I *am* going to have a baby! And I'm going into seclusion just like these silly women here, and not have to go to a single formal dinner, or Spice Hunt, or Harp Circle, for six cycles! So there!"

Matt Ferguson leaned across the seat. His fingers bit

hard into her arm and his voice sounded hoarse. "Elizabeth! Look at me—" he commanded. "Didn't you *promise*—haven't you been taking your anti shots?"

"N-no," Beth faltered, "I wanted to—oh, Matt, I'm alone so much, and we've been married now almost four years—"

"Oh, my God," said Matt slowly, and let go her arm. "Oh, my God!" he repeated, and sank back, the color draining from his face.

"Will you stop saying that!" Beth raged. "When I tell you a thing like—" her voice caught on the edge of a sob, and she buried her face in her scarf.

Matt's hand was rough as he jerked her head up, and the gray pallor around his mouth terrified the girl. "You damn little fool," he shouted, then swallowed hard and lowered his voice. "I guess it's my fault," he muttered. "I didn't want to scare you—you promised to take the shots, so I trusted you—like an idiot!" He released her. "It's classified top-secret, Beth, but it's why this place is closed to colonization, and it's why Terran men don't bring their wives here. This damned, stinking, freak atmosphere! It's perfectly harmless to men, and to most women. But for some reason, it plays hell with the female hormones if a woman gets pregnant. For 60 years—since Terra set up the Legation here—not one Terran baby has been born alive. Not *one*, Beth. And eight out of ten women who get pregnant—oh, God, Betty, I trusted you!"

She whispered "But this—this was a Terran colony, once—"

"They've adapted—maybe. We've never found out why Centaurian women go into seclusion when they're pregnant, or why they hide the children so carefully."

He paused, looking down at the thinning jungle of roofs. There would not be time to explain it all to Beth. Even if she lived—but Matt did not want to think about that. They never *sent* married men to this planet, but Centaurian custom could not admit a single man to be mature enough to hold a place in government. He had succeeded at this post where single men, twice his age, had been laughed at by the Archons. But what good was that now?

"Oh, God, Beth," he whispered, and his arms went out blindly to hold her close. "I don't know what to do—"

She sobbed softly, scared, against him. "Oh, Matt, I'm afraid! Can't we go home—home to Terra? I want—I want to go home—to go home—"

"How can we?" the man asked drearily. "There won't be a star-ship leaving the planet for three months. By that time, you wouldn't be able to live through blastoff. Even now, you couldn't pass a physical for space." He was silent for minutes, his arms strained around her, and his eyes looked haunted. Then, almost visibly, he managed to pull himself together.

"Look, the first thing tomorrow, I'll take you to the Medical HQ. They've been working on it. Maybe—don't worry, darling. We'll get along." His voice lapsed again, and Beth, wanting desperately to believe him, could find no reassurance in the words. "You're going to be all right," he told her again. "Aren't you?" But she clung to him and did not answer. After a long, strained silence, he roused a little, and let her go, glancing from the windbreak of the cariole cabin.

"Beth, darling, fix your face—" he urged her gently. "We'll be late, and you can't go down looking like that—"

For a minute Beth sat still, simply not believing that after what she had told him, he would still make her go to the detested dinner. Then, looking at his tense face, she suddenly knew it was the one thing on earth—no, she corrected herself with grim humor, the one thing on Theta Centaurus IV, Megaera, that she *must* do.

"Tell him not to land for a minute," she said shakily. She unfastened her wrist compact, and silently began to repair the wreckage of her cosmetics. Above the Archonate, the cariole maneuvered frantically for place with another careening skycab, and after what seemed an imminent clash of tangled gyroscopes, slid on to the skyport only seconds before it. Beth shrieked, and Matt flung the door open and abused the pilot in choice Centaurian.

"I compliment you on your perfect command of our language," murmured a soft creamy voice, and Matt flushed darkly as he saw the Archon standing at the very foot of the roofport. He murmured confused apology; it was hardly the way to begin a formal evening. The Archon lipped a buttery smile. "I pray you do not think of it. I disregard speech of yours. It is again not spoken." With an air of esthetic unconcern, he gestured welcome at Beth, and she stepped down, feeling clumsy and awkward. "I stand where you expect me not, only because I think Senior Wife mine in cariole this one," the Archon continued. Out of courtesy to his guests, he was speaking a mangled dialect of Galactic Standard; Beth wished irritably that he would talk Centaurian. She understood it as well as Matt did. She also had the uncomfortable feeling that the Archon sensed her irritation and that it amused him; a sizable fraction of the Megaeran population was slightly telepathic.

"You must excusing Cassiana," the Archon offered languidly as he conducted his guests across the great open skycourt which was the main room of a Centaurian home. "She went to the City, one of our families visiting, for she is rhu'ad, and must be ever at their call when she is needed. And Second Wife is most fortunately in seclusion, so you must excusing her also," he continued as they approached the lighted penthouse. Beth murmured the expected compliments on Nethle's coming child. "Youngest wife then be our hostess, and since she not used to formal custom, we be like barbarian this night."

Matt gave his wife a vicious nudge in the ribs. "Cut that out," he whispered, savagely, and with an effort that turned her face crimson, Beth managed to suppress her rising giggles. Of course there was nothing even faintly informal in the arrangement of the penthouse room into which they were conducted, nor in the classic and affected poses of the other guests. The women in their stiff metallic robes cast polite, aloof glances at Beth's soft drapery, and their greetings were chilly, musical murmurs. Under their slitted, hostile eyes, Beth felt despairingly that she and Matt were intruders here, barbaric atavisms; too big and muscular, too burned by yellow sun, blatantly and vulgarly colorful. The Centaurians were little and fragile, not one over five feet tall, bleached white by the red-violet sun, their foamy, blue-black hair a curious metallic halo above stiff classicized robes. Humans? Yes—but their evolution had turned off at right angles a thousand years ago. What had those centuries done to Megaera and its people?

Swathed in a symbolic costume, Rai Jeth-san's youngest wife Wilidh sat stiffly in the great Hostess Chair. She spoke to the guests formally, but her mouth quirked up at Beth in the beginnings of a giggle. "Oh, my good little friend," she whispered in Galactic Standard, "I *die* with these formals! These are Cassiana's friends, and not mine, for no one knew she would not be here tonight! And they laugh at me, and stick up their backs, all stiff, like this—" she made a rude gesture, and her topaz eyes glinted with mischief. "Sit here by me, Beth, and talk of something very dull and stupid, for I *die* trying not to disgrace me by laughing! When Cassiana comes back—"

Wilidh's mirth was infectious. Beth took the indicated seat, and they talked in whispers, holding hands after the fashion of Centaurian women. Wilidh was too young to have adopted the general hostility toward the Terran woman; in many ways, she reminded Beth of an eager school girl. It was hard to remember that this merry child had been married as long as Beth herself; still more incredible that she was already the mother of three children.

Suddenly Wilidh turned color, and stood up, stammering confused apologies. "Forgive me, forgive me, Cassiana—"

Beth also rose, but the Archon's Senior Wife gestured for them to resume their seats. Cassiana was not dressed for formal dining. Her gray street wrap was still folded over a plain dress of dark thin stuff, and her face looked naked without cosmetics, and very tired. "Never mind, Wilidh. Remain hostess for me, if you will." She smiled flittingly at Beth. "I am sorry I am not here to greet you." Acknowledging their replies with a weary politeness, Cassiana moved past them like a wraith, and they saw her walking across the skycourt, and disappearing down the wide stairway that led to the lower, private parts of the house.

She did not rejoin them until the formal dinner had been served, eaten and removed, and the soft-footed servants were padding around the room with bowls and baskets of exotic fruit and delicacies and gilded cups of frosty mountain nectar. The penthouse shutters had been thrown wide, so that the guests could watch the flickering play of lightning from the giant magnetic storms which were almost a nightly occurrence on Megaera. They were weirdly beautiful and the Centaurians never tired of watching them, but they terrified Beth. She preferred the rare calm nights when Megaera's two immense moons filled the sky with uncanny green moonlight; but now thick clouds hid the faces of Alecto and Tisiphone, and the jagged bolts leaped and cast lurid shadows on the great massy clouds. Through the thunder, the eerie noise which passed, on Megaera, for music, was wailing from the slitted walls. In its shadow, Cassiana ghosted into the room and sat down between Beth and Wilidh. She did not speak for minutes, listening with evident enjoyment to the music and its counterpoint of thunder. Cassiana was somewhat older than Beth, small and exquisite, a filigree dainty woman fashioned of gilded silver. Her ash blonde hair had metallic lights, and her skin and eyes had almost the same hue, a gold-cream, smudged with gilt freckles, and with a sort of luminous, pearly glow . . . the distinguishing mark of a curious mutation called rhu'ad. The word itself meant only *pearl;* neither Beth nor any other Terran knew what it implied.

The servants were passing around tiny baskets, curiously woven of reeds from the Sea of Storms. Deferentially, they laid a basket before the three women. "Oh, *sharigs!*" Wilidh cried with a childish gusto. Beth glanced into the basket at the wriggling mass of small, greenish-gold octopods, less than three inches long, writhing and struggling in their nest of odorous seaweed and striking feebly at each other with the stumps of claws they did not know had been snapped off. The sight disgusted Beth, but Wilidh took a pair of tiny tongs and picked up one of the revolting little creatures, and as Beth watched with fascinated horror, thrust it whole into her mouth. Daintily, but with relish, her sharp small teeth crunched the shell; she sucked, and fastidiously spat the empty shell into her palm.

"Try one, Bet'," Cassiana suggested kindly. "They are really delicious."

"N-no, thank you," Beth said weakly—and suddenly disgraced herself and all her conditioning by turning aside and being very completely and excruciatingly sick on the shimmering floor. She barely heard Cassiana's cry of distress, although she was conscious of a prim offended murmur, and knew she had outraged custom beyond all credibility. Through helpless spasms of retching, she was conscious of hands and voices. Then she was picked up in strong familiar arms, and heard Matt's worried "Honey, are you all right?"

She knew she was being carried across the skycourt and into a lower room, and opened her eyes sickly to see Cassiana and Matt standing over her. "I'm—I'm so sorry—" she whispered. Cassiana's thin hand patted hers, comfortingly. "Do not think of it," she reassured, "Legate Furr-ga-soon, your wife will be well enough, you may return to the other guests," she said, gently, but in a tone that unmistakably dismissed him. There was no polite way to protest. Matt went, looking back doubtfully. Cassiana's strange eyes looked rather pitying. "Don't try to talk," she admonished.

Beth felt too sick and weak to move and being alone with Cassiana terrified her. She lay quiet on the big divan, tears slipping weakly down her face. Cassiana's hand still clasped hers; in a kind of childish petulance, Beth pulled her hand away, but the slender fingers only closed more tightly around Beth's wrist. "Be still," said Cassiana, not unkindly, but in a tone of absolute command, and she sat there, looking down at Beth with a staring intensity, for some minutes. Finally she sighed and freed Beth's hand.

"Do you feel better now?"

"Why—yes!" said Beth, surprised. Quite suddenly, the nausea and the pain in her head were altogether gone. Cassiana smiled. "I am glad. No—lie quiet. Bet', I think you should not ride in cariole tonight, why not stay here? You can visit Nethle—she has missed you since she went into seclusion."

Beth almost cried out with surprise. This *was* rare—for an outsider to be invited into a Centaurian house any further than the skycourt and penthouse reserved for social affairs. Then, with a stab of frightened memory, she recalled the reason for Nethle's seclusion—and her own fears. Nethle was her friend, even Cassiana had shown her kindness. Perhaps in a less formal atmosphere she might be able to ask something about the curious taboo which surrounded the birth of children on Megaera, perhaps learn some way of averting her own danger . . . she closed her eyes and leaned against the cushions for a moment. If nothing else, it meant reprieve. For a little while she need not face Matt's gallantly concealed fear, his reproach. . . .

Matt, returning with Cassiana, quickly gave consent. "If that's what you really want, honey," he said gently. As she looked up into his tense face, Beth's impulse suddenly changed. She wanted to cry out "No—don't leave me here, take me home—"a night here in this strange place, alone with Centaurian women who were, however friendly they might be, entirely alien, seemed a thing too fearful to contemplate. She felt inclined to cry. But Cassiana's eyes on her proved rather steadying, and Beth's long conditioning in the ceremonial life necessary on Megaera triumphed over emotions she knew to be irrational.

Her husband bent and kissed her lightly. "I'll send a cariole for you tomorrow," he promised.

The lower portions of a Centaurian home were especially designed for a polygamous society in harmony with itself. They were carefully compartmented, and the only entrance from one to the other was from the great common stairway which led to the roof and skycourt. Roughly a third of the house was sectioned off for the habitation of Rai Jeth-san and his seasonal consort. The remainder was women's quarters, and the Archon himself might not enter them without specific invitation. In effect, Megaera's polygamous society was a rotational monogamy, for although Rai Jeth-san had three wives—the legal maximum was five—he had only one at a time and their alteration was strictly regulated by tradition. The surplus women lived together, always on terms of the most cordial friendship. Cassiana took precedence over the others, by custom, but there was the closest affection among all three—which had surprised Beth at first, especially when she found out that this was by no means rare; the bond between the wives of one man was traditionally the strongest family tie in existence, far stronger than the tie between natural sisters.

Beth had discovered long ago that she was not alone in her awe of Cassiana, who was one of the peculiar patriciate of the planet. Men and women fought for the privilege of serving the rhu'ads; Beth, relaxing into the almost sybaritic luxury of the women's quarters, wondered again—what was Cassiana's strange power over the Centaurians? She knew Cassiana was one of the rare telepaths who were found in the Darkovan planets, but that alone would not have explained it, nor would Cassiana's odd beauty. On Megaera there were perhaps 10,000 women like Cassiana: curiously beautiful, more curiously revered. There were no male rhu'ad. Beth had seen both men and women throw themselves to the ground in a burst of spontaneous emotion as one of the small, pearl-colored women passed, but had never understood, or dared to ask.

Cassiana asked her, "Would you like to see Nethle before you sleep—and our children?"

This was, indeed, a strange relaxation of tradition; Beth knew no Terran had ever seen a Centaurian child. Astonished, she followed Cassiana into a lower room.

It seemed full of children. Beth counted; there were nine, the youngest only a baby in arms, the oldest about ten. They were pale, pretty children, like hot-house flowers reared in secret. Seeing the stranger, they clustered together, whispering to each other timidly, staring with wide eyes at her strange hair and curious garments.

"Come here, my darlings," said Cassiana in her soft pleasant voice. "Don't stare." She was speaking in Centaurian, a further gesture of friendliness.

One little boy—the rest of the children were all girls—piped up valiantly, "Is she another mother for us?"

Cassiana laughed. "No, my son. Aren't three mothers enough?"

Nethle rose from a cushiony chair and came to Beth, her hands outstretched in welcome. "I thought you had forgotten me! Of course, you poor Terran women, only one wife to look after a husband, I cannot see how you ever have time for *anything!*"

Beth blushed—Nethle's outspoken references to Beth's "unhappy" state as a solitary wife, always embarrassed her. But she returned Nethle's greeting with genuine pleasure—Nethle Jeth-san was perhaps the only Centaurian whom Beth could tolerate without that sense of uneasy dislike.

She said, "I've missed you, Nethle," but secretly she was dismayed at the change in her friend. Since Nethle had gone into seclusion, months ago, she had changed frighteningly. In spite of the distortion of pregnancy, Nethle seemed to have lost weight, her small face looked haggard, and her skin was a ghastly color. She walked shakily, and sat down almost at once after greeting Beth, but her gay manner and brilliant joyous eyes belied her illness. She and Beth talked quietly, about inconsequential things—Centaurian custom almost outlawed serious conversation—while Cassiana curled up, kittenlike, in a nest of soft pillows, picking up the littlest baby.

Two toddlers came and tried to crawl up on her knees at once, so Cassiana laughed and slid down on the floor, letting the children climb all over her, snuggle against her shoulder, tug at her garments and her elaborately arranged hair. She was so tiny that she looked like a little girl with a lapful of dolls. Beth asked her—hesitantly, for she did not know if it was polite to ask—"Which are your children, Cassiana?"

Cassiana glanced up. "In a way, all, and in another way, none," she said curtly and Beth thought she had trespassed on courtesy; but Nethle put her hand on the solitary boy's head. "Cassiana has no children, Beth. She is rhu'ad, and rhu'ad women do not bear children. This is my son, and the oldest girl, and the girl with long hair. Those," she indicated the twin toddlers and the baby in Cassiana's lap, "are Wilidh's. The rest are Clotine's. Clotine was our sister, who died many cycles ago."

Cassiana gently put the children aside and came to Beth. She looked at one of the little girls playing in the corner. She made no sound, but the child turned and suddenly ran to Cassiana, flinging her arms around the rhu'ad. Cassiana hugged her, then let her go, and—to Beth's surprise—the tiny girl came and tugged at Beth's skirt, clambering into her lap. Beth put an arm around her, looking down in astonishment.

"Why, she—" she broke off, not knowing, again, whether she should remark on the extraordinary likeness. The tiny girl—she seemed about four—had the same, pearly, lustrous skin; her hair was a silvery eiderdown, pallid and patrician. Cassiana noted her discomfiture and laughed gaily. "Yes, Arli is rhu'ad. She is mine."

"I thought—"

"Oh, Cassiana, stop it," Nethle protested, laughing. "She doesn't understand!"

"There are many things she does not understand," said Cassiana abruptly, "but I think she will have to learn to understand them. Bet', you have done a terribly unwise thing. Terran women *cannot* have children here in safety!"

Beth could only blink in amazement. The self test taken the day before had shown her pregnancy to be less than a month advanced. "How *ever* did you know?" she asked.

"Your poor husband," Cassiana's voice was gentle. "I felt his fear like a gray murk, all evening. It is not pleasant to be telepath, sometimes. It is why I try not to go in crowds, I cannot help invading the privacy of others. Then, when you were so sick, I knew."

Nethle seemed to freeze, to go rigid. Her arms fell to her sides. "So that is it!" she whispered almost inaudibly. Then she burst out, "And that is the way with the women of Terra! That is why your Earthmen will never take this planet! As long as they despise us and come as conquerors, they cannot come here where their women—die!" Her eyes glared. She rose and stood, heavy, distorted, menacing, over Beth, her lips drawn back in an animal snarl, her arm raised as if to strike. Cassiana gasped, sprang up, and with a surprising strength, she pushed Nethle back into her chair.

"Bet', she is raving—even women here, sometimes—"

"Raving!" Nethle said with a curl of her lip. "Wasn't there a day when our women and their unborn children died by the hundreds because we did not know the air was poison? When women died, or were kept in airtight rooms and given oxygen till their children were born, and then left to die? When men married a dozen wives to be sure of one living child? Did the Terrans help us then, when we begged hem to evacuate the planet? No! They had a war on their hands—

for 600 years they had a war on their hands! Now they've finished their private wars, they try to come back to Megaera—"

"Nethle! Be quiet!" Cassiana commanded angrily. Beth had sunk into the cushions, but through her cupped hands she saw that Nethle's face blazed, a contorted mask of fury. "Yes, yes, Cassiana," her voice was a mocking croon, "Bet' condescends to make friends with me—and now she will see what happens to the women of Terra who mock our customs instead of finding out why we have them!" The wildness of her hysteria beat and battered at Beth. "Oh, yes, I liked you," she snarled, "but could you really be friends with a Centaurian woman? Don't you think I know you mock our rhu'ad? Could you live equal to us? Get out!" she shouted. "Get off our world! Go away, all of you! Leave us in peace!"

"Nethle!" Cassiana grasped the woman's shoulders and shook her, hard, until the wildness went out of her face. Then she pushed Nethle down in the cushions, where she lay sobbing. Cassiana looked down at her sorrowfully. "You hate worse than she hates. How can there ever be peace, then?"

"You have always defended her," Nethle muttered, "and she hates you worst of all!"

"That is exactly why I have more responsibility," Cassiana answered. She went to the curtained door at the end of the room. At her summons, a servant came and began unobtrusively to shepherd the children out of the room. They went obediently, the older ones looking scared and bewildered, glancing timidly at the weeping Nethle; the little ones reluctant, clinging to Cassiana, pouting a little as she gently pushed them out the door. Cassiana drew the curtain firmly down behind them; then went back to Nethle and touched her on the shoulder. "Listen," she said.

Then Beth had the curious feeling that Nethle and Cassiana were conversing through some direct mental exchange from which she was excluded. Their changing expressions, and faint gestures, told her that, and a few emphatic, spoken words seemed to give point to the soundless conversation—it made Beth's flesh crawl.

"My decisions are always final," Cassiana stated.

Nethle muttered ". . . cruel of you . . ."

Cassiana shook her head.

After long minutes of speech-silence, Cassiana said aloud, quietly, "No, I have decided. I did it for Clotine. I would do it for you—or for Wilidh, if you were fool enough to try what Bet' has done."

Nethle flared back, "I wouldn't *be* fool enough to try to have a baby *that way*—"

Cassiana checked her with a gesture, rose, and went to Beth, who was still lying huddled in the pillows of the big divan. "If I, who am rhu'ad, do not break the laws," she said, "then no one will ever dare to break them, and our planet will stagnate in dead traditions. Bet', if you can promise to obey me, and to ask me no questions, then I, who am rhu'ad, promise you this: you may have your child without fear, and your chance of life will be—" she hesitated, "equal to a Centaurian woman's."

Beth looked up. speechless, her eyes wide. A dozen emotions tangled in some secret part of her mind, fear, distrust—anger. Yet reason told her that Cassiana was showing disinterested kindness in the face of what must certainly have been obvious to her, Beth's own dislike. At the moment Beth was unaware that proximity to the telepath was sharpening her own sense perceptions, but for the first time in months she was thinking reasonably, unblurred by emotion.

Cassiana insisted, "Can you promise? Can you promise, especially, not to ask me questions about what I have to do?"

And Beth nodded soberly. "I'll promise," she said.

The pale pink, watery sunlight looked feeble and anachronistic on the white, sterile, characteristically Terran walls, floors and furnishings of the Medical HQ; and the white indoor face of the old doctor looked like some sun-sheltered slug.

"He's lived here so long, he's half Centaurian himself," Matt Ferguson thought irrelevantly, and threw down the chart in his hand. "You mean there's nothing to be done!" he said bluntly.

"We never say that in my profession," Dr. Bonner told him simply. "While there's life, and all the rest of it. But it looks bad. You never should have left it up to the girl to make sure she took her anti shots. Women aren't reliable about that kind of thing—not normal women. A woman's got to be pretty damned abnormal, to be conscientious about contraceptives." He frowned. "You know, it's not a question of adapting, either. If anything, the third, fourth, fourteenth generations are more susceptible than the first. The planet seems so perfectly healthy that women simply don't believe it until they *do* get pregnant, and then it's too late."

"Abortion?" Matt suggested, lowering his head. Dr. Bonner shrugged. "Worse yet. Operative shock on top of the hormone reaction would just kill her now, instead of later." He leaned his head on his hands. "Whatever it is in the air, it doesn't hurt anybody until we get the flood of female hormones released in pregnancy. We've tried everything—manufacturing our own air—chemically pure, but we can't get that stink out of it, and we can't keep it pure. There's just something linked into the atomic structure of the whole damned planet. It doesn't bother test animals, so we can't do any experimenting. It's just the human, female hormones of pregnancy. We've even tried locking the women in airtight domes, and giving them pure oxygen, the whole nine months. But we get the same reaction. Pernicious vomiting, weight loss, confusion of the balance centers, convulsions—and if the foetus isn't aborted, it's oxygen-starved and a monster. I've lived on Megaera 40 years, Matt, and I haven't delivered a live baby yet."

Matt raged, "Then how do the Centaurians manage? They have children, all right!"

"Have you ever seen one?" asked Dr. Bonner tersely.

At Matt's denial, he continued, "Neither have I—in 40 years. For all I know, Centaurian women cultivate their babies in test tubes. Nobody's ever seen a pregnant Centaurian woman, or a child under about ten years old. But one of our men—ten, twelve years ago—got a Centaurian girl pregnant. Of course, her family threw her out—right in the damn' street. Our man married the girl—he'd wanted to, anyhow. The man—I won't tell you his name—brought her in to me. I thought maybe—but the story was just *exactly* the same. Nausea, pernicious vomiting—all the rest. You wouldn't believe the things we tried to save that girl. I didn't know I had so much imagination myself." He dropped his eyes, bitter with an old failure. "But she died. The baby lived. It's up in the incurable ward."

"Jesus!" Matt shuddered uncontrollably. "What can I *do?*"

Dr. Bonner's eyes were very sorrowful. "Bring her in, Matt, right away. We'll do our damnedest for her." His hand found the younger man's shoulder as he rose, but Matt was not conscious of the touch. He never knew how he got out of the building, but after a reeling walk through streets that twisted around his bleared eyes, he heard the buzz of a descending cariole, and Cassiana Jeth-san's level voice.

"Legate Furr-ga-soon?"

Matt raised his head numbly. She was about the last person he cared to see. But Matt Ferguson was a Legate of the Terran Empire, and had undergone strenuous conditioning for this post. He could no more have been rude to anyone to whom courtesy was required, than he could have thrown himself from a moving cariole. So he said with careful graciousness, "I greet you, Cassiana."

She signaled the pilot to set the hovering skycab down.

"This meeting is fortunate," she said quietly. "Get into this cariole, and ride with me."

Matt obeyed, mostly because he lacked, at the moment, the ingenuity to form an acceptable excuse. He climbed in; the skycab began to ascend again over the city. It seemed a long time before Cassiana said, "Bet' is at the Archonate. I have made a finding the most unfortunate. Understand me, Legate, you are in situation of the baddest."

"I know," Matt said grimly. His wife's dislike of Cassiana suddenly became reasonable to him. He had never been alone with a telepath before, and it made him a little giddy. There was almost a physical vibration in the small woman's piercing gaze. Cassiana's mangling of Galactic Standard—she spoke it better than her husband, but still abominably—was another irritation which Matt tried to hide. As if in answer to his unspoken thought, Cassiana switched to her own language. "Why did you come to Megaera?"

What a fool question, Matt thought irritably. Why did any man take a diplomatic post? "My government sent me."

"But not because you liked Megaera, or us? Not because you wanted to live here, or cared about Terrans and Centaurians getting along? Not because you cared about the space station?"

Matt paused, honestly surprised. "No," he said, "I suppose not." Then annoyance triumphed. "How *can* we live together? Your people don't travel in space. Ours can't live in health or ordinary comfort on this—this stinking planet! How can we do anything but live apart and leave you to yourselves?"

Cassiana said slowly, "We wanted, once, to abandon this colony. For all Terra cared, we could live or die. Now they have found out their lost property might be worth—"

Matt sighed. "The Imperialists who abandoned Megaera have all been dead for hundreds of years," he pointed out wearily. "Now, we have to have some contact with your planet, because of the political situation. You know that. No one is trying to exploit Megaera."

"I know that," she admitted. "Perhaps 50 other people on the whole planet realize that. The rest are one seething mass of public opinion, and under the anti-propaganda laws, we can't change that." She stopped. "But I didn't want to talk politics. Why did you bring Bet' here, Legate?"

Matt bit his lip. Under her clear eyes he told the truth. "Because I knew a single man couldn't succeed at this post."

Cassiana mused. "It's a pity. It's almost certain that this affair will close out the Legation here. No married man will want to come, and we cannot accept a single man in such an important position. It is against our most respected tradition for a man to remain single after he is mature. Our only objection to your space station is the immense flood of unattached personnel who will come here to build it—drifters, unmarried men, military persons—such an influx would throw Megaera into confusion. We would be glad to accept married colonists who wanted to settle here."

"You *know* that's impossible!" Matt said.

"Maybe," Cassiana said thoughtfully. "It *is* a pity. Because it is obvious that the Terrans need Megaera, and Megaera needs some outside stimulus. We're turning stagnant." She was silent for a minute. Then she continued, "But I'm talking politics again. I suppose I wanted to see if it was in you to be honest. Perhaps, if you had grown angry sooner, been less concerned with polite formalities—angry men are honest men. We like honesty, we rhu'ad."

Matt's smile was bitter. "We are conditioned in courtesy. Honesty comes second."

"A proof that you are not suited to a society where any fraction of the population is telepathic," said Cassiana bluntly. "But that is not important. This is—Bet' is in very real danger, Legate. I promise nothing—even we Centaurians die sometimes—but if you will let her live at the Archonate for three, maybe four of your months—I think I can promise you she'll live. And probably the baby, too."

Hope seethed in Matt. "You mean—go into seclusion—"

"That, and more," said Cassiana gravely. "You must not attempt to see her yourself, and you must keep your entire Legation from knowing where she is, or why. That includes your personal friends and your officials. Can you do this? If not, I promise nothing."

"But that isn't possible—"

Cassiana dismissed the protest. "It is your problem. I am not a Terran, I don't know how you will manage it."

"Does Beth want to—"

"At this moment, no. You are her husband, and it is your child's life at stake. You have authority to order her to do it."

"We don't think of things that way on Terra. I don't—"

"You are not on Terra now," Cassiana reminded him flatly.

"Can I see Beth before I decide? She'll want to make arrangements, pack her things—"

"No, you must decide here, now. It may already be too late. As for her 'things,' " the pearly eyes held delicate scorn, "she must have nothing from Terra near her."

"What kind of rubbish is that?" Matt demanded. "Not even her clothes?"

"I will provide anything she needs," Cassiana assured him. "Believe me, it is necessary. No—don't apologize. Anger is honesty."

"Look," Matt suggested, still trying to compromise acceptably. "I'll want her to see a Terran doctor, first, the authorities—"

Without warning, Cassiana lost her temper.

"You Terrans," she exploded, in a gust of fury that was like a physical blow. "You stupid lackwit from a planet of insane authoritarians, I *told* you, you must say nothing to anyone! This isn't a political matter, it's her *life*, and your child's! What can your so-called *authorities* do?"

"What can *you* do?" Matt shouted back. Protocol

went overboard. The man and woman from two alien star systems glared at each other across a thousand years of evolution.

Then Cassiana said coldly, "That is the first sensible question you have asked. When our planet was—jettisoned as useless—we had to acquire certain techniques the hard way. I can't tell you exactly what. It isn't allowed. If that answer is not adequate, I am sorry. It is the only answer you will ever get. Wars have been fought on Megaera because the rhu'ad have refused to answer that question. We've been hounded and stoned, and sometimes worshiped. Between science and religion and politics, we've finally worked out the answer, but I have never told even my husband. Do you think I would tell a—a bureaucrat from Terra? You can accept my offer or refuse it—now."

Matt looked over the windbreak of the cariole at the wideflung roofs of the city. He felt torn with terrible indecision. Reared in a society of elaborately delegated responsibilities, it went against all his conditioning—how could one man make a decision like this? How could he explain Beth's absence? What would his government say if they discovered that he had not even consulted the medical authorities? Still, the choice was bald—Bonner had made it very clear that he had no hope. It was: trust Cassiana, or watch Beth die.

And the death would be neither quick nor easy.

"All right," he said, pressing his lips together. "Beth—Beth doesn't like you, as you probably know, and I'll be—I'll be everlastingly damned if I know why you are doing this! But I—I can't see any other way out. This isn't a very polite way to put it, but it was you who insisted on honesty. Go ahead. Do what you can. I—" his voice suddenly strangled, but the little rhu'ad did not take the slightest notice of his losing struggle for self-control. With an air of remote detachment, she directed the driver of the cariole to set him down before the Residence.

During the brief ride there, she did not speak a word. Only when the cariole settled on the public skyport did she raise her head. "Remember," she said quietly, "you must not call at the Archonate, or attempt to see Bet'. If you have business with the Archon, you must arrange to meet him elsewhere. That will not be easy."

"Cassiana—what can I say—"

"Say nothing," she advised, not smiling, but there was a glint in the pearly eyes. In a less reserved face, it might have been friendly amusement. "Sometimes men are more honest that way."

She left him staring dumbly upward as the cariole climbed the sky once more.

When Cassiana—no longer friendly, but reserved and rigid—had brought the news that Matt had commanded her to stay, Beth had disbelieved—had shouted her hysterical disbelief and terror until Cassiana turned and walked out, locking the door behind her. She did not return for three days. Beth saw no one but an old lady who brought her meals and was, or pretended to be, deaf. In that time, Beth lived through a million emotions; but at the end of three days, when Cassiana came back, she looked at Beth with approval.

"I left you alone," she explained briefly, "to see how you reacted to fear and confinement. If you could not endure it, I could have done nothing for you. But I see you are quite calm."

Beth bit her lip, looking down at the smaller woman. "I was angry," she admitted. "I didn't think it was necessary to treat me like a child. But somehow I don't think you would have done it without good reason."

Cassiana's smile was a mere flicker. "Yes. I can read your mind a little—not much. I'm afraid you will be a prisoner again, for some time. Do you mind much? We'll try to make it easy for you."

"I'll do whatever you say," Beth promised calmly, and the rhu'ad nodded. "Now, I think you mean that, Bet'."

"I meant it when I said it before!" Beth protested.

"Your brain, and your reason, said it. But a pregnant woman's reasoning faculties aren't always reliable. I had to be certain that your emotions would back up your reason in the event of a shock. Believe me, you'll get some shocks."

But so far there had been none, although Cassiana had not exaggerated in the slightest when she said Beth would be a prisoner. The Terran woman was confined closely in two rooms on the ground floor—a level rarely used in a Centaurian house—and saw no one but Cassiana, Nethle and a servant or two. The rooms were spacious—even luxurious—and the air was filtered by some process which—while it did not diminish the distinctive smell—was somehow less sickening, and easier to breathe. "This air is just as dangerous, chemically, as that outdoors," Cassiana cautioned her. "Don't think that this, alone, makes you safe. But it may make you a little more comfortable. Don't go outside these rooms."

But she kept her promise to make imprisonment easy for Beth. Nethle, too, had recovered from her hysterical attack, and was punctiliously cordial. Beth had access to Cassiana's library—one of the finest tape collections on the planet—although, from a little judicious searching—Beth decided that Cassiana had removed tapes on some subjects she thought the Terran woman should not study too closely—and when Cassiana learned that Beth knew the rather rare art of three-dimensional painting, she asked her guest to teach her. They made several large figures, working together. Cassiana had a quick, artistic sensitivity which delighted Beth, and she swiftly mastered the complicated technique. The shared effort taught them a good deal about each other.

But there was much inconvenience which Cassiana's kindness could not mitigate. With each advancing day, Beth's discomfort became more acute. There was pain, and sickness, and a terrible feeling of breathlessness— for hours she would lie fighting for every breath. Cassiana told her that her system, in the hormone allergy, had lost the ability, in part, to absorb oxygen from the bloodstream. She broke out in violent rashes which never lasted more than a few hours, but recurred every few days. The ordinary annoyances of early pregnancy were there, too, magnified a hundred times. And during the electric storms, there was a strange reaction, a taut pain as if her body were a conductor for the electricity itself. She wondered if this pain were psychosomatic or genuinely symptomatic, but she never knew.

For some reason, the sickness receded when Cassiana was in the room, and as the days slid past. Cassiana was with her almost constantly, once or twice even sleeping in the same room, on a cot pushed close to Beth's. Unexpectedly, one day, Beth asked her, "Why do I always feel better when you are in the room?"

Cassiana did not answer for a minute. All the morning, they had been working on a three-dimensional painting. The floor was scattered with eyepieces and pigments, and Cassiana picked up an eyepiece and scanned a figure in the foreground before she even turned around to Beth. Then she disengaged her painting cone, and began to refill it with pigment.

"I wondered when you would ask me that. A telepath's mind controls her body, to some extent—that's a very rough way of putting it, but you don't know enough about psychokinetics to know the difference. Well—when we are working together, as we have been today, your mind is in what we telepaths call vibratory harmony with mine, and you are able to pick up, to a very slight degree, my mental projections. And they, in turn, react on your body."

"You mean you control your body by *thinking*?"

"Everybody does that." Cassiana smiled faintly. "Yes, I know what you mean. I can, for instance, control reflexes which are involuntary in—in normal people. Just as easily as you would flex or relax a muscle in your arm, I can control my heartbeat, blood pressure, uterine contractions—" she stopped abruptly, then finished, "and I can control gross reflexes, such as vomit-

ing, in others—if they come within the kinetic field."
She put down the spinning-cone. "Look at me, and
I'll show you what I mean."

Beth obeyed. After a moment, Cassiana's gilt hair
began to darken. It grew darker, darker, till the shining strands were the color of clear honey. Cassiana's
cheeks seemed to lose their pearly luster, to turn pinker.
Beth blinked and rubbed her eyes. "Are you control-
ling my mind so I think your skin and hair are changing color?" she asked suspiciously.

"You overestimate my powers! No, but I concen-
trated all the latent pigment in my skin into my hair.
We rhu'ad can look almost as we choose, within certain limits—I couldn't, for instance, make my hair as
dark as yours. There simply isn't enough melanin in
my pigment. Even this much color wouldn't last, unless I wanted to alter my adrenalin balance permanently. I could do that, too, but it wouldn't be sensible.
My hair and skin will change back to rhu'ad during the
day—we keep our distinctive coloring, because it's a
protection against being harmed or injured acciden-
tally. We are important to Megaera—" abruptly she
stopped again, and a mask of reticence slid down on
her face. She re-engaged the spinning-cone and began
to weave a surface pattern in the frame.

Beth persisted. "Can you control my body too?"

"A little," said Cassiana shortly. "Why do you think
I spend so much time with you?"

Snubbed, Beth took up her spinning-cone and began to weave depth into Cassiana's surface figure.
After a minute, Cassiana relented and smiled, "Oh,
yes, I enjoy your company too—I did not at first, but I
do now."

Beth laughed, a little shamefacedly. She had begun
to like Cassiana very much—once she had grown accustomed to Cassiana's habit of answering what Beth
was thinking, instead of what she had said.

Weeks slid into months. Beth had now lost all desire
to go out of doors, although she dutifully took what

slight exercise Cassiana required of her. The rhu'ad now remained with her almost continually. Although Beth was far too ill to study Cassiana, it finally became apparent even to her that Cassiana herself was far from well. The change in the rhu'ad was not marked; a tenseness in her movements, a pallor—Beth could not guess the nature of her ailment. But in spite of this, Cassiana watched over Beth with careful kindliness. Had she been Cassiana's own child, Beth thought, the rhu'ad could not have cared for her more solicitously.

Beth did not know that she was so dangerously ill as to shock Cassiana out of her reserve. She could not walk more than a step or two without nausea and a shooting, convulsive pain. The nights were a horror. She knew faintly that they had given her oxygen several times, and even this had left her half asphyxiated. And although it was now past the time when her child should have quickened, she had felt no stir of life.

Half the time she was dizzy, as if drugged. In her rare moments of lucidity, it disturbed her that Cassiana should spend her strength in tending her. But when she tried to voice this, Cassiana returned only a terse, hostile, "You think of yourself and I will take care of myself, and you too."

But once, when Cassiana thought Beth asleep, Beth heard her mutter aloud, "It's too slow! I can't wait much longer—I'm afraid!"

No news from the Terran sector penetrated her seclusion. She missed Matt, and wondered how he had managed to conceal her long absence. But she did not spend much time wondering; life, for her, had been stripped bare of everything except the fight for survival in each successive day. She had slipped so far down into this vegetable existence that she actually shuddered when Cassiana asked her one morning, "Do you feel well enough to go out of doors?" She dressed herself obediently, but roused a little when Cassiana held a heavy bandage toward her. There was compassion in her eyes.

"I must blindfold you. No one may know where the kail' rhu'ad is. It is too holy."

Beth frowned pettishly. She felt horribly ill, and Cassiana's mystical tone filled her with disbelieving disgust. Cassiana saw, and her voice softened.

She said persuasively, "You must do this, Bet'. I promise I will explain everything some day."

"But why blindfold me? Won't you trust me not to tell, if it's secret?"

"I might trust you and I might not," Cassiana returned coldly. "But there are 10,000 rhu'ad on Megaera, and I am doing this on my single responsibility." Then suddenly her hands clenched so tightly on Beth's that the Terran woman almost cried out with pain, and she said harshly, "I can die too, you know! The Terran women who have died here, don't you think anyone ever tried—" her voice trailed off, indistinct, and suddenly she began to cry softly.

It was the first time since Beth had known her that the rhu'ad had betrayed any kind of emotion. Cassiana sobbed, "Don't fight me, Bet', don't! Both our lives may depend on your personal feelings about me in the next few days—I can't reach you when you're hating me! Try not to hate me so much—"

"I don't hate you, Cassiana," Beth breathed, shocked, and she drew the Centaurian girl close and held her, almost protectingly, until the stormy weeping quieted and Cassiana had herself under control again.

The rhu'ad freed herself from Beth's arms, gently, her voice reserved again. "You had better calm yourself," she said briefly, and handed Beth the scarf. "Tie this over your eyes. I'll trust you to do it securely."

Sometimes Beth tried to remember in detail what happened after Cassiana removed the blindfold, and she found herself in a vast, vaulted room of unbelievable beauty. The opalescent dome admitted a filtered, frosty glimmer of pallid light. The walls, washed in some light pigment which both absorbed and reflected colors too vague to be identified, drifted with hazy shadows. Beth was oblivious to the emotional appeal of the place—she was too alien for that—but the place was unmistakably a temple, and Beth began to be afraid. She had heard about some of the extra-terrestrial religions, and she had always suspected that the rhu'ad filled some religious function. But the beauty of the place touched even her, and gradually she became conscious of a low vibration, almost sound, pervading the entire building.

Cassiana whispered, "That's a telepathic damper. It cuts out the external vibrations and allows the augmentation of others."

The vibration had a soothing effect. Beth sat quietly, waiting, and Cassiana was altogether silent, her eyes closed, her lips moving as if she prayed, but Beth realized afterward that she was simply conversing telepathically with some unseen person. Later, she arose and led Beth through a door which she carefully closed and fastened behind them.

This inner chamber was smaller, and was furnished only with a few immense machines—Beth assumed they were machines, for they were enclosed anonymously in metallic casings, and dials and controls and levers projected chastely from a covering of gray paint—and a few small couches, arranged in pairs. Here three rhu'ad were waiting—slight patrician women who ignored Beth entirely and only glanced at Cassiana.

Cassiana told Beth to lie down on one of the couches, and, leaving her there, went to the other rhu'ad. They stood, their hands laced together, for minutes. Beth, by now habituated to Cassiana's moods, could guess that her friend was disturbed, even defiant. The others seemed equally disturbed; they shook their heads and made gestures that looked angry, but finally Cassiana's fair face looked triumphant and she came back to Beth.

"They are going to let me do what I planned. No, lie still—" she instructed, and to Beth's surprise, Cassiana lay down on the other couch of the pair. This one was located immediately beneath one of the big machines; the control panel was located in such a way that Cassiana could reach up and manipulate the dials and levers. This she proceeded to do, assuring herself that all were within easy reach; then reached across and touched Beth's pulse lightly. She frowned.

"Too fast—you're excited, or frightened. Here, hold my hand for a minute." Obediently Beth closed her hand around the one Cassiana extended. She forced back her questions, but Cassiana seemed to sense them. "Sssh. Don't talk, Bet'. Here, where the vibrations are dampered, I can control your involuntary reactions too." And, after a few minutes, the Terran woman actually felt her heartbeat slowing to normal, and knew that her breathing was quiet and nataral again.

Cassiana took her hand away, reached upward, and began to adjust a dial, her delicate fingers feeling for a careful calibration. "Just lie quietly," she warned Beth, but Beth felt not the slightest desire to move. Warmth and well-being held her lapped in comfort. It was not a perceptible thing, but an intangible vibration, almost but not quite sensible to her nerves. For the first time in months, she was wholly free of discomfort.

Cassiana was fussing with the dials, touching one control, discarding another, playing the vibration now upward until it was almost visible, no downward until it disappeared into sound. Beth began to feel a little dizzy. Her senses seemed augmented, she was so wholly conscious of every nerve and muscle in her body that she could *feel* Cassiana's presence, a few feet away, through the nerves of her skin. The particular sensation identified Cassiana as completely as her voice. Beth even felt it—an odd little coldness—when one of the other rhu'ad approached the couch . . . and when she moved away again.

I suppose, she thought, this is what it feels like to be telepathic. And Cassiana's thoughts seemed to penetrate her brain like so many tiny needles: *Yes, almost like that. Actually, it's just the electrical vibration of your body being put into phase with mine. That's a kind of short-term telepathy. Each individual has his own per-*

sonal wave-length. We're tuned in to each other now. We used to have to do this telepathically, and it was a horrible ordeal. Now we use the dampers, and it's easy.

Beth seemed to float somewhere, weightless, above her body. A rhu'ad had walked through the edge of the vibratory field; Beth felt the shock of their out-of-phase bodies, as a painful electric jolt which gradually lessened as they adjusted into the vibration. Then she smelled a sharp-sweet smell, and with her augmented consciousness knew it was a smell of anesthetic—*what were they going to do?* In a spasm of panic she began to struggle; felt steady hands quieting her, heard strange voices—

Her body exploded in a million fragments of light.

The room, the machines and the rhu'ad were gone. Beth was lying on a low, wide shelf, built into the wall of a barren cubicle. She felt sick and breathless, and tried to sit up, but pain shot through her body and she lay still, blinking back tears of agony. She lay gasping, feeling the weight of her child holding her like a vise of iron.

As details came back to her clearing sight, she made out a second shelf across the room. What she had at first taken for a heap of padding was the body of a woman—it was Cassiana—sprawled face downward in an attitude of complete exhaustion. As Beth looked, the rhu'ad turned over and opened her eyes; they looked immense and bloodshot in the whiteness of her face. She whispered hoarsely, "How—do you—feel?"

"A little sick—"

"So do I." Cassiana struggled upright, got to her feet, and walked, with heavy deliberation, toward Beth. As she approached, Beth felt a sort of echo of the soothing vibration, and the pain slackened somewhat. Cassiana sat down on the edge of the shelf, and said quietly, "We are not out of danger. There is still to be—" she paused, seeking a word, and finally used the Galactic standard term, "still to be *allergic reaction*. We have to stay close together—in same kinetic field— days till the reaction is desensitized, and our body develop tolerance to the grafted—" she stopped and said sharply in Centaurian, "I have told you you must not ask me questions! You want your baby to live, don't you? Then just do as I say! I—I am sorry, Bet'—I do not mean to be angry, I do not feel very well either."

Beth knew already that Cassiana never exaggerated, but even knowing this she had not expected the violence of the next few hours. After they reached the Archonate, the world seemed to dissolve around her in a burning fever, a nausea and pain that made her previous illness seem like comfort by comparison. Cassiana, deathly pale, her hands as hot as Beth's own, did not leave her for an instant. They seemed unable to remain apart for an instant. When they were very close together, Beth felt a brief echo of the miasmic vibration which had eased her in the room of the machines; but at best this was faint, and when Cassiana drew away from her, by even a few feet, a vague, all-over trembling began in every nerve of her body, and the spasms of sickness were aggravated unbearably. The critical distance seemed about twelve feet; at that distance, the pain was almost intolerable. For hours, Beth was too miserable to notice, but it finally dawned on her that Cassiana was actually sharing this same torture. She clung to Beth in a kind of dread. Had they been less ill, Beth thought, they might have found it funny. It was a little like having a Siamese twin. But it was not funny at all. It was a grim business, urgent as survival.

They slept that night on the narrow cots pushed close to gether. Half a dozen times in her fitful sleep Beth woke to find Cassiana's hand nestled into hers, or the rhu'ad girl's arm flung over her shoulder. Once, in a moment of intimacy, she asked, "Do all women suffer like this—here?"

Cassiana sat up, and pushed back her long pale hair. Her smile was wry and the drawn face, in the flicker of lurid lightning that leaped and danced through the shutters, looked bitter and almost old. "No, or I fear there would be few children. Although, I'm told, when Megaera was first colonized, it was pretty bad. More than half the—the normal women, died. But we found out that sometimes a normal woman could go through a pregnancy, if she was kept close to a rhu'ad constantly. I mean *constantly*. Almost from the minute of conception, she had to stay close to the rhu'ad who was helping her. It was confining for both of them. If they didn't like each other to start with—" suddenly, softly, Cassiana chuckled. "You can imagine, the way you used to feel about me!"

"Oh, Cassiana, *dear*—" Beth begged.

Cassiana went on laughing. "When they didn't hate us, they worshiped us, and that was worse. But now— well, a woman will have a little discomfort—inconvenience—you saw Nethle. But you—if I had not taken you to the kail' rhu'ad when I did, you would have died very soon. As it was I delayed almost too long, but I had to wait, because my child was not—"

"Cassiana," Beth asked her in sudden understanding, "are you going to have a baby too?"

"Of course," Cassiana said impatiently. "How could I help you if I wasn't?"

"You said, rhu'ad don't—"

"They don't usually, it's a waste of time," said Cassiana unguardedly. "Married rhu'ad are not allowed to go through a pregnancy, for now, during all the six cycles of my pregnancy and two more while I recover, no woman in our family group can have a child"—suddenly her anger came back and closed down like a black cloud between their brief intimacy. "Why do you torment me with questions?" she flung furiously at Beth. "You know I mustn't answer them! Just let me alone, let me alone, let me alone!"

She threw up her arm over her eyes, turned on her side and lay without speaking, her back to Beth; but the other, sinking into a restless doze, heard through her light sleep the sound of stifled crying . . .

* * *

Beth thought it was the next day—she had lost consciousness of time—when she started out of sleep with the vague, all-over pain that told her Cassiana was not close to her. Voices filtered through a closed door; Cassiana's voice, muted and protesting, and Wilidh's high childish treble.

" . . . but to suffer so, Cassiana, and for *her*! Why?"

"Perhaps because I was tired of being a freak!"

"Freak?" Wilidh cried, incredulous. "Is that what you call it?"

"Wilidh, you're only a child," Cassiana's voice sounded inexpressibly tender. "If you were what I am, you would know just how much we hate it. Wilidh—since I was younger than you, I have had the burden of four families on my head. In all my life, am I not to do one thing, just one, because I myself wished for it? You have had children of your own. Can't you try to understand me?"

"You have Arli—" Wilidh muttered, sulky.

"She isn't mine—not as Lassa and the twins are yours. Do you know what it's like to carry a child—to watch it die—" Cassiana's voice broke. The voices sank, were indistinct—then there was a sudden sound like a slap, and Cassiana cried out furiously, "Wilidh, tell me what Nethle has done! I'm not *asking* you, I am ordering you to tell—"

Beth heard Wilidh stammering something—then there was a stifled scream, a wailing sound, and Cassiana, her face drained of color, pushed the door and came with groping steps to Beth's side. "Bet'—wake up!"

"I'm awake—what's happened, Cassiana?"

"Nethle—*false friend, false sister*—" Cassiana's voice failed her. Her mouth moved, but no words came. She looked ghastly, sick and worn, and she had to support herself with one hand against the frame of Beth's cot. "Listen—there are—Terrans here, looking for you. They are looking for you—days now—your husband could not lie well enough, and Nethle told—" she clutched at Beth's hand. "You *cannot* leave here now.

We might both die—" she stopped, her face gone impassive. There was a knock on the door.

Beth lay quiet, her eyes burning, as the door swung wide. Cassiana, a stony, statue-still figure of offended tradition, stared coldly at the two intruders who crossed the threshold. In 600 years no man had penetrated these apartments. The Terrans stood ill at ease, knowing they violated every tradition, law, custom of the planet.

"Matt!" Beth whispered, not believing.

In two strides he was beside her, but she drew away from his arms. "Matt, you promised!" she said unsteadily.

"Honey, honey—" Matt moaned. "What have they *done* to you here?" He looked down, tormented, at her thinner cheeks, and touched her forehead with disbelieving dismay. "Good God, Dr. Bonner, she's burning with fever!" He straightened and whirled on the other. "Let's get her out of here, and talk afterward. She belongs in a hospital!"

The doctor thrust the protesting Cassiana unceremoniously aside. "I'll deal with you later, young woman," he said between his teeth. He bent professionally over Beth; after a moment he turned on Cassiana again. "If this girl dies," he said slowly, "I will hold you personally responsible for denying her competent medical attention. I happen to know she hasn't been near any practitioner on the planet. If she dies, I will haul you into court if I have to take it to Galactic Center on Rigel!"

Beth pushed Matt's hand away. "Please—" she begged. "You don't realize—Cassiana's been good to me, she's tried to— she sat up, clutching her night robe—one of Nethle's a little too small for her—about her bare shoulders. "If it hadn't been for her—"

"Then why all this secrecy?" the doctor asked curtly. He thrust a message capsule into Cassiana's hands. "Here. This will settle it." Like a sleepwalker, Cassiana opened it, drew out the slip of flexible plastic, stared, shrugged and tossed it to Beth. Incredulous, Beth

Ferguson read the legal words. Under the nominal law of the Terran Empire, they could be enforced. But this—to the wife of the Chief Archon of Megaera—she opened her mouth in silent indignation.

Matt said quietly, "Get dressed, Betty. I'm taking you to the hospital. No—" he checked her protest, "don't say a word. You aren't capable of making decisions for yourself. If Cassiana meant you any good, there wouldn't be all this business of hiding you."

Cassiana caught Beth's free hand tight. She looked desperate—trapped. "Leave her with me for three days," she made a final appeal. "She'll die if you take her away now!"

Dr. Bonner said tersely, "If you can give me a full explanation of that statement, I'll consider it. I'm a medical man. I think I'm a reasonable man." Cassiana only shook her head silently. Beth blinked hard, almost crying, "Cassiana! Can't you *tell* them—"

"Leave her with me for three days—and I'll try to get permission to tell you—" Cassiana begged helplessly. Before her despairing eyes, Matt lowered his own. "Look, Doc, we could be making a big mistake—"

"We're only delaying," the doctor said tersely. "Come on, Mrs. Ferguson, get dressed. We're taking you to Medical HQ. If we find that this—this delay hasn't really hurt you any—" he turned and glared at Cassiana, "then maybe we'll do some apologizing. But unless you can explain—"

Cassiana said bitterly, "I am sorry, Bet'. If I were to tell now, without permission, I would not live till sunset. And neither would anyone who heard what I said."

"Are you threatening us?" Matt asked ominously.

"Not at all. Only stating a fact." Cassiana's eyes held cold contempt.

Beth was sobbing helplessly. Dr. Bonner rasped, "Pull yourself together! You'll go, or be carried. You're a sick girl, Mrs. Ferguson, and you'll do as you're told."

Cassiana said softly, "Leave her alone with me for just a few minutes, at least, while I get her dressed—"

51

Matt started to leave the room, but the doctor put a hand on his shoulder. "Stay with your wife. Or I will."

"Never mind," said Beth wearily, and began to get out of bed. Cassiana hovered near her, not speaking, her face sick with despair, while the Earth-woman managed to dress herself after a fashion. But as Beth, still protesting helplessly, leaned on Matt, Cassiana suddenly found her voice.

"You will do justice to remember," she said, very low, "that I have warn' you. When there come thing which you do not understand, remember. Bet'—" she looked up imploringly, then without warning she broke down and collapsed, a limp rag, on the tumbled bed. The servant women, spitting Centaurian curses, hastened to her. Beth struggled to free Matt's hands, but the two men carried her from the room.

It was like dying. It was like being physically pulled into pieces. Beth clawed and fought, knowing in some subconscious, instinctive way that she was fighting for her life, feeling strength drain out of her, second by second. The world dissolved in red fog, and she slumped down fainting in her husband's arms.

Time and delirium passed over her head. The white sterile smells of the Medical HQ surrounded her, and the screens around her bed bounded her sight except when Matt or a puzzed doctor bent over her. She was drugged, but through the sedatives there was pain and a fearful sickness and she cried and begged Matt incoherently, "Cassiana—I had to be near her, can't you understand—" and Matt only patted her hand and whispered gentle words. She dived down deep into delirium again, feeling her body burning, while faces, familiar and strange, multiplied around her, and once she heard Matt shouting in a voice that cracked like a boy's, "Damn it, she's worse than she was when we found her, *do* something, can't any of you *do* anything?"

Beth knew she was dying, and the idea seemed pleasant. Then quite suddenly, she came up to the surface of her fogged dreams to see the pallid stern face of a rhu'ad above her.

Beth's eyes and brain cleared simultaneously. The room was otherwise empty. Pinkish sunlight and a cool, pungent breeze filled the white spaces, and the rhu'ad's face was colorless and alien but full of reserved friendliness. Not only the room but the whole building seemed oddly silent; no distant voices, no hurrying footsteps, nothing but the distant hum of skycabs outside the windows, and the faint rustle of the ventilators. Beth felt a sort of drowsy, lazy comfort. She smiled, and said without surprise, "Cassiana sent you."

The rhu'ad murmured, "Yes. She nearly died too, you know. Your Terrans are—" she used a word which did not appear in Megaerean dictionaries "—but she did not forget you. I have done a fearful thing, so you must promise not to tell anyone that I've been here. I brought a damper into the building and hypnotized all the nurses on this floor. I've got to leave before they wake up. But you will get well now."

Beth pleaded, "Why is this secrecy so necessary? Why can't you just tell them what you've done? I know they didn't think I'd live, the fact that I feel better should be enough proof!"

"They would try to make me tell them, and then they would not believe me. After they see your baby, they will believe it. Then we will tell them."

Beth asked her, "Who are you?"

The rhu'ad smiled faintly and mentioned the name of one of the most important men of Megaera. Her eyes twinkled at Beth's astonishment. "They sent me rather than an unknown—in the event I *am* found here, your Terrans might hesitate to cause an international incident. But just the same I don't intend to let them see me."

"But what was the matter with me?"

"You developed an allergy to the baby. Alien tissue—blood types that didn't mix—but you'll be all right now. I haven't time to explain it," the rhu'ad finished impatiently and turned, without another word, and hurried out of the room.

Beth felt free and light, her body in comfort, without a trace of sickness or pain. She lay back on her pillows, smiling, feeling the faint stir and quickening of the child within her, then adjusted the smile to the proper angle as a nurse—one of Dr. Bonner's hard-faced old Darkovan assistants—tiptoed in, her face sheepish, and peered round the corner of the screen. Beth had to force back a spontaneous laugh at the change which came over the old lady's face as she gasped, "Oh—Mrs. Ferguson—you—you *do* look better this morning, don't you? I—I—I think Dr. Bonner had better have a look at you—" and she turned and actually ran out of the cubicle.

"But what did they *do* to you? Surely you must know what they did to you," Dr. Bonner protested tiredly for the hundredth time. "Just tell me what you remember. Even if it doesn't make sense to you."

Beth felt sorry for the old man's puzzlement. It couldn't be pleasant for him, to admit he'd failed. She said gently, "I've told you everything." She paused, trying to put it into words he could accept; she had tried to tell him about the manner in which Cassiana's physical presence had soothed her, but he had shrugged it off angrily as delirium.

"This place where they took you. Where was it?"

"I don't know. Cassiana blindfolded me." She paused again. From prolonged mental contact with Cassiana, she had come from the kail' rhu'ad with a subdued sense of having taken part in a religious ritual, but it meant nothing to her as religion, and she could only give incoherent scraps of her impressions. "A big domed room—and a room full of machines—" at his request, she described the machines in as much detail as she could remember, but he shook his head. Trying to help, she ventured, "Cassiana called one of them a telepathic damper—"

"Are you *sure?* Those things are made on Darkover, and their export is generally discouraged—even the Darkovans won't talk about them very much. The

54

other thing could have been a Howell C-5 Electropsychometer. It must have been a special hopped-up model, though, if it could put your cell waves into phase with a telepath's!" His eyes were thoughtful. "I wonder what they did that for? It must have hurt like hell!"

"Oh, no!" Beth tried to explain just how it had felt, but he only shrugged and looked dissatisfied again. "When I examined you," he told her, and glanced sidewise at Matt, "I found an incision, about four inches long, in the upper right groin. It was almost healed over, and they'd pulled it together with a cosmetic lacquer—even under a magnifying glass, it was hard to see."

Beth said, struggling for a dim memory, "Just as I was going under the anesthetic, one of the rhu'ad said something. It must have been a technical term, because I didn't understand it. *Aghmara kedulhi varrha.* Does that mean anything to you, Dr. Bonner?"

The man's white head moved slightly. "The words mean, *placenta graft.* Placenta graft," he repeated, slowly. "Are you absolutely certain those were the words?"

"Positive."

"But that doesn't make sense, Mrs. Ferguson. Even a partial detachment of the human placenta would have caused miscarriage."

"I definitely haven't miscarried!" Beth laughed, patting her swollen body.

The old man smiled with her. "Thank God for that!" he said sincerely. But his voice was troubled. "I wish I was sure of those words."

Beth hesitated, "Maybe it was—*Aghmarda kedulhiarra va?*"

Bonner shook his head, almost smiling. "*Kedulhi*—placenta—is bad enough," he said. "*Kedulhiarra*—who ever heard of grafting a baby? No, you must have had it right the first time, I guess. Maybe they grafted, subcutaneously, some kind of placental tissue from a Centaurian. That would even explain the allergy. Possibly, Mrs. Jeth-san acted as the donor?"

"Then why did she have the allergy too?" Beth asked. Dr. Bonner's heavy shoulders lifted and dropped. "God knows. All I can say is that you're a lucky, lucky girl, Mrs. Ferguson." He looked at her in unconcealed wonder, then turned to Matt. "You might as well take your wife home, Legate. She's perfectly all right. I've never seen a Terran woman look so healthy on Megaera. But stay close to home," he advised her. "I'll come over and have a look at you now and then. There must be some reason why the Centaurians go into seclusion. We'll try it with you—no sense in taking chances."

But Beth's sickness did not return. Contentedly secluded in the Residence, as snugly celled as a bee in her hive, she made tranquil preparations for the birth of her child. Nature has a sort of anesthesia for the pregnant woman; it smoothed Beth's faint disquiet about Cassiana. Matt was tender with her, refusing to discuss his work, but Beth detected lines of strain in his face and voice, and after a month of this she asked him pointblank, "Is something wrong, Matt?"

Matt hesitated—then exploded. "Everything's gone wrong! Your friend Cassiana has really messed us up properly with Rai Jeth-san! I'd counted on his cooperation, but now—" he gave a despondent shrug. "He just says, in that damned effeminate voice of his," Matt's husky baritone rose to a thin mocking echo of the Archon's accent, "peaceful settlement is what we want. Terran colonists with their wives and children we will accept, but on Megaera we will not accept floods of unmarried and unattached personnel to disturb the balance of our civilization." Matt made a furious gesture. "He knows Terrans can't bring their women here! The hell with this place, Betty—space station and all! They can blow the planet into the Milky Way, for all I care! As soon as Junior is born, and you're clear for space, I'm going to throw this job right in the Empire's face! I'll take a secretaryship somewhere—we'll probably have to go out on the fringe of the Galaxy—but at least I've got you!" He bent down to kiss his wife. "It serves me right for bringing you here in the first place!"

Beth hugged him, but she said in a distressed tone, "Matt, Cassiana saved my life! I simply can't believe that she'd turn the Archon against you. We don't deserve what Cassiana did for me—the Empire's been treating Megaera like a piece of lost-and-found property!"

Matt laughed, guilty. "Are you going in for politics?"

Beth said hotly, "You have authority to make recommendations, don't you? Why not, once, just once, do what's fair, instead of what the diplomatic manual recommends? You *know* that if you resign now, Terra will close out the Legation here, and put Megaera under martial law as a slave state! I know, the official term is protectorate satellite, but it means the same thing! Why don't you make a formal recommendation that Megaera be given dominion status, as an independent, affiliated government?"

Matt began, "To achieve that distinction, a planet has to make some important contribution to Galactic Civilization—"

"Oh, comet dust!" Beth snapped. "The fact of their survival proves that their science is ahead of ours!"

Matt said dubiously, "The Empire might agree to an independent buffer state in this end of the Galaxy. But they've been hostile to the Empire—"

"They sent a petition to Terra, 600 years ago," Beth said quietly. "Their women died by thousands while the petition was being pigeonholed. I think they'd die all over again before they asked anything of Terra. It's Terra's turn to offer something. The Empire owes them something! Independence and affiliation—"

"Cassiana's certainly got *you* sold on Megaeran politics," Matt said sourly.

"Politics be damned!" Beth said with such heat that her husband stared. "Can't you *see* what it means, idiot—what Cassiana did? It proves that Terran women *can* come here in safety! It means that we *can* send colonists here for peaceful settlement! Can't you see, you half-wit, that's the opening Rai Jeth-san was leaving for you? Cassiana's proved a concession on their side—it's up to Terra to make the next move!"

Matt stared at her in blank surprise.

"I hadn't thought of it that way. But, honey, I believe you're right! I'll put through the recommendation, anyway. The planet's almost a dead loss now, things couldn't be worse. We've nothing to lose—and we might gain a good deal."

Beth's baby was born at the Residence—the Medical HQ did not have maternity ward facilities, and Dr. Bonner thought Beth would be more comfortable at home—on the first day of the brief Megaeran winter. She came, alert and awake, out of a brief induced sleep, and asked the usual questions.

"It's a girl." Mr. Bonner's lined old face looked tired and almost angry. "A little over three pounds, in this gravity. Try to rest, Mrs. Ferguson."

"But is she—is she all right?" Beth caught weakly at his hand. "Please tell me—please, please let me see her—"

"She's—she's—" the old doctor stumbled over a word, and Beth saw him blink hard. "She's—we're giving her oxygen. She's perfectly all right, it's just a precaution. Go to sleep, like a good girl. You can see her when you wake up." Abruptly, he turned his back and walked away.

Beth struggled against the lassitude that forced her head back. "Dr. Bonner—please—" she called after him weakly. The nurse bent over and there was the sharp prick of a needle in her arm. "Go to sleep, now, Mrs. Ferguson. Your baby's all right. Can't you hear her squalling?"

Beth sobbed, "What's the matter with him? *Is there something wrong with my baby?*" The nurse could not hold her back. Before her fierce maternity the old woman hesitated, then turned and crossed the room. "All right, I guess one look won't hurt you. You'll sleep better if you've seen her." She picked up something and came back to the bed. Beth reached out hungrily, and after a minute, smiling faintly, the Darkovan woman put the baby down on the bed beside Beth.

"Here. You can hold her for a minute. The men don't understand, do they?"

Beth smiled happily, folding back the square of blanket that lay lapped over the small face. Then her mouth fell open and she uttered a sharp cry.

"This isn't my baby! It's not—she isn't, you don't—" her eyes blurred with panicky tears. Rebelliously, scared, she looked down in terror at the baby she held.

The infant was not red or wrinkled. The smooth soft new skin was white—a shining, lustrous, *pearly* white. The tight-screwed eyes were a slaty silver, and a pallid, gilt-colored down already curled faintly on the little round head.

Perfect. Healthy. But—a rhu'ad.

The nurse dived for the baby as Beth fainted.

It was nearly a month before Beth was strong enough to get up during the day. Shock had played vicious havoc to her nerves, and she was very ill indeed. Her mind acquiesced, and she loved her small perfect daughter, but the unconscious conflict forced itself inward, and took revenge on every nerve of her body. The experience had left a hidden wound, too raw to touch. She sheltered herself behind her weakness.

The baby—over Matt's protest, Beth had insisted on calling the child Cassy—was more than a month old when one afternoon her Centaurian servant came into her room and announced, "The Archon's wife has come to visit you, Mrs. Legate Furr-ga-soon."

Beth had forced the memory so deep that she only thought that Nethle or Wilidh had come to pay a formal call. She sighed and stood up, sliding her bare feet into scuffs, and padding across to her dressing panel. She twisted buttons, playing out lengths of billowing nylene to cover her short indoor chemise, and slid her head into the brusher which automatically attended to her short hair. "I'll go up. Take Cassy down to the nursery, will you?

The Centaurian girl murmured, "She has her baby— with her."

Beth stared in stupefaction. No wonder the servant girl had seemed thunderstruck. A baby outside its own home, on Megaera?

"Bring her down here, then—" she directed. But that did not dull her surprise when a familiar, lightly moving form shrouded in pale robes, ghosted into the room.

"Cassiana!" she said tremulously.

The rhu'ad smiled at her affectionately as they clasped hands. Then suddenly Beth threw her arms around Cassiana and broke down in a tempest of stormy crying.

"Don't, don't—" Cassiana pleaded, but it was useless. All the suppressed fear and shock had broken loose at once, and Cassiana held her, awkwardly, as if unused to this kind of emotion, trying to comfort, finally bursting into tears herself. When she could speak again steadily, she said, "Can you believe me, Beth, if I say I know how you are feeling? Look, you must try to pull yourself together, I have promised I'd explain to you—"

She freed herself gently, and from the servant's arms she took a bundle, carefully shielded in tough, transparent plastic, with double handles for carrying. She opened the package carefully and from the depths of this ingenious cradle she lifted a wrapped baby, held it out and put it into Beth's arms.

"This is my little boy—"

Beth finally raised her eyes to Cassiana, who was standing, fascinated, by Cassy's crib. "He—he—he looks like—" Beth faltered, and Cassiana nodded. "That's right. He is a Terran child. But he's mine. Rather— he's ours." Her earnest eyes rested on the other in something like appeal. "I promised to explain—Dhe mhári, Bet', don't start to cry again . . ."

* * *

"We rhu'ad would probably have been killed, anywhere except on Megaera," Cassiana began, a few minutes later, when they had settled down together on a cushioned divan, the babies snuggled down in pillows between them. "Here, we saved the colony. Originally, I think, we were a cosmic ray mutation. We were part of the normal population then. We hadn't adapted quite so far." She paused. "Do you know what Genetic Drift is? In an isolated population, hereditary characteristics just drift away from normal. I mean—suppose a colony had, to begin with, half blonde people, and half brunette. In a normal society, it would stay distributed like that—about 50-50 per cent. But in one generation, just by chance, it might vary as far as 60-40. In the next generation, it could go back to normal, or—the balance once having been changed—it could keep drifting, and there would be 70 per cent of blondes and only 30 per cent of brunettes. That's oversimplified, of course, but if that keeps up for eight or ten generations, with natural selection working hard too, you get a distinct racial type. We had two directions of drifting, because we had the normal population, and—we had the rhu'ad. Our normal women were dying—more in every generation. The rhu'ad could have children safely, but somehow, we had to preserve the normal type."

She picked up Cassy and snuggled her close. "Did you name her for me, then?" she asked. "Well—I started to explain. A rhu'ad is human, and perfectly normal, except—they will find it out about Cassy some day—we have, in addition to our other organs, a *third* ovary. And this third ovary is parthenogenetic—self-reproducing. We could have perfectly, human, normally sexed children, either male or female, who would breed true to the normal human type. They were even normally susceptible to the poisonous reaction in this air. These normal children were carried, in the normal way, except that a rhu'ad mother was immune to the hormone reaction, and could protect a normal child. Or, a rhu'ad woman could, from the *third* ovary, *at*

61

her own will—we have control over all our reflexes, including conception—have a *rhu'ad*, female child. Any rhu'ad can reproduce, duplicate herself, without male fertilization. I never had a father. No rhu'ad does."

"Is *Cassy*—"

Cassiana paid no attention to the interruption. "But the mutation is female. While the normal women were dying, and only the rhu'ad could have children—even these children died when they grew up—we were afraid that in three or four generations we would end with an all-female, parthenogenetic, all-rhu'ad society. No one wanted that. Least of all the rhu'ads themselves." She paused. "We have all the instincts of normal women. I *can* have a child without male fertilization," she looked searchingly at Beth, "but that does not change the fact that I—I love my husband and I want *his* children— like any other woman. Perhaps more—being telepathic. That's an emotional problem, too. We have done our part for Megaera, but we—we want to be women. Not sexless freaks!"

She paused again, then continued, evidently searching for words. "The rhu'ad are almost completely adaptable. We tried implanting rhu'ad gametes—ova—from our normal ovaries, into normal women. It didn't work, so finally they evolved the system we have today. A rhu'ad becomes pregnant in the normal way—" for the first time Beth saw her blush slightly, "and carries her child for two, maybe three months. By that time, the unborn child builds up a *temporary* immunity against the toxins released by the hormone allergy. Then they transfer this two-month embryo into the host mother's womb. The immunity lasts long enough that the baby can be carried to full term, and birthed. Then, of course, there's no more danger at all, for a male child—or, for a female child, no more danger until she grows up and herself becomes pregnant.

"Another thing: After a woman has her first child like that, she also builds up a very slight immunity to the hormone reaction. For a woman's second child, or third, or more, it is sufficient to transplant a fertilized ovum of six or seven days . . . provided that there is a rhu'ad within immediate call, to stabilize the chemistry in case anything goes wrong. One or more of my families always has a woman who is pregnant, so I must be continuously available."

"Isn't that terribly hard on you?" Beth asked.

"Physically, no. We've done what they do with prize cattle all over the Empire—hyperovulation. At certain days in each cycle, rhu'ads are given particular hormone and vitamin substances, so that we release not one ovum, but somewhere between four and twelve. Usually they can be transferred about a week later, and the operation is almost painless—"

"Then *all* the children in your four—families, are *yours,* and your husband's?"

"Why, no! Children belong to the woman who bears them and gives birth to them—and to the man who loves that woman, and mates with her!" Cassiana laughed. "Oh, I suppose all societies adapt their morals to their needs. To me, it's a little—nasty, for a man to have just one wife, and live with her all year. And aren't you terribly lonely, with no other women in your house?"

It was Beth's turn to blush. Then she asked, "But you said those were normal children. Cassy—Cassy is a rhu'ad—"

"Oh yes. I couldn't do with you what I'd have done with a Centaurian. You had no resistance at all, and you were already pregnant. Women *do* become pregnant sometimes, in the ordinary way, on Megaera—we are strict about contraceptive laws, but nothing is entirely reliable—and when they do, they die, unless a rhu'ad will take for them the risk I took for you. I had done it once before, for Clotine, but the baby I had died—well, during those three days while you were shut up alone, I went to the kail' rhu'ad, and put myself under a damper—and became pregnant. By myself."

A thousand tiny hints were suddenly falling into place in Beth's mind. "Then you did graft—"

Cassiana nodded. "That's right. When we went together to the kail' rhu'ad, the dampers put us into phase—so the cellular wave lengths wouldn't vary enough to throw the babies into shock—and just exchanged the babies."

Beth had been expecting this; but even so, Cassiana's casual tone was a shock. "You really—"

"Yes. My little boy is—by heredity alone—your child and the Legate's. But he is mine. He lived because I—being rhu'ad—could carry him in safety, and manage to stabilize his reactions to the hormone allergy with the atmosphere. There was no question of Cassy's safety: a rhu'ad baby, even a rhu'ad embryo, is perfectly adaptable, even to the alien environment of a Terran body. The first few days were so crucial because you and I both developed allergies to the grafted alien tissue; our bodies were fighting the introduction of a foreign kind of substance. But once we mother-hosts began to develop a tolerance, I could stabilize myself, and my little boy, and you—and when you were taken from me too soon, I could send another rhu'ad to complete the stabilization. There was no need to worry about Cassy; she simply adapted to the poisonous condition which would have killed a normal child."

She picked up Cassy and rocked her almost wistfully. "You have a most unusual little daugher, Bet'. A perfect little parasite."

Beth looked down at Cassiana's little boy. Yes, she could trace in his face a faint likeness to the lines of Matt's, and yet—hers? No. Cassy was hers, borne in her body—she wanted to cry again.

Cassiana leaned over and put an arm around her. "Bet'," she said quietly, "I have just come from the Legation HQ, where—with full permission of the Council of Rhu'ad—I have laid before them a complete, scientific account of the affair. I have also been allowed to assure the Terran authorities that when Terran colonists come here to build the Space Station, their women will be safe. We have suggested that colonists be limited to families who have already had children, but we will give assurance that an accidental pregnancy need not be disastrous. In return I received assurance, forwarded from Galactic Center, that Megaera will receive full dominion status as an independent planetary government associated with the Empire. And we are being opened to colonization."

"Oh, how wonderful!" Beth cried impulsively. Then doubt crept into her voice. "But so many of your people hate us—"

The rhu'ad smiled. "Wait until your women come. Unattached men, on Megaera, could only make trouble. Men have so many different basic drives! An Empire man from Terra is nothing like a Centaurian from Megaera, and a Darkovan from Thendara is different from either—take ten men from ten different planets, and you have ten different basic drives—so different that they can only lead to war and ruin. But women—all through the Galaxy, Terran, Darkovan, Samarran, Centaurian, Rigelian—women are all alike, or at least they have a common basic area. A baby is the passport to the one big sorority of the universe. And admission is free to every woman in the Galaxy. We'll get along."

Beth asked numbly, "And you were convinced enough of that to risk your life for a Terran who—hated you? I'm ashamed, Cassiana."

"It wasn't entirely for you," Cassiana admitted. "You and your husband were Megaera's first and last chance to avoid being a backwater of the Galaxy. I planned this from the minute I first saw you. I—I wasn't your friend, either, at first."

"You—you *couldn't* have known I'd get pregnant—"

Cassiana looked shamed and embarrassed. "Bet'. I—I planned it, just as it happened. I'm a telepath. It was my mental command that made you stop taking your anti shots."

Beth felt a sudden surge of anger so great that she could not look at Cassiana. She had been manipulated like a puppet—

She felt the rhu'ad's thin hand on her wrist. "No. Only a fortuitous accident in the way of destiny. Bet', look at them—" Her free hand touched the two babies, who had fallen asleep, cuddled like two little animals. "They are sister and brother, in more than one way. And perhaps you will have other children. You belong to us, now Bet'."

"My husband—"

"Men will adapt to anything, if their women accept it," Cassiana told her. "And your daughter is a rhu'ad—who will grow up in a Terran home. There will be others like her. In her turn she will help the daughters of Terran families who come here, until science finds a new way and each woman can bear her own children again—or until Centaurians take their place, moving out into the Galaxy with the rest—"

And Beth knew in her heart that Cassiana was right.

(1954)

The Climbing Wave

Brian Kearns knew to the second, by his ship-time chronometer and by the faint, almost imperceptible humming of a monitor screen, when the limit of gravity tolerance was reached. Giving himself a round ten seconds for safety margin—Brian was a practical and methodical young man, and had spent twelve years training for this work and four and a half years doing it—he unfastened the straps on his skyhook, the free-swinging, nest-like lounge cradle where he had been lying with ears and eyes fastened on the complex controls. He inched patiently, fly-like, down the wall, braced himself to a handhold, and threw a certain switch to the farthest position leftward.

The barely perceptible humming stopped.

Brian Kearns had just put himself out of a job.

He picked up the stylus chained to the logbook, held a floating page down with his right hand, and wrote swiftly and expertly with his left:

"1676th day of voyage; have just thrown switch which cut the interstellar drives. Our calculations were correct and there appear to have been no visible shock effects as the IS units went out of function. We are now standing fourteen hundred miles off Mars. Relinquished control of ship at—" he glanced at the chronometer again, and wrote "—0814 hours. Position . . ." He added a series of complicated numerals, scribbled his initials beneath his entry, then picked up the hook of the intercabin communicator and waggled it.

A dim rasping voice said from the other end of the starship, almost half a mile away, "That you, Kearns?"

"Right, Caldwell."

"We're standing by with atomics back here, Brian. Were the figures right?"

"All calculations appear to have been correct," Brian answered stiffly. "The drives have been cut according to the schedule previously worked out."

"Yippee!" the voice shouted from the loudspeaker, and Brian frowned and coughed reprovingly. The faraway voice appeared to be stifling an expletive, but inquired correctly: "Standing by for orders, Captain Kearns?"

"All right, Captain Caldwell," Brian said; "she's your ship, as of—" he stopped, glanced at the chronometer again, and after a few seconds said, *"now!"*

He put down the hook, and looked around the main control room, in which he had spent the best part of the *Homeward*'s long voyage. The tremendous interstellar drives were silent now, their dim hum stilled, and the metal surfaces faced him with a blank, metallic unresponsiveness. Brian had a curious feeling of anticlimax while he recapped the stylus, slid a moving panel over the logbook, and clung there to the handhold, wondering with the back part of his mind if he had left anything undone, while knowing, with the sureness of long habit, that he had not.

It is impossible to shrug one's shoulders in free fall; the motion sends you flying across the cabin, and Brian was too well-trained to make waste motions of that sort. But his eyebrow lifted a little, and a sort of elated grin spread across his face; for a minute, unobserved, he looked almost as young as he was. Then, re-schooling his expression to the gravity he always wore in the presence of his crew, he inched back across the wall, methodically unstrapped his rubber sandals from their place in the skyhook, worked his feet into them with the skill of long practice, and, pulling himself swiftly across the remaining section of wall, wriggled the forward part of his body through the sphincter lock which led to the forward part of the great starship.

There he paused, his middle clasped firmly by the expanding diaphragm, looking down the narrow, cylindrical corridor. He could feel, now, the faint vibration all around him, as far away in the nose of the *Homeward* the atomic rockets began firing. He allowed himself to grin again, this time with the secret contempt of a hyperdrive technician for rockets, however necessary, and slowly hauled the rest of his long, narrow body through the sphincter; then, pushing his feet hard against the diaphragm which had snapped tight behind him, he arrowed down, in a straight line, his body rocketing weightless down the corridor. He braked himself with strong hands at the far end, then paused; there was a musical mewing behind him, and the ship's cat, Einstein—actually a Centaurian mammal more nearly resembling a dwarf kangaroo—somersaulted dizzily through the air toward him.

"Brian—catch him!" a girl's voice called, and Brian turned, hooking one rubber sandal through a strap, and made a wide sweeping grab for the creature. He caught it by one spindly leg; it squalled and thrashed to get away, and the girl called anxiously "Hang on, I'm coming." She propelled herself down the corridor, and hurriedly snatched the little animal, who immediately quieted and snuggled under her chin.

"He went crazy when the rockets started," she murmured apologetically. "It must be the vibration or something."

Brian grinned down at the girl, who was small and slight, her curly fair hair standing weirdly around her head and her prim brief coverall floating out in odd billows. They had all lived at free fall conditions for so long that he barely noticed this, but he did see the disquiet in her brown eyes—Ellinor Wade was a food culturist, and knew rather less about the drives than the Centaurian cat.

"It's all right, Ellie; maybe Einstein's a hyperdrive technician. I just cut the IS units and turned the ship over to Caldwell."

She whispered, "Then we're almost there! Oh,

Brian!" and her eyes were a double star, first magnitude. He nodded. "It's Caldwell's command now, so I don't know what he'll do," Brian added, "but you'd better keep your ears lapped over for instructions. We'll have to strap in, in a few minutes, for deceleration, if he's going to brake in at Mars."

"Brian, I'm scared . . ." Ellie whispered, and let the Centaurian cat float free, fumbling around for his hand. "It would be—hideously ironical, if this old ship traveled to Centaurus and back, and then cracked up in atmosphere—"

"Relax," Brian advised her genially. "He may decide to go on to Earth, anyway—Caldwell knows his business, Ellie. And I know the *Homeward*."

"You certainly do." The girl attempted a smile, which somehow missed its purpose. "You're in love with this old wreck!"

Brian grinned disarmingly. "I won't deny it," he answered. "But it's just a kind of substitute passion till I can get you down to earth!"

The girl blushed and turned her face away from him. The twelve members of the *Homeward*'s crew were all young, and the confined quarters aboard generated strong attachments; but men and women were carefully segregated aboard ship, for an excellent and practical reason which had nothing to do with morality. The trip from Centaurus, even at hyperspeeds, took the best part of five years. And no one has yet discovered any method for delivering a baby in free fall.

Brian unhooked his rubber shoe. "Going into the lounge?"

"No . . . " She hung back. "I've got to feed Einstein, after—Paula's still in the Food Culture unit, and there's no public address system in there—I'd better go and tell her we may have to strap in. Go on ahead, and I'll tell Paula—"

"I'll come with you. I'm hungry and I want to snatch a bite before we go out, anyhow—"

"No!" The sharpness of her voice amazed him. "Go on out in the lounge, I'll bring you something."

He stared at her. "What—"

"Go on. Paula's—Paula's—" Ellie fumbled and finished, "—she's dressing in there."

"What the devil—" Brian, suddenly suspicious, shoved hard against the handhold, and barreled across the corridor to the open lock of the Food Culture unit. Ellie gave a wordless cry of warning as Brian fell through the doorway, and in the aftermath of that cry, beneath Brian's intrusive stare, two fused figures jerked convulsively and thrust apart, Paula Sandoval flung her arms over her face and grabbed at a floating garment, while Tom Mellen jackknifed upright and glared belligerently at Brian.

"Get the hell out of here!" he roared, simultaneous with Brian's needle-voiced, "What's going on in here?"

There was blue vitriol in Paula Sandoval's taut voice. "I think you can *see* what goes on, Captain!" and her black eyes snapped fire at him.

"Brian—" Ellie implored, her hand on his wrist with a gentle, repressive force. He threw it off with a violence that flung her halfway across the cabin.

He said, with icy command, "You'd better get up front, Paula. Caldwell will need his figures checked. As for you, Mellen, regulations—"

"Regulations go jump in a hot jet, and you too!" Tom Mellen stormed. He was a loose-limbed young fellow, well over six feet tall and looking longer. "What the hell do you think you're doing anyway, pushing your weight around?"

"Look," Brian said tersely, and jerked around to the girls, "Paula, get up front—*that's an order*! Tom, this part of the ship is off limits for men except at regular meal periods. This is the fifth time—"

"The sixth to be exact, Captain's Log-book, and four times you didn't catch me. So what? What the hell are *you*, a blasted—"

"We'll leave my personal habits out of the matter,

Mister Mellen. *Sandoval!*" he flung at Paula. "I gave you an order!"

Ellie had her arms around Paula, who was sobbing harshly, but the small dark girl pulled away from Ellie, her eyes ablaze. "Give him another one for me, Tom," she said bitterly, and scooted out of the cabin. Brian added, more quietly, "You go too, Ellie. I'll settle this with Mellen right now."

But Ellie did not move. "Brian," she said quietly, "this is a pretty stupid time to be enforcing that regulation."

"As long as the *Homeward* is in space," Brian said tightly, "that particular regulation—and all others based on principles of necessity—will be enforced."

"You listen here—" Mellen began furiously, then abruptly, his face suffusing with violent color, he flung himself upward at Brian, before Kearns realized what was coming. "The atomics are on," he grated. "Which means Caldwell's captain! And for three years I've been waiting for this—"

Brian dodged in a queer, jerky gesture, and Mellen hurtled over his head, thrown on by the momentum of his own blow. *"Brian! Tom!"* Ellie begged, diving toward them and thrusting her rubber-sandaled feet between the men, but Mellen shoved her aside.

"I'm warning you, Ellie, get out of the way—" he panted. Brian started "Look here—" then, as Mellen plunged at him again, put out both hands and shoved hard.

Momentum met momentum. Brian and Mellen spun apart with such violence that heads cracked at opposite ends of the Food Culture unit, and Brian, half-stunned, dragged himself groggily upright.

Mellen's laughter, wry and ironical, filled the cabin. "Okay, damn it," he said bitterly. "I suppose there's no use having it out here and now. But just wait till I get you down to Earth—"

Brian rubbed his head and blinked dizzily, but his voice was precise, giving no hint of the shooting stars that were chasing themselves before his eyes. "By that time," he answered coldly, there will no longer be occasion for fighting, since my command will have terminated."

Mellen tightened his mouth, and Ellie interceded anxiously: "Tom, Brian is perfectly right, theoretically—don't stir up hard feelings now, when we're almost home—"

"Yeah, that's right . . ." Tom Mellen suddenly grinned, and his face was good-natured. "Hey, Brian how about it? No hard feelings, huh?"

Brian turned away. He said frigidly, "Why should there be hard feelings? It's my duty to enforce regulations until the *Homeward* is down."

"God damn—" Mellen muttered under his breath at Brian's rigid back, and even Ellie looked troubled. Then Mellen made a useless movement and started toward the front of the ship.

"Come on. I expect Caldwell will be wanting us," he said tightly, and propelled himself in quick, wrathful jerks toward the forward lounge.

II

The technique of braking into atmosphere had been perfected a hundred years before the old *Starward* rose from Earth to aim at Centaurus. However, it was new to the *Homeward*'s crew, and the tediousness of the process set nerves to jittering. Only Brian, strapped into one of the skyhooks in the lounge, was really calm, and Ellie, in the cradle next to his, absorbed a little of his calm confidence; Brian Kearns had been trained aboard the *Homeward* for twelve years before the trip began.

It had taken four generations for the stranded crew of the original ship, the *Starward,* to repair the hyperdrives smashed in landing, and to wrest from the soil of Θ Centauri fourth planet—Terra Two, they called it—enough cerberum to take a pilot crew back to earth with news of their success. A hundred and thirty years, subjective time. Taking account of the timelags engendered by their hyperspeeds, it was entirely possible that four or five hundred years had elapsed, objectively, on the planet their ancestors had left. Ellie, looking across at Brian's calm face, at his mouth that persisted in grinning with some personal, individual elation when he thought himself unwatched, wondered if he felt no regrets at all. Ellie struggled with a moment of blinding homesickness, remembering their last view of the little dark planet spinning around the red star. They had left a growing colony of 400 souls, a world to which they could never return, for, after five years of subjective time in hyperspeeds, it was entirely possible that everyone they had known on Terra Two had already lived out a full lifetime.

But Brian's thoughts were moving forward, not backward, and he could not keep them to himself.

"I suppose by now they've discovered a better method for braking into atmosphere," he mused. "If anybody's watching us, down there, we probably look like living fossils—and I suppose we are. In their world, we'll be so obsolete that we'll feel like stone-age man!"

"Oh, I don't know," Ellie protested. "People don't change—"

"But civilizations do," Brian insisted. "There was less than a hundred years between the first rocket to Luna and the launching of the *Starward*. That's how fast a scientific civilization can move."

"But how can you be sure they've moved along those lines?" Ellie wanted to know.

"Have you ever heard of time-binding?" he asked derisively. "When each generation accumulates the knowledge of the one before it, progress is a perfectly cumulative, straightforward thing. When the *Starward* left—"

"Brian—" she began, but he rushed on: "I grant you that man progressed at random for thousands of years, but when he acquired the scientific method, it was less than a hundred years from jet plane to rocketship. A race which had interstellar travel could progress in only one direction. If we wanted to take the time, we could sit down with an electronic calculator and add it all up, and predict exactly what we'd find down there."

"It seems," Ellie said slowly, "That you're leaving out the human element. The crew of the *Starward* were all scientists, hand-picked for compatibility, and the Terra Two colony is probably the nearest thing to a homogeneous society that ever existed. You can't make that kind of prediction for a normally populated planet."

"The human element—"

"Will you two quit it?" shouted Langdon Forbes angrily from his skyhook. "I'm trying not to get spacesick, but Kearns sounding off about progress is about all I can take! Does he have to pick a time when we're strapped in, and can't get away?"

Brian grumbled something unintelligible and lapsed into morose silence. Ellie reached dragging fingers, newly clumsy, toward him, but he pushed the hand away.

A dismal wailing came from beneath Ellie's skyhook; Einstein was getting reacquainted with gravity, and didn't like it. Ellie scooped up the miserable little animal and held it cuddled tight against her straps. It was silent in the lounge; the steady, low vibration of the atomic drives was a sound already so deeply embedded in their consciousness that they did not think of it as sound at all. There was still no feeling of motion, but there was an unpleasant, dragging sensation as the enormous starship made its wide braking circles, first grazing the atmosphere for a second or two, as it swung elliptically, like a crazy comet; then entering atmosphere for a few seconds, then a full minute, then a few minutes—coming "down" in slow, careful spirals.

"I hope they've found some way to put artificial gravity in spaceships," Judy Keretsky moaned, half-laughing, from the skyhook where she swung, upside down, from what was now the ceiling of the lounge.

He long, curly hair fell down over her head in a thick curtain; she alone of the starship's crew did not keep her hair clipped functionally short. She batted futilely at the waving curls as she wailed, "Oh, my poor head, I'm getting di-i-zzy up here!"

"You're getting dizzy! What about this poor cat!" Ellie jibed.

"Say, whose idea was it to bring that animal along, anyhow?" someone demanded.

"Very valuable contribution to science," Judy burlesqued. "Why didn't you bring a pair of them, Ellie!"

"Brian wouldn't let her," Marcia van Schreeven jeered, with an undertone of bitterness.

Ellie patted Einstein's darkish fur defensively, reminding Marcia in her peaceful voice: "Einstein is one of the third gender. When conditions are right, he'll reproduce in the first and second."

"Lucky animal," Brian said half-seriously, and Ellie glanced at him with unusual shyness as she murmured, "Well, Einstein will be unique on Earth, anyhow!"

"You'll see things much weirder than Einstein," Brian said offhandedly. "We've only been on one planet, and by now, Earth has probably colonized all the nearer stars. The people of Earth will be cosmopolitan in the largest sense—"

"Speaking of Earth," Langdon forcibly headed him off before he could hold forth again, "where on the planet are we going to set this thing down?"

"We won't know that till we contact the surface," Judy said irritably, batting her hair back. "We have the map the Firsts gave us, but it's unthinkable that the old spaceport at Denver would still be in use, and if it is, it would probably be so changed that we wouldn't know how to land—and too crowded for an IS ship this size."

"You've been listening to Brian," Langdon grinned. "According to him, it's a wonder we haven't already bumped into the local rocket for the second galaxy!"

Brian ignored the confusion of technical terms and answered seriously, "That's why I suggested landing on Mars. There are enough desert areas on Mars where we could have landed without any danger of damaging urbanized sections. I doubt if the population there is quite so centralized—"

"Well, why *didn't* we?" Marcia queried sharply, and Langdon, frowning, twisted his head to her. "We tried to radio them from space," he answered, "but they evidently didn't pick up our signals. So Caldwell and Mellen decided to bring us in to Earth instead of wasting time braking in at Mars and maybe having to pick up again. We haven't enough fuel for more than one landing and pick-up."

"We could certainly have refueled at Mars—" Brian began, but was interrupted by an apologetic cough from the loudspeaker in the center of the lounge.

"Hey, Kearns," it said in a puzzled rasp. "Brian Kearns, come on up forward, will you? Kearns, please come up to the front control room, if you can."

Brian scowled, and started painfully unbuckling the straps on his skyhook. "Now what does Mellen want—" he wondered aloud.

"What's the matter?" Judy squeaked, "Are we in trouble?"

"Oh, hush!" Ellie commanded. "If we are, we'll be told!" She watched, with vague disquiet, as Brian crawled over the side of his skyhook and abruptly tumbled two feet, not very hard, to the floor. "Weight's on the axis now," he announced wryly to no one in particular. "Good thing I wasn't up where Judy is, or I'd have broken my neck! Somebody will have to lift her down—"

Judy squeaked again, but Ellie snapped at her: "Just stay where you are until we find out what's going on!" and watched, disturbed, as Brian crawled clumsily on hands and knees across the wall which lay along the central axis of the starship and therefore "down." He pushed at the refractory sphincter lock—it worked perfectly only in free fall—and forced his head and shoulders through into the forward control room.

Tom Mellen, his short hair bristling upright around

his head, twisted around as Brian wriggled his shoulders through. "We've tried to raise them by FM, AM and wavicle," he said, scowling, "but they don't answer. Not a sign of a signal. What do you think of that, Brian?"

Brian looked deliberately around the cabin. Paula Sandoval, strapped in before the navigation instruments, hunched her bare, tanned shoulders and refused to meet his eyes; Caldwell, the gray-haired veteran who had repaired the atomic rockets, grinned truculently. Mellen's face was puzzled and defensive.

"I said it off Mars," Brian told them, "and I say it again; we're just wasting time trying to raise them with any communication devices aboard. By now, they're probably using something so far beyond radio or wavicles that they can't pick us up. Their equipment would be too fine for our clumsy primitive devices to—"

"Clumsy primitive—" Caldwell broke off, visibly summoning patience, and Mellen interrupted fiercely. "Look, Kearns, there are just so many ways of transmitting electric impulses."

"The first spacemen said that all fuels had to be chemical or atomic, didn't they?" Brian snapped. "And we came on cerberum. The world didn't end when the *Starward* left! You've got to realize that we've been stranded in what amounts to a time-warp for five hundred years or so, and we're hopelessly obsolete!"

"Maybe so . . ." Mellen said slowly, and waggled the switch again. Brian irritably flipped it shut.

"Why keep fussing with it, Tom? If they'd picked up our signals, they'd have answered by now. Have you seen any rockets entering or leaving?"

"Nothing larger than twelve centimeters since we entered the orbit," Mellon told him.

Brian frowned. "Where are we, Paula?"

The girl gave him a venomous look, but she glanced at her instruments and replied, "Orbiting at forty miles, velocity five point six m.p.s."

Kearns glanced at Caldwell. "You're the captain."

"In a limited sense," Caldwell said slowly, and returned his steady gaze. "That's why I wanted you up here. There are two things we can do. We can go down under the cloud layer and maybe risk getting shot at—to find a place to set down, or else go on a permanent orbit, and send somebody down in the pickup."

"The pickup," Brian decided immediately. "Can you imagine trying to land a ship this size without instructions from outside? For all we know, there may be laws about landing spaceships. The pickup can set down in a few square yards. Whoever goes down can locate a spaceport big enough to handle the *Homeward* and see about getting the necessary permissions."

"You're overlooking one thing." Mellen forced the words out. "Suppose they haven't any spaceports!"

"They'd have to have spaceports, Tom," Caldwell protested, "even for interplanetary ships." And Brian added, "It's impossible that we'd have been the only interstellar ship—"

"That isn't what I mean," Mellen protested. "Surely one of the planets, Mars or Earth, would have picked up our signals. Someone must use radio for something, even if it's purely local. That is, if there's anyone down there at all!"

Brian snorted laughter. "You mean some kind of end-of-the-world disaster?" he asked, elaborately sarcastic, but Mellen took him seriously. "Something like that."

"There's one way we can find out," Caldwell interrupted, "Do you want to take the pickup down, Brian? We won't be using the IS drives again—there's nothing more you can do aboard."

"I'll go," Brian said shortly, but he could barely conceal his eagerness, and even forgot his animosity toward Mellen for a minute. "Shall I take Tom to handle the radio?"

Caldwell frowned, and answered half practically and half tactfully, "I'll need Tom, and Paula too, to bring the ship down when we're ready. Langdon can handle the radio in the pickup. And take a couple of others too; Mellen may or may not be right, but I don't think any crew members ought to go down alone until we know exactly what we'll find down there."

Caldwell's seriousness made little impression on Brian, but he realized that he would need someone to pilot the pickup in any case; his own training had fitted him only to handle the complex interstellar drives. And Langdon should, they decided, keep the radio at his fingertips, to report instantly to the *Homeward* in case of any unforeseen events.

So it was Ellinor Wade who took the controls of the small jet-driven stratoplane which had been designed for ship-to-surface shuttling, and used during the final stages of repair on the *Homeward*. She let the small plane sink through the thick clouds, and asked, "Where do we want to set down?"

Langdon bent over the carefully copied map. "Judy's scribbled all over this thing," he complained. "But try North America, midwest. That's where the first rocket ranges were built, and we all speak English, after a fashion."

"Unless the language has changed too much," Brian murmured. Ellie frowned as she brought the swift little jet down, arcing across an unfamiliar land-mass; Brian and Langdon squeezed their hands to their eyes as the clouds thinned, for the sudden blaze of yellow light was like a stab in the eyeballs. Lighting aboard ship, of course, was keyed to the familiar crimson noon of Terra Two, under which the crew had lived all their lives. Ellie squinted over the instrument panel, using an unladylike word under her breath.

The ship dived over rolling hills, and Brian let out his breath slowly as the serried regular skyline of massive buildings cleaved the horizon, and said in an edgy voice, "I was beginning to wonder if Mellen had been right about those atomic deserts!"

Ellie warned, "From what the Firsts have told us, I don't care to get tangled up in a city airport! Let's find an open space and set down there." She headed northward from the city, and asked, "Have either of you seen anything that looks like transportation? Planes, rockets, anything on the ground?"

"Nothing at all with the naked eye," Langdon frowned, "and nothing moving that beeps the radar. And I've been watching pretty close."

"Funny . . ." Ellie murmured.

From this height everything was clear, and as they swerved groundward, details became sharply incised in miniature: wide plowed fields, scattered, toy-like houses, clusters of small buildings. There seemed to be animals in the fields. Langdon smiled. "Just like home," he said happily, meaning Terra Two. "Regular rural community, except that everything looks *green!*"

"That's this ridiculous yellow light!" Ellie said, absently, and Brian scoffed, "Just like home! Better get set for a shock, Langdon!"

"It might be you that gets the shock," Langdon answered unexpectedly, and peered over Ellie's shoulder at the controls. "The ground's level here, Ellie."

The pickup bumped ground and rolled gently; Langdon's fingers moved delicately on the radio panel, and he made a brief report in staccato speech while Brian unsealed the door. Strange smells wafted in to the cabin, and the three crowded together in the entrance, eyes squinted against the stabbing light, strangely reluctant, at the last, to set foot on the unfamiliar soil.

"It's cold . . ." Ellie shivered in her thin garment.

Langdon looked down, dismayed. "You've set down in somebody's grainfield!" he reproached. Food was still conserved carefully on Terra Two, more from habit than from serious privation; Man's conquest of the new planet was uncertain, and the colony took no chances. The three felt a twinging guilt as they looked down at the blackened spears of grain, and Ellie clutched at Brian's arm. "Someone's coming—" she faltered.

Across the evenly plowed ridges, between rows of ripening wheat, a boy of thirteen walked, steadily and unhurried. He was not very tall, but looked sturdy; his face was deeply tanned under square-cut dark hair, and he was wearing a loose shirt and breeches tucked into low boots, all the same rich deep-brown color. Even Brian was silent as the boy advanced to the very foot of the pickup plane, paused and looked up at it, then glanced up indifferently at the three in the doorway, and began to move around to the tail, toward the smoking jets.

Brian quickly dropped Ellie's hand and scrambled to the ground. "Hey there!" he called, forgetting the prepared speech on his lips. "Better not go around there, it's dangerous—*hot!*"

The boy desisted at once, turning to gaze at him, and after a moment he said in slurred but perfectly understandable English, "I saw the streak, and hoped that a meteor had fallen." He laughed, turned and began to walk away from them.

Brian looked blankly up at Ellie and Langdon. The man jumped down and gave Ellie a hand as she called after the boy "Please—wait a minute—"

He looked around, politely, and before his indifferent courtesy Brian felt the words, melting from his lips. It was Langdon who finally said, in an empty voice, "Where can we—We have a message for the— the Government. Where can we get—transportation—to the City?"

"The City?" The boy stared. "What for? Where did you come from? The—the *City?*"

Brian quietly assumed command of the situation again. "We are from the first Centaurian expedition, the *Starward,*" he said. "We or rather our ship, left this planet hundreds of years ago."

"Oh?" The boy smiled in a friendly way. "Well, I suppose you are glad to be back. Over that hill," he pointed, "you will find a road which goes toward the City." He turned again, this time with a definite air of finality, and started to walk away.

The three travelers stared at one another in blank indignation. Brian finally took a step forward and shouted: "Hey, come back here!"

With an irritated jerk of his head, the boy turned. "*Now* what do you want?" he demanded.

Ellie said conciliatingly, "This is only the pickup of our ship. We have to—to find someone who can tell us where to bring the spaceship down. As you can see," she gestured toward the ruined wheat, "our jets have destroyed a part of the crop here. Our spaceship is much larger, and we don't want to do any more damage. Perhaps your father—"

The boy's face, puzzled at first, had cleared while she was talking. "My father is not in our village now," he informed them, "but if you will come with me, I will take you to my grandfather."

"If you could tell us where the nearest spaceport is—" Brian suggested.

The boy frowned, "Spaceport?" he repeated. "Well, maybe my grandfather can help you."

He turned again, and led the way across the field. Langdon and Ellie followed at once; Brian hung back, looking uneasily at the pickup. The boy glanced over his shoulder. "You need not be anxious about your plane," he called, laughing. "It's too large to be stolen!"

Brian stiffened; the boy's attitude was just derisive enough to put him on the defensive. Then, realizing the futility of anger, he broke into a run to catch up with the others. When he came near them, the boy was saying, a little sulkily, "I thought that I would be fortunate enough to find a fallen meteor! I have never seen a meteorite." Then, making a tardy attempt to remember his manners, he added politely, "Of course, I have never seen a spaceship either—" but it was evident that a spaceship was a very poor substitute.

Ellie's thinly shod feet stumbled on the uneven ground, and all three were glad when they came out on a smoothed road which wound between low flowering trees. There seemed to be no vehicles of any kind for the road was just wide enough to permit the four to walk abreast. The boy's walk was rapid, and he kept moving, almost unconsciously, ahead of them, then looking back and deliberately slowing his steps.

Once when he had forged ahead, Langdon murmured, "Evidently vehicular traffic has been completely diverted from rural neighborhoods!" and Brian whispered, "This is incredible! Either the boy's half-witted, or else even the children here are so blasé that the first star-expedition doesn't mean anything to them!"

"I wouldn't be too sure," Ellie said slowly. "There's something that we don't understand. Let's not try to figure things out ahead, Brian. Let's just take them as they come."

III

Muscles virtually unused for nearly five years were aching by the time the narrow road wound into a village of low clustered houses, built of what seemed to be grayish field stone. A profuse display of flowers bloomed in elaborate geometrical patterns around nearly every doorstep, and little groups of children, dressed in smocks of dark yellow or pale reddish-gray, were chasing one another haphazardly on the lawns, shouting something rhythmic and untuneful. Most of the houses had low trellised porches, and women in short light dresses sat in little groups on the porches. The street was not paved, and the women did not appear busy; their low-pitched conversation was a musical hum, and all down the street the three strangers could hear a sound of singing. A man's voice, singing in a low, monotonous rise and fall of notes. It was toward this sound of singing that the boy led them, up the steps of a porch which was not trellised but roofed, and through an open door.

They stepped into a wide, light room. Two walls seemed to open in slatted shutters, giving a view of an evenly patterned garden; on another wall was a large fireplace, where embers flickered quietly, and there was a gleaming kettle of some light, brilliant metal swung on a crane over the embers. It reminded Brian of a picture in one of his oldest history books, and he blinked at the anachronism. The other furniture in the room was unfamiliar, low cushioned seats built against the walls, and a few closed doors on the fourth wall. From an inner room, the singing filled the house: a baritone voice, rich and resonant, rising and falling in slow, unfamiliar harmonic patterns.

The boy called: "Grandpa!"

The singer finished one of the odd phrases; then the song ceased, and the three strangers heard slow, deliberate steps behind the closed door. It swung back, and a tall old man came out into the main room.

He looked like the boy. His hair was clipped short, but grew down along his cheeks, although his chin was shaven clean; he wore a shirt and breeches of the same rich brown, and his feet were thrust into slippers of stitched leather. He looked strong and vigorous; his hands, tanned and knotty, were extremely well-kept, though somewhat stained, and he stood very erect, surveying them with great composure, while his deep-set dark eyes studied them from their clipped and tended hair to their rubber-sandaled feet. The composure gradually gave way to a quizzical smile, and he came forward a few steps. His voice was a singer's voice, full and very strong.

"Be welcome, friends. You are home. Destry, who are our guests?"

The boy said calmly, "They came down in a space-ship, Grandpa, or rather, part of one. That streak wasn't a meteor at all. They said they wanted to go to the City. So I brought them along to you instead."

The man's face did not change by a fraction. Brian had been looking for surprise, or some more tangible emotion, but the man only surveyed them equably.

"Please be seated," he invited graciously. "I am Hard Frobisher, friends, and this is my grandson Destry."

The three sank on one of the cushioned seats, feeling a little like children in their first learning-period before the Firsts. Only Brian had presence of mind enough to murmur their names.

"Brian Kearns—Ellinor Wade—Langdon Forbes—"

The old man repeated the names, bowing courteously to Ellie, at which the girl could barely conceal her amazement. He inquired, smiling, "Can I be of assistance to you?"

Brian stood up. "The boy didn't tell you, sir, but we're from the first Centaurus expedition—the *Starward*."

"Oh?" A faint flicker of interest crossed Hard Frobisher's face. "That was a good long time ago, I am told. Did the Barbarians have some means, then, of prolonging life beyond its appointed limits?"

Brian's patience had already gone a long way beyond its appointed limits, and now, abruptly, it deserted him.

"Look sir. We're from the first expedition into interstellar space. The *first*. None of us left Earth on the *Starward*. We weren't born. Our hyperspeeds, if you know what they are—which I'm beginning to doubt—threw us into a time-lag. There's no need to call us Barbarians, either. The ship's drives were smashed when they landed, and we've been four generations, *four generations*, getting it in operable condition to come back to Earth. None of us have ever been on Earth before. We're strangers here, understand? We have to ask our way around. We asked a civil question. Now if we could kindly have a civil answer—"

Hard Frobisher raised a placating hand. "I am sorry," he said calmly. "I didn't understand. Just what do you want me to do about it?"

Brian made a visible attempt to keep his temper. "Well, first, we want to get in touch with the authorities. Then I want to find a place where we can bring our spaceship down—"

Frobisher was frowning, and Brian fell silent.

"Frankly," the old man said, "I don't know whom you'd contact about a thing like that. There is plenty of open island to the south, nearer the city, where you might land your ship—"

"Now look—" Brian started, but Langdon touched his arm. So Brian only asked, "If you could tell us how to get in touch with the Government . . ."

"Well," the old man said neutrally, "there are three governors in our village, but they only regulate the school hours, and make rules about locking houses. I wouldn't want to bother them about something foolish like this. I don't think they'd have much to say about your . . . oh, yes, spaceship."

That silenced Brian and Langdon completely. Ellie, feeling as if they were being tangled into a giant spiderweb, asked desperately, "Could we go to some other, perhaps some larger place?"

Frobisher looked at her, frankly puzzled.

"It's a half a day's walk to Camey," he said, "and when you got there, they would tell you the same thing. You are perfectly welcome to put your spaceship down on our barrens, if you want to."

Brian stiffened belligerently. "Now let's get this straight. There's a city over there. There must be someone there in authority!"

"Oh, the City!" Frobisher's voice held dismissal, "Nobody's lived in any of the cities for years! Why should you want to go there?"

Langdon said, baffled, "Look, Mr. Frobisher. We've come all the way from Centaurus, to bring Earth the news about our expedition. We'd expected to be surprised at what we found—after all, it has been a long time since the *Starward* left. But are we supposed to understand from this run-around you're giving us that there's nobody to listen, that the first of the interstellar expeditions doesn't mean anything to anyone?"

"Should it?" asked Frobisher, and his face was even more baffled than Brian's. "I can understand your personal predicament somewhat—after all, you've come a long way, but why? Didn't you like it where you were? There is only one reason why people move from one place to another—and it seems to me that you have overdone it."

The room was silent. Hard Frobisher stood up, looking indecisively at his guests, and Brian half expected him to repeat Destry's move and walk away, uninterested; but he merely went to the fireplace and peered into the kettle.

"Food is prepared," he remarked. "Can I invite you to join us? Good food is ill-seasoned by dissension, and there is no wisdom in an empty belly."

Brian and Langdon just sat and looked dumbly at Frobisher. It was Ellie who said firmly, "Thank you, Mr. Frobisher," and dug an elbow into Brian's ribs, whispering savagely, "Behave yourself!"

The boy Destry came and helped his grandfather bring food from the fireplace and from an inner room; he conducted the strangers to seats around a sort of table. The food was unfamiliar and not altogether pleasant to the strangers, accustomed to the elaborate synthetics of the ship; Brian, altogether out of humor, made almost no effort to conceal his distaste, and Langdon ate listlessly; Hard and Destry ate with the unfeigned appetite of men who spend much time in the open air, and neither spoke much during the meal except to urge food upon their guests. Ellie, finding the curious liquids and semi-solids fascinating, if strange, tasted them with an interested professional curiosity, wondering how they were prepared.

It was not very long before Hard Frobisher nodded to Destry, and the boy rose and began taking dishes from the table. Frobisher pushed back his chair and turned to Brian. "We can now discuss your problem, if you wish," he said pleasantly. "Full stomachs make wise decisions." He glanced at Ellie, smiling. "I regret that there is no woman in my house to entertain you while we talk, young lady," he said regretfully, and Ellie dropped her eyes. On the *Homeward*—as on Terra Two—men and women were equals and neither deferred to the other. Hard's polite deference was new, and his bland assumption that she could have no part in their talk was a somewhat distasteful surprise. Langdon clenched his fists, while Brian seemed about to explode. Ellie summed up the situation at a glance, and swiftly intervened by rising and glancing shyly at Destry. "Can I help you?" she offered diffidently, the boy grinned.

"Sure, come ahead," he told her. "You carry the dishes and I'll bring the kettle."

Frobisher settled back, taking a leather pouch from his pocket and meticulously stuffing a pipe of carved amber which swiftly revised Langdon's ideas of the present level of civilization. Smoking was a habit on Terra Two as well; only the smell of the tobacco was unfamiliar. Both young men stifled coughs and refused his offer of the sack, taking out their own grayish cigarettes and inhaling the sweetish-sour smoke avidly to shut out the rank stench of the pipe. Somewhere, behind closed doors, they heard a splashing of water and the uncertain falsetto of the boy's voice, mingled with Ellie's merry soprano laughter. Brian scowled and leaned forward, his arms on his knees.

"See here, Mr. Frobisher," he said truculently. "I know you are trying to be hospitable, but if you don't mind, let's talk business. We have to bring the ship down, and after that—" He stopped and stared at the floor, wondering suddenly if he were on some kind of reservation for half-wits. No: the room was tastefully, if simply, furnished; everything was plain, but nothing crude. The wood of the furniture was beautifully stained and polished, and the hand-woven rug on the floor matched the thick draperies at the slatted windows. The house showed comfort, even a moderated luxury, and Frobisher's accents were those of a cultured man. Nor was he merely an eccentric, judging from what Brian had briefly seen of the other houses and the glimpsed people. Destry hadn't seemed surprised at the plane—he'd known what it was, and yet it hadn't impressed him. No, it wasn't savagery. But it was radically different from what he had expected, and the change bewildered him. He looked up at one of the many pictures which hung about the room, and there, for the first time, sensed a note of eccentricity; they were mostly sketches of birds, very precisely drawn, but the colors were combined in a fashion which only a madman could endure. . . . Then Brian realized that it was this bright, unfamiliar light which made the colors bizarre to him, and simultaneously he became conscious that his eyes were stinging and watering, and that he had a violent headache. He rested his forehead on his clenched hands, closing his eyes.

"It isn't that you aren't welcome here," Frobisher said thoughtfully, pulling at his pipe. "We realize that there is only one reason why you would leave your home planet, and that would, of course, be because you were unhappy there. And so we understand—"

"Of all the stupid, unjustified assumptions—" Brian began furiously, then checked himself. What was happening to his caution? He and Langdon were effectively cut off from the rest of the crew; they couldn't afford to get into trouble. He rubbed his aching eyes.

"Sorry, Mr. Frobisher," he said tiredly. "I didn't mean to be offensive."

"No offense taken," Frobisher assured him. "And certainly none was intended by me. Am I mistaken—"

"We came here for one reason," Langdon informed him. "To advance man's knowledge of the world outside the solar system. In other words, to finish what the Firsts started."

"And, judging by appearances—" Brian's voice was bitter, "—we've wasted our time!"

"Yes, I'm afraid you have." Something new in Frobisher's voice made both young men look up. "Whether you realize it or not, I am quite aware of your problems, Mr. Kearns. I have read a good deal about the Bar—excuse me, about the past." He tapped his pipe meditatively on a projecting corner of the fireplace. "I suppose it would be impossible for you to return to Centaurus in your lifetimes?"

Brian bit his lip. "In our lifetimes—no, not impossible," he answered, "but in the lifetimes of anyone we had known, assuming that we could *get* back. Our fuel reserves are not great—" He looked questioningly at Frobisher.

"Then I don't quite know what to do with you," the old man said, and there was a genuine personal concern in his voice. And that friendly concern was the last thing needed to bring Brian to critical mass. Ignoring the warning pressure of Langdon's hand on his knee, he stood up.

"Look, Frobisher," he said tensely, "just who in hell gave you the authority to make this decision, anyhow?"

Frobisher's face did not change by a fraction. "Why, you landed in our field and my grandson brought you here."

"So you're just taking responsibility for the whole matter? Do you rule Earth?"

The man's mouth dropped open. *"Do I rule . . . Ha, ha, ha!"* Frobisher leaned back in his chair, holding his sides and rocking suddenly with uncontrollable laughter. *"Do I rule . . ."* He collapsed into chuckles again, his mirth literally shaking the floor, and the large expansive laughter was so infectious that Langdon finally glanced up with a faint, puzzled grin, and even the worst of Brian's fury began to drain away a little. "I'm sorry," Frobisher said weakly at last, and there were tears in his eyes. "But that—that is the funniest thing I've heard since spring sowing! *Do I . . .* ha, ha, ha, ha! *Wait* until I tell my son—I'm sorry, Mr. Kearns, I can't help it. *Do I rule Earth!*" he chuckled again, "Heavens forbid! I have enough trouble ruling my grandson!" He laughed again, irrepressibly. Brian couldn't see what was so funny and said so.

With an effort, Frobisher controlled his laughter and his eyes sobered—but not much—as he looked at Brian. "You did come to me," he pointed out, "and that makes it my responsibility. I'm not a man to evade responsibility or refuse you hospitality, but frankly, I wish you had found somebody else!" A tiny snort of laughter escaped him again, "I can see you'll make trouble here! But if you don't listen to me, you'll only have to find somebody else, and I'm afraid that whoever you found would tell you just about the same thing!" He smiled, and the anxious friendliness in his face took the edge from Brian's anger, although annoyed puzzlement remained.

Frobisher added quietly, "There is no reason that Norten village shouldn't have this problem, as well as any other." He stood up. "I expect the remainder of your ship's crew will be anxious about you. Do I assume correctly that you have a communication device?" At Langdon's exasperated nod, Frobisher twitched a loose coat from a peg. "Then why not report to them? We can talk further on the way—you don't mind if I come, do you?"

"No, not at all," Brian said weakly. "Not at all."

IV

Mindful of Caldwell's words about not getting separated, Brian insisted that Ellie should accompany them back to the pickup. Destry, apparently uninterested, at first refused his grandfather's invitation to join them, then changed his mind. He ran to fetch a warm jacket, but surprisingly, instead of donning it, he laid it about Ellie's shoulders. "She's cold," he explained briefly to his grandfather, and without waiting for thanks, strode ahead of them, along the road.

The sun was dropping westward, and the light was almost unbearable; Brian's eyes were squinted tight, and Langdon's forehead furrowed in deep-plowed lines; Ellie held one across her forehead, and Brian put his arm around her.

"Headache, darling?" he asked tenderly.

She grimaced. "Will we get used to this light, do you think, or are we going to have to put up with this all along?"

Langdon said wryly, "I suppose the Firsts felt like this under Theta Centauri!"

Ellie smiled faintly. "No one spread out a welcome for them."

Frobisher walked ahead of them, with long, swinging steps, and Brian said in a savage undertone, "I still think this whole thing is an elaborate bluff of some sort. Or else we're on a primitive reservation. The whole world *can't* be like this!"

"Oh, don't be silly," Ellie said wearily, rubbing her aching eyes. "How could anyone have known that we'd choose to land here?"

Some of the women on the porches called familiarly to Frobisher, and he waved gaily to them in return, but no one paid any attention to the strangers, except for one plump woman, her hair in curly sausages all over her head, who waddled from her steps and toward the road. "I see you have guests, Hard," she called cheerfully. "If your house is too full, mine is empty!"

Frobisher faced around, smiling. "Your hospitality may be required," he said. "There are others, and they have come a long way."

The woman looked at Ellie with a sharp female glance, noting her fair cropped hair, the smooth spun-synthetic coverall beneath the boy's jacket, the molded sandals and bare legs. Then she put out a fat warm hand. "Are you planning to settle in our village, my dear?" she asked.

"They haven't decided," Frobisher answered noncommittally, but Ellie said with a shy, impulsive friendliness, "I do hope so!" and squeezed the offered hand.

"Well, I hope so too, dear. It isn't often we have young neighbors," the plump woman replied. "You and your husband" (Ellie blushed at the forthright archaism) "be sure and call on us, now, if you need anything before you get settled." She smiled and waddled back to her doorway.

Langdon said, low-voiced, "It's like being on Terra Two, except that everything—everything—"

Brian said, "There must have been some inconceivable disaster! Culturally, they're a thousand years behind the world when the *Starward* left. Why, even Terra Two is more civilized than they seem to be! Cooking with fire—and these little villages—and the cities empty—"

"Oh, I don't know," Ellie murmured surprisingly. "How do you measure culture? Isn't it possible that they've progressed in ways we don't know anything about? The difference might be in viewpoint."

Brian shook his head stubbornly.

"It's regression," he protested, but Ellie had no time to answer, for they had come within sight of the pickup, and Frobisher dropped back to walk with them.

"There is your plane," he said. "Do you intend to communicate from here, or will you rejoin your spaceship?"

Brian and Langdon looked at one another. "We haven't thought about it," Langdon said at last, "but— Brian—without a spaceship or at least a radio beaming device, how are they going to land?"

Brian frowned. "I don't know much about rockets," he said at last; "the hyperdrives are my job. How much landing room do they need?"

Langdon said, troubled, "Paula and Caldwell, between them, could land the *Homeward* in great-grandfather Kearn's biochemistry lab, if they had to, without breaking a test tube. But they'd have to have a fix. If they land blind, they're apt to set down right on the village." He paused, and clarified, "That is, if they just aim at our general direction from what we transmit here."

"In that case," Brian suggested, "we'd better take up the pickup and rejoin the ship—and hunt up a good big desert to land blind."

"Rejoining the ship would be quite a problem in this light," Ellie said, troubled. "It's going to be dark in less than an hour, I'd say—and I have a feeling that we're going to find ourselves completely night-blind."

Frobisher had considerately withdrawn while they were talking, and Brian snapped, "What's the matter with your brain, Ellie? You can go around to sunward, and match velocities with the *Homeward* there!"

"But then we might not find this place again," Langdon said surprisingly, and Ellie added, "If we go hurtling all around the planet, who knows if we'd find this again?"

"For the love of—who *cares*?"

"I do," said Langdon firmly. "According to Frobisher, conditions are pretty much the same everywhere, and—I kind of like that old guy, Brian. I like it here. I'd like to land here. Maybe settle down here."

Brian stared. "Are you crazy?

Langdon said, "Not at all. If we want to look around after the *Homeward* is down, fine—we have the pickup, we can do all the exploring we want to. We've plenty of fuel for the pickup. We're down, let's stay down."

Brian's face lost a little of its self-confidence; it was the first time that any of the crew had ever questioned his judgment, although many had resented his methods. He shrugged in a sudden futile misery. "I'm outvoted! And anyhow I resigned command when the atomics went on! Settle it with Caldwell by radio!" He lurched away from them and around toward the other side of the pickup. He heard the staccato bark of the radio inside, but paid no attention until he suddenly became conscious of Ellie, close beside him.

She raised her face, with an affectionate smile. Brian, even distracted by a thousand irritated thoughts, found time to wonder at the new mystery of her fair hair in the golden sun: the red was dimmed out, here, and the short curls seemed a pure, delicate silver; she was very white and fragile in this new light, and Brian reached impulsively to pull her close. She responded eagerly, her arms going around him and her face lifted with a simplicity that he had not quite expected.

"Journey's end," she said gently. "We've waited a long time for this, Brian, even if that electronic calculator was off-beam about what we'd find down here. Kiss me, you idiot."

The strength in his arms was astonishing, and she

gave a little cry. "Hey, I'm not used to weighing so much, take it easy—" she protested, laughing and the laughter trailed away as he bent his head down to hers. She was conscious of the sun in her eyes, of the physical fatigue from unaccustomed exercise, and the dragging feel of too much gravity—Terra Two was a small, light world. There was a crushing urgency in Brian's arms, and he strained her desperately close for a frantic minute, then abruptly pushed her away, his voice roughened.

"Where did Frobisher go? Damn it, Ellie, I need a clear head right now! The way it looks, we'll have the rest of our lives for that kind of thing!"

Hurt, but sensing the plea for help that begged her from behind the facade of his taut control, Ellie swallowed the pain of the personal rejection, and forced herself to think beyond the immediate moment. "He and Destry went to see how much of the grain had been ruined—"

"Hell, we can pay for the grain. There they come now—" Brian kicked out at a stalk of wheat, a curiously futile movement, and said in an odd, quenched voice, looking at his foot, "It's going to take months for us to get back in shape, after so long in free fall. We're coordinated all wrong for so much gravity. Notice the way Frobisher walks? Like he owned the world—" Resentment and envy mingled in his voice, and he stopped, then finished in a surprised tone, "—or as much of it as he wants!"

He said abruptly as the grandfather and grandson joined them, "Mr. Frobisher, we'll be glad to pay for what wheat we ruined."

"I would not have mentioned it," Frobisher said, and for the first time there was something like respect in his voice, "but it shows a good spirit that *you* have mentioned it. I have abundance, and you will have much to do after your crew lands. But if you insist upon payment, you can contribute task-work next season, after you are settled."

Brian was puzzled, but decided not to press the

point. Langdon rejoined them, and he asked, "What did Caldwell say?"

"He'll try it, if we'll fix up some kind of radio beam," Langdon responded. "Where do you want us to land, Mr. Frobisher?"

Hard Frobisher began to draw a sketch-map with a long stick in the dirt. "Over that rise—"

"We'll move the pickup over there," Ellie decided, then abruptly proffered the invitation, "Ride over there with us?"

Hard Frobisher looked speculatively at the plane, then toward the horizon. "Oh, it isn't a long walk," he said, but Destry said eagerly, "I believe I'd like it, grandpa."

The old man smiled deprecatingly. "The young are enthusiastic, Miss Wade," he said, almost in apology, "but—very well."

Brian logged another point of bewilderment. Could any educated humans be so trusting? Even on Terra Two, a well-united colony, there was a certain individual wariness, and strangers—how did Frobisher and Destry know they wouldn't be kidnapped?

It was an incredible relief to get back inside the pickup and switch on the familiar crimson light. Destry expressed mild surprise at the lighting, but Frobisher asked no questions and did not seem impressed when the pickup rose straight upward and circled before relanding at the edge of the large barren tract where they were to bring the *Homeward* down. At only one point in the whole maneuver did Frobisher show the slightest surprise, and that was when Ellie took the controls; he glanced at Brian, then at Langdon, and then, in frank amazement, at the small slim girl at the controls; but he made no comment.

They landed, and Langdon touched the radio. Brian took it from his hand. "Hello? Hello the *Homeward*? Kearns talking. That you, Tom?"

Tom Mellen's husky voice, very far away, asked thinly, "Was I right about no spaceports?"

"You were." Brian did not elaborate.

"We've got the direction of your beam. But Paula says if we follow it in, we'll land straight on the pickup. And if we don't, how are we going to hit the spot you've picked out for us?" Tom sounded puzzled. "In the last few seconds of braking, this hulk isn't very easy to steer."

"Hell!" Brian swore. "Hold on a minute!" He explained the situation briefly to Langdon. "I told you so!"

Langdon said grimly, "There's only one way to handle it. Take the fuel out of the pickup—impact would blow it up—move it out where we want them to land, and let them land on it. The pickup's expendable. The crew isn't. They'd land hard, but the crew will be in skyhooks, and Caldwell in a crash cockpit. Nobody'll be hurt."

"We're going to need the pickup later," Brian argued stubbornly.

"Well, have you a better idea?" Langdon asked. "If they follow the beam in part way, and try to swerve in the last few seconds, they're apt to miscalculate by a degree or two, and burn up the village."

"I still think we ought to hunt up a good-sized desert," Brian insisted.

Destry interrupted suddenly, in a tone of disgust, "Say, when you want a kingfisher to dive, you throw a hunk of bread where you want him to dive—you don't stand and hold it! If your radio—what is it—beam comes from that," he gestured at the transmitter, "why not just rip that thing out of the plane, fix it to send out a steady signal, and take it out where you want your spaceship to land? It won't hurt the spaceship to land on anything that small, will it?"

Brian stared at the boy in amazement for a minute, and Langdon's mouth dropped open.

"Destry," Ellie said after a brief silence, "*you* have the makings of a scientist."

"Look," the boy said uncomfortably. "The idea may not be much good, but why insult me?"

"It *is* good," Langdon interrupted. "I don't know

why I didn't think of it myself, except that I'm half-witted in this light! Brian, that's *it*. Ellie, while I send word to Mellen—before I rip this out—get under the seat and find the radio kit; I may have to resolder a few wires. Looks like we'll be in the dark by the time we finish, too; better get out the small lamps. Come on, get busy—" He flipped the switch open. *"Home-ward? Forbes speaking. Tom? Listen, in about twenty minutes we'll have a fix set up—"*

Brian and Ellie were struggling to lift the heavy seat; the unaccustomed gravity made it almost impossible to budge. Destry caught one end and heaved it up easily, and Ellie and Brian bent over the equipment stored there. The girl murmured in Brian's ear, "There goes your theory about regression! That kid knew what he was talking about."

Brian snorted. "And used an analogy from natural history! It was obvious enough, knowing the purpose of the radio. If either Langdon or I had been thinking, we'd have hit on it."

Ellie did not answer; there seemed no use in making Brian angry again. She went and stood watching Langdon working swiftly and expertly to dismantle and readjust the radio set to emit a self-contained, steady signal. He had to switch on the lights in the pickup before he finished, and before the impromptu homing device was completed, the sun had gone down. As they stood in the doorway of the pickup, Langdon scowled.

"I can't see my hand before my eyes!" he protested, and took one of the small red handlamps Ellie handed him. He looked at it disgustedly. "I can set the signal up with this, yes—but I don't know the lay of the land!" He gestured to the vast empty tract of barren land, and added, "I'll get lost there, or set it up on a side hill!"

Destry volunteered: "I know this place like my own hand—I'll come along and find a flat space."

"Need any help?" Brian offered, but Langdon shook his head. "No thanks. No sense in both of us getting tangled up in this murk." He picked up the homing device and, with Destry, moved away across the field which, to Brian and Ellie, was inky-dark, although in actuality it was bathed in clear moonlight. They stood in the door of the pickup, straining their eyes for the reddish, bobbing glimmer of Langdon's light, and Ellie shuddered in the rough warmth of Destry's coat. Brian's arm stole round her in the darkness.

She said tremulously, "What would have happened if we'd gone in at Mars!"

Frobisher, behind them, drew a harsh breath. "You're certainly lucky you didn't!" he said thankfully. "You couldn't have lived there three days, unless you stayed with your ship—I assume the ship is self-contained?"

"Oh, yes," Brian told him. "But—Mars was a sizable colony when the *Starward* left!"

Frobisher shrugged. "Everybody came in from Mars before the spacers stopped running. There's no water there at all, now."

Brian murmured, ". . . and by now you should have had all the planets colonized, and reached most of the nearer stars!"

The older man's voice lost its pleasant inflection. "You say some very surprising things, Mr. Kearns," he said dryly. "You don't say that we *could* have colonized the planets—which, of course, is true—but that we *should* have. Do you mind telling me why? The planets are not exactly suited for human habitation, except this one—and I would hate to have to live on any other."

Brian asked almost savagely, "You mean there is *no* space travel?"

"Why, no," Frobisher said slowly. "No one cares to go to the planets."

"But . . . the planets had already been reached, conquered, when the *Starward* left!"

Frobisher shrugged. "The Barbarians did a great many things which we regard as stupid," he said. "But why should it be called conquest, to encourage men to go out to worlds for which they are not biologically adapted? I have read much about the Barbarians, their insatiable egotism, their idle, childish curiosity, their continual escapism and refusal to face their problems, but—forgive me for saying this, no personal offense is intended—I had never believed it until today!"

Ellie took Brian's arm before he could answer. "Look there, Langdon's signaling—they must have the transmitter set up," she said, and moved her lamp in a wide circle. Before long, Langdon and Destry emerged from the bath of inky darkness, and sank down on the ground, in the little flood of reddish light from the pickup's windows. "That did it," Langdon said. "Now we sit and wait while Paula pinpoints the beam, and Caldwell will put her down right where we want."

"I hope somebody remembers to look after Einstein," Ellie worried. "I'd hate to have him break his neck in the last few seconds of the trip!"

"Judy will take care of him," Langdon reassured, and they waited in the red-cast darkness. Brian was mustering all the arguments he had heard from the Firsts about the necessity that had backed developing space travel.

"What about overpopulation? What about diminishing food supplies and natural resources?"

Frobisher's laugh was loud in the darkness. "Certainly not even the Barbarians expected to find natural food supplies on Mars or Venus!" he chuckled. "Interstellar travel might have solved it, but at prohibitive cost. Still, once man decided to stop squandering natural resources on vast theoretical projects, and throwing them irrecoverably out into space, that problem was easily solved."

"But what forced the decision?" Brian asked almost timidly.

"I wouldn't know," Frobisher said thoughtfully, "but when a decision is really necessary, as a rule, some one makes it. Probably the overpopulation reached such extremes—the solar system as a whole, of course, since Earth had to feed Mars and Venus too—that for one or two whole generations, every able-bodied man and woman had to put all his efforts into foodmaking instead of theoretical astronomy or whatever they called it. And by the time they had that problem solved, people were thinking of science in terms of human benefits, and probably realized that their resources could be handled more efficiently here on Earth. That—I mean thinking in terms of cost and human benefits—did away with war, too. It doesn't take long for attitudes to grow up. Then, too, during the over-populated generations, the population was almost entirely neurotic. The scientists of that day simply made it possible, I imagine, for women to avoid having the children they didn't want anyway, so that no one had children except the healthy-minded women whose primary interest was in children. The neurotic deathwish in the others effectively reduced the population in only two or three generations. You might say that the neurotics committed race suicide. Is that your ship, or another of Destry's meteors?"

They scrambled down, stumbling in the darkness, as the incredible rocket-roar sounded, and, on a collapsing telescope of fire, the *Homeward* screamed down to its resting-place. Brian, standing between Destry and Ellie, wondered—but was too weary and too overexcited to ask—if Destry still regretted his failure to find a meteor.

V

Explanations, introductions and much rapid-fire conversation made the landing a babble of noise.

"Hey, we're here!"

"Who thought up that homing device?"

"Hey, I'm blind! No light on this planet? Couldn't we have landed sunward?"

"What, in China?"

"Damned gravity, I can't walk!"

"Ellie!" (More imperatively than the other voices.) "Come here and get this devil-ridden cat of yours!"

102

Ellie dashed to Judy, who was carrying the squirming Einstein as she stumbled, clumsy-footed, down the ladder. "Here, take this animal!" she said crossly. "He's pulling my hair out by the roots!" She shoved the thick curls back over her shoulder, and fretted, "Hair's a worse nuisance in gravity than out of it!"

Ellie gently unwound her pet's suckers from Judy's ringlets, and the animal clung to her shoulder, squirming in crazy anticipation, struggling to get to the ground. She climbed the ladder painfully, wondering if she would ever adjust to the heavy gravity again, and, shoving into the lounge, ripped a strip of cloth from her skyhook to make a leash for the little animal. It was docile, but the prospect of running freely might tempt it to wildness.

As she came down again, she heard Frobisher's rich voice. "I offer the hospitality of our village and my home, for as long as you wish."

Stumbling on the final rung, Ellie almost fell against Mellen and Paula, standing silently in each other's arms at its foot. Their faces glowed dimly in the reddish shimmer from the open door of the ship, and a pang of envy stabbed through Ellie. They had only one emotion about the landing. They didn't care what they found—they were here, and together. She turned swiftly, not wanting to violate their moment, but Tom looked up at her and smiled with a joyfulness that made his gaunt good-natured face almost handsome. Paula reached out and hugged Ellie, cat and all. "It's all over!" she whispered jubilantly. "We're here!" But her dark eyes were a little sad, too, as she added, "I only wish there was some way we could let—our mothers and fathers—know that we came safely."

"They would be sure of that," Ellie comforted softly.

Tom Mellen scowled. "What's Kearns sounding off about now? Shush, girls—"

Brian was protesting, "Look, we can't all go. Some of us ought to stay aboard the *Homeward*. I suggest that we sleep aboard, and visit the village in the morning—"

"You stay if you like," Caldwell said mutinously. "I've seen enough of the *Homeward* for a lifetime!"

Then open rebellion burst out. Little Judy set off the reaction by proclaiming violently. "If I ever go aboard the *Homeward* again, they'll have to carry me and tie me!" and Mellen shouted, "The trip's over and we're private citizens again, Kearns, so stop pulling your rank on us!" In the storm of voices, the Centaurian cat went wild and clawed its way from Ellie's shoulder, tumbling with a queer, staggering gait across the rough dark grass. Ellie screamed, "Catch him, catch him!" and Paula made a grab for the creature, but missed, to trip and fall in the darkness. She lay there, laughing hysterically, watching the cat as it dived into the ring of lights. It stumbled and weaved on its spindly legs, thrusting pouch and tail weirdly to balance against the unfamiliar gravity; it sniffed the grass, with a musical caterwauling, then rolled over and over in the dark grass of the barrens, like a crazy asteroid tumbling in a wildly erratic orbit.

Brian didn't have a chance after that. The *Homeward*'s crew, barely more than adolescents, and semi-hysterical anyway with release from strain and the euphoria of journey's end, lay on the grass and rolled and stretched like children, paying less than no attention to Brian's harangue. By the time Ellie had managed to recapture the staggering Einstein, and the laughter-drunk youngsters had calmed a little, Brian had only one desire; to restore some semblance of dignity to himself and his crew. Livid and all but speechless, he tersely requested Caldwell, the calmest of the group, to accept Frobisher's hospitality on behalf of all, and watched, leaning somberly against the ladder, as they trooped away, guided by Destry with a lantern, still laughing wildly at nothing, and hanging on to each other's hands in the darkness to keep from falling.

Hard Frobisher walked steadily toward him, and on an impulse Brian asked him, "Would you like to come aboard?"

Hard answered unexpectedly, "Yes, I believe I'd be interested to see the inside of your ship," and followed Brian up the ladder, navigating the rungs with more ease than Brian himself, and into the lounge.

He looked curiously at the skyhooks and the complicated recreation devices, inspected the cabins without much comment, gave an interested hum in the Food Culture department. Finally Brian led him upward, into the enormous cabin where he himself had spent most of the voyage, handling the incredibly complex IS drives.

And here, before the tremendous machinery, Frobisher seemed at last impressed. He broke his silence with a wondering, "And you—you know all about this—this gimcrackery?"

Since the IS drives weighed upwards of a hundred tons, Brian laughed tolerantly at this understatement. "Yes, I'm a drive technician. I spent some time training."

"It must take a lifetime to learn all this!"

Brian condescended, "No, only about twelve years."

"Twelve years!" Frobisher repeated. "Twelve years, and how many—four?—on the way here, wasted on a room full of machines!" And now Brian uncomfortably recognized the emotion in his voice. It was pity. "You poor boy," Frobisher said, and repeated "Poor boy! To waste sixteen years on these metal levers and things! No wonder you are—" He broke off, perhaps aware of the tightness of Brian's clenched jaw.

Brian said in a low and deadly voice, "Oh, don't stop there! No wonder I am—what!"

"Neurotic," Frobisher said quietly. "Of course you must give yourself some reason why you have not wasted your life." And sadly he shook his head. "Fortunately, you are still young—"

"This ship," Brian said stiffly, "is the greatest accomplishment of the human race! If I live to be twice your age, I shall never—" Abruptly he rose and flicked a switch. The great dome cleared, and the immense magnifiers brought down the newly blossoming stars so that the man and boy stood under a vast, blazing galaxy of fire. "Damn it," Brian said huskily and his voice caught. "Man, we brought this little ship across nine light-years of nothing, nothing, *nothing!* We stepped on worlds where no human being had ever been before! You can't make out that that's nothing! It's the biggest thing humanity ever did—and I had the privilege to be part of it—" He was stammering, and, aware of it, he stopped.

Frobisher looked sad and embarrassed. "Poor lad, and what for? What did you, personally, get from it? What good did it do—not you alone—any single human being?"

Brian shouted suddenly, "You senile, half-witted old imbecile. I don't suppose you ever heard of abstract knowledge!"

"It isn't wholly unknown to me," Frobisher said coldly, but added, again with the same anxious friendliness, "Well my boy, I suppose you believe as you've been taught—but can you show me one single human, now *or* in the past, who was benefited by the trip of the *Starward,* except in his personal vanity? I think, if you carefully examined the matter, you'd find that the building, launching and cost of the *Starward* defrauded quite a large number of people."

Brian said almost desperately, "Individuals don't matter. Knowledge—any knowledge—is for the good of the race as a whole—to lift humanity out of the mud of the sea bottom—toward the stars—"

"I can't breathe such thin air," Frobisher said lightly. "The mud is much more comfortable."

"And where would you be," Brian almost shouted, "if your remote ancestor had never crawled down a tree trunk because he was *comfortable* where he was?"

"Why," Frobisher returned, looking up at the stars that were brilliant in the dome, "I should be very happily scratching myself and swinging by my tail. Do you think the great apes have any ambition to be human? Unfortunately, I've come too far to be happy in a treetop or a cave. But it seems to me that it's important, for any individual human, to find the absolute minimum with which he can recover that state of effortless happiness he lost when he left the treetops. Do you know what this ship reminds me of?"

"No!" Brian snapped.

"A brontosaurus." Frobisher did not elaborate, and in surly silence Brian snapped a switch. The stars went out.

"Come on," he muttered, "let's get out of here."

Brian slept little that night. At daybreak he stole into the room where the six women of the crew were sleeping, and quietly woke them; one by one, wrapping themselves sleepily in blankets, they tiptoed into the men's bedroom, where the crew gathered close, listening to Brian's soft, savage whispers.

"Kids, we've got to do something—anything to get away from this madhouse!"

"Go easy, Brian," Mellen interrupted. "That's strong language, and I don't like it. These people aren't crazy, from what we saw and heard last night. They think we're a little off course, though."

Caldwell muttered, "They're probably right. They used to say that being too long in space drove men crazy."

Brian said bitterly, "You all seem insane!"

"I don't blame them," Ellie said unexpectedly. "What *is* the good of going shooting all over the galaxy? It was fine, back in the days when it made people happy, but these people are happy without it."

"Brian's right, of course," said Don Isaacs, a quiet boy who had never grown too friendly with any of the crew except Marcia, and who never had much to say. "But there's this. Let's be practical. We're here. We can't go back to Terra Two. And we can't start reforming them. So let's just make the best of it."

Mellen said shortly, "Good for you, Don. And one more thing: if Kearns keeps shooting off his big mouth, we're apt to land in the local equivalent of the lock-up, for disturbing the peace or something. The peace seems to be valued pretty highly around here."

"But what are we going to do?" Brian wanted to know. "We can't just *live* here, can we?"

"And why not?" Paula's voice was defiant, and Judy murmured, "There aren't as many gadgets and things as there are on Terra Two, but it's certainly a better place than the Ship!"

Mellen pulled Paula's small shadowy form upright beside him. "I don't know why you came on the trip, Brian," he said. "But I came for one reason: because the Firsts trained me for it, and because if I'd begged off, somebody else would have had to. This isn't home, but it's as close to it as we're apt to find. I like it. Paula and I are going to settle down, and build a house or something."

Langdon added, "It's no secret that Judy and I and Don and Marcia,—" he paused, "and Brian and Ellie too—have been waiting a lot longer than we wanted to wait. There are a couple of hundred people in this village. Nice people, too, I'll bet. I like that old fellow. He reminds me of great-grandpa Wade. Anyhow, that's almost as many as they have on Terra Two. And I'll bet they don't all spend their time knocking themselves out, synthesizing food and exploring and cataloguing the whole planet, either!"

"They certainly don't!" Ellie slid her arm through Brian's. "They are, now, where Terra Two is, without the struggle. They've conquered the planet. They can quit trying."

But Mellen murmured derisively, "Kearns is heartbroken! He wanted to find mechanical computers telling everybody when to spit, and robots doing all the housework!"

"Yes . . ." Brian said thickly. "I guess I did . . ."

He turned his back on them and slammed out.

Ellie thrust her way through the others and ran out into the new day. She plunged her way through the gradually thinning darkness after his retreating shadow, and found him, huddled at the foot of the pickup. She knelt close to him and put her warm hands over his cold ones.

"Brian—oh, my dearest—"

"Ellie, Ellie!" He flung his arms around her, hiding his head against her thin dress. The girl held him tight, without speaking. How young he was, she thought, how very young. He'd started training for this work before he could read. Twelve years, training for the biggest job in the world he knew. And now it all collapsed under him.

Brian said bitterly, "It's the waste, Ellie. Why—we might as well have stayed on Terra Two!"

"That's exactly what Frobisher said," Ellie told him gently. She glanced at the reddening clouds in the east, and such a wave of homesickness wrenched at her that she nearly sobbed.

"Ellie—why?" he insisted. "Why? What makes a culture just stop, go dead, stagnant? They were right on the borders of conquering the whole universe! *What made them stop?*" The agonized earnestness of the question made Ellie's voice very tender.

"Maybe they didn't stop, Brian. Maybe they just progressed in another direction. Space travel was right for the culture we knew—or maybe it wasn't. Remember what the Firsts told us, about the Russo-Venusian War, and the Mars Raids? These people—maybe they've achieved what all cultures were looking for, and never found."

"Utopia!" Brian sneered, and pushed her away.

"No," said Ellie very low and put her arms about him again. "Arcadia."

"You're just the same, anyway. . . . Ellie, whatever happens, don't *you* leave me too—" he begged.

"I won't," she promised. "Never. Look, Brian, the sun's coming up. We should go back."

"Yeah, big day ahead," he said, and his mouth was too young to twist into such bitter lines. Then it relaxed, and he smiled and pulled her close to him.

"Not just yet . . ."

VI

Paula and Ellie stood on a knoll, near the abandoned *Homeward*, and watched the skeletal houses going up almost visibly beneath them. "The entire village has turned out!" Paula marveled. "Our house will be finished before night!"

"I'm glad there was land near the village for us," Ellie murmured. "Don't you feel as if you'd always lived here? And in only four months!"

The dark girl's face was sad. "Ellie, can't you do anything to keep Brian from—from sounding off at Tom? One day Tom will up and paste him one, and then you know what will happen to us!"

Ellie sighed. "And I'd hate to have either of us turned out of the village! It isn't all Brian's fault, Paula—" But then she paused, smiled sadly, and finished "I'm afraid he usually starts it, though. I'll do what I can, of course—"

"Brian is crazy!" Paula said emphatically. "Ellie—is it really true, that you and Brian will go on living in the *Homeward*?" She glanced distastefully at the black mass of the starship, and went on, "Why do you stand for it?"

"I'd live with Brian in a worn-out hydroponics tank, Paula. You would too, if it were Tom," Ellie said wearily. "And Brian's right, some one should keep the ship from being dismantled. Any of you had the same choice."

Paula murmured, "I like our house better, especially now—" and she put her head close to Ellie and whispered. Ellie hugged her delightedly, then asked, "Are you feeling all right, Paula?"

The girl hesitated before answering: "I tell myself it's all my imagination," she said at last. "This planet belonged to our ancestors, our race; my body should adapt to it easily. But after being born and growing up on Terra Two where I weighed half what I do here, and then so long in free fall—I know it's hard for all of us, this gravity, but since the baby . . . My body is one damned enormous ache, night and day!"

"You poor thing—" Ellie put an arm around her friend. "And I think I have troubles because my eyes still hurt in this light!"

Judy, heavy-footed, puffed up the slope. She had wound her heavy hair into a coil on her neck, and would have been pretty, in her light synthetic ship's coverall, had her eyes been less painfully screwed up against the brilliant sunlight. "Lazy things," she called gaily. "The men are hungry!"

"In a minute," Ellie answered, but did not move. She still found it more convenient to prepare food in the culture units of the *Homeward*, but disliked doing so now. However, on occasions such as today, when the villagers had turned out *en masse*, making a holiday of building the five new houses, it would make it easy to feed almost three hundred.

Langdon and Brian came up the hill, Hard Frobisher striding easily beside them. Langdon squinted at the women and finally pretended to identify Judy. "You women are getting spoiled," he teased. "On Terra Two, you'd be working along with the men, Judy!"

Judy tossed her head. "I enjoy being spoiled," she said pertly, "and I'll have enough to do, learning what women do here!"

There was a derisive twist in Brian Kearns' smile. "I came off lucky," he commented sourly. "Ellie at least had training for this kind of life. What about you, Paula, are you sorry not to be playing nurse to your electronic calculator?"

Paula gave an eloquent shrug. "The women of the *Starward* chose to be scientists and were chosen *because* they were scientists! I learned navigation because my grandmother learned to fix a cyclotron before she had her babies on Terra Two! I'm shedding no tears."

"Well, suppose you two come and have a lesson in food culture," Ellie admonished, and the three women turned toward the ship. At the foot of the ladder, however, Ellie paused. "Paula, dear, you shouldn't climb these steps now. Go on back, we'll manage by ourselves," she offered gently, and Paula gratefully turned back to rejoin the men.

Meanwhile, Frobisher sat looking down at the rising houses. "Soon you will be part of our village," he commented. "I think you have all done well."

Brian nodded curtly in acknowledgment. He had not been prepared to find the village operating as a self-contained colony, very much like the one at Terra Two—the crew of the *Homeward* had expected to re-enter the complex financial structure of the world the *Starward* had left. But the system seemed simplicity itself. Every man owned as much land as he, alone, was able to work, and owned whatever else he made with his own hands. A man gave his work wherever it was needed, and in return was entitled to take what he needed; food from those who grew it, clothes from those who made them, and so forth. Whatever he needed beyond the necessities of life must be earned by industry, good management and private arrangements. Brian found the system easy and congenial, even enjoying the job he did—a carpenter in Norten had given him work, and Brian, whose training had familiarized him with tools and machinery, had found no trouble in adapting his specialized skills to carpentry and building. There was always building going on somewhere in the village, it seemed. Brian made a good living.

And yet, for all its simplicity, the system seemed remarkably inefficient. Brian said, looking down at the sprawled houses, "I would think it would be easier if you had some kind of central distribution system."

"It's been tried, often," the old man answered patiently. "Every few years, a group of villages will consolidate, to exchange services, or set up communications systems for private individuals, or distribute foods that can't be grown locally, or luxury goods of one kind or another. But that means devising a means of exchange, and keeping account of credits, and so forth. As a rule, the disadvantages are so much greater than the advantages that the consolidation breaks down again within a year or two."

"But there's no law against it?" Brian asked.

"Oh, no!" Frobisher sounded shocked. "What would be the sense of that? The purpose of the whole system is to leave each man as free as possible! Most places are just about like Norten—the maximum of comfort, and the minimum of trouble."

Brian murmured, "I should think, then, that you'd want all kinds of labor-saving devices. You cook with fire—isn't it easier to have food culture units, such as we have on the Ship?"

Frobisher gave the matter grave attention. "Well, a wood fire imparts a fine flavor to food," he remarked. "Most people prefer it. And a cook must take pride in what she cooks, or why cook at all? And, although food culture units may be easier, if one is lazy, for those who use them, no one wants to take the time to manufacture them. One man can build a fireplace in a day, with a neighbor to help, and cook with it for the rest of his life. For a food culture unit, a man would have to spend years in learning to build it, and dozens of skilled and unskilled workers take months to build it; and, in order to make them cheaply enough for one man to buy, millions of them must be made, which means hundreds and thousands of people crowded together, just making them, having no time to grow or cook their own food, or live their own lives. The cost is too high. It's more trouble than it's worth."

Langdon asked him suddenly, "Just what is the population now?"

Frobisher frowned. "You people certainly are full of questions! Who knows? Collectively, people are nothing but statistics, which are no good to anyone. People are individuals. A few years ago, a philosopher in Camey—that's where Destry was born—worked out what he called the critical factor in population: the point where a village becomes too large to be efficient as a self-contained unit, and starts to break down. It's a nice problem, if you're interested in abstract mathematics—which I'm not."

"But I am," Paula said behind them, lowering herself carefully to the grass beside the men. "It sounds interesting."

Frobisher looked at her with fatherly friendliness. "You and Tom can come with me, next time I go to Camey," he invited. "I'll introduce you to Tuck—but all I know is, if a village gets too large, it's more trouble than convenience, and about half the population will go away and start a new one, or move to a smaller place."

"It doesn't sound very workable," Brian said with sour skepticism.

"It works," Frobisher answered equably. "That's the final test of any theory—hullo, here's Tom. We're not lying down on the job, Tom—just waiting for the women to bring dinner."

Mellen thrust a penciled scrap of paper into Langdon's hands. "Is Judy around? I can't read this—her writing is half Russian and half Arabic!"

"She's in the ship with Kearns' wife," Frobisher answered, not noticing how Paula winced at the word which, on Terra Two, had acquired an ignominious connotation of servitude and sexual inferiority. The three men from the *Homeward* tried to ignore the vulgarity, and Langdon gave a self-conscious laugh. "I think I can translate for you."

"What have you got there?" Brian asked, interested against his will—Judy had been an electrician aboard the *Homeward,* responsible for all lighting circuits, and her work was capable and excellent. He squinted toward the paper. Langdon scowled. "I can't see a thing in this cussed sunlight! What's it supposed to be, Tom?"

"Wiring diagram. There are red bulbs in the *Homeward,* and Judy's going to put lighting in our house—and yours, too. Didn't she tell you?"

"I thought you'd both gone all out on the primitive life," Brian muttered. Langdon snorted mockingly, and Mellen clenched his fists, then relaxed, with an easy grin.

"It's a free country," he said. Then suddenly he added, "Brian, it's none of my business, but are you and Ellie really going to stick to this damn foolishness? You'll be lonely up here. We could start on a house for you tomorrow."

"Somebody's got to keep the ship from being dismantled," Brian said stiffly. "And that reminds me, if Judy's going to do any wiring, she'd better use spare parts. No more trying to dismantle the drive units!"

Langdon laughed softly, but Mellen's face darkened in annoyance. He said shortly, "You aren't captain any more. The *Homeward* isn't your personal property, Brian."

"I'm aware of that," Brian rasped. "Neither does it belong to the crew collectively. It's being held in trust. And since nobody else has any sense of responsibility, I'm acting as caretaker."

Frobisher looked up as if he were about to speak, but Paula forestalled him, asking gently, "What for? We've no fuel, we'll never take off again."

The nightmare settled down on Brian again. He was fighting—but fighting an intangible, unresisting opponent! If they had been malicious, it would have been easier. They weren't malicious, they were only stupid—unable to understand just why the *Homeward* must be safeguarded as their only link with civilized life. A year or two, he thought grimly, and they'll realize just what I'm doing, and why. Just now, this primitivism is new, novel. But they are basically intelligent, sooner or later they will get tired of this. They can't live from day to day, like the villagers—but how do the villagers live this way? Frobisher's a cultured man. Destry's a bright boy. How can they stand it, living like nice clean animals?

"What deep imponderable are you meditating?" Ellie mocked his serious expression with a gay grimace, and thrust a basket into his hands, loaded with hot food. "Langdon, Paula, Mr. Frobisher—all hands needed to carry food. Here, Destry, you take a basket too," she commanded, handing one to the boy. "Bring this down to the village, now. Dinner is ready. And hurry up before it all gets cold."

Brian absent-mindedly picked up a biscuit-like cake of protein and munched at it as they descended the hill, his mind still halfway circling the continual problem. Ellie offered her basket, in turn, to Destry and Frobisher, and the old man politely took a cake, but Destry shook his head. "Thanks, I don't care for synthetics, Ellie."

"Destry!" His grandfather said with unnecessary sharpness, while Ellie murmured, "I didn't know you'd ever tasted them."

Destry stumbled over a rock in the path and used a couple of unfamiliar expletives; by the time he had picked himself up, retrieved the luckily unhurt basket, and apologized unnecessarily for the words he had used—he might have saved the trouble, for Ellie had never heard them and did not know whether they were sacred or profane—Ellie had forgotten her question for another.

"Have you ever been out of Norten, Destry?"

"Once or twice. I went to Camey with my father, when he went to teach a man there how to weave a rug. He weaves beautiful rugs—much better ones than ours."

"I see," Ellie murmured.

"He wanted me to come with him this time, but one place is pretty much like another, and I had my gardens to look after, so I stayed with grandpa. Besides, I had to—" Destry abruptly stopped. They were nearing the site of the new houses, and he called loudly. "Dinner!" and watched the villagers swarm off their scaffolds and beams. He took one of the baskets and scooted away to hand it around.

The food from the *Homeward*'s culture units was distributed, and the villagers ate it with polite thanks, but without much enthusiasm; only the children seemed to enjoy the elaborate synthetics, and even the *Home-*

ward's crew seemed to have lost their taste for it. Brian, sitting on a half-finished wooden step and munching absent-mindedly, abruptly made a face and flung the cake into the grass. Ellie cooked better, he decided, without the food machines. She liked the primitive cooking, and he had to admit she did it well. Still he felt disquieted. The food culture units synthesized their food out of a raw carbon, water, and almost infinitesimal amounts of raw chemicals; the whole process of *growing* food seemed, to Brian, wasteful and inefficient. It took so much time. Of course, he reflected, it was pleasant, outdoor work, and the people who did it seemed to enjoy it. It wasn't so confining as standing over the machines, and you didn't grow so deathly bored, month after month, with nothing to do except push a lever now and then, and between the lever-pushings, scan films and play endlessly complicated mental games. Brian had been expert at a certain three-dimensional board game which had to be played with the aid of an electronic computation device; now he felt a curiously disloyal thought that his proficiency had been born of boredom. When you enjoyed your work, he thought, you didn't have to invent things to do in your spare time.

But I enjoyed my work, he told himself in confusion, I enjoyed working on the IS units.

Didn't I?

Furiously scattering the remaining synthetics on his disposable plate, he crumpled up the bit of plastic and flung it angrily away, grabbing up his tools—the new hammer, plane and level which the village smith had made in exchange for roofing a chicken-house and repairing his cellar steps—and shouted to Caldwell.

"Come on, let's get back at work, I want to get this floor laid by sundown!" He walked catlike across the empty beams, squatted where he had left off, and began sliding boards into place and nailing them with fierce, angrily precise blows.

VII

He was still tersely angry and short-worded when, a few weeks later, he walked down through the village, a box in his hands. The houses were completed now, even to the steps, although still scantily furnished— Brian was still working, after each day's work, helping Caldwell build furniture.

He turned in at one still-raw, trampled muddy lawn, where brief spikes of summer grass were just beginning to peep through the wet earth, and knocked roughly.

Paula, a loose hand-woven smock wrapped about her body—she was beginning to grow clumsy and heavy now—opened the door, and her squinted, drawn face relaxed suddenly in a quick impulsive smile which made Brian feel ashamed and almost defensive.

"Brian—yes, Ellie's here, but—" She paused, hesitant, then invited shyly, "Won't you come in for a few minutes? We don't see much of you."

"I came down to see Tom—" Brian said uneasily, and followed Paula into the large reddish-lighted room. Before the fireplace he saw, to his intense dismay, that not only Ellie was there with Tom Mellen, but Langdon and Judy, Marcia and Don Isaacs, Destry, and—Hard Frobisher. Frobisher! It seemed that Hard Frobisher was continually underfoot, as if the crew of the *Homeward* needed his continual surveillance, assistance, advice! Brian frowned in annoyance; Frobisher acted like a self-appointed guardian to the newcomers. Yet it was impossible not to like the old fellow, even when he inquired genially, "And what have you in that big, interesting box, Mr. Kearns?"

"Just more of our top-heavy science," Brian said rudely, and undoing the box, took from it several pairs of red-lensed glasses in bent-plastic frames. He handed one pair to Mellen and donned one himself. "Turn out these lights, and see if these help any in the sun, will you?"

Tom looked at the glasses, puzzled, for a moment, then hooked the frames behind his ears and switched out the red lights, stepping to the west door and looking into the setting sun. Then he turned, grinning.

"They work, all right! What did you do, Brian? Just red glass wouldn't work—remember, we tried it?"

Brian shrugged. "There's a polarized layer inside. I couldn't find selenium, so I used an oxide of gold for the red color. It's a thin quartz filter . . . oh, never mind. I'd have had them before, but it took a damned long time to grind them."

Langdon took a pair from the box. "That's right," he said slowly. "I remember, Miguel Kearns made lenses for some of the old *Starward* instruments, when they broke, and when we were duplicating instruments for the strip. Did you help him?"

"Some," Brian returned. He met Frobisher's eyes, and said truculently, "So you have no use for science. Well, as you pointed out yourself, it's a free country, and my crew have been going around with sore eyes— and I don't like it!"

Paula's strained face relaxed as she slipped the filter glasses over her eyes, and she smiled. "This is wonderful, Brian," she said, and Ellie's face glowed with pride. Langdon mocked in a friendly voice, "The old fellow's human after all!" and flung a companionable arm around Brian's shoulders. "When are you and Ellie going to come down off your lofty peak and live with the rest of the pack?"

Brian stiffened, but the tone of approbation warmed him, and he came back, half-unwilling, to the fireplace, and listened to Frobisher, who said, laughing faintly, "It isn't science itself we don't like. It's the use of science as an end in itself, rather than a means. I mentioned a brontosaurus. I assume you know what that is?"

"We had them, alive, on Terra Two—or something like them. They're big, but not dangerous—they're too dumb," Brian told him.

"Exactly," Frobisher said. "But they're not much

good to themselves, are they?" He smiled; then his face sobered. "The brontosaurus, with his titanic body-mass, had outgrown the logical use of a development which had, originally, been good and useful. Science," he proceeded, "was developed to make life easier for man. The individual man. The light body-armor of the Barbarian soldier was developed for more formidable weapons, and finally the armor had to be so cumbersome that the armored man must be lifted on his horse with a derrick. And if he fell down—well, there he was. It helped along the army, as a unit—but it certainly made life a mess, for the individual. And science gave so much time and thought to units—the Nation, the Race, Humanity-as-a-Whole—that it laid terrific burdens on humanity as individuals. To benefit the monster of Humanity-as-a-Whole, they even fought wars—which killed off humanity, individually, at a fearful rate. Eventually—well, the knight fell down inside his armor, and couldn't get up again. I think the collapse started even before the *Starward* left. The brontosaurus died along with his protective nuisances, but nature was a little kinder to men—individually. Humanity-as-a-Whole died out pretty thoroughly, even as a concept. The individuals who were left knew enough not to start the whole dreary process all over again. Science took its rightful place with the other arts and crafts—instead of using it to serve a hypothetical whole, we use each art, or science, to enrich the personal, private life of each individual." He gestured around the room. "The sawmill and pottery. Tom's red lighting in here. And—your red-lensed glasses, Brian. I think the time has come when I can tell you why—"

But Brian had already risen, and flung away from him.

"I didn't come down here to be lectured!" he shouted at Frobisher, and strode to the door. "There are the glasses, Tom. You hand them out. Tell everybody not to break them; they take forever to grind."

The door slammed behind him.

Now that he had defied Frobisher, he felt a little better, but as the days came and went, he felt tormented by the uselessness of his life. He spent more and more time in vicious, expert hammering and sawing—in solitude, now—at furniture, finding a sort of satisfaction in substituting physical activity for insoluble mental problems; Ellie never dared to broach the subject of moving away from the *Homeward* again, until one night when Brian was sitting hunched over in the former lounge, listlessly watching Einstein clamber around the axis beams. The Centaurian cat's suckers were not strong enough to support his weight, in this gravity; he had developed a queer shambling gait on his hind feet, amusing to watch, but clumsy and painful, and Ellie picked up her pet and patted him as she passed through the lounge.

"Poor Einstein doesn't know what to make of this," she observed. "Gravity, in here where there ought to be no gravity at all. He'd be happier in a regular house."

"I suppose so," Brian said sourly. "I suppose you would too. But look, Ellie; the crew would dismantle the ship inside a year or two."

"Well, why not let them?" Ellie asked, matter-of-factly.

Brian shrugged, helplessly. "I suppose, sooner or later—but still, some day Terra Two will go out into space again, too—*they* haven't reverted to savagery!"

Ellie only smiled. "It won't happen in our lifetime."

"You're worse than the others!" Brian shouted in sudden furious anger. She only murmured uncritically, "Come in and have dinner."

Brian morosely rose and followed her. He had to edge by a machine, suddenly stumbled over Einstein, and exploded violently, "It's too damn cramped in here!"

Ellie did not answer, and Brian finally said, "I suppose—it won't happen in our lifetime, no."

"What are you going to do then, pass this great secret on to your sons?" Ellie inquired, and Brian started to answer before apprehending the dry irony in her voice. It had taken him twelve years to learn even the basics of interstellar operation.

He applied himself grimly to his food; but his mood softened as he ate, and he finally looked up and said, "Frobisher can like it or not, but I'll make a scientist out of Destry yet. The kid's always underfoot. Ever since you taught me to fly the pickup—I took him up one day, and let him take the controls for a few minutes; they aren't very complicated." He spoke with a sort of satisfaction; it was a point of self-respect in his continual struggle to maintain himself in Frobisher's presence. "The boy's nuts on airplanes. He must have read a lot in old books."

Ellie asked suddenly, "I wonder what Destry's father is like?"

Brian scoffed, "He makes rugs!"

Ellie looked unconvinced. "Maybe he makes the rugs the way Frobisher paints those birds he has all over the house. Look what I found in Frobisher's bookcase. Destry loaned it to me when I asked him." She handed him a book, nicely handbound in red cloth. Brian opened it curiously, skipping over the name—John D. Frobisher—penned neatly on the cover. He had seen few books in Norten village, and those were mostly blank-books filled with recipes, musical notations, or diaries—diary-keeping was a favorite pastime among young people here. But this was printed, and filled with elaborate, exquisitely reproduced diagrams which reminded Brian of Judy's scrawls when she was working out a wiring diagram. He tried to read a page or two, but, although the language was only loosely technical, Brian's education had been so rigidly specialized that the vocabulary was beyond him. He shut it up, and asked, "Did you show this to Judy?"

"Yes. It's a text, she says, on radio and radar, and not an elementary one either."

"Funny . . ." Brian mused.

"Here's something funnier," Ellie said. "Have you seen Caldwell lately? Or Marcia and Don Isaacs?"

"Come to think of it, I haven't. I never saw much of Don, though—"

"They went away, that night you and Frobisher had a fight. Marcia told me they were going so that Don could work in another village. That's what they always say—like Destry's father. People seem to come and go, here, all the time! Almost every day, somebody picks up a clean shirt and a pair of stockings, and walks off down the road. And nobody sees him again for three or four months—then he walks in again, as casually as I do when I go down to Paula's and back!"

"And the standard of living . . ." Brian mused, "comfortable enough—but primitive—"

Ellie laughed. "Oh, Brian! We were happy enough on Terra Two, without quite so much. The ship is super-mechanized. We're spoiled—we've developed a lot of artificial wants—"

"Frobisher converting you, too?" he asked glumly.

Her laugh was gay. "Maybe."

Brian was silent, staring at the book. He felt trapped. It was an insidious poison, the temptation to relax, rest, dream and die in this—Ellie had called it Arcadia, but a fragment of poetry from an old book in the ship's library teased his brain; not Arcadia, he thought drearily, but the isle of the lotus eaters, who tasted the poison flower and forgot all that they had been before. . . .

The words of the ancient poet sang insidiously in his brain. He rose and fetched the book from behind a panel in the lounge, and sat with it on his knees, the words of defeat staring him in the face.

Hateful is the dark-blue sky,
Vaulted o'er the dark-blue sea;
Death is the end of life; ah, why
Should life all labor be?
Let us alone; Time driveth onward fast. . . .

How could a man who had mastered space live like

this, in animal content, year after year? He wondered if among the lotus eaters there had been anyone who had refused the poison—and finally eaten it from starvation, or because he could not endure the loneliness of being the only sane man among a crew abandoned to their dreams?

> Let us alone . . . what pleasure can we have
> To war with evil? Is there any peace
> In ever climbing up the climbing wave?
> Give us long rest or death, dark death or dreamful
> ease . . .

Brian scowled and let the book fall to the floor. There was nothing easy about life in Norten! In the last few days, weeks, months, he had worked harder than ever in his life. His hands, once sensitive and smooth, alert to the quiver of a lever, were hard and callused and brown. And yet there was something satisfying about it. He no longer found himself inventing elaborate leisure-time pursuits, no longer felt impelled by continual anxiety about his crew, lest some minor infringement of a rule should lead to catastrophe. And Ellie—he had Ellie, and that, if nothing else, was something to hold him here.

And yet—after he had crossed space—his body thrived, but his brain was starving. Or was it, he asked himself. He'd gotten almost as much satisfaction—the guilty thought came—out of seeing his crew's eyes get well again, with the special glasses he'd made, as he had in piloting the *Homeward* safely through a dangerous cloud of radioactive gas. Maybe—again the guilt—maybe more.

The glasses. But they couldn't go around wearing red goggles for the rest of their lives. There ought to be some way of gradually altering the filters, maybe at monthly intervals, so that they became gradually accustomed to the light. He pulled a stylus toward him, vainly rummaged for a loose sheet of paper, then irritably climbed into his old control room, searched, and at last slid open the moving panel over the log book. His hands hesitated at the vandalism, then he shrugged and swore—the voyage was finished, the log book closed out! He ripped a blank sheet from the back, sat down then and there on the edge of the skyhook, and began to sketch out, roughly, a plan for glasses with changeable filters.

The yellow dawn was a glare in the sky when he finally came down; Ellie was sleeping in the cabin, her curly hair scattered over her face, and he quietly tiptoed past her and down the ladder. The air was cold and clear, and he stretched and yawned, suddenly realizing that he was very sleepy.

Against the brightening sky, a man's form was silhouetted as he gradually came over the knoll, and Tom Mellen called to him, "Is that you, Brian?" and came toward him with swinging strides. He had long ago discarded the shorts and sandals of the ship in favor of boots and long dyed breeches, and he wore one of his uniform shirts tucked into them. The ship's synthetics were not long-wearing or practical, although they were simply produced, but a few of the younger women in Norten had liked the thin pretty stuff, and exchanged lengths of it for the sturdier and more practical hand-made variety.

As he came near, Brian asked him, "Where are you going so early?"

"I'm going to work awhile in another town," Tom told him casually. "I've a letter to a friend of Frobisher's. I came up to ask a favor. I don't suppose Ellie's up yet? Well, don't bother her, but—" He paused, then added, "I meant for Paula to come along with me. But she's not very well, and she doesn't want to be with strangers. She'd particularly miss Ellie. But I hate to have her alone—"

Brian said abruptly, "Tom, we're going to move down into the village. I've—" He glanced around at the *Homeward* and all his pent-up resentment suddenly spilled over and he shouted, "I'm tired of caretaking the damned old—brontosaurus! I'm through!"

Tom whistled. "What's gotten into you? I thought you were dedicated to maintaining a nice snug little island of culture." Then at Brian's expression, the sarcasm left his voice, and he said eagerly, "Brian, if you mean that, why don't you and Ellie move down with Paula while I'm gone? I'll be back before the baby comes, and we can get started on a house for you two."

Brian stood thinking it over for a minute, and finally nodded. "All right. I'm sure Ellie will want to; she worries about Paula."

Tom stood looking at the ground. "Well, I'll shove along and tell Paula to expect you and then I'll get on my way." He paused, then said, low-voiced, "Brian—I thought, on the ship, you were just throwing your rank, about—well, about the girls. But now—" He stopped again, and said finally, embarrassed, "You know the baby was—started—before we landed?"

"I guessed that," Brian said coldly.

"I thought it was all right because we'd be landing within a month or two. But now—and the change in gravity, I'm afraid—if Paula and I had had the sense to wait—Judy's pregnant, you know, and she's not having any trouble at all, while Paula—" He stopped, and finally got out, "I guess I owe you an apology, Brian."

"You might better apologize to Paula," Brian said, but he had appreciated the spirit in which Tom spoke. So Tom finally realized that Brian had a good reason for what he'd done!

Tom added quietly, "I owe an apology for something else, too, Brian. It's my fault they've been leaving you out of things around here. I had the idea you were still trying to rehabilitate the natives."

"Don't bother apologizing," Brian said frigidly. So Tom had missed the point after all! "I'm not particularly interested in 'things around here,' and sooner or later I expect the natives will need rehabilitating, as you put it. When that day comes, I'll be here."

Mellen's mouth hardened. "I guess Frobisher's right

about you!" he said tightly. "So long, then." He put out his hand, rather unwillingly, and Brian shook it, without enthusiasm. He watched as Tom descended the hill, wondering where he was going and why. Was it just part of the local irresponsibility? Tom was irresponsible anyhow—the way he'd behaved toward Paula was shameful. And who, here, was going to look after her? The local witch-doctor? He scowled, and went in to tell Ellie about their impending move.

VIII

Paula was almost pathetically grateful for Ellie's company, and even Einstein settled down near the new fireplace as cozily as any of the ordinary Norten cats with whom he had a continual feud. Brian located a site for the house he intended to build and, aided by Destry, began a rough workshop of fieldstone. In return for the boy's help, Brian took him, nightly, into the dome of the *Homeward* and taught him the names and positions of the fixed stars. The boy was filling a blank-book with astronomical data; Brian offered to present him with one of the astronomy texts duplicated in the ship, but Destry politely refused the gift. "I like to make my own. That way I'm sure of what's in it," he explained.

Brian himself was painstakingly perfecting his lens-grinding equipment. The workshop had gradually become his refuge and, now that he knew he was working on something which was worth doing, he slowly began to come out of the closed shell he had originally thrown about himself, forbidding intimacy with the life of the village. He relaxed from the painstaking lens-grinding by beginning something he had not done since his early teens; glass-blowing. He made a set of fancy bottles for Ellie, and when Judy admired them, made one for her as well. Both Ellie and Judy had many friends in the village, and within a few weeks Brian found that so many men and women were asking him to make them that he could switch his full-time work from carpentry to glass-making. There was a potter in the village, who made extremely fine crockery, but at present the local glass-maker was—again the omnipresent phrase—"working in another village." Brian found the work congenial, and felt that he had approval.

However, privately, anxiety piled on anxiety. He actually saw very little of Paula, for there was still a certain stiffness between them; however, he felt disturbed at her obvious weakness. Ellie, too, was expecting a child by now, although as yet she had told no one but him, and Paula's condition filled him with panic for Ellie.

There had not been a medical man on the *Homeward:* none of them had ever been ill. Marcia had nominally been responsible for their health, but even Marcia wasn't here now. And judging from what little talk Brian had heard here in Norten, it was simply a matter of any woman's helping out when asked. Ellie had vigorously defended the system when Brian attacked it, protesting that having children was a natural function, and that the medical and surgical atmosphere with which the Terra Two colony surrounded it was enough to make any woman neurotic. Brian was unconvinced; that might be true when everything was normal, but Paula definitely needed care. He wondered how Ellie could be so unconcerned; Paula was her closest friend.

But even Brian was not prepared for the suddenness with which mere anxiety turned to disaster. At noon that day Paula was her usual self: pale and pathetically heavy of step, but gay and bright-eyed. In the evening she was quieter than usual, and went to bed early. And some time during the night Brian was roused by Ellie's hand on his shoulder and her scared voice: "Brian—*wake up!*"

Brian drew himself upright, instantly alert, seeing Ellie's tensely drawn face and hearing the near-hysteria in her voice. "It's Paula—I've never seen anything like it—she was all right this evening—oh, Brian, please come!"

Brian pulled a robe about his shoulders, thinking, what could have happened so suddenly? He heard the low, incessant moans even before he stepped into the inner room and stopped, aghast at Paula's face. It was altogether drained of color; even the lips were white and sunken, but a curious dark line marred their edges. She had always been excessively thin, but now her hands seemed suddenly shrunken into claws, and when Brian touched one, it was fire-hot. Brian cast his mind rapidly over what little he had been taught about the relationship of gravity and pregnancy—just enough to know that in free fall, a dangerous condition could develop suddenly. He wished he had known more, but they had taught him just enough that he was thoroughly convinced of the wisdom of enforcing strict celibacy in spaceship personnel. His brain, strictly specialized for one limited aspect of science, retained only a few fragments of knowledge. They fluttered and teased at the edge of his mind: imperfect placental junction without the cohesive effect of gravity, hormone malfunction under the added strain of pregnancy, extensive damage to internal tissues—all this was at free fall conditions. But what about Paula, who was adapted to the light gravity of Terra Two, whose child had actually been conceived in free fall, and who was being brutally punished by the dragging gravity of Earth? Something in the delicate balance of cohesions had evidently kicked loose. Brian looked down at the unconscious girl and spoke violently.

"Damn Mellen for an insubordinate idiot!"

"Where's Tom?" Paula whispered rackingly. "I want Tom!" The feverish bony fingers clutched at Brian's, and she begged, "I want Tom!" Her eyes opened, but she was looking past Brian into space. Brian felt the old cold anger knotting inside him. He bent over and promised quietly, "I'll get him."

Ellie whispered, "But—I don't know where he's gone, Brian. Paula might be—"

Brian straightened savagely. "I'll find him if I have to take my fists to Frobisher! Thank God we still have the pickup! And I'll find out where Don and Marcia were sent; yes, *sent!* All along I've had the feeling—"

"Brian—" Ellie caught at his hand, but he pushed her away. "Frobisher's going to listen to *me* for once! He can damn science all he wants to. But if Paula dies on our hands because nobody on this dark-ages planet knows what to do for her, then by the living God I'm going to personally raise such hell in this god-forsaken little Utopia of theirs that Frobisher and his pals will snap out of their daydream and start living like human beings again!" Without another word he strode out of the room, dressed hastily and went out of the house, his long-repressed anger boiling up and stiffening his back as he hurried toward the village. He went up Frobisher's steps and across his porch at a single bound, thrust the door open without knocking, and stormed inside.

"Frobisher!" he bellowed unceremoniously.

In the darkness there was a surprised noise; then steps, a door flung open and a light shining in Brian's eyes—and Hard Frobisher, half-dressed, came swiftly into the main room. Another opening door showed the half-naked Destry, surprised and angry. Frobisher's face, dim in the firelight, was surprised, too, but there was no anger, and he asked calmly, "Is something wrong?"

And as always, his calm brought Brian's anger to the exploding point. "You're right there's something wrong," he raged, and advanced on Frobisher so violently that the old man retreated a step or two. "I've got a girl on my hands who looks as if she were going to die," Brian roared, "And I want to know where on this devil-ridden planet you packed Tom off to, and where Marcia's gone! And then I want to know if there's a decent medical man anywhere in this damned backward dark-ages Utopia of yours!"

Frobisher's face swiftly lost its calm.

"Tom's wife?"

"And there's no need to talk smut!" Brian shouted, "Paula!"

"Paula Sandoval, then, if you like it better. What's the trouble?"

"I doubt if you'd understand," Brian snapped, but Frobisher said steadily, "I suppose it's the gravity sickness. Tom mentioned it before he left. It's easy to get hold of him. Destry—" He turned to the boy in the doorway. "Quick, go down and get the Center on the wire. Tell them to fly Mellen back here, inside an hour if they can. And—where's your father, Destry? This sounds like something for him."

Destry had disappeared inside his room while his grandfather was talking; almost instantly he came out again, stuffing his shirt into trousers. "He was in the Marilla Center last week, too," Destry said quickly, "but he's in Slayton now. And there's no regular transit plane there. Hey, Mr. Kearns—" He turned quickly to Brian. "You can fly the *Homeward*'s plane now, can't you? Or shall we get Langdon? They'll fly Tom in from the Marilla Center, but we'll have to fly over and pick up my father."

"What the—what the *hell*—!" Brian started, but Destry was already hurrying down a flight of stairs. Hard Frobisher put a compulsive hand on Brian's shoulder and shoved him after the boy. Brian stumbled on the steps and blinked in the raw light of an electric arcbulb. On a rough wood workbench, with Destry's notebooks and a few ordinary boy-type oddments, the stupefied Brian recognized what was unmistakably a radio transmitter. And not a simple one. Destry was already adjusting earphones and making a careful calibration of an instrument which looked handmade but incredibly delicate. He moved a key and said in a hurried voice, "Marilla Center, please, second-class priority, personal. Hello—Betty? You've got a man in the Center working on radio? Mellen? That's the man. This is Destry Frobisher talking from Norten. Fly him over here—as fast as you can make it. His wife's ill—yes, I know, but it's a special case. Thanks—" A long pause. "Thanks again, but we'll manage. Look, Betty, I have to get Slayton. Clear the stations, will you?" Another pause, and he said, "My father. Why? Oh—thanks, Betty, thanks a lot. Tell them we'll bring a plane over there for him." He closed the key and ripped off the headphone, standing up, and Brian exploded again.

"Just what's going on?" he demanded. *"What kind of a bluff have you people been putting up on us?"*

"No bluff," Frobisher said calmly. "I've told you, all along, that we use science, in its proper place. I've tried to tell you, two or three times, but you always shouted at me and shut me up before I could explain. Tom Mellen has been working in one of the Centers for a month. Didn't you wonder why he wasn't worried about leaving Paula, in her state of health? He's known that if any serious complication developed, he'd be sent for right away." He turned and started toward the stairs. "Don't you realize this is the first time you've ever shown the slightest *personal* concern for anyone or anything? Before this, you've been concerned with scientific accomplishments for their own sake. Now look, you can stand here staring like a brainless fool, or you can come with me to the Center to fetch my son—Destry's father—who is one of the most skillful medical men in this section." As Brian stood stonestill, unable to move before the onslaught of ideas, Frobisher urgently took his arm. "Snap out of it!" he commanded harshly. "I *can* fly a plane, but I would hate to have to manage that jet of yours! And I'll have to come with you, because you don't know the way! Destry, you stay close to the radio, just in case," he added.

Brian, too dazed to speak, stumbled with him across the dark fields toward the pickup, but by the time they reached it, his reactions were in operable condition; he climbed in at the controls, advised Frobisher to fasten a safety strap, put the pickup in the air, and listened intelligently to Frobisher's instructions for reaching the place he called Slayton Center. Then he turned his head.

"Look," he said grimly, "I'm a little stunned. Just what has been going on?"

Frobisher looked equally puzzled. "What do you mean?"

"All this—"

"Oh, this!" Frobisher dismissed it with a shrug. "You had fire extinguishers on your spaceship, I remember. Did you keep them out on your dinner tables, or did you leave them out of sight until they were needed in a hurry?"

"I mean—you let me go on thinking that people here didn't know much about science—"

"Listen, Kearns," Frobisher said abruptly, "you've been jumping to conclusions all along. Now don't jump to another one, that we've been bluffing, and concealing our civilization from you. We live the way we like to live."

"But radio—planes—you have all those things, and yet—"

Frobisher said, with barely concealed disgust, "You have the Barbarian viewpoint, I see. Radio, for instance. We use it for emergency needs. The Barbarians used to listen to keep from doing things—I know, they even had radio with pictures, and used to sit and listen and look at other people doing things instead of doing them themselves. Of course, they led rather primitive lives—"

"Primitive! Brian interrupted. "You have airplanes, and yet people walk—"

Frobisher said irritably, "Why not? Where is there to go in such a hurry—as long as we have fast transport for those few times when it is really necessary?"

"But even when the *Starward* left, each man had his own private copter—"

"Private baby carriage!" Frobisher snorted. "When I go anywhere, I go on my feet like a man! Stupid, primitive Barbarians, living huddled in cities like big

133

mechanical caves, never seeing the world they lived in, hidden away behind glass and steel and seeing their world on television screens and through airplane windows! And to make all those things they had to live huddled in their caves and do dirty smelly jobs with metal nuts and bolts, and never see what they were doing, never have any pride or skill—they lived like dirty animals! And what for? Mass men for mass production—to produce things they didn't need, to have money to buy other things they didn't need! Top-heavy brontosaurs! Who wants to live that way, or do that kind of work? There are a few craftsmen who build airplanes, or design them, because that's what they would rather do, and they'd be unhappy if they couldn't. They're artisans. And we can always use a *few* planes. But there aren't many, so we keep the planes for necessary work. And most people like doing simpler things, things with personal satisfaction. We don't force them to mass-produce airplanes simply because it's possible!" He checked his vehemence with an almost apologetic cough. "I didn't mean to get angry—that's the Slayton Center down there. You can land inside that rectangle of lights."

Brian set the pickup down easily—it seemed to be rolling over a velvety carpet—and they got down and walked in silence, across the darkly luxuriant grass, toward a low frame building of dark wood. Inside, by the warm glow of a fireplace, a man sat at a large table, lighted by an expertly rigged system of miniature spotlights, looking down at what appeared to be a large relief map. A headphone was on his ears; he glanced up as they came through the door, but motioned them into silence, listening intently, and after a moment groped blindly into a box fixed on the side of the desk and came out with a large black pin which he stabbed accurately into the relief map. "Tornado reported between Camey and Marilla. All right, then, ring off and send Robinson up to put a bomb in the center of it before it hits the farms out that way." He replaced the headphone, and inquired courteously. "What can I do for you gentlemen?"

"Hello, Halleck," Hard Frobisher said, and, advancing to the desk, shook hands with the man, "This is Brian Kearns—came in from space."

"Oh, are they still coming in, down your way? The last one we had here was in my grandfather's time," the man Halleck observed casually. "No, come to think of it, down there in Marilla they have a man called Mellen, been working the weather station. Do you know him, Mr. Kearns? I'm glad to meet you."

Brian murmured something noncommittal, and looked around, dazed. Halleck added, "I suppose you came to pick up Dr. Frobisher? He's on his way over. Won't you sit down?"

"Thanks." Frobisher sank down in a comfortable armchair, motioned Brian into another. The man at the desk hung up his headset and came to stand by Frobisher's chair. "Good to see you, Hard. When do you come up here again?"

"Not for a month or so. You'll be off by then?"

"I should say so! I've a couple of good cows calving, and I want to be home."

"Those blacks?" Frobisher asked. "Drive a few through Norten some day, and we'll see if we can't make a deal. I could use a good bull, and there are some new families with children, could use a milk cow."

Brian didn't try to follow the conversation after that; it seemed to be mostly about cows and the luck a mutual friend was having in breeding chickens which laid black-shelled eggs. Frobisher finally took pity on his blank face. "He's never been at a Center, before, Halleck," he told the stranger, who grinned. "Pretty dull, aren't they, Mr. Kearns? I'm always glad to come up here when it's time, but I'm always glad to get back to the farm."

Brian said, "I'm a little stunned at all this—" and added, "I'd understood your—your civilization wasn't scientific—"

"It isn't," Frobisher said sternly. "It definitely is not. We use science; it doesn't use us. Science, Mr. Kearns, is no longer the plaything of powerful war-mongers, nor is it enslaved to an artificial standard of living, keyed to an unhealthy, neurotic population who want to be continually amused, rocked in a cradle of overstimulation! It is not playing for pressure groups, so-called educators, fanatics, adolescents, egocentric exhibitionists, or lazy women! Men are no longer under pressure to buy the products of commercialized science to create employment and keep the cities running. Anyone who's interested, and who has talents and skills which go beyond day-to-day living, which is more than half of the population, spends a few months every year doing the things which need doing, not just in science. Halleck here knows more about weather conditions than anyone else in the South Plains. About four months out of the year, he sits over there, or works out in a weather plane, fighting tornados before they get started, working on reforestation, handling drought conditions. The rest of the year, he lives like anybody else. Everybody lives an easy, balanced life. Man's a small animal, and has to have a small horizon. There's a definite limit to his horizon, which is why a village breaks down and starts having internal trouble when it gets too big. But groups of people, as a whole, have to have some idea of the world over the horizon, if they're going to avoid the development of false ideas, superstitions and fears of strangers. So every man leads a secure, balanced life in the small horizon of his village, where he is responsible for himself, and responsible to every person he knows—and also, if he is capable, he lives a larger life *beyond* the village, working for others—but still and always for individuals, not for ideals." Brian opened his mouth to speak, but Frobisher quietly forestalled him. "And before he can work in the Centers, he has to prove himself as a responsible individual in the villages. There's a place waiting for you, Brian. How would you like to teach a course in the mechanics of interstellar space?"

"What?" Brian spluttered. "You mean—space travel?"

Frobisher laughed heartily. He glanced at his watch and said inconsequentially, "My son will probably be here in a few minutes—but still, I've time to explain—"

He turned to Brian again. "For two or three months a year," he reminded him. "There is always a use for knowledge, whether we can use it immediately or not. Our present way of life won't endure forever. At best it's an interim device, a probationary period, a sort of resting stage while man returns to sanity before he starts climbing again. Some day, man will probably take to space again, even the stars, but this time, we hope he'll do it with a sense of perspective, counting the cost and weighing it against individual advantages." He paused, and added quietly, "I think he will."

After a long silence, he added, "I'm a historian. Back in the First Renaissance, man was starting to outgrow his atavistic notion about survival of the strong and powerful instead of the best. Then, unluckily for Europe, and also unluckily for the Redmen, the so-called New World was discovered. It's always easier to escape across a frontier, and drive your misfits out instead of learning to live with your problems. When that frontier was finally conquered, man had a second chance to learn to live with himself and with what he'd done. Instead, after wars and all kinds of trouble, he escaped again, this time to the planets. But he couldn't escape from himself—and eventually that frontier was filled up to the saturation point, too. So he escaped again, this time by launching the *Starward*—but that time he went just one step too far. And then the crash came. Every man had the choice: die in his armor, or take it off." He grinned. "I thought for a while, Brian, that you were a brontosaur."

Brian mopped his forehead. "I feel pretty extinct," he murmured.

"Well, you can try teaching interstellar mechanics for awhile. The rest of the time—"

"Say—" Brian interrupted anxiously. "I don't have to start right away, do I? I'm fixing up a new set of lenses for the crew—"

Frobisher laughed, heartily and kindly, and put a hand on his shoulder. "Take your own time, my boy. The stars won't be bridged again for centuries. It's a lot more important to get your crew's eyes in good condition again." He rose abruptly. "Good—here is John, and I suppose by now, Mellen's on his way to Paula."

Brian quickly got to his feet as a tall dark-haired man in a white jacket came into the room. Even in the dim light the resemblance to Frobisher was obvious; he looked like an older, maturer Destry. Frobisher introduced the men, and Dr. John Frobisher gave Brian's hand a quick, warm hand shake.

"Glad to meet you, Kearns. Tom Mellen spoke about you, last time I was in Marilla. Shall we be on our way?" As they turned outward, and crossed the lighted airfield, he and his father spoke in low tones, and for once Brian had nothing to say. Even his thoughts were not working as he put the pickup in the air. The reversal had been too fast. Then, abruptly, a memory hit him and he turned his head around to ask sharply, "Listen here, if you can receive radio signals, *how is it that no one answered the* Homeward's *call from space!*"

Frobisher looked a trifle embarrassed. He said gently, at last, "We use a special, tight-beam transmission. Your signals are the old wide-band ones, and they came in as bursts of static."

For some reason Brian felt incredibly relieved, and his relief exploded in laughter.

"I *told* Tom our radio devices would be obsolete. . ." he choked.

"Yes," Frobisher said quietly. "Obsolete, only in a way you hadn't planned for. The whole crew of the *Homeward* was obsolete—and you've been on probation all along. But you've come out of that now, I think. Wait a bit—don't go to Norten just yet. Turn north—just a mile or two. There's something I want you to see."

Brian protested, "Paula—"

John Frobisher leaned forward. "Mellen's wife—" and this time Brian did not bridle at the vulgarism, "—will be all right, Kearns. We don't get the gravity sickness very often, now, but any danger in it was knocked out even before the spacers quit running. The girl's probably uncomfortable, and it looks terrible, but it isn't dangerous. We'll have her fixed up within an hour."

And somehow Brian's anxiety slid away. The words didn't mean much to him, but his training had taught him one thing, at least; he recognized competence when he met it, and it was in every inflection of John Frobisher's voice. Acquiescently he swung the skip to the northeast. The rising sun broke in a wave of brightness over the horizon, revealing the far-away line of ruined buildings that looked down drearily over a too-flat strip of dismal, barren land where nothing grew, a straight level plain of gray concrete. For miles it seemed to stretch away; Brian, flying low, could see the grass that pushed its way upward through the crumbling concrete, the dreary gap-windowed buildings softened a little by ivy. And then he saw them: eight tall regular shapes, straight and still gleaming a little. . . .

"There are only two laws in our culture," Frobisher said quietly. "One is that no man shall enslave another. And the second—" he paused, looking straight at Brian, "—is that no man shall enslave himself. Which is why we have never destroyed these ships. This was the old spaceport, Brian. Does it look very majestic? Would you care to land?"

Brian looked, thinking: this was what he had expected to see first. And yet, somehow, this was what seemed greatest to him: that man, having created this monster, should have the common sense to abandon its dreary domination—and the courage to leave it there. Men destroy only what they fear.

"Come on," Brian said steadily. "Quit riding me.

Let's get back home—and I do mean home. There's a sick girl waiting for you, doctor. And even if it isn't dangerous, they're going to be worrying until you tell them it isn't." Abruptly he gunned the jets and turned the ship southeast toward Norten Village, into the rising sun. He was not aware that he had passed the final test. He was thinking about Paula, and about Ellie, waiting and worrying. He knew in the back of his mind that he'd come back here some day, look around a little, maybe even mourn a little; you couldn't put away the biggest part of your life. But he wouldn't come right away. He had work to do.

The pickup of the *Homeward* flew away, into the morning. Yet behind them the mighty symbols remained, cold and masterful, a promise and a threat: eight great starships, covered from nose to tail with green-growing moss and red rust.

(1955)

Exiles of Tomorrow

"A very strange thing happened when I was born,"
Carey Kennaird told me.

He paused and refilled his wine glass, looking at me
with a curious appraisal in his young and very blue
eyes. I returned his glance as casually as I could,
wondering why he had suddenly decided to confide in
me.

I had known Carey Kennaird for only a few weeks.
We were the most casual of acquaintances; a word in
the lobby of our hotel, a cup of coffee in a lunchroom
he liked, mugs of beer in the quiet back room of the
corner bar. He was intelligent and I had enjoyed his
conversation. But until now it had consisted entirely of
surface commonplaces. Today, he seemed to be opening up a trifle.

He had volunteered the information, unasked, that
he was the son of a well-known research physicist, and
that he was in Chicago to look for his father who had
disappeared mysteriously a week or so before. Young
Kennaird seemed oddly unworried about his father's
plight. But I was pleased at the way his reserve appeared to be dropping.

As I say, Carey Kennaird had a casual way with
him, and he puzzled me. He did not, somehow, seem
emotionally in sympathy with the hectic tempo of the
rushed age in which he had grown up.

"Well," I told him noncommitally, "childhood memories often make quite normal events seem strange.
What was it?"

The appraisal in his eyes was franker now. "Mr. Grayne, do you ever read science-fiction?"

"I'm afraid not," I told him. "At least, only very occasionally."

He looked a little crestfallen. "Oh—well, do you know anything about the familiar science-fiction concept of traveling in time?"

"A little," I finished my drink, wishing the waiter would bring us another bottle of wine. "It's supposed to involve some quite staggering paradoxes, I believe. I'm thinking of the man who goes back in time and kills his own grandfather."

He looked disgusted. "That's at best a trite layman's idea!"

"Well, I'm a layman," I said genially. The arrogance of young people always strikes me as being pathetic rather than insulting. I did not think young Kennaird could have been more than nineteen. Twenty, perhaps. "Now then, young fellow, don't tell me you've actually invented a time machine!"

"Good Lord, no!" The denial was so laughingly spontaneous that I had to laugh with him, "No, just an idea that interests me. I don't really believe there's much paradox involved in time-travel at all."

He paused, his eyes still on my face. "See here, Mr. Grayne, I'd like to—well, do you mind listening to something rather fantastic? I'm not drunk, but I've got a good reason for wanting to confide in you. You see, I know a great deal about you, really."

I wasn't surprised. In fact, I'd been prepared for just such a statement. I grinned a strained grin at the boy. "No, go ahead," I told him. "I'm interested." I leaned back in my chair, preparing to listen.

You see, I knew what he was going to say.

II

Ryn Kenner sat in his cell, his head buried in his hands.

"Oh, God—" he muttered to himself, over and over.

There were so many unpredictable risks involved. Even though he had spent three years coaching Cara, teaching her to guard against every possible contingency, he still might fail. If only he could have eliminated the psychic block. But that, of course, was the most necessary risk of all.

Sometimes, in spite of his humanitarian training, Ryn Kenner thought the old, primitive safeguards had been better. Executing murderers, locking maniacs up in cells was certainly better than exiling men in this horrible new way. Ryn Kenner knew that he would have preferred to die. Two or three times he had even thought of slashing his wrists with a razor before the Exile. Once he had actually set a razor against his right wrist, but his early training had been too strong for him. Even the word *suicide* could set off a mental complex of quivering nerve reactions impossible to control.

The tragedy, Kenner thought despondently, resided in the paradox that civilization had become too enlightened. There had been a time when men had thought that traveling backward in time would upset the framework of events and change the future. But it had been a manifestly mistaken idea, for in this year, 2543 A.D. the whole past had already occurred, and the present moment contained within itself the entire past, including whatever rectifying attempts time-travelers had made in that past.

Kenner shivered as he realized that his own acts had all occurred in the past. He, Ryn Kenner, had already died—six centuries before.

Time-travel—the perfect, the most humane way of banishing criminals! He had heard all the arguments which sophistry could muster. The strong individualists were clearly misfits in the enlightened twenty-sixth century. For their own good, they should be exiled to eras psychologically congenial to them. A good many of them had been sent to California in the year 1849. They thus took a one-way trip to an era where murder was not a crime, but a social necessity, the respectable business of a gentleman. Religious fanatics were exiled to the First Dark Ages, where they could not disturb the tranquil materialism of the present century; too aggressive atheists, to the twenty-third century.

Kenner rose and began to pace his cell, which was a prison in fact, if not in appearance. Outside the wide window spread a spacious view of Nyor Harbor, and the room was luxuriously furnished. He knew, however, that if he stepped a foot past the lines which had been drawn around the door, he would be instantly overpowered by a powerful sleeping gas. He had tried it once, with almost disastrous results.

This hour of high decision was his last in the twenty-sixth century. In fifty minutes, in his own personal, subjective time from now, he would be somewhere in the twentieth century, the era to which his rashness had condemned him when he had been apprehended by the psycho police while attempting to rediscover the fabulous atomic isotopes. And he wouldn't remember enough to get back. He would be permitted to keep all his training—all his knowledge, and memory—but there would be a fatal reservation.

Never, for the rest of his life, would Kenner be able to remember that he had come from the future. For the three weeks during which he had been confined to the cell the radiant suggestor had been steadily beaming at his brain. No defense his mind could devise had sufficed to stay its slow inroads into his thought.

Already his brain was beginning to grow fuzzy and he knew that the time was short. He drew a long breath, hearing steps in the corridor, and the whistle which meant the hypnotic gas was being momentarily turned off.

He stopped pacing.

Abruptly the door opened, and a psycho-supervisor entered the cell. Framed in the radiance behind him—

"Cara!" Kenner almost sobbed, and ran forward to catch his wife in his arms, and hold her with hungry violence. She cried softly against him. "Ryn, Ryn, it won't be long—"

The supervisor's face was compassionate. "Kenner," he said, "you may have twenty minutes alone with your wife. You will be unsupervised." The door closed softly behind him.

Kenner led Cara to a seat. She tried to hold back her tears, looking at him with wide, frightened eyes. "Ryn, darling, I thought you might have—"

"Hush, Cara," he whispered. "They may be listening. Just remember everything I've told you. You *mustn't* risk being sent to a different year. You already know what to do."

"I'll—find you," she promised.

"Let's not talk about it," Kenner urged gently. "We haven't long. Grayne promised he'd look after you until—"

"I know. He's been good to me while you were here."

The twenty minutes didn't seem long. The supervisor pretended not to notice while Cara clung to Kenner in a last agony of farewell. Ryn brushed the tears away from her eyes, softly.

"See you in nineteen forty-five, Cara," he whispered, and let her go.

"It's a date, darling," were her last words before she followed the supervisor out of the prison. Kenner, in the last few moments remaining to him, before he sank into sleep again, desperately tried to marshal what little knowledge he possessed about the twentieth century.

His brain felt dark now, and oppressed, as if someone had wrapped his mind in smothering folds of wool. Dimly he knew that when he woke, his prison would be yet unbuilt. And yet, all the rest of his life he would be in prison—the prison of a mind that would never let him speak the truth.

III

"—and of course, this hypothetical psychic block would also contain a provision prohibiting marriage with anyone from the past," Carey Kennaird finished. "It would naturally be inconvenient for children to be born of the time exiles. But if my hypothetical man from the future should actually find the wife he'd arranged to have exiled with him, there'd be no psychic block against marrying *her*." He paused, staring at me steadily. "Now, what would happen to the kid?"

My own glass stood empty. I signaled to the waiter, but Kennaird shook his head. "Thanks, I've had enough."

I paid for the wine. "Suppose we walk to the hotel together, Kennaird?" I said. "You've got a fascinating theory there, my boy. It would make a fine plot for a science-fiction novel. Are you a writer? Of course, what happened to the boy—" we passed together into the blinding sunlight of the Chicago Loop, "—would be the climax of your story."

"It would," Kennaird agreed.

We crossed the street beneath the thundering El trains, and stood in front of Marshall Field's while Carey lit a cigarette.

"Smoke?" he asked.

I shook my head. "No thanks. You said you had a reason for confiding in me, young man. What is it?"

He looked at me curiously. "I think you know, Mr. Grayne. You weren't born in the Twentieth Century. I was, of course. But you're like Dad and Cara. You're a time exile, too, aren't you?"

"I know you can't *say* anything; because of the psychic block. But you don't have to deny it. That's how Dad told me. He made me read science-fiction. Then he made me ask him leading questions—and just answered yes or no." Young Kennaird paused. "I don't have the psychic block. Dad was trying to help me discover the time-travel device. He came up to Chicago, and disappeared. But I'm on the right track now. I'm sure of it. I think Dad got back somehow."

Even though I'd known what he was going to say, I swallowed hard.

"Something very strange *did* happen when you were born," I said. "You put a peculiar strain on the whole framework of time. It was something that never should have happened, because of—" my voice faltered, "the psychic block against marrying anyone from the past."

Carey Kennaird looked at me intently. "Hard to talk about the psychic block, isn't it? Dad never could."

I nodded without speaking. We climbed the hotel steps together. "Come up to my room," I urged. "We'll talk it over. You see, Carey—I'm going to call you that—Kenner used to be my friend."

"I wonder," Carey said, "If Dad got home in the twenty-sixth century."

"He did."

Carey stared. "Mr. Grayne! Is he all right?"

Regretfully, I shook my head. The elevator boy let us off on the fourth floor. I wondered if he, too, were an exile. I wondered how many people in Chicago were exiles, sullen behind the mask of a mental block which clamped a gag on their lips when they tried to speak the truth.

I wondered how many men, and how many women, were living such a lie, day in, and day out, lonely, miserable exiles from their own tomorrow, victims of a fate literally worse than death. Small wonder they would do *anything* to avoid such a fate.

My door closed behind us. While Carey stared, wide-eyed, at the device which loomed darkly in one corner of the room, I went to my desk, and removed the shining disk. I walked straight up to him. "This is from your father," I told him. "Look at it carefully."

He accepted it eagerly, his eyes blazing with excitement, sensing at once that it had come from the twenty-sixth century.

He died instantly.

Hating my work, hating time-travel, hating the whole chain of events, which had made me an instrument of justice, I stepped into the device that would return me to the twenty-sixth century.

Carey Kennaird had told the truth. A very strange thing *had* happened at his birth. Like an extra electron bombarding an unstable isotope, he had broken the link that held the framework of time together. His birth had started a chain reaction that had ended, for me, a week before in 2556, when Kenner and Cara had reappeared in the twenty-sixth century and been murdered in a panic by the psycho-supervisors. I, already condemned to time exile, had won a free pardon for my work, a commutation of my sentence to a light reprimand and the loss of my position. It was ugly work and I hated it, for Kenner and Cara *had* been my friends. But I had no freedom of choice. Anything was better than exile into time.

Anything, anything.

Besides, it had been necessary.

It isn't lawful for children to be born before their parents.

(1955)

Death Between the Stars

They asked me about it, of course, before I boarded the starship. All through the Western sector of the Galaxy, few rules are stricter than the one dividing human from nonhuman, and the little Captain of the *Vesta*—he was Terran, too, and proud in the black leather of the Empire's merchant-man forces—hemmed and hawed about it, as much as was consistent with a spaceman's dignity.

"You see, Miss Vargas," he explained, not once but as often as I would listen to him, "this is not, strictly speaking, a passenger ship at all. Our charter is only to carry cargo. But, under the terms of our franchise, we are required to transport an occasional passenger, from the more isolated planets where there is no regular passenger service. Our rules simply don't permit us to discriminate, and the Theradin reserved a place on this ship for our last voyage."

He paused, and re-emphasized, "We have only the one passenger cabin, you see. We're a cargo ship and we are not allowed to make any discrimination between our passengers."

He looked angry about it. Unfortunately, I'd run up against that attitude before. Some Terrans won't travel on the same ship with nonhumans even when they're isolated in separate ends of the ship.

I understood his predicament, better than he thought. The Theradin seldom travel in space. No one could have foreseen that Haalvordhen, the Theradin from Samarra, who had lived on the forsaken planet of

Deneb for eighteen of its cycles, would have chosen this particular flight to go back to its own world.

At the same time, I had no choice. I had to get back to an Empire planet—*any* planet—where I could take a starship for Terra. With war about to explode in the Procyon sector, I had to get home before communications were knocked out altogether. Otherwise—well, a Galactic war can last up to eight hundred years. By the time regular transport service was reestablished, I wouldn't be worrying about getting home.

The *Vesta* could take me well out of the dangerous sector, and all the way to Samarra—Sirius Seven—which was, figuratively speaking, just across the street from the Solar System and Terra. Still, it was a questionable solution. The rules about segregation are strict, the anti-discriminatory laws are stricter, and the Theradin had made a prior reservation.

The captain of the *Vesta* couldn't have refused him transportation, even if fifty human, Terran women had been left stranded on Deneb IV. And sharing a cabin with the Theradin was ethically, morally and socially out of the question. Haalvordhen was a non-human telepath; and no human in his right senses will get any closer than necessary even to a human telepath. As for a nonhuman one—

And yet, what other way was there?

The captain said tentatively, "We *might* be able to squeeze you into the crewmen's quarters—" he paused uneasily, and glanced up at me.

I bit my lip, frowning. That was worse yet. "I understand," I said slowly, "that this Theradin—Haalvordhen—has offered to allow me to share *its* quarters."

"That's right. But, Miss Vargas—"

I made up my mind in a rush. "I'll do it," I said. "It's the best way, all around."

At the sight of his scandalized face, I almost regretted my decision. It was going to cause an interplanetary scandal, I thought wryly. A human woman—and a Terran citizen—spending forty days in space and sharing a cabin with a nonhuman!

The Theradin, although male in form, had no single attribute which one could remotely refer to as sex. But of course that wasn't the problem. The nonhuman were specifically prohibited from mingling with the human races. Terran custom and taboo were binding, and I faced, resolutely, the knowledge that by the time I got to Terra, the planet might be made too hot to hold me.

Still, I told myself defiantly, it was a big Galaxy. And conditions weren't normal just now and that made a big difference. I signed a substantial check for my transportation, and made arrangements for the shipping and stowing of what few possessions I could safely transship across space.

But I still felt uneasy when I went aboard the next day—so uneasy that I tried to bolster up my flagging spirits with all sorts of minor comforts. Fortunately the Theradin were oxygen-breathers, so I knew there would be no trouble about atmosphere-mixtures, or the air pressure to be maintained in the cabin. And the Theradin were Type Two nonhumans, which meant that the acceleration of a hyperspeed ship would knock my shipmate into complete prostration without special drugs. In fact, he would probably stay drugged in his skyhook during most of the trip.

The single cabin was far up toward the nose of the starship. It was a queer little spherical cubbyhole, a nest. The walls were foam-padded all around the sphere, for passengers never develop a spaceman's skill at maneuvering their bodies in free-fall, and cabins had to be designed so that an occupant, moving unguardedly, would not dash out his or her brains against an unpadded surface. Spaced at random on the inside of the sphere were three skyhooks—nested cradles on swinging pivots—into which the passenger was snugged during blastoff in shock-absorbing foam and a complicated Garensen pressure-apparatus and was thus enabled to sleep secure without floating away.

A few screw-down doors were marked LUGGAGE. I immediately unscrewed one door and stowed my personal belongings in the bin. Then I screwed the top down securely and carefully fastened the padding over it. Finally, I climbed around the small cubbyhole, seeking to familiarize myself with it before my unusual roommate arrived.

It was about fourteen feet in diameter. A sphincter lock opened from the narrow corridor to cargo bays and crewmen's quarters, while a second led into the cabin's functional equivalent of a bathroom. Planet-bound men and women are always surprised and a little shocked when they see the sanitary arrangements on a spaceship. But once they've tried to perform normal bodily functions in free-fall, they understand the peculiar equipment very well.

I've made six trips across the Galaxy in as many cycles. I'm practically an old hand, and can even wash my face in freefall without drowning. The trick is to use a sponge and suction. But, by and large, I understand perfectly why spacemen, between planets, usually look a bit unkempt.

I stretched out on the padding of the main cabin, and waited with growing uneasiness for the nonhuman to show. Fortunately, it wasn't long before the diaphragm on the outer sphincter lock expanded, and a curious, peaked face peered through.

"Vargas Miss Hel-len?" said the Theradin in a sibilant whisper.

"That's my name," I replied instantly. I pulled upward, and added, quite unnecessarily, "You are Haal-vordhen, of course."

"Such is my identification," confirmed the alien, and the long, lean, oddly-muscled body squirmed through after the peaked head. "It is kind, Vargas Miss, to share accommodation under this necessity."

"It's kind of you," I said vigorously. "We've all got to get home before this war breaks out!"

"That war may be prevented, I have all hope," the nonhuman said. He spoke comprehensibly in Galactic Standard, but expressionlessly, for the vocal chords of the Theradins are located in an auxiliary pair of inner lips, and their voices seem reedy and lacking in resonance to human ears.

"Yet know you, Vargas Miss, they would have hurled me from this ship to make room for an Empire citizen, had you not been heart-kind to share."

"Good heavens!" I exclaimed, shocked, "I didn't know that!"

I stared at him, disbelieving. The captain couldn't have legally done such a thing—or even seriously have entertained the thought. Had he been trying to intimidate the Theradin into giving up his reserved place?

"I-I was meaning to thank *you*," I said, to cover my confusion.

"Let us thank we-other, then, and be in accord," the reedy voice mouthed.

I looked the nonhuman over, unable to hide completely my curiosity. In form the Theradin was vaguely humanoid—but only vaguely—for, the squat arms terminated in mittened "hands" and the long sharp face was elfin, and perpetually grimacing.

The Theradin have no facial muscles to speak of, and no change of expression or of vocal inflection is possible to them. Of course, being telepathic, such subtleties of visible or auditory expression would be superfluous on the face of it.

I felt—as yet—none of the revulsion which the mere presence of the Theradin was *supposed* to inspire. It was not much different from being in the presence of a large humanoid animal. There was nothing inherently fearful about the alien. Yet he was a telepath—and of a nonhuman breed my species had feared for a thousand years.

Could he read my mind?

"Yes," said the Theradin from across the cabin. "You must forgive me. I try to put up barrier, but it is hard. You broadcast your thought so strong it is impossible to shut it out." The alien paused. "Try not to be embar-rass. It bother me too."

Before I could think of anything to say to that a

crew member in black leather thrust his head, unannounced, through the sphincter, and said with an air of authority, "In skyhooks, please." He moved confidently into the cabin. "Miss Vargas, can I help you strap down?" he asked.

"Thanks, but I can manage," I told him.

Hastily I clambered into the skyhook, buckling the inner straps, and fastening the suction tubes of the complicated Garensen apparatus across my chest and stomach. The nonhuman was awkwardly drawing his hands from their protective mittens and struggling with the Garensens.

Unhappily the Theradin have a double thumb, and handling the small-size Terran equipment is an almost impossibly delicate task. It is made more difficult by the fact that the flesh of their "hands" is mostly thin mucous membrane which tears easily on contact with leather and raw metal.

"Give Haalvordhen a hand," I urged the crewman. "I've done this dozens of times!"

I might as well have saved my breath. The crewman came and assured himself that *my* straps and tubes and cushions were meticulously tightened. He took what seemed to me a long time, and used his hands somewhat excessively. I lay under the heavy Garensen equipment, too inwardly furious to even give him the satisfaction of protest.

It was far too long before he finally straightened and moved toward Haalvordhen's skyhook. He gave the alien's outer straps only a perfunctory tug or two, and then turned his head to grin at me with a totally uncalled-for-familiarity.

"Blastoff in ninety seconds," he said, and wriggled himself rapidly out through the hook.

Haalvordhen exploded in a flood of Samarran which I could not follow. The vehemence of his voice, however, was better than a dictionary. For some strange reason I found myself sharing his fury. The unfairness of the whole procedure was shameful. The Theradin had paid passage money, and deserved in any case the prescribed minimum of decent attention.

I said forthrightly, "Never mind the fool, Haalvordhen. Are you strapped down all right?"

"I don't know," he replied despairingly. "The equipment is unfamiliar—"

"Look—" I hesitated, but in common decency I had to make the gesture. "If I examine carefully my own Garensens, can you read my mind and see how they should be adjusted?"

He mouthed, "I'll try," and immediately I fixed my gaze steadily on the apparatus.

After a moment, I felt a curious sensation. It was something like the faint, sickening feeling of being touched and pushed about, against my will, by a distasteful stranger.

I tried to control the surge of almost physical revulsion. No wonder that humans kept as far as possible from the telepathic races. . .

And then I saw—did I *see*, I wondered, or was it a direct telepathic interference with my perceptions?—a second image superimpose itself on the Garensens into which I was strapped. And the realization was so disturbing that I forgot the discomfort of the mental rapport completely.

"You aren't nearly fastened in," I warned. "You haven't begun to fasten the suction tubes—oh, *damn* the man. He must have seen in common humanity—" I broke off abruptly, and fumbled in grim desperation with my own straps. "I think there's just time—"

But there wasn't. With appalling suddenness a violent clamor—the final warning—hit my ears. I clenched my teeth and urged frantically: "Hang on! Here we go!"

And then the blast hit us! Under the sudden sickening pressure I felt my lungs collapse, and struggled to remain upright, choking for breath. I heard a queer, gagging grunt from the alien, and it was far more disturbing than a human scream would have been.

Then the second shockwave struck with such violence that I screamed aloud in completely human terror. Screamed—and blacked out.

I wasn't unconscious very long. I'd never collapsed during takeoff before, and my first fuzzy emotion when I felt the touch of familiar things around me again was one of embarrassment. What had happened? Then, almost simultaneously, I became reassuringly aware that we were in free fall and that the crewman who had warned us to alert ourselves was stretched out on the empty air near my skyhook. He looked worried.

"Are you all right, Miss Vargas?" he asked, solicitously. "The blastoff wasn't any rougher than usual—"

"I'm all right," I assured him woozily. My shoulders jerked and the Garensens shrieked as I pressed upward, undoing the apparatas with tremulous fingers. "What about the Theradin?" I asked urgently. "His Garensens weren't fastened. You barely glanced at them."

The crewman spoke slowly and steadily, with a deliberation I could not mistake. "Just a minute, Miss Vargas," he said. "Have you forgotten? I spent *every moment* of the time I was in here fastening the Theradin's belts and pressure equipment."

He gave me a hand to assist me up, but I shook it off so fiercely that I flung myself against the padding on the opposite side of the cabin. I caught apprehensively at a handhold, and looked down at the Theradin.

Haalvordhen lay flattened beneath the complex apparatus. His peaked pixie face was shrunken and ghastly, and his mouth looked badly bruised. I bent closer, then jerked upright with a violence that sent me cascading back across the cabin, almost into the arms of the crewman.

"You must have fixed those belts *just now*," I said accusingly. "They *were not* fastened before blastoff! It's malicious criminal negligence, and if Haalvordhen dies—"

The crewman gave me a slow, contemptuous smile. "It's my word against yours, sister," he reminded me.

"In common decency, in common humanity—" I found that my voice was hoarse and shaking, and could not go on.

The crewman said humorlessly, "I should think you'd be glad if the geek died in blastoff. You're awfully concerned about the geek—and you know how *that* sounds?"

I caught the frame of the skyhook and anchored myself against it. I was almost too faint to speak. "What were you trying to do?" I brought out at last. "*Murder* the Theradin?"

The crewman's baleful gaze did not shift from my face. "Suppose you close your mouth," he said, without malice, but with an even inflection that was far more frightening. "If you don't, we may have to close it for you. I don't think much of humans who fraternize with geeks."

I opened and shut my mouth several times before I could force myself to reply. All I finally said was, "You know, of course, that I intend to speak to the captain?"

"Suit yourself." He turned and strode contemptuously toward the door. "We'd have been doing you a favor if the geek had died in blastoff. But, as I say, suit yourself. I think your geek's alive, anyhow. They're hard to kill."

I clutched the skyhook, unable to move, while he dragged his body through the sphincter lock and it contracted behind him.

Well, I thought bleakly, I had known what I would be letting myself in for when I'd made the arrangement. And since I was already committed, I might as well see if Haalvordhen were alive or dead. Resolutely I bent over his skyhook, angling sharply to brace myself in free-fall.

He wasn't dead. While I looked I saw the bruised and bleeding "hands" flutter spasmodically. Then, abruptly, the alien made a queer, rasping noise. I felt helpless and for some reason I was stirred to compassion.

I bent and laid a hesitant hand on the Garensen apparatus which was now neatly and expertly fastened. I was bitter about the fact that for the first time in my life I had lost consciousness! Had I not done so the crewman could not have so adroitly covered his negligence. But it was important to remember that the circumstance would not have helped Haalvordhen much either.

"Your feelings do you nothing but credit!" The reedy flat voice was almost a whisper. "If I may trespass once more on your kindness—can you unfasten these instruments again?"

I bent to comply, asking helplessly as I did so, "Are you sure you're all right?"

"Very far from all right," the alien mouthed, slowly and without expression.

I had the feeling that he resented being compelled to speak aloud, but I didn't think I could stand that telepath touch again. The alien's flat, slitted eyes watched me while I carefully unfastened the suction tubes and cushioning devices.

At this distance I could see that the eyes had lost their color, and that the raw "hands" were flaccid and limp. There were also heavily discolored patches about the alien's throat and head. He pronounced, with a terribly thick effort:

"I should have—been drugged. Now it's too late. *Argha maci*—" the words trailed off into blurred Samarran, but the discolored patch in his neck still throbbed sharply, and the hands twitched in an agony which, being dumb, seemed the more fearful.

I clung to the skyhook, dismayed at the intensity of my own emotion. I thought that Haalvordhen had spoken again when the sharp jolt of command sounded, clear and imperative, in my brain.

"Procalamine!" For an instant the shock was all I could feel—the shock, and the overwhelming revulsion at the telepathic touch. There was no hesitation or apology in it now, for the Theradin was fighting for

his life. Again the sharp, furious command came: *"Give me procalamine!"*

And with a start of dismay I realized that most nonhumans needed the drug, which was kept on all spaceships to enable them to live in free-fall.

Few nonhuman races have the stubbornly persistent heart of the Terrans, which beats by muscular contraction alone. The circulation of the Theradin, and similar races, is dependent on gravity to keep the vital fluid pulsing. Procalamine gives their main blood organ just enough artificial muscular spasm to keep the blood moving and working.

Hastily I propelled myself into the "bathroom" —wiggled hastily through the diaphragm, and unscrewed the top of the bin marked FIRST AID. Neatly pigeonholed beneath transparent plastic were sterile bandages, antiseptics clearly marked HUMAN and— separately, for the three main types of nonhuman races, in one deep bin—the small plastic globules of vital stimulants.

I sorted out two purple fluorescent ones—little globes marked *procalamine*—and looked at the warning, in raised characters on the globule. It read: FOR ADMINISTRATION BY QUALIFIED SPACE PERSONNEL ONLY. A touch of panic made my diaphragm catch. Should I call the *Vesta's* captain, or one of the crew?

Then a cold certainty grew in me. If I did, Haalvordhen wouldn't get the stimulant he needed. I sorted out a fluorescent needle for nonhuman integument, pricked the globule and sucked the dose into the needle. Then, with its tip still enclosed in the plastic globe, I wriggled myself back to where the alien still lay loosely confined by one of the inner straps.

Panic touched me again, with the almost humorous knowledge that I didn't know where to inject the stimulant, and that a hypodermic injection in space presents problems which only space-trained men are able to cope with. But I reached out notwithstanding and gingerly picked up one of the unmittened "hands." I didn't stop to think how I knew that this was the proper site for the injection. I was too overcome with strong physical loathing.

Instinct from man's remote past on Earth told me to drop the nonhuman flesh and cower, gibbering and howling as my simian antecedents would have done. The raw membrane was feverishly hot and unpleasantly slimy to touch. I fought rising queasiness as I tried to think how to steady him for the injection.

In free-fall there is no steadiness, no direction. The hypodermic needle, of course, worked by suction, but piercing the skin would be the big problem. Also, I was myself succumbing to the dizziness of no-gravity flight, and realized coldly that if I couldn't make the injection in the next few minutes I wouldn't be able to accomplish it at all.

For a minute I didn't care, a primitive part of myself reminding me that if the alien died I'd be rid of a detestable cabinmate, and have a decent trip between planets.

Then, stubbornly, I threw off the temptation. I steadied the needle in my hand, trying to conquer the disorientation which convinced me that I was looking both up and down at the Theradin.

My own center of gravity seemed to be located in the pit of my stomach, and I fought the familiar space voyaging instinct to curl up in the foetal position and float. I moved slightly closer to the Theradin. I knew that if I could get close enough, our two masses would establish a common center of gravity, and I would have at least a temporary orientation while I made the injection.

The maneuver was unpleasant, for the alien seemed unconscious, flaccid and still, and mere physical closeness to the creature was repellent. The feel of the thick wettish "hand" pulsing feebly in my own was almost sickeningly intimate. But at last I managed to maneuver myself close enough to establish a common center of gravity between us—an axis on which I seemed to hover briefly suspended.

I pulled Haalvordhen's "hand" into this weight-center in the bare inches of space between us, braced the needle, and resolutely stabbed with it.

The movement disturbed the brief artificial gravity, and Haalvordhen floated and bounced a little weightlessly in his skyhook. The "hand" went sailing back, the needle recoiling harmlessly. I swore out loud, now quite foolishly angry, and my own jerky movement of annoyance flung me partially across the cabin.

Inching slowly back, I tried to grit my teeth, but only succeeded with a snap that jarred my skull. In tense anger, I seized Haalvordhen's "hand," which had almost stopped its feverish pulsing, and with a painfully slow effort—any quick or sudden movement would have thrown me, in recoil, across the cabin again—I wedged Haalvordhen's "hand" under the strap and anchored it there.

It twitched faintly—the Theradin was apparently still sensible to pain—and my stomach rose at that sick pulsing. But I hooked my feet under the skyhook's frame, and flung my free arm down and across the alien, holding tight to the straps that confined him.

Still holding him thus wedged down securely, I jabbed again with the needle. It touched, pricked—and then, in despair, I realized it could not penetrate the Theradin integument without weight and pressure behind it.

I was too absorbed now in what had to be done to care just how I did it. So I wrenched forward with a convulsive movement that threw me, full-length, across the alien's body. Although I still had no weight, the momentum of the movement drove the hypodermic needle deeply into the flesh of the "hand."

I pressed the catch, then picked myself up slowly, and looked around to see the crewman who had jeered at me with his head thrust through the lock again, regarding me with the distaste he had displayed toward the Theradin, from the first. To him I was lower than the Theradin, having degraded myself by close contact with a nonhuman.

Under that frigid, contemptuous stare, I was unable to speak. I could only silently withdraw the needle and hold it up. The rigid look of condemnation altered just a little, but not much. He remained silent, looking at me with something halfway between horror and accusation.

It seemed years, centuries, eternities that he clung there, just looking at me, his face an elongated ellipse above the tight collar of his black leathers. Then, without even speaking, he slowly withdrew his head and the lock contracted behind him, leaving me alone with my sickening feeling of contamination and an almost hysterical guilt.

I hung the needle up on the air, curled myself into a ball, and, entirely unstrung, started sobbing like a fool.

It must have been a long time before I managed to pull myself together, because before I even looked to see whether Haalvordhen was still alive, I heard the slight buzzing noise which meant it was a meal-period and that food had been sent through the chute to our cabin. I pushed the padding listlessly aside, and withdrew the heat-sealed containers—one set colorless, the other set nonhuman fluorescent.

Tardily conscious of what a fool I'd been making of myself, I hauled my rations over to the skyhook, and tucked them into a special slot, so that they wouldn't float away. Then, with a glance at the figure stretched out motionless beneath the safety-strap of the other skyhook, I shrugged, pushed myself across the cabin again, and brought the fluorescent containers to Haalvordhen.

He made a weary, courteous noise which I took for acknowledgment. By now heartily sick of the whole business, I set them before him with a bare minimum of politeness and withdrew to my own skyhook, occupying myself with the always-ticklish problem of eating in free-fall.

At last I drew myself up to return the containers to the chute, knowing we wouldn't leave the cabin during the entire trip. Space, on a starship, is held to a rigid minimum. There is simply no room for untrained outsiders moving around in the cramped ship, perhaps getting dangerously close to critically delicate equipment, and the crew is far too busy to stop and keep an eye on rubbernecking tourists.

In an emergency, passengers can summon a crewman by pressing a call-button. Otherwise, as far as the crew was concerned, we were in another world.

I paused in midair to Haalvordhen's skyhook. His containers were untouched and I felt moved to say, "Shouldn't you try to eat something?"

The flat voice had become even weaker and more rasping now, and the nonhuman's careful enunciation was slurred. Words of his native Samarran intermingled with queer turns of phrase which I expected were literally rendered from mental concepts.

"Heart-kind of you, *thakkava* Varga Miss, but late. Haalvordhen-I deep in grateful wishing—" A long spate of Samarran, thickly blurred followed, then as if to himself, "Theradin-we, die nowhere only on Samarra, and only a little time ago Haalvordhen-I knowing must die, and must returning to home planet. *Saata.* Knowing to return and die there where Theradin-we around dying—" The jumble of words blurred again, and the limp "hands" clutched spasmodically, in and out.

Then, in a queer, careful tone, the nonhuman said, "But I am not living to return where I can stop-die. Not so long Haalvordhen-I be lasting, although Vargas-you Miss be helping most like *real* instead of alien. Sorry your people be most you unhelping—" he stopped again, and with a queer little grunting noise, continued, "Now Haalvordhen-I be giving Vargas-you stop-gift of heritage, be needful it is."

The flaccid form of the nonhuman suddenly stiffened, went rigid. The drooping lids over the Theradin's eyes seemed to unhood themselves, and in a spasm of

163

fright I tried to fling myself backward. But I did not succeed. I remained motionless, held in a dumb fascination.

I felt a sudden, icy cold, and the sharp physical nausea crawled over me again at the harsh and sickening touch of the alien on my mind, not in words this time, but in a rapport even closer—a hateful touch so intimate that I felt my body go limp in helpless fits and spasms of convulsive shuddering under the deep, hypnotic contact.

Then a wave of darkness almost palpable surged up in my brain. I tried to scream, *"Stop it, stop it!"* And a panicky terror flitted in my last conscious thought through my head. *This is why, this is the reason humans and telepaths don't mix—*

And then a great dark door opened under my senses and I plunged again into unconsciousness.

It was not more than a few seconds, I suppose, before the blackness swayed and lifted and I found myself floating, curled helplessly in mid-air, and seeing, with a curious detachment, the Theradin's skyhook below me. Something in the horrid limpness of that form stirred me wide awake.

With a tight band constricting my breathing, I arrowed downward. I had never seen a dead Theradin before, but I needed no one to tell me that I saw one now. The constricting band still squeezed my throat in dry gasps, and in a frenzy of hysteria I threw myself wildly across the cabin, beating and battering on the emergency button, shrieking and sobbing and screaming. . .

They kept me drugged all the rest of the trip. Twice I remember waking and shrieking out things I did not understand myself, before the stab of needles in my arm sent me down into comforting dreams again. Near the end of the flight, while my brain was still fuzzy, they made me sign a paper, something to do with witnessing that the crew held no responsibility for the Theradin's death.

It didn't matter. There was something clear and cold and shrewd in my mind, behind the surface fuzziness, which told me I must do exactly what they wanted, or I would find myself in serious trouble with the Terran authorities. At the time I didn't even care about that, and supposed it was the drugs. Now, of course, I know the truth.

When the ship made planetfall at Samarra, I had to leave the *Vesta* and transship for Terra. The *Vesta*'s little captain shook me by the hand and carefully avoided my eyes, without mentioning the dead Theradin. I had the feeling—strange, how clear it was to my perceptions—that he regarded me in the same way he would regard a loaded time bomb that might explode at any moment.

I knew he was anxious to hurry me aboard a ship for Terra. He offered me special reservations on a lino-cruiser at a nominal price, with the obvious lie that he owned a part interest in at. Detachedly I listened to his floundering lies, ignored the hand he offered again, and told a lie or two of my own. He was angry. I knew he didn't want me to linger on Samarra.

Even so, he was glad to be rid of me.

Descending at last from the eternal formalities of the Terran landing zone, I struck out quickly across the port city and hailed a Theradin ground-car. The Theradin driving it looked at me curiously, and in a buzzing voice informed me that I could find a human conveyance at the opposite corner. Surprised at myself, I stopped to wonder what I was doing. And then—

And then I identified myself in a way the Theradin could not mistake. He was nearly as surprised as I was. I clambered into the car, and he drove me to the queer, block-shaped building which my eyes had never seen before, but which I now knew as intimately as the blue sky of Terra.

Twice, as I crossed the twisting ramp, I was challenged. Twice, with the same shock of internal surprise, I answered the challenge correctly.

At last I came before a Theradin whose challenge crossed mine like a sure, sharp lance, and the result was startling. The Theradin Haalvamphrenan leaned backward twice in acknowledgment, and said—not in words—"Haalvordhen!"

I answered in the same fashion. "Yes. Due to certain blunders, I could not return to our home planet, and was forced to use the body of this alien. Having made the transfer unwillingly, under necessity, I now see certain advantages. Once within this body, it does not seem at all repulsive, and the host is highly intelligent and sympathetic.

"I regret the feeling that I am distasteful to you, dear friend. But, consider. I can now contribute my services as messenger and courier, without discrimination by these mind-blind Terrans. The law which prevents Theradin from dying on any other planet should now be changed."

"Yes, yes," the other acquiesced, quickly grasping my meaning. "But now to personal matters, my dear Haalvordhen. Of course your possessions are held intact for you."

I became aware that I possessed five fine residences upon the planet, a private lake, a grove of Theirry-trees, and four hattel-boats. Inheritance among the Theradin, of course, is dependent upon continuity of the mental personality, regardless of the source of the young. When any Theradin died, transferring his mind into a new and younger host, the new host at once possessed all of those things which had belonged to the former personality. Two Theradin, unsatisfied with their individual wealth, sometimes pooled their personalities into a single host-body, thus accumulating modest fortunes.

Continuity of memory, of course, was perfect. As Helen Vargas, I had certain rights and privileges as a Terran citizen, certain possessions, certain family rights, certain Empire privileges. And as Haalvordhen, I was made free of Samarra as well.

In a sense of strict justice, I "told" Haalvamphrenan

how the original host had died. I gave him the captain's name. I didn't envy him, when the *Vesta* docked again at Samarra.

"On second thought," Haalvamphrenan said reflectively, "I shall merely commit suicide in his presence."

Evidently Helen-Haalvordhen-I had a very long and interesting life ahead of me.

So did all the other Theradin.

(1956)

Bird of Prey

It would be an hour before I could board the starship. Straight ahead, an open gateway led to the spaceport, and the white skyscraper which was the Headquarters of the Terran Empire on Wolf; behind me, Phi Coronis was dipping down over the roofs of the Kharsa—the Old Town—which lay calm in the bloody sunset, but alive with the sounds and the smells of human, nonhuman and half-human life. The pungent reek of incense from an open street-shrine made my nostrils twitch, and a hulked form inside, not human, cast me a surly green glance as I turned aside into the cafe at the spaceport gates.

It wasn't crowded inside. A pair of furred chaks lounged beneath the mirrors at the far end. One or two spaceport personnel, in storm gear, were drinking coffee at the counter, and a trio of Dry-towners, rangy lean men in colorful shirtcloaks, stood at a wall-shelf, eating Terran food with aloof dignity. In my neat business clothes I felt more conspicuous than the furred and long-tailed chaks; an Earthman, a civilian. I ordered, and by unconscious habit, carried my food to a wall-shelf near the Dry-towners, the only native humans on Wolf.

They were tall as Earthmen, weathered by the fierce sun of their parched cities of dusty salt stone—the Dry Towns which lie in the bleached bottoms of Wolf's vanished oceans. Their dialect fell soft and familiar on my ears. One, without altering his expression or his easy tone, had begun to make elaborate comments on

169

my entrance, my appearance, my ancestry and probable personal habits, all defined in the colorfully obscene dialect of the Dry Towns.

I leaned over and remarked, in the man's own dialect, that at some future and unspecified time I would appreciate an opportunity to return their compliments.

By custom they should have apologized, and laughed at a jest decently reversed on themselves. Then we would have bought each other a drink, and that would have been that. But it didn't happen that way. Not this time.

Instead, to my dismay, one of them fumbled inside the clasp of his shirtcloak; I edged backward, and found my own hand racing upward, seeking a skean I hadn't carried in six years. It looked like a rough-house.

The chaks in the corner moaned and chattered. Then I became aware that the three Dry-towners were gazing, not at me, but at something, or someone, just behind me. Their skeans fumbled back into the clasps of their cloaks, and they surged back a pace or two.

Then they broke ranks, turned and ran. They *ran*—blundering into stools as they went, leaving a havoc of upset benches and broken crockery in their wake. I let my breath go, turned, and saw the girl.

She was slight, with waving hair like spun black glass, circled with a tracery of stars. A black glass belt imprisoned her waist, like clasped hands, and her robe, stark white, bore an ugly sprawl of embroidery across the breasts—the hideous Toad-god, Nebran. Her face was all human, all woman, but the crimson eyes held a hint of alien mischief.

Then she stepped backward, and with one swift movement she was outside in the dark street. A smudge of incense from the street-shrine blurred the air; there was a little stirring, like the rising of heat waves in the salt desert at noon. Then the shrine of Nebran was empty, and nowhere in the street was there a sign of the girl; she simply was not there.

I turned toward the spaceport, slowly, walking through a dragging reluctance, trying to file the girl away in memory as just another riddle of Wolf that I'd never solve.

I'd never solve another riddle on Wolf. I'd never see it again. When the starship lifted at dawn, I'd be on it, outbound from Phi Coronis—the red sun of Wolf.

I strode toward the Terran H.Q.

No matter what the color of the sun, once you step inside an H.Q. building, you are on Terra. The Traffic Division was efficiency made insolent, in glass and chrome and polished steel. I squinted, readjusting my eyes to the cold yellowness of the light, and watched myself stride forward in a dozen mirrors; a tall man with a scarred face, bleached by years spent under a red sun. Even after six years, my neat civilian clothes didn't fit quite right, and, with unconscious habit, I still walked with the lean stoop of the Dry-towners I had impersonated. The clerk, a rabbitty little man, raised his head in civil inquiry.

"My name's Cargill," I told him. "Have you a pass for me?"

He stared. A free pass aboard a starship is rare except for professional spacemen, which I obviously wasn't. "Let me check my records," he hedged, and punched scanning buttons on the mirror top of the desk. "Brill, Cameron—ah, yes, Cargill—are you *Race* Cargill of the Secret Service, sir? *The* Race Cargill? Why, I thought—I mean—everybody took it for granted that you were—"

"You thought I'd been killed a long time ago because my name never turned up in the news? Yes, I'm Race Cargill. I've been working upstairs on Floor 38 for six years, holding down a desk any clerk could handle."

He gawped. "You, the man who went to Charin in disguise and routed out The Liess? And you've been working upstairs all these years? It's—hard to believe, sir!"

My mouth twitched. It had been hard for me to believe while I was doing it. "The pass?"

"Right away, sir." There was respect in his voice

now, despite those six years. Six years of slow death since Rakhal Sensar had left me a marked man, my scarred face making me a target for all my old enemies, and ruining my career as a Secret Service man.

Rakhal Sensar—my fists knotted with the old, impotent hate. And yet, it had been Rakhal Sensar who had first led me into the secret byways of Wolf, teaching me a dozen alien languages, coaching me in the walk and step of a Dry-towner, perfecting a disguise which had become deep second nature to me. Rakhal was a Dry-towner from Shainsa, and he had worked in the Terran Secret Service, my partner since we were boys. Even now I was not sure why he had erupted, one day, into the violence that ended our friendship. Then he had simply disappeared, leaving me a marked man, my usefulness to the Secret Service ended . . . a bitter man tied to a desk . . . and a lonely man—Juli had gone with him.

With a small whirring noise, a chip of plastic emerged from a slot on the desk. I pocketed the pass, and thanked the clerk.

I went down the skyscraper steps, and across the vast expanse of the spaceport, avoiding or ignoring the last-minute bustle of cargo loading, process crews, curious spectators. The starship loomed over me, huge and hateful.

A steward took me to a cabin, then strapped me into the bunk, tugging at the acceleration belts until my whole body ached. A long needle went into my arm—the narcotic that would keep me safely drowsy during takeoff. Doors clanged, men moved and talked in the corridors with a vague excitement. All I knew about Theta Centaurus, my destination, was that it had a red sun, and the Legate on Megaera could use a trained Secret Service man. And *not* pin him down at a desk. My mind wandered and it was a pair of crimson eyes, and hair like spun black glass, that tumbled down with me, down to the bottomless pit of sleep. . .

. . . someone was shaking me.

"Ah, come on, Cargill. Wake up, fella."

My eyes throbbed, and when I got them open I saw two men in the black leather of spaceforce guards, mingled with some vague memory of a dream. We were still inside gravity. I came all the way awake with a rush, swinging my legs out of the bunk, flinging aside the belts somebody had unfastened.

"What the devil—Is something wrong with my pass?"

He shook his head. "Magnusson's orders. Ask him about it. Can you walk?"

I could, although my feet were a little shaky on the ladders.

I knew it made no sense to ask what was going on. They wouldn't know. I asked anyway. "Are they holding the ship for me?"

"Not that one," he answered.

My head was clearing fast, and the walk speeded up the process. As the elevator swooped up to Floor 38, my anger mounted. Magnusson had been sympathetic when I resigned; he'd arranged the transfer and the pass himself. What right did he have to grab me off an outbound starship at the last minute? I barged into his office without knocking.

"What's this all about, chief?"

Magnusson was at his desk, a big bull of a man who always looked as if he'd slept in his rumpled uniform. He said, not looking up, "Sorry, Cargill, but there was just time to get you off the ship—no time to explain."

There was somebody in the chair in front of his desk; a woman, sitting very straight, her back to me. But when she heard my voice, she twisted around, and I stared, rubbing my eyes. Then she cried out, "Race, *Race!* Don't you *know* me?"

I took one dazed step forward. Then she had flown across the space between us, her thin arms tangling around my neck, and I caught her up.

"Juli!"

"Oh, Race, I thought I'd die when Mac told me you were leaving tonight, it was the only thing that kept me going, the thought of seeing you," she sobbed and laughed at once. I held my sister at arm's length, looking down at her. I saw the six years that divided us, all of them, printed plain on her face. Juli had been a pretty child; six years had fined her features into beauty, but there was tension in the set of her shoulders, and the gray eyes had looked into horrors.

I said, "What's wrong, Juli? Where's Rakhal?"

I felt her shiver, a deep thing that I could feel right up through my own arms.

"I don't know. He's gone. And—oh, Race, he's taken Rindy with him!"

"Who's Rindy?"

She didn't move.

"My daughter, Race. Our little girl."

Magnusson's voice sounded low and harsh. "Well, Cargill? Should I have let you go?"

"Don't be a damned fool!"

"Juli, tell Race what you told me—just so he'll know you didn't come for yourself."

I knew that, already. Juli was proud, and she *had* always been able to live with her own mistakes. This wouldn't be any simple complaint of an abused wife.

She said, "You made your big mistake, Mac, when you turned Rakhal out of the Service. He was one of the best men you had."

"Matter of policy. I never knew how his mind worked. Do *you*, Juli? Even now? That final episode— Juli, have you taken a good look at your brother's face?"

Juli raised her eyes, and I saw her wince. I knew just how she felt; for almost three years I'd kept my mirror covered. Then she said, almost inaudibly, "Rakhal's face is—is just as bad."

"That's some satisfaction," I said.

Mac looked baffled. "Even now I don't know what it was all about."

"And you never will," I said for the dozenth time. "Nobody could understand it, unless he'd lived in the Dry Towns. Let's not talk about that. *You* talk, Juli. What brought you here? And what about the kid?"

"At first Rakhal worked as a trader in Shainsa,"

174

Juli began. I wasn't surprised. The Dry Towns were the core of Terran trade on Wolf. "Rakhal didn't like what the Empire was doing. But he tried to keep out of it. There were times—they'd come to him and ask for information, information he could have given them, but he never told anything—"

Mac grunted, "Yeah, he's an angel. Go ahead."

Juli didn't, not immediately; instead, she asked, "Is it true what he told me—that the Empire has a standing offer of a reward for a working model of a matter-transmitter?"

"That offer's been standing for five hundred years, Terran reckoning. Don't tell me he was going to invent one!"

"I don't think so, no. But he heard rumors—he knew *about* one. He said he was going to try to find it—for money and Shainsa. He started coming in at odd times—wouldn't talk to me about it. He was queer about Rindy. Funny thing. Crazy. He'd brought her some kind of nonhuman toy from one of the inland towns, Charin, I think. It was a weird thing, scared me. He'd talk to her about it and Rindy would gabble all kinds of nonsense about little men and birds and a toymaker—it *changed* him, it—"

Juli swallowed hard, twisting her thin fingers in her lap. "A weird thing—I was afraid of it, and we had a terrible fight. He threw it out and Rindy woke up and shrieked, she screamed for hours and hours. Then she dug it up out of a trashpile, she broke all her fingernails but she kept on digging for it, we never knew where or why, and Rakhal was like a crazy man—" abruptly Juli checked herself, and visibly caught at vanishing self-control.

Magnusson broke in, very gently. "Juli, tell Race about the riots in Charin."

"In Charin—oh. I think he led the rioting; he came back with a knife cut in his thigh. I asked him if he was mixed up in the anti-Terran movements, and when he wouldn't answer—that was when I threatened to leave him, and he said if I came there—I'd never see Rindy again. The next day he was gone—"

Suddenly the hysteria Juli had been forcing back broke free and she rocked back and forth in her chair, torn and shaken with great strangling sobs. "He—took— Rindy! Oh, Race, he's crazy, crazy, I think he hates Rindy, he took—he smashed her toys, Race, he took every toy she had and broke them one by one, smashed them into powder, every toy she had—"

"Juli. Juli, please—" Magnusson pleaded. I looked at him, shaken. "If we're dealing with a maniac—"

"Mac, let me handle this. Juli. Shall *I* find Rakhal for you?"

A hope was born in her ravaged face, and died there, while I looked. "He'd have you killed. Or kill you."

"He'd try, you mean," I amended. I stooped and lifted Juli, not gently, my hands gripping at her shoulders in a sort of rage.

"And I won't kill him—do you hear? He may wish I had, when I get through with him—*hear me, Juli?* I'll beat the living daylights out of him, but I'll settle it with him like an Earthman."

Magnusson stepped toward me and pried my crushing hands off her shoulders. He said, "Okay, Cargill. So we're all crazy. I'll be crazy too—try it your way."

A month later, I found myself near the end of a long trail.

I hadn't seen an Earthman or a Dry-towner in five days. Charin was mostly a chak town; not many humans lived there, and it was the core and center of the resistance movement. I'd found that out before I'd been there an hour.

I crouched along the shadow of a wall, looking toward the gypsy glare of fires, hot and reeking at the far end of the Street of the Six Shepherds. My skin itched from the dirty shirtcloak I hadn't changed in days—shabbiness is wise in nonhuman parts, and Dry-towners from the salt lands think too highly of water to spend much of it in washing, anyway.

It had been a long and difficult trail. But I'd been lucky. And if my luck held, Rakhal would be somewhere in the crowd around those fires.

A dirty, dust-laden wind was blowing up along the street, heavy with the reek of incense from a street-shrine. I took a few steps toward the firelight, then stopped, hearing running feet.

Somewhere, a girl screamed.

Seconds later, I saw her; a child, thin and barefoot, a tangle of dark hair flying loose as she darted and twisted to elude the lumbering fellow at her heels. His outstretched paw jerked cruelly at one slim wrist. The girl sobbed and wrenched herself free and threw herself straight on me, wrapping herself around my neck with the violence of a stormwind. Her hair got in my mouth, and her small hands gripped at my back like a cat's flexed claws. "Oh, help me," she sobbed, "don't let him, don't—" And even in that broken cry, I took it in; the brat did not speak the jargon of the slum, but the pure, archaic Shainsa dialect.

What I did then was just as automatic as if it had been Juli; I pulled the kid's fists loose, shoved her behind me, and scowled at the pig-eyed fellow who lurched toward us. "Make yourself scarce," I advised.

The man reeled; I smelled sour wine and the rankness of his rags as he thrust one grimy paw at the girl. I thrust myself between them and put my hand on the skean quickly.

"Earthman!" The man spit out the word like filth.

"Earthman!" Someone took up the howl; there was a stir, a rustle, all along the street that had seemed empty, and from nowhere, it seemed, the space in front of me was crowded with shadowy forms, human and—otherwise.

"Grab him, Spilkar! Run him outa Charin!"

"Earthman!"

I felt the muscles across my belly knotting into a hard band of ice. I didn't believe I'd given myself away as an Earthman—the bully was using the old

Wolf tactic of stirring up a riot in a hurry—but just the same I looked quickly round, hunting a path of escape.

"Put your skean in his guts, Spilkar!"

"Hai-ai! Earth man! *Hai-ai!"*

It was that last sound that made me panic, the shrill yelping *Hai-ai* of the Ya-men. Through the sultry glare of the fires, I could see the plumed and taloned figures, leaping and rustling; the crowd melted open.

"Hai-ai! Hai-ai!"

I whirled, snatching the girl up, and high-tailed it back the way I'd come, only faster. I heard the yelping shrieks of the Ya-men behind me, and the rustle of their stiff plumes; I dived headlong around the corner, ducked into an alley, and set the girl on her feet.

"Run, kid!"

"No, no! This way!" she urged in a hasty whisper, and her small fingers closed like a steel trap around my wrist; she jerked hard, and I found myself plunging forward into the shelter of a street-shrine.

"Here—" she panted, "stand in—close to me, on the stone—" I drew back, startled.

"Oh, don't stop to argue," she whimpered. "Come *here!* Quick!"

"Hai-ai! Earthman! *There he is—"*

The girl's arms flung round me again; I felt her slight, hard body pressing on mine, and she literally hauled me toward the center of the shrine.

The world tilted. The street disappeared in a cone of spinning lights, stars plummeted crazily, and I plunged down—locked in the girl's arms—spun—dropped head-over-heels through reeling lights and shadows that wheeled around us. The yelping of the Ya-men whispered away in unimaginable distances, and for a second I felt the swift unmerciful blackout of a powerdive, with blood breaking from my nostrils and filling my mouth. . . .

Light flared in my eyes. I was standing square on my feet in a little street-shrine—but the street was gone. Coils of incense still smudged the air, the God squatted, toadlike, in his recess; the girl was still hanging limp, locked between my clenched arms. As the floor straightened under my feet, I staggered forward, thrown off balance by the sudden return of the girl's weight, and grabbed, blindly, for support.

"Give her to me," said a voice at my ear, and the girl's light sagging body was lifted from my arms. A strong hand grasped my elbow; I found a chair beneath my knees, and sank gratefully into it.

"The transmission isn't smooth between such distant terminals," the voice remarked, "I see that Miellyn has fainted again. A weakling, the girl, but useful."

I spat blood, trying to get the room in focus. For I was inside a room; windowless, but with a transparent skylight, through which pink daylight streamed in thin long splinters. Daylight—and it had been midnight in Charin! I'd come halfway around the planet in a few seconds!

From somewhere, the room was filled with a sound of hammering; tiny, bell-like hammering, a fairy's anvil. I looked up and saw a man—a man?—watching me.

On Wolf you see all kinds of human, nonhuman and half-human life. I consider myself an expert on all three. But I had never seen anyone who so closely resembled the ordinary human—and so obviously wasn't. He, or it, was tall and lean, humanoid, but oddly muscled, a vague suggestion of something less than human in the lean hunch of his body. Manlike, he wore tight-fitting trunks, and a shirt of green fur that revealed bulging biceps where they shouldn't be, and angular planes where there should have been swelling muscles. The shoulders were high and hunched, the neck unpleasantly sinuous, and the face, only a little narrower than human, was handsomely arrogant, with a kind of wary, alert mischief that was the least human thing about him.

He bent, tilted the girl's inert body on to a divan of some sort, and turned his back on her, lifting his hand in an impatient gesture.

All the little tinkling hammers stopped as if their switch had been turned out.

"Now," said the nonhuman, "we can talk."

Like the waif, he spoke the archaic Shainsa, with its lilting, sing-song rise and fall. I asked in the same language, "What happened? Who are you? And where am I?"

The nonhuman crossed his hands. "Do not blame Miellyn. She acted under orders. It was imperative to bring you here, and we had reason to believe you might ignore an ordinary summons. You were clever at evading our surveillance—for a while. But there would not have been two Dry-towners in Charin tonight. You *are* Rakhal Sensar?"

Rakhal Sensar!

Shaken, I pulled a rag from my pocket and wiped the blood from my mouth. As far as I knew, there was no resemblance between Rakhal and myself—but it occurred to me, for the first time, that any casual description would fit either of us. Humans, tall and lean and without distinctive coloring, with the Dry-towner's walk and speech, and the same scars across face and mouth—and I'd been hanging around in Rakhal's old haunts. The mistake was natural; and natural or not, I wasn't going to deny it.

"We knew," the nonhuman continued, that if you remained where you were, the Earthman who has been trailing you—Cargill—would have made his arrest. We knew about your quarrel with Cargill—among other things—but we did not consider it necessary that you should fall into his hands."

I was puzzled. "I still don't understand. Exactly where am I?"

"This is the Master-shrine of Nebran."

Nebran! Knowing what Rakhal would have done, I hastily made the quick good-luck gesture, gabbling a few archaic words.

Like every Earthman on Wolf, I'd seen blanked impassive faces at mention of the Toad-god. Rumor made his spies omniscient, his priesthood virtually om-

nipotent, his powers formidable. I had believed about
a tenth of what I heard, but even that was consider-
able. Now I was in his shrine, and the device which
had brought me here, without a doubt, was a working
model of a matter-transmitter.

A matter-transmitter—a working model—Rakhal was
after it.

"And who," I asked slowly, "are you, Lord?"

The green-clad creature hunched his shoulders in a
ceremonious bow. "My name is Evarin. Humble servant of Nebran and yourself, honorable sir," he added,
but there was no humility in his manner. "I am called
the Toymaker."

Evarin. That was another name given weight by
rumor; a breath of gossip in a thieves market, a scrawled
name on a torn scrap of paper—a blank folder in
Terran Intelligence. A Toymaker . . .

The girl on the divan sat up, passing slim hands over
her disheveled hair. "My poor feet," she mourned,
"they are black and blue with the cobbles, and my hair
is filled with sand and tangles! Toymaker, I will do no
more of your errands! What way was this to send me
to entice a man?"

She stamped one small bare foot, and I saw that she
was not nearly as young as she had looked in the
street; although immature by Terran standards, she
had a fair figure for a Dry-town girl. Her rags fell
around her slim legs in graceful folds, her hair was
spun black glass, and I suddenly saw what the confusion in the filthy street had kept me from seeing before.

It was the girl of the spaceport café—the girl with
the Toad-god embroidered on the breast of her robes,
who had sent the Dry-towners to running madly, insane with terror.

I saw that Evarin was watching me, and turned idly
away. Evarin said, with a kind of rueful impatience,
"You know you enjoyed yourself, Miellyn. Run along
and make yourself beautiful again."

She danced out of the room.

The Toymaker motioned to me. "This way," he

directed, and led me through a different door. The offstage hammering I had heard, tiny bell-tones like a fairy xylophone, began again as the door opened, and we passed into a workroom which made me remember nursery tales from a half-forgotten childhood on Terra. For the workers were tiny, gnarled—*trolls!* They were chaks—chaks from the Polar mountains, furred and half-human, with witchlike faces, but transformed, dwarfed. Tiny hammers pattered on miniature anvils, in a tinkling, jingling chorus of musical clinks and taps. Beady eyes focused, like lenses, over winking jewels and gimcraks. Busy elves. Makers of—

Toys!

Evarin jerked his hunched shoulders with an imperative gesture; I recalled myself, following him through the fairy workroom, casting lingering glances at the worktables. A withered leprechaun set eyes into the head of a minikin hound; delicate fingers worked precious metals into invisible filigree for the collarpiece of a dainty dancing doll with living emerald eyes; metallic feathers were thrust in clockwork precision into the wings of a skeleton bird no larger than a fingernail. The nose of the hound wobbled sensitively, the bird's wings quivered, the eyes of the little dancer swiveled to follow me as I passed.

Toys?

"Come along." Evarin rapped, and a door slid shut behind us. The clinks and taps grew faint, fainter. But never ceased.

"Now you know, Rakhal, why I am called Toymaker. Is it not strange—the Masterpriest of Nebran a maker of Toys, the shrine of the Toad-god a workshop for children's playthings?" Evarin didn't wait for an answer. From a sliding cabinet, he took out a doll.

She was, perhaps, the length of my longest finger, molded to the precise proportions of woman, and costumed in the bizarre fashion of the Shainsa dancers. Evarin touched no button or key visible to me, but when he set the figurine on its feet, it executed a whirling, arm-tossing dance, in a familiar and tricky tempo.

"I am, perhaps, in a sense, benevolent," Evarin murmured. He snapped his fingers and the doll sank to her knees and posed there, silent. "Moreover, I have the means and—let us say—the ability to indulge my small fancies. The small daughter of the President of the Federation of Trade Cities was sent such a doll recently. What a pity that Paolo Arimengo was so suddenly impeached and banished!" The Toymaker clucked his teeth commiseratingly, "Perhaps a little companion—such as this—may comfort little Carmela for her adjustment to her new—position."

He replaced the dancer and pulled down something like a whirligig. "This might interest you," he mused, and set it spinning. I stared, entranced, at the wheeling pattern of lights and shadows that flowed and disappeared, melting in and out of visible patterns . . . Suddenly I realized what the thing was doing. I wrested my eyes away with an effort. *Had* I blanked out?

Evarin arrested the compelling motion with one finger. "Several of these harmless toys are available to the children of important men," he said absently, "an export of value for our impoverished and exploited world. Unfortunately, an incidence of nervous breakdowns is—ah—interfering somewhat with their sale. The children, of course, are unaffected, and—ah—love them." Evarin set the hypnotic wheel moving again for an instant, glanced sidewise at me, and set it carefully back.

"Now—" Evarin's voice, hard with the silkiness of a tiger-snarl, clawed across sudden silence. "We'll talk business!"

He had something concealed in one hand. "You are probably wondering how we recognized and found you?" A panel cleared in the wall, and became translucent; confused flickers moved on the surface, then dropped into focus and I realized that the panel was an ordinary television screen and that I was looking down into the well-known interior of the Cafe of Three Rainbows, in the small Terran Colony at Charin. The focus gradually sharpened down on the long, Earth-type bar, where a tall man in spaceman's leathers was talking with a pale-haired Terran girl.

Evan said at my ear, "By now, Race Cargill has decided that you fell into his trap and the hands of the Ya-men."

It seemed so unbearably funny that my shoulders twitched. Since I landed in Charin, I'd gone to great pains to avoid the Terran colony. And Rakhal, somehow, discovering this, had conveniently filled my empty place. By posing as me.

Evarin rasped, "Cargill meant to leave the planet—and something stopped him. *What?* You could be of great use to us, Rakhal—but not with this blood-feud unsettled!"

That needed no elucidation. No Wolfan in his senses will make any bargain with a Dry-towner carrying an unresolved blood-feud. By law and custom, formal blood-feud takes precedence over any other business, public or private, and is sufficient and legal excuse for broken promises, neglected duties—even theft or murder.

"We want this feud settled, once and for all," Evarin's voice was low, and unhurried, "and we're not above weighting the scales. This man Cargill can, and has, posed as a Dry-towner. We don't like Earthmen who can spy on us that way. In settling your blood-feud, you would do us a service, and we would be grateful. Look."

He opened his closed hand, displaying something small, curled, inert.

"Every living being emits a characteristic pattern of electrical nerve impulses. As you may have guessed, we have methods of recording these individual patterns, and we have had you and Cargill under observation for a long time. We've had plenty of opportunity to key this—Toy—to Cargill's personal pattern."

On his palm the curled, inert thing stirred and spread

wings; a fledgling bird lay there, small soft body throbbing slightly; half-hidden in a ruff of metallic feathers, I glimpsed a grimly elongated beak. The tiny pinions were feathered with delicate down less than a quarter of an inch long; they beat, with rough insistence, against the Toymaker's prisoning fingers.

"This is not dangerous—to you. Press this point"—he showed me—"and if Race Cargill is within a certain distance—it is up to you to be within that distance—it will find Cargill and kill him. Unerringly, inescapably and untraceably. We will not tell you the critical distance. And we give you three days."

He checked my startled exclamation with a gesture. "It is only fair to tell you; this is a test. Within the hour, Cargill will receive a warning. We want no incompetents who must be helped too much. Nor do we want cowards! If you fail, or try to evade the test—" there was green and inhuman malice in his eyes—"we have made another bird."

He was silent, but I thought I understood the complexity of Wolf illogic. "The other bird is keyed to *me?*"

With slow contempt, Evarin shook his head.

"You? You are used to danger and fond of a gamble. Nothing so simple! We have given you three days. If, within that time, the bird you carry has not killed, the other bird will fly, and it will kill. Rakhal Sensar— you have a wife. . ."

Yes, Rakhal had a wife. They could threaten his wife. . . . And his wife was my sister Juli. . .

Everything after that was anticlimax. Of course I had to drink wine with Evarin, the elaborately formal ritual without which no business agreement on Wolf is valid, and go through equally elaborate courtesies and formalities. Evarin entertained me with gory and technical descriptions of the methods by which the birds— and others of his hellish Toys—did their killing and their other tasks. Miellyn danced into the room and upset our sobriety by perching on my knee and drinking sips from my cup, and pouting prettily when I paid her less attention than she thought she merited. She even whispered something about a rendezvous in the Cafe of the Three Rainbows.

But eventually it was over, and I stepped through a door that twisted, and I spun again through a queer giddy blackness, and found myself outside a blank, windowless wall, back in Charin. I found my way to my lodging in a filthy chak hostel, and threw myself down on the verminous bed.

Believe it or not, I slept.

Later I went out into the reddening morning. I pulled Evarin's toy from my pocket, unwrapped the silk slightly, and tried to make some sense from my predicament.

The little thing lay innocent and silent in my palm. It couldn't tell me whether it had been keyed to me, the real Cargill, or to Rakhal, using my name and reputation in the Terran Colony. If I pressed the stud, it might hunt down Rakhal, and all my troubles would be over. On the other hand, if it killed me, presumably the other bird, keyed to Juli, would never fly—which would save her life, but would not get Rindy back for her. And if I delayed past Evarin's deadline, one of the birds would hunt down Juli, and give her a swift and not too painless death.

I spent the day lounging in a chak dive, juggling a dozen plans frantically in my head. Toys, innocent and sinister. Spies, messengers. Toys which killed—and horribly. Toys which could be controlled by the pliant mind of a child—*and every child hates his parents now and again!*

I kept coming back to the same conclusion. Juli was in danger, but she was half a world away, while Rakhal was here in Charin, calmly masquerading as me. There was a child involved, Juli's child, and I had made a promise involving that child; the first step was to get inside Charin's Terran Colony, and see how the land lay.

Charin is a city shaped like a crescent moon, encircling the small Colony of the Trade City; a miniature spaceport, a miniature skyscraper of an HQ, the clustered dwellings of the Terrans who worked there and those who lived with them and catered to their needs.

Entry from one to another—since Charin is in hostile territory, and far beyond the impress of the ordinary Terran law—is through a guarded gateway; but the gate stood wide open, and the guards looked lazy and bored. They carried shockers, but they didn't look as if they'd ever used them. One raised an eyebrow at his companion as I shambled to the gate and requested permission to enter the Terran Zone.

They inquired my name and business. I gave a Dry-towner name I'd used when I was known from Shainsa to the Polar Mountains, and tacked one of the Secret Service passwords to the end of it. They looked at each other again, and one said, "Yeah, this is the guy," and they took me into the booth beside the gate and one of them used an intercom device. Presently they took me along into the HQ building, and into an office that said LEGATE.

Evidently I had walked straight into another trap. One of the guards asked me, straight out, "All right, now. Just what, exactly, is your business in the Terran Colony?"

"Terran business. You'll have to make a visicall to check on me. Put me straight through to Magnusson's office at Central HQ. The name's Race Cargill."

The guard made no move. He was grinning. He said to his partner. "Yeah, that's the guy, all right, the one we were told to watch out for." He put a hand on my shoulder and spun me around.

There were two of them, and spaceforce guards aren't picked for their good looks. Just the same, I gave a good account of myself, until the inner door burst open and a man stormed out.

"What's all this racket?"

One of the guards got a hammerlock on me, giving my arm a twist. "This Dry-towner bum tried to talk us into making a priority call to Magnusson—the Secret

Service Chief, that is. He knew one or two of the Secret Service passwords—that's how he got through the gate. Remember, Cargill passed the word that someone might turn up trying to impersonate him?"

"I remember." The strange man's eyes were wary and cold.

I found myself seized by the guards, and frog-marched to the gate; one of the men pushed my skean back into its clasp, the other pushed me, hard, and I stumbled, and fell sprawling on the chinked street.

First round to Rakhal. He had sprung the trap on me, very neatly.

The street was narrow and crooked, winding along between double rows of untidy pebble-houses. I walked for hours.

It was dusk when I realized that I was being followed.

At first it was a glance out of the corner of my eye, a head seen a little too frequently behind me for coincidence. It developed into a too-persistent footstep in an uneven rhythm; tap-*tap*-tap, tap-*tap*-tap.

I had my skean handy, but I had a hunch this wasn't anything I could settle with a skean. I ducked into a side street, and waited for my follower.

Nothing.

After a time, I went on, laughing at my imagined fears.

Then, after a time, the soft and persistent footfall thudded behind me again.

I fled down a strange street, where women sat on flower-decked balconies, their open lanterns flowing with fountains and rivulets of gold and orange fire; I raced down quiet streets where furred children crept to doors and watched me pass, with great golden eyes that shone in the dusk.

I dodged into an alley and lay there. Someone not two inches away said softly, "Are you one of us, brother?"

I muttered something surly in his dialect, and a hand seized my elbow. "This way, then."

Tap*tap*tap. TapTAPtap.

I let my arm relax in the hand that guided me. Wherever I was being taken, it might shake off my follower. I flung a fold of my shirtcloak over my face, and went along.

I stumbled over steps, then took a jolting stride downward and found myself in a dim room, jammed with dark figures, human and nonhuman. The figures swayed in the dimness, chanting in a dialect not altogether familiar to me; a monotonous wailing chant, with a single recurrent phrase: *"Kamaina! Kamaina!"* beginning on a high note, descending in a series of weird chromatics to the lowest tone the human ear could resolve. The sound made me draw back; even Dry-towners shunned the orgiastic rituals of Kamaina.

My eyes were adapting to the dim light and I saw that most of the crowd were Charin plainsmen and chaks; one or two wore Dry-towner shirtcloaks, and I even thought I saw an Earthman. They were all squatting around small crescent shaped tables, and all intently gazing at a flickery spot of light near the front. I saw an empty place at one table, and let myself drop there, finding the floor soft, as if cushioned. On each table, small, smudging pastilles were burning, and from these cones of ash-tipped fire came the steamy, swimmy smoke that filled the darkness with strange colors. Beside me, an immature chak girl was kneeling, her fettered hands strained tightly back at her sides, her naked breasts pierced with jeweled rings; beneath the pallid fur, cream-colored, flowing around her pointed ears, the exquisite animal face was quite mad.

There were cups and decanters on the table, and another woman tilted a stream of pale phosphorescent fluid into one cup, and proffered it to me.

I took a sip, then another; it was cold and pleasant, and not till the second swallow turned bitter on my tongue did I know what I tasted. I pretended to swallow while the woman's phosphorescent eyes were fixed on me, then somehow contrived to spill the foul stuff down my shirt. I was wary even of the fumes, but there was nothing else I could do. It was *shallavan*, the reeking drug outlawed on every half-way decent planet in the Galaxy.

The scene itself looked like the worst nightmare of a drug-dreamer, ablaze with the colors of the smoking incense, the swaying crowd and their monotonous cries. Quite suddenly there was a blaze of orchid light and someone screamed in raving ecstasy, *"No ki na Nebran n'hai Kamaina!"*

"Kamaieeeeeeeeeeeeeeeeeeeeena!" shrilled the entranced mob.

Evarin stood in the blaze of the lights.

The Toymaker was as I had seen him last, cat-smooth, gracefully alien, shrouded in a ripple of giddy crimsons. Behind him there was a blackness. I waited until the painful blaze of the lights abated, then, straining to see past him, I got my worst shock.

A woman stood there, naked to the waist, her hands ritually fettered with little chains that stirred and clashed musically as she walked, stiff-legged, in a frozen dream. Hair like black glass combed into metallic waves banded her brow, and naked shoulders, and her eyes were crimson . . .

. . . and her eyes lived, in the dead face. They lived and they were mad with terror although the lips curved in a placid, dreaming smile.

Miellyn.

I realized that Evarin had been speaking for some time in that dialect I could barely understand. His arms were flung high, and his cloak went spilling away from them, rippling like something alive.

"Our world—an old world—"

"Kamaieeeena!" whimpered the shrill chorus.

" . . . humans, all humans, nothing but humans. They would make slaves of us all, slaves to the Children of the Ape . . ."

I blinked and rubbed my eyes to clear them of the incense fumes. I hoped what I saw was an optical illusion, drug-born. Something huge, something dark, was hovering over the girl. She stood placid, hands clasped on her chains, the wreathing smoke glimmering around her jewels, but her eyes writhed and implored in the still, frozen face.

Then something, I can only call it a sixth sense, warned me that there was someone outside that door. I'd been followed, probably by the Legate's orders; my follower, tracing me here, had gone away and returned, with reinforcements.

Someone struck a blow on the door, and a stentorian voice bawled. "Open up, there! In the name of the Terran Empire!"

The chanting broke off in ragged quavers. Evarin glanced around, startled and wary. Somewhere a woman screamed; the lights abruptly went out, and a stampede started in the room. I thrust my way forward, with elbows and knees and shoulders, butting through the crowd. A dusky emptiness opened, and yawned, and I got a glimpse of sunlight and open sky, and knew that Evarin had stepped into *somewhere* and was gone. The banging on the door sounded like a whole regiment of spaceforce. I dived toward the shimmer of little stars which marked Miellyn's tiara in the darkness, braving that black horror which hovered above her, and encountered rigid girl-flesh, cold as death.

I grabbed her, and ducked to the side. Every native building on Wolf has half-a-dozen concealed entrances and exits, and I know where to look for them. I pushed one, and found myself standing in a dark, peaceful street. One lonely moon was setting, low over the rooftops. I put Miellyn on her feet, but she moaned and leaned limply against me. I took off my shirtcloak and put it around her naked shoulders, then hoisted her in my arms. There was a chak-run cookshop down the street, a place I had once known, with an evil reputation and worse food, but it was quiet, and stayed open all night. I turned in at the door, bending under the low lintel.

The inside room was smoky and foul-smelling; I dumped Miellyn on one of the circular couches, sent the frowsy waiter for two bowls of noodles and coffee, handed him a few more coins than the food would warrant, and told him to leave us alone. He drew down the shutters and went.

I stared at the inert girl for a few seconds, then shrugged and started to eat one bowl of the noodles; my own head was still swimming with the fumes of incense and drug, and I wanted it clear. I wasn't quite sure what I would do, but I had Evarin's right-hand girl, and I meant to use her.

The noodles were greasy, but they were hot, and I ate all of one bowl before Miellyn stirred and whimpered and put up one hand, with a little musical clashing of chains, to her hair. Finding that the folds of my shirtcloak interfered, she made a convulsive movement and stared around her with growing bewilderment and dismay.

"You! What am I—"

"There was a riot," I said briefly, "and Evarin ditched you. And you can stop thinking what you're thinking. I put my cloak on you because you were bare to the waist and it didn't look so good." I stopped to think that over, then grinned and amended, "I mean, I couldn't haul you around the street that way, it looked good enough."

To my amazement she gave a shaky giggle. "If you'll—"and held out her fettered hands. I chuckled and snapped the links. It didn't take much strength— they were symbolic ornaments, not real chains, and many Wolf women wear them all the time.

Miellyn drew up her draperies and fastened them so that she was decently covered, then tossed me back my shirtcloak. "Rakhal, when I saw you there—"

"Later." I shoved the bowl of noodles toward her.

"Eat it," I ordered, "you're still doped; the food will clear your head." I picked up one of the mugs of coffee, and emptied it at a single swallow. "What were you doing in that place?"

Without warning she flung herself across the table, throwing her arms around my neck. For a minute, startled, I let her cling, then reached up and firmly unfastened her hands. "None of that, now. I fell for it once, and it landed me in the middle of the mudpie."

Her fingers clutched at me with a feverish, tense grip. "Please, please listen to me! Have you still got the bird, the Toy? You haven't set it off, yet? Don't, don't, don't, don't, Rakhal, you don't know what Evarin is, what he's doing—" the words poured out of her in a flood, uncontrollable and desperate. "He's won so many men like you—don't let him have you too, they say you're an honest man, you worked once for Terra, the Terrans would believe you if you went to them and told them—Rakhal, take me to the Terran zone, take me there, take me there where they'll protect me from Evarin—"

At first I had leaned forward to protest, then waited and let the torrent of entreaty run on and on. At last she lay quiet, exhausted, her head fallen forward against my shoulder, her hands still clutching at me. The musky *shallavan* mingled with the flower-scents of her hair. At last, heavily, I said, "Kid, you and your Toymaker have both got me all wrong. I'm not Rakhal Sensar."

"You're not—" she drew back, regarding me in dismay and disbelief. "Then who—?"

"Race Cargill. Terran Intelligence."

She stared at me, her mouth wide like a child's.

Then she laughed. She *laughed*—I thought she was hysterical, and stared at her in consternation. Then, as her wide red eyes met mine, with all the mischief of Wolf illogic—I started to laugh.

"Cargill—you can take me to the Terrans where Evarin—"

"Damn!" I exploded, "I can't take you anywhere, girl, I've got to find Rakhal!" I hauled out the Toy and slapped it down on the greasy table. "I don't suppose you know which of us this is supposed to kill?"

"I know nothing about the Toys."

"You know plenty about the Toymaker," I said sourly.

"I thought so. Until last night." She burst out, in an

explosion of passionate anger, "It's not a religion! It's a *front!* For drugs and politics and—and every other filthy thing! I've heard a lot about Rakhal Sensar! Whatever you think of him, he's too decent to be mixed up in that!"

The pattern was beginning to take shape in my mind. Rakhal had been on the trail of the matter-transmitter, and had fallen afoul of the Toymaker. Evarin's words, *you were very clever at escaping our surveillance for a while*, made sense to me now; Juli had given me the clue. *He smashed Rindy's Toys.* It had sounded like the act of a madman, but it made plain, good sense.

I said, "There's some distance limitation on this thing, I understand. If I lock it inside a steel box and drop it in the desert, I'll guarantee it won't bother anybody. Miellyn, I don't suppose you'd care to have a try at stealing the other one for me?"

"Why should *you* worry about Sensar's wife?" she flashed.

For some reason it seemed important to set her straight. "My sister," I explained. "The thing to do, I suppose, is to find Rakhal first—" I stopped, remembering something. "I can find Rakhal with that scanning device in the workshops. Take *me* to the Master-shrine, will you? Where's the nearest street-shrine?"

"No! Oh, no, I don't dare!"

I had to argue and plead, and finally threaten her, reminding her that except for me she would have been torn to pieces or worse, by a crowd of drugged and raving fanatics, before she finally consented to take me to a transmitter. She was shaking when she set her foot into the patterned stones. "I *know* what Evarin can do!" Then her red mouth twitched, in tremulous mischief. "You'll have to stand closer than that, the transmitters are meant for only one person!"

I stooped and put my arm round her. "Like this?"

"Like this," she whispered, pressing herself against me. A swirl of dizzy darkness swung around my head; the street vanished, and we stepped out into the terminal room in the Master-shrine, under a skylight darkened with the last splinters of the setting sun. Distant little hammering noises made a ringing in my ears.

Maellyn whispered, "Evarin's not here, but he might jump through at any minute!" I paid no attention.

"Exactly where on the planet are we?"

Miellyn shook her head. "No one knows that except Evarin himself. There are no doors, just the transmitters—when we want to go outside, we jump through them. The scanning device is through there—we'll have to go through the Little Ones' workroom." She opened the door of the workroom, and we walked through.

Not for years had I known that special feeling—thousands of eyes, all boring holes in the center of my back. I was sweating by the time we reached the farther door and it closed, safe and blessedly opaque behind us. Miellyn was shivering with reaction.

"Steady," I warned. "We've still got to get out. Where's that scanner?"

She touched the panel. "I'm not sure I can focus it accurately, though. Evarin's never let me touch it."

"How does it work?"

"The principle is just the same as the matter-transmitter; that is, it lets you look through to anywhere, but without jumping. It uses a tracer mechanism, just as the Toys do," she added. "If Rakhal's electrical-impulse pattern were on file anywhere, I could—wait! I know how we can do it! Give me the Toy." I drew it out; she took it quickly and unwrapped it. "Here's a good, quick way to find out which of you this bird is intended to kill!"

I looked at the fledgling thing, soft and innocent in her palm. "Suppose it's turned on me?"

"I wasn't going to set it off." Miellyn pushed aside the feathers, revealing a tiny crystal set into the bird's skull. "The memory-crystal. If it's tuned to your nerve-patterns, you'll see yourself in the scanner, as if it were a mirror. If you see Rakhal—"

She touched the crystal against the surface of the screen. Little flickers of "snow" danced across the clearing panel; then, abruptly, a picture dropped into focus, the turned-away back of a man in a leather jacket. The man turned, slowly, and I saw first, a familiar profile, then saw the profile become a scarred mask, more hideous than my own. His lips were moving; he was talking to someone beyond the range of the lens.

Miellyn asked, "Is that—"

"It's Rakhal, yes. Move the focus, if you can, try to get a look out of a window, or something. Charin's a big city. If we could get a look at a landmark—"

Rakhal went on talking, soundlessly, like television without sound. Abruptly Miellyn said "There!" She had brought the scanning device within range of a window; Rakhal was inside a room that looked out on a high pylon and two or three uprights that looked like a bridge. I recognized the place at once, and so did Miellyn.

"The Bridge of Summer Snows, in Charin. I can find him now. Come on, turn if off, and let's get out of here." I was turning away from the screen when Miellyn gave a smothered scream.

"Look!"

Rakhal had turned his back on our scanning device, and for the first time we could see the person he was talking to. A hunched and catlike shoulder, twisted, revealing a sinuous neck, a handsome and arrogant face—

"Evarin!" I swore. "He knows, then, that I'm not Rakhal. He's probably known all along. Come on, girl, we're getting out of here." She shoved the silk-wrapped bird into her skirt pocket and we ran through the workroom. We banged the workroom door shut behind us, and I shoved a heavy divan against it, barricading it shut.

Miellyn was already inside the recess where the Toad-god squatted. "There is a street-shrine just beyond the Bridge of Summer Snow. Hold me, hold me tight, it's a long jump—" suddenly she froze in my arms, with a convulsive shudder. "Evarin—he's jumping in! Quick!"

Space reeled around us.

We landed inside a street-shrine; I glimpsed the pylon, and the bridge, and the rising sun; then there was the giddy, internal wrench, a blast of icy air whistled around us; and we found ourselves gazing out at the Polar mountains, ringed in their eternal sunlight.

We jumped again, the wrenching sickness of disorientation forcing a moan from the girl, and dark clouds shivered around us; I looked out on an unfamiliar expanse of sand and wasteland and dust-bleared stars. Miellyn whimpered. "Evarin knows what I'm doing, he's jumping us all around the planet, he can work the controls with his mind . . . Psychokinetics . . . I can do it, a little, only I've never . . . oh, hang on to me, tight, tight, I've never dared do this—"

Then began one of the most amazing duels ever fought. Miellyn would make some tiny movement; we would fall, blind and dizzy, through the blackness, half-way through the giddy spin, a new direction would wrench at us, and we would be thrust *elsewhere*—and look out on a different street. One instant we were in the Kharsa—I actually saw the door of the spaceport cafe, and smelled hot coffee—and an instant later it was blinding noon, with crimson fronds waving overhead, over the roofs of gilt temples. We froze and burned, moonlight, noon, dim twilight, in the terrible giddiness of hyperspace.

Then, suddenly, I caught a glimpse of the pylon, the bridge; luck or an oversight had landed us again for half a second in Charin. The blackness started to reel down again, but my reflexes are fast, and I made one swift, scrabbling step forward. We lurched, then sprawled, locked together, on the sharp stones of the bridge outside the street-shrine; bruised and bloody, but alive—and at our destination!

I lifted Miellyn to her feet; her eyes were dizzy with pain. Clinging together, the ground swaying madly under our feet, we fled along the Bridge of Summer

Snows. At the far side, I looked up at the pylon. Judging by the angle, the place where we'd seen Rakhal couldn't be far away. In this street there was a wine-shop, a silk market, and one small private house. I walked up, and banged on the door.

Silence. I knocked again. From within there came a child's shrill question, a deeper voice hushing it, and the door opened, to reveal a scarred face that drew back into a hideous facsimile of a grin.

"I thought it might be you, Cargill," Rakhal said. "You've taken longer than I expected. Come in."

He hadn't changed much, except for the crimson, ugly scars that drew up mouth and nostril and jawline. His face *was* worse than mine. The mask tensed as he saw Miellyn, but he backed away to let us in, and shut the door behind us.

A little girl, in a fur smock, stood watching us. She had red hair like Juli's, and evidently she knew just who I was, for she looked at me quite calmly, without surprise. Had Juli told her about me?

"Rindy," Rakhal said quietly, "go into the other room." The little girl, still staring at me, did not move. Rakhal added, in a gentle, curiously moderate voice, "Do you still carry a skean, Race?"

I shook my head. "That's Juli's daughter. I'm not going to kill her father under her eyes." Suddenly my rage spilled over. "To hell with your damned Dry-town blood-feud and codes and your filthy Toad-god!"

Rakhal's voice was harsher now. "Rindy. I told you to get out."

I took a step toward the little girl. "Don't go, Rindy. I'm going to take her to Juli, Rakhal. Rindy, don't you want to go to your mother?" I held out my arms to her.

Rakhal made a menacing gesture; Miellyn darted between us, and picked up Rindy in her arms. The child struggled and whimpered, but Miellyn took two quick steps and carried her bodily through an open door.

Rakhal began, slowly, to laugh.

"You're as stupid as ever, Cargill. You still don't realize—I knew Juli would come straight to you, if she was frightened enough. I thought it would lure you out of hiding—you filthy coward! Six years hiding in the Terran zone! If you'd had the guts to walk out with me when I engineered that final deal, we would have had the biggest thing on Wolf!"

"Doing Evarin's dirty work?"

"You know damn well that had nothing to do with Evarin. It was for us—and Shainsa. Evarin—I might have known he'd get to you! That girl—if you've spoiled my plans—" Abruptly he whipped out his skean and came at me. "Son of the ape! I might have known better than to depend on you! I'll finish your meddling, this time!"

I felt the skean drive home, slicing flesh and ribs, and staggered back, grunting with pain. I grappled with him, forcing back his hand. My side burned furiously, and I wanted to kill Rakhal and I couldn't, and at the same time I was raging because I didn't want to fight the crazy fool, I wasn't even mad at him—

Miellyn flung the door open, shrieking. There was a flutter of silk, and then the Toy was darting, a small whirring droning horror, straight at Rakhal's eyes. There was no time even to warn him. I bent and butted him in the stomach; he grunted, doubled, and fell, out of the path of the diving Toy. It whirred in frustration, hovered, dived again. Rakhal writhed in agony, drawing up his knees, clawing inside his shirt. "You damned—I didn't want to use this—" He opened his closed fist, and suddenly there was another Toy in the room. An identical fledgling bird, and this one was diving at me—and in a split second I understood. Evarin had made the same arrangment with Rakhal, as with me.

From the door came a child's wild shriek.

"Daddy!"

Abruptly the birds collapsed in mid-air and went limp. They fell, inanimate, to the floor, and lay there, quivering. Rindy dashed across the room, her small skirts flying, and grabbed one of the vicious things in each hand.

She stood there, tears pouring down her little face. Dark veins stood out like narrow cords on her temples. "Break them, quick. I can't hang on to them any longer—"

Rakhal grabbed one of the Toys from a little fist, and smashed it under his heel. It shrilled and died. The other screamed like a living bird as his foot scrunched on the tiny feathers. He drew an agonized breath, his hands clutching his belly where I'd butted him.

"That blow was foul, Cargill, but I guess I know why you did it. You—" he stopped and said shame-facedly," You saved my life. You know what that means. Did you know you were doing it?"

I nodded. It meant the end of the blood-feud. How-ever we had wronged one another, this ended it, fi-nally and forever.

He said, "Better get that skean out of your ribs, you damn' fool. Here—" with a quick jerk he drew it out. "Not more than half an inch. Your rib must have turned it. Just a flesh wound. Rindy—"

She sobbed noisily, hiding her head on his shoulder. "The other Toys . . . hurt you . . . when I was mad at you, Daddy, only . . ." she dug her fists in her red eyes. "I wasn't that mad at you, I wasn't that mad at anybody . . . not even . . . him . . ."

He said over her head, "The Toys activate a child's subconscious resentments against his parents. That also means a child can control them—for a few seconds; no adult can."

"Juli told me you threatened Rindy—"

He chuckled. "What else could I have done that would have scared Juli enough to send her to you? Juli's proud, nearly as proud as you, you stiffnecked son of the ape! She had to be desperate."

He tossed it all aside with a shrug. "You've got Miellyn to take you through the transmitters. Go back to the Mastershrine, and tell Evarin I'm dead. In the

Trade City, they think *I'm* Cargill; I can go in and out as I choose. I'll 'vise Magnusson, and have him send soldiers to guard the street-shrines; Evarin may try to escape through one of them."

"Terra hasn't enough guards on all Wolf to cover the street-shrines in Charin alone," I objected, "and I can't go back with Miellyn." I explained why, and Rakhal pursed his lips and whistled when I described the fight in the transmitters.

"You have all the luck! I've never been near enough to be sure how the transmitters work, and I'll bet you didn't begin to understand! Well, we'll do it the hard way. We'll face Evarin down in his own shrine—if Rindy's with us, we needn't worry."

I was shocked at his casual suggestion. "You'd take a child into that?"

"What else is there to do?" Rakhal inquired logically, "Rindy can control the Toys, and neither you nor I could do that, if Evarin should decide to throw his whole arsenal at us!" He called Rindy to him again, and spoke softly. She looked from her father to me, and back again to her father, then smiled, and stretched out her small hand to me.

While we hunted for another street-shrine—Miellyn had some esoteric reason for not wanting to use the same one we'd landed in—I asked Rakhal point-blank, "Are you working for Terra? Or for the resistance movement? Or for the Dry-towns?"

He shook his head. "I'm working for myself. I just want one thing, Race. I want the Dry-towns, and the rest of Wolf, to have a voice in their own government. Any planet which makes a substantial contribution to Galactic science, by the laws of the Terran Empire, gets the status of an independent commonwealth. If a Dry-towner discovers anything as valuable as a matter-transmitter, Wolf gets dominion status. And incidentally, I get a nice fat bonus, and an official position."

Before I could answer, Miellyn touched my arm. "This is the shrine."

Rakhal picked up Rindy, and the three of us crowded

close together. The street swayed and vanished, and I felt the familiar dip and swirl of blackness. Rindy screamed with terror and pain, then the world straightened out again. Rindy was crying, dabbing smeary fists at her face. "Daddy, my nose is bleeding—"

Miellyn bent and wiped the blood from the snubby nose. Rakhal set his daughter on her feet.

"The chak workroom, Race. Smash everything you see. Rindy, if anything comes at us, stop it—stop it, quick!"

Her wide round eyes blinked, and she nodded, a solemn little nod. We flung open the door of the elves' workshop with a shout. The ringing of the fairy anvils shattered into a thousand dissonances as I kicked over a workbench and half-finished Toys smashed in confusion to the floor.

The chaks scattered like rabbits before our advance. I smashed half-finished Toys, tools, filigree and jewels, stamping everything out with my heavy boots. A tiny doll, proportioned like a woman, dashed at me, shrilling in a high supersonic shriek; I put my foot on her and ground the life out of her. She screamed like a living woman as she came apart. Her blue eyes rolled from her head and lay on the floor watching me, still alive; I crushed the blue jewels under my foot.

I was drunk with crushing and shattering and ruining when I heard Miellyn shriek in warning, and turned to see Evarin standing in the doorway. He raised both hands in a sardonic gesture, then turned, and with a queer, loping, inhuman run, headed for the transmitter.

"Rindy," Rakhal panted, "can you block the transmitter?"

Instead Rindy screamed. "We've got to get out! The house is falling down! It's going to fall on us—look—look at the roof!"

Transfixed by her horror, I looked up, to see a wide rift opening in the ceiling. The skylight shattered, broke, and daylight poured through the cracking, translucent walls. Rakhal snatched up Rindy, protecting her from the falling debris with his head and shoulders; I grabbed

Miellyn around the waist, and we ran for the rift that was widening in the cracking wall. We shoved through, just before the roof caved in, the walls collapsed and we found ourselves standing on a bare, grassy hillside, looking down in shock and horror, as, below us, secton after section of what was, apparently, bare hill and rock caved in and collapsed into dusty rubble.

Miellyn cried hoarsely, "Run! Run—hurry!"

I didn't understand, but I ran.

Then the shock of a great explosion rocked the earth, hurling me to the ground, Miellyn falling in a heap on top of me. Rakhal stumbled, went down to his knees. When I could see again, I looked at the hillside.

There was nothing left of Evarin's hideaway, or of the Master-shrine of Nebran, but a great, gaping hole, still oozing smoke and black dust.

"Destroyed! All destroyed!" Rakhal raged. "The workroom, all the science of the Toys, the secret of the transmitters—" He beat his fists furiously. "Our one chance to learn—"

"You're lucky you got out alive," said Miellyn quietly. "Where are we?"

I looked down, and stared in amazement. Spread out below us lay the Kharsa, and straight ahead, the white skyscraper of the Terra HQ and the big spaceport. I pointed.

"Down there. Rakhal, you can make your peace with the Terrans, and with Juli. And you, Miellyn—"

Her smile was shaky. "I can't go into the Terran Zone like this. Have you a comb? Rakhal, lend me your shirtcloak, my robes are torn, and—"

"Stupid female, worrying about a thing like that at a time like this!" Rakhal's look was like murder. I put my comb into her hand, then, abruptly saw something in the symbols embroidered across her breasts.

I reached out, and ripped the cloth away.

"Cargill!" she protested angrily, turning crimson and covering her bared breasts with both hands. "Is this the place—and before a child, too—"

I hardly heard her. "Look," I exclaimed, snatching at Rakhal's sleeve, "look at the symbols embroidered into the God! You can read the old nonhuman glyphs, I've seen you do it! I'll bet the formula is written out there for everyone to read! Look here, Rakhal! I can't read it, but I'll bet it's the equations for the matter-transmitter."

Rakhal bent his head over the torn robe. "I believe you have it! he exclaimed, shaken and breathless. "It may take years to translate the glyph, but I can do it! I'll do it, or die trying!" His scarred face looked almost handsome, and I grinned at him.

"If Juli leaves enough of you, once she finds out what you did to her. Look, Rindy's asleep. Poor little kid, we'd better get her down to her mother."

We walked abreast, and Rakhal said softly, "Like old times, Race."

It wasn't like old times, and I knew he would see it, too, once his exultation sobered. I had outgrown my love for intrigue, and I had a feeling this was Rakhal's last adventure, too. It would take him, as he said, years to work out the equations for the transmitter. And I had a feeling that my own solid, ordinary desk was going to look pretty good to me in the morning.

But I knew now, that I'd never leave Wolf. It was my own beloved sun that was rising. My sister was waiting down below, and I'd given her back her child. My friend was walking at my side. What more could a man want?

I looked at Miellyn, and smiled.

(1957)

The Wind People

It had been a long layover for the *Starholm's* crew, hunting heavy elements for fuel—eight months, on an idyllic green paradise of a planet; a soft, windy, whispering world, inhabited only by trees and winds. But in the end it presented its own unique problem.

Specifically, it presented Captain Merrihew with the problem of Robin, male, father unknown, who had been born the day before, and a month prematurely, to Dr. Helen Murray.

Merrihew found her lying abed in the laboratory shelter, pale and calm, with the child beside her.

The little shelter, constructed roughly of green planks, looked out on the clearing which the *Starholm* had used as a base of operations during the layover; a beautiful place at the bottom of a wide valley, in the curve of a broad, deep-flowing river. The crew, tired of being shipbound, had built half a dozen such huts and shacks in these eight months.

Merrihew glared down at Helen. He snorted, "This is a fine situation. You, of all the people in the whole damned crew—the ship's doctor! It's—it's—" Inarticulate with rage, he fell back on a ridiculously inadequate phrase. "It's—criminal carelessness!"

"I know." Helen Murray, too young and far too lovely for a ship's officer on a ten-year cruise, still looked weak and white, and her voice was a gentle shadow of its crisp self. "I'm afraid four years in space made me careless."

Merrihew, brooded, looking down at her. Something about ship-gravity conditions, while not affecting potency, made conception impossible; no child had ever been conceived in space and none ever would. On planet layovers, the effect wore off very slowly; only after three months aground had Dr. Murray started routine administration of anticeptin to the twenty-two women of the crew, herself included. At that time she had been still unaware that she herself was already carrying a child.

Outside, the leafy forest whispered and rustled, and Merrihew knew Helen had forgotten his existence again. The day-old child was tucked up in one of her rolled coveralls at her side. To Merrihew, he looked like a skinned monkey, but Helen's eyes smoldered as her hands moved gently over the tiny round head.

He stood and listened to the winds and said at random, "These shacks will fall to pieces in another month. It doesn't matter, we'll have taken off by then."

Dr. Chao Lin came into the shack, an angular woman of thirty-five. She said, "Company, Helen? Well, it's about time. Here, let me take Robin."

Helen said in weak protest, "You're spoiling me, Lin."

"It will do you good," Chao Lin returned. Merrihew, in a sudden surge of fury and frustration, exploded. "Damn it, Lin, you're making it all worse. He'll die when we go into overdrive, you know, as well as I do!"

Helen sat up, clutching Robin protectively. "Are you proposing to drown him like a kitten?"

"Helen, I'm not proposing anything. I'm stating a fact."

"But it's not a fact. He won't die in overdrive because he won't be aboard when we go into overdrive!"

Merrihew looked at Lin helplessly, but his face softened. "Shall we—put him to sleep and bury him here?"

The woman's face turned white. "No!" she cried in passionate protest, and Lin bent to disengage her frantic grip.

"Helen, you'll hurt him. Put him down. There."

Merrihew looked down at her, troubled, and said, "We can't just abandon him to die slowly, Helen—"

"Who says I'm going to abandon him?"

Merrihew asked slowly, "Are you planning to desert?" He added, after a minute, "There's a chance he'll survive. After all, his very birth was against all medical precedent. Maybe—"

"Captain"—Helen's voice sounded desperate—"even drugged, no child under ten has ever endured the shift into hyperspace drive. A newborn would die in seconds." She clasped Robin to her again and said, "It's the only way—you have Lin for a doctor, Reynolds can handle my collateral duties. This planet is uninhabited, the climate is mild, and we couldn't possibly starve." Her face, so gentle, was suddenly like rock. "Enter my death in the log, if you want to."

Merrihew looked from Helen to Lin, and said, "Helen, you're insane!"

She said, "Even if I'm sane now, I wouldn't be long if I had to abandon Robin." The wild note had died out of her voice, and she spoke rationally, but inflexibly. "Captain Merrihew, to get me aboard the *Starholm*, you will have to have me drugged or taken by force; I promise you I won't go any other way. And if you do that—and if Robin is left behind, or dies in overdrive, just so you will have my services as a doctor—then I solemnly swear that I will kill myself at the first opportunity."

"My God," said Merrihew, "you *are* insane!"

Helen gave a very tiny shrug. "Do you want a madwoman aboard?"

Chao Lin said quietly, "Captain, I don't see any other way. We would have had to arrange it that way if Helen had actually died in childbirth. Of two unsatisfactory solutions, we must choose the less harmful." And Merrihew knew that he had no real choice.

"I still think you're both crazy," he blustered, but it was surrender, and Helen knew it.

Ten days after the *Starholm* took off, young Colin Reynolds, technician, committed suicide by the messy procedure of slicing his jugular vein, which—in zero gravity—distributed several quarts of blood in big round globules all over his cabin. He left an incoherent note.

Merrihew put the note in the disposal and Chao Lin put the blood in the ship's blood bank for surgery, and they hushed it up as an accident; but Merrihew had the unpleasant feeling that the layover on the green and windy planet was going to become a legend, spread in whispers by the crew. And it did, but that is another story.

Robin was two years old when he first heard the voices in the wind. He pulled at his mother's arms and crooned softly, in imitation.

"What is it, lovey?"

"Pretty." He crooned again to the distant murmuring sound.

Helen smiled vaguely and patted the round cheek. Robin, his infant imagination suddenly distracted, said, "Hungry. Robin hungry. Berries."

"Berries after you eat," Helen promised absently, and picked him up. Robin tugged at her arm.

"Mommy pretty, too!"

She laughed, a rosy and smiling young Diana. She was happy on the solitary planet; they lived quite comfortably in one of the larger shacks, and only a little frown line between her eyes bore witness to the terror which had closed down on her in the first months, when every new day had been some new struggle—against weakness, against unfamiliar sounds, against loneliness and dread. Nights when she lay wakeful, sweating with terror while the winds rose and fell again and her imagination gave them voices, bleak days when she wandered dazedly around the shack or stared moodily at Robin. There had been moments—only fleeting, and penanced with hours of shame and regret—when she thought that even the horror of losing Robin in those first days would have been less than the horror of spending the rest of her life alone here, when she had wondered why Merrihew had not realized that she was unbalanced, and forced her to go with them; by now, Robin would have been only a moment's painful memory.

Still not strong, knowing she had to be strong for

Robin or he would die as surely as if she had abandoned him, she had spent the first months in a somnambulistic dream. Sometimes she had walked for days at a time in that dream; she would wake to find food that she could not remember gathering. Somehow, pervasive, the dream voices had taken over; the whispering winds had been full of voices and even hands.

She had fallen ill and lain for days sick and delirious, and had heard a voice which hardly seemed to be her own, saying that if she died the wind voices would care for Robin . . . and then the shock and irrationality of that had startled her out of delirium, agonized and trembling, and she pulled herself upright and cried out, "No!"

And the shimmer of eyes and voices had faded again into vague echoes, until there was only the stir of sunlight on the leaves, and Robin, chubby and naked, kicking in the sunlight, cooing with his hands outstretched to the rustle of leaves and shadows.

She had known, then, that she had to get well. She had never heard the wind voices again, and her crisp, scientific mind rejected the fanciful theory that if she only believed in the wind voices she would see their forms and hear their words clearly. And she rejected them so thoroughly that when she heard them speak, she shut them away from her mind, and after a time heard them no longer, except in restless dreams.

By now she had accepted the isolation and the beauty of their world, and begun to make a happy life for Robin.

For lack of other occupation last summer—though the winter was mild and there was no lack of fruits and roots even then—Helen had patiently snared male and female of small animals like rabbits, and now she had a pen of them. They provided a change of diet, and after a few smelly unsuccessful experiments she had devised a way to supply their fur pelts. She made no effort at gardening, though when Robin was older she might try that. For the moment, it was enough that they were healthy and safe and protected.

Robin was *listening* again. Helen bent her ear, sharpened by the silence, but heard only the rustle of wind and leaves; saw only falling brightness along a silvered tree-trunk.

Wind? When there were no branches stirring?

"Ridiculous," she said sharply, then snatched up the baby boy and squeezed him before hoisting him astride her hip. "Mommy doesn't mean *you,* Robin. Let's look for berries."

But soon she realized that his head was tipped back and that he was listening, again, to some sound she could not hear.

On what she said was Robin's fifth birthday, Helen had made a special bed for him in another room of the building. He missed the warmth of Helen's body, and the comforting sound of her breathing; for Robin, since birth, had been a wakeful child.

Yet, on the first night alone, Robin felt curiously freed. He did something he had never dared do before, for fear of waking Helen; he slipped from his bed and stood in the doorway, looking into the forest.

The forest was closer to the doorway now; Robin could fuzzily remember when the clearing had been wider. Now, slowly, beyond the garden patch which Helen kept cleared, the underbrush and saplings were growing back, and even what Robin called "the burned place" was covered with new sparse grass.

Robin was accustomed to being alone during the day—even in his first year, Helen had had to leave him alone, securely fastened in the house, or inside a little tight-fenced yard. But he was not used to being alone at night.

Far off in the forest, he could hear the whispers of the other people. Helen said there were no other people, but Robin knew better, because he could hear their voices on the wind, like fragments of the songs Helen sang at bedtime. And sometimes he could almost see them in the shadowy spots.

Once when Helen had been sick, a long time ago, and Robin had run helplessly from the fenced yard to the inside room and back again, hungry and dirty and furious because Helen only slept on the bed with her eyes closed, rousing up now and then to whimper like he did when he fell down and skinned his knee, the winds and voices had come into the very house; Robin had hazy memories of soothing voices, of hands that touched him more softly than Helen's hands. But he could not quite remember.

Now that he could hear them so clearly, he would go and find the other people. And then if Helen was sick again, there would be someone else to play with him and look after him. He thought gleefully, *Won't Helen be surprised?* and darted off across the clearing.

Helen woke, roused not by a sound but by a silence. She no longer heard Robin's soft breaths from the alcove, and after a moment she realized something else:

The winds were silent.

Perhaps, she thought, a storm was coming. Some change in air pressure could cause this stillness—but Robin? She tip-toed to the alcove; as she had suspected, his bed was empty.

Where could he be? In the clearing? With a storm coming? She slid her feet into handmade sandals and ran outside, her quivering call ringing out through the silent forest:

"Robin—oh, Robin!"

Silence. And far away a little ominous whisper. And for the first time since that first frightening year of loneliness, she felt lost, deserted in an alien world. She ran across the clearing, looking around wildly, trying to decide which way he could have wandered. Into the forest? What if he had strayed toward the riverbank? There was a place where the bank crumbled away, down toward the rapids—her throat closed convulsively, and her call was almost a shriek:

"Oh, Robin! Robin, darling! Robin!"

She ran through the paths worn by their feet, hearing snatches of rustle, winds and leaves suddenly vocal in the cold moonlight around her. It was the first time

211

since the spaceship left them that Helen had ventured out into the night of their world. She called again, her voice cracking in panic.

"Ro-bin!"

A sudden stray gleam revealed a glint of white, and a child stood in the middle of the path. Helen gasped with relief and ran to snatch up her son—then fell back in dismay. It was not Robin who stood there. The child was naked, about a head shorter than Robin, and female.

There was something curious about the bare and gleaming flesh, as if she could see the child only in the full flush of the moonlight. A round, almost expressionless face was surrounded by a mass of colorless streaming hair, the exact color of the moonlight. Helen's audible gasp startled her to a stop: she shut her eyes convulsively, and when she opened them the path was black and empty and Robin was running down the track toward her.

Helen caught him up, with a strangled cry, and ran, clasping him to her breast, back down the path to their shack. Inside, she barred the door and laid Robin down in her own bed, and threw herself down shivering, too shaken to speak, too shaken to scold him, curiously afraid to question. *I had a hallucination,* she told herself, *a hallucination, another dream, a dream. . .*

A dream, like the other Dream. She signified it to herself as The Dream because it was not like any other dream she had ever had. She had dreamed it first before Robin's birth, and been ashamed to speak of it to Chao Lin, fearing the common-sense skepticism of the older woman.

On their tenth night on the green planet (the *Starholm* was a dim recollection now), when Merrihew's scientists had been convinced that the little world was safe, without wild beasts or diseases or savage natives, the crew had requested permission to camp in the valley clearing beside the river. Permission granted, they had gone apart in couples almost as usual, and even those who had no enduring liaison at the moment had found a partner for the night.

It must have been that night . . .

Colin Reynolds was two years younger than Helen, and their attachment, enduring over a few months of shiptime, was based less on mutual passion than on a sort of boyish need in him, a sort of impersonal feminine solicitude in Helen. All her affairs had been like that, companionable, comfortable, but never passionate. Curiously enough, Helen was a woman capable of passion, of great depths of devotion; but no man had ever roused it and now no man ever would. Only Robin's birth had touched her deeply pent emotions.

But that night, when Colin Reynolds was sleeping, Helen stayed restlessly awake, hearing the unquiet stirring of wind on the leaves. After a time she wandered down to the water's edge, staying a cautious distance from the shore—for the cliff crumbled dangerously—and stretched herself out to listen to the wind-voices. And after a time she fell asleep, and had The Dream, which was to return to her again and again.

Helen thought of herself as a scientist, without room for fantasies, and that was why she called it, fiercely, a dream; a dream born of some undiagnosed conflict in her. Even to herself Helen would not recall it in full.

There had been a man, and to her it seemed that he was part of the green and windy world, and he had found her sleeping by the river. Even in her drowsy state, Helen had suspected that perhaps one of the other crew members, like herself sleepless and drawn to the shining water, had happened upon her there, such things were not impossible, manners and mores being what they were among starship crew's.

But to her, half dreaming, there had been some strangeness about him, which prevented her from seeing him too clearly even in the brilliant green moonlight. No dream and no man had ever seemed so living to her; and it was her fierce rationalization of the dream which kept her silent, months later, when she discovered (to her horror and secret despair) that she was with child. She had felt that she would lose the haze and secret delight of the dream if she openly acknowledged that Colin had fathered her child.

But at first—in the cool green morning that followed—she had not been at all sure it was a dream. Seeing only sunlight and leaves, she had held back from speaking, not wanting ridicule; could she have asked each man of the *Starholm*, "Was it you who came to me last night? Because if it was not, there are other men on this world, men who cannot be clearly seen even by moonlight."

Severely she reminded herself, Merrihew's men had pronounced the world uninhabited, and uninhabited it must be. Five years later, hugging her sleeping son close, Helen remembered the dream, examined the content of her fantasy, and once again, shivering, repeated, "I had a hallucination. It was only a dream. A dream, because I was alone . . ."

When Robin was fourteen years old, Helen told him the story of his birth, and of the ship.

He was a tall, silent boy, strong and hardy but not talkative; he heard the story almost in silence, and looked at Helen for a long time in silence afterward. He finally said in a whisper, "You could have died— you gave up a lot for me, Helen, didn't you?" He knelt and took her face in his hands.

She smiled and drew a little away from him. "Why are you looking at me like that, Robin?"

The boy could not put instant words to his thoughts; emotions were not in his vocabulary. Helen had taught him everything she knew, but she had always concealed her feelings from her son. He asked at last, "Why didn't my father stay with you?"

"I don't suppose it entered his head," Helen said. "He was needed on the ship. Losing me was bad enough."

Robin said passionately, "I'd have stayed!"

The woman found herself laughing. "Well—you did stay, Robin."

He asked, "Am I like my father?"

Helen looked gravely at her son, trying to see the half-forgotten features of young Reynolds in the boy's face. No, Robin did not look like Colin Reynolds, nor like Helen herself. She picked up his hand in hers; despite his robust health, Robin never tanned; his skin was pearly pale, so that in the green sunlight it blended into the forest almost invisibly. His hand lay in Helen's palm like a shadow. She said at last, "No, nothing like him. But under this sun, that's to be expected."

Robin said confidently, "I'm like the *other* people."

"The ones on the ship? They——"

"No," Robin interrupted, "you always said when I was older you'd tell me about the other people. I mean the other people *here*. The ones in the woods. The ones you can't see."

Helen stared at the boy in blank disbelief. "What do you mean? There are no other people, just us." Then she recalled that every imaginative child invents playmates. *Alone*, she thought, *Robin's always alone, no other children, no wonder he's a little—strange.* She said quietly, "You dreamed it, Robin."

The boy only stared at her in bleak, blank alienation. "You mean," he said, "you can't *hear* them, either?" He got up and walked out of the hut. Helen called, but he didn't turn back. She ran after him, catching at his arm, stopping him almost by force. She whispered, "Robin, Robin, tell me what you mean! There isn't anyone here. Once or twice I thought I had seen—something, by moonlight, only it was a dream. Please, Robin—please—"

"If it's only a dream, why are you frightened?" Robin asked, through a curious constriction in his throat. "If they've never hurt you . . ."

No, they had never hurt her. Even if, in her long-ago dream, one of them had come to her. *And the sons of God saw the daughters of men that they were fair*—a scrap of memory from a vanished life on another world sang in Helen's thoughts. She looked up at the pale, impatient face of her son, and swallowed hard.

Her voice was husky when she spoke. "Did I ever

tell you about rationalization—when you want something to be true so much that you can make it sound right to yourself?"

"Couldn't that also happen to something you wanted *not* to be true?" Robin retorted with a mutinous curl of his mouth.

Helen would not let go his arm. She begged, "Robin, no, you'll only waste your life and break your heart looking for something that doesn't exist."

The boy looked down into her shaken face, and suddenly a new emotion welled up in him and he dropped to his knees beside her and buried his face against her breast. He whispered, "Helen, I'll never leave you, I'll never do anything you don't want me to do, I don't want anyone but you."

And for the first time in many years, Helen broke into wild and uncontrollable crying, without knowing why she wept.

Robin did not speak again of his quest in the forest. For many months he was quiet and subdued, staying near the clearing, hovering near Helen for days at a time, then disappearing into the forest at dusk. He heard the winds numbly, deaf to their promise and their call.

Helen too was quiet and withdrawn, feeling Robin's alienation through his submissive mood. She found herself speaking to him sharply for being always underfoot; yet, on the rare days when he vanished into the forest and did not return until after sunset, she felt a restless unease that set her wandering the paths herself, not following him, but simply uneasy unless she knew he was within call.

Once, in the shadows just before sunset, she thought she saw a man moving through the trees, and for an instant, as he turned toward her, she saw that he was naked. She had seen him only for a second or two, and after he had slipped between the shadows again common sense told her it was Robin. She was vaguely shocked and annoyed; she firmly intended to speak to him, perhaps to scold him for running about naked and slipping away like that; then, in a sort of remote embarrassment, she forbore to mention it. But after that, she kept out of the forest.

Robin had been vaguely aware of her surveillance and knew when it ceased. But he did not give up his own pointless rambles, although even to himself he no longer spoke of searching, or of any dreamlike inhabitants of the woods. At times it still seemed that some shadow concealed a half-seen form, and the distant murmur grew into a voice that mocked him; a white arm, the shadow of a face, until he lifted his head and stared straight at it.

One evening toward twilight he saw a sudden shimmer in the trees, and he stood, fixedly, as the stray glint resolved itself first into a white face with shadowy eyes, then into a translucent flicker of bare arms, and then into the form of a woman, arrested for an instant with her hand on the bole of a tree. In the shadowy spot, filled only with the last ray of a cloudy sunset, she was very clear; not cloudy or unreal, but so distinct that he could see even a small smudge or bramble scratch on her shoulder, and a fallen leaf tangled in her colorless hair. Robin, paralyzed, watched her pause, and turn, and smile, and then she melted into the shadows.

He stood with his heart pounding for a second after she had gone; then whirled, bursting with the excitement of his discovery, and ran down the path toward home. Suddenly he stopped short, the world tilting and reeling, and fell on his face in a bed of dry leaves.

He was still ignorant of the nature of the emotion in him. He felt only intolerable misery and the conviction that he must never, never speak to Helen of what he had seen or felt.

He lay there, his burning face pressed into the leaves, unaware of the rising wind, the little flurry of blown leaves, the growing darkness and distant thunder. At last an icy spatter of rain aroused him, and cold, numbed, he made his way slowly homeward. Over his head the boughs creaked woodenly, and Robin, under

217

the driving whips of the rain, felt their tumult only echoed his own voiceless agony.

He was drenched by the time he pushed the door of the shack open and stumbled blindly toward the fire, only hoping that Helen would be sleeping. But she started up from beside the hearth they had built together last summer.

"Robin?"

Deathly weary, the boy snapped, "Who *else* would it be?"

Helen didn't answer. She came to him, a small swift-moving figure in the firelight, and drew him into the warmth. She said, almost humbly, "I was afraid— the storm—Robin, you're all wet, come to the fire and dry out."

Robin yielded, his twitching nerves partly soothed by her voice. *How tiny Helen is,* he thought, *and I can remember that she used to carry me around on one arm; now she hardly comes to my shoulder.* She brought him food and he ate wolfishly, listening to the steady pouring rain, uncomfortable under Helen's watching eyes. Before his own eyes there was the clear memory of the woman in the wood, and so vivid was Robin's imagination, heightened by loneliness and undiluted by any random impressions, that it seemed to him Helen must see her too. And when she came to stand beside him, the picture grew so keen in his thoughts that he actually pulled himself free of her.

The next day dawned gray and still, beaten with long needles of rain. They stayed indoors by the smoldering fire; Robin, half sick and feverish from his drenching, sprawled by the hearth too indolent to move, watching Helen's comings and goings about the room; not realizing why the sight of her slight, quick form against the gray light filled him with such pain and melancholy.

The storm lasted four days. Helen exhausted her household tasks and sat restlessly thumbing through the few books she knew by heart—they had allowed her to remove all her personal possessions, all the things she had chosen on a forgotten and faraway Earth for a ten-year star cruise. For the first time in years, Helen was thinking again of the life, the civilization she had thrown away, for Robin who had been a pink scrap in the circle of her arm and now lay sullen on the hearth, not speaking, aimlessly whittling a stick with a knife (found discarded in a heap of rubbish from the *Starholm*) which was his dearest possession. Helen felt slow horror closing in on her. *What world, what heritage did I give him, in my madness? This world has driven us both insane. Robin and I are both a little mad, by Earth's standard's. And when I die, and I will die first, what then?* At that moment Helen would have given her life to believe in his old dream of strange people in the wood.

She flung her book restlessly away, and Robin, as if waiting for that signal, sat upright and said almost eagerly, "Helen—"

Grateful that he had broken the silence of days, she gave him an encouraging smile.

"I've been reading your books," he began diffidently, "and I read about the sun you came from. It's different from this one. Suppose—suppose there were actually a kind of people here, and something in this light, or in your eyes, made them invisible to you."

Helen said, "Have you been seeing them again?"

He flinched at her ironical tone, and she asked, somewhat more gently, "It's a theory, Robin, but it wouldn't explain, then, why *you* see them."

"Maybe I'm—more used to this light," he said gropingly. "And anyway, you said you thought you'd seen them and thought it was only a dream."

Halfway between exasperation and a deep pity, Helen found herself arguing, "If these other people of yours really exist, why haven't they made themselves known in sixteen years?

The eagerness with which he answered was almost frightening. "I think they only come out at night, they're what your book calls a primitive civilization." He spoke the words he had read, but never heard, with an odd hesitation. "They're not really a civilization at all, I think, they're like—part of the woods."

"A forest people," Helen mused, impressed in spite of herself, "and nocturnal. It's always moonlight or dusky when you see them—"

"Then you *do* believe me—oh, Helen," Robin cried, and suddenly found himself pouring out the story of what he had seen, in incoherent words, concluding, "and by daylight I can hear them, but I can't see them. Helen, Helen, you have to believe it now, youll have to let me try to find them and learn to talk to them . . ."

Helen listened with a sinking heart. She knew they should not discuss it now, when five days of enforced housebound proximity had set their nerves and tempers on edge, but some unknown tension hurled her words at Robin. "You saw a woman, and I—a man. These things are only dreams. Do I have to explain more to you?"

Robin flung his knife sullenly aside. "You're so blind, so stubborn."

"I think you are feverish again." Helen rose to go.

He said wrathfully, "You treat me like a child!"

"Because you act like one, with your fairy tales of women in the wind."

Suddenly Robin's agony overflowed and he caught at her, holding her around the knees, clinging to her as he had not done since he was a small child, his words stumbling and rushing over one another.

"Helen, Helen darling, don't be angry with me," he begged, and caught her in a blind embrace that pulled her off her feet. She had never guessed how strong he was; but he seemed very like a little boy, and she hugged him quickly as he began to cover her face with childish kisses.

"Don't cry, Robin, my baby, it's all right," she murmured, kneeling close to him. Gradually the wildness of his passionate crying abated; she touched his forehead with her cheek to see if it was heated with fever, and he reached up and held her there. Helen let him lie against her shoulder, feeling that perhaps after the violence of his outburst he would fall asleep, and she was half-asleep herself when a sudden shock of realization darted through her; quickly she tried to free herself from Robin's entangling arms.

"Robin, let me go."

He clung to her, not understanding. "Don't let go of me, Helen. Darling, stay here beside me," he begged, and pressed a kiss into her throat.

Helen, her blood icing over, realized that unless she freed herself very quickly now, she would be fighting against a strong, aroused young man not clearly aware of what he was doing. She took refuge in the sharp maternal note of ten years ago, almost vanished in the closer, more equal companionship of the time between: "No, Robin. Stop it at once, do you hear?"

Automatically he let her go, and she rolled quickly away, out of his reach, and got to her feet. Robin, too intelligent to be unaware of her anger and too naive to know its cause, suddenly dropped his head and wept, wholly unstrung. "Why are you angry?" he blurted out. "I was only loving you."

And at the phrase of the five-year-old child, Helen felt her throat would burst with its ache. She managed to choke out, "I'm not angry, Robin—we'll talk about this later, I promise," and then, her own control vanishing, turned and fled precipitately into the pouring rain.

She plunged through the familiar woods for a long time, in a daze of unthinking misery. She did not even fully realize that she was sobbing and muttering aloud, "No, no, no, no!"

She must have wandered for several hours. The rain had stopped and the darkness was lifting before she began to grow calmer and to think more clearly.

She had been blind not to foresee this day when Robin was a child; only if her child had been a daughter could it have been avoided. Or—she was shocked at the hysterical sound of her own laughter—if Colin had stayed and they had raised a family like Adam and Eve!

But what now? Robin was sixteen; she was not yet forty. Helen caught at vanishing memories of society; taboos so deeply rooted that for Helen they were instinctual and impregnable. Yet for Robin nothing existed except this little patch of forest and Helen herself—the only person in his world, more specifically at the moment the only woman in his world. *So much,* she thought bitterly, *for instinct. But have I the right to begin this all over again? Worse; have I the right to deny its existence and, when I die, leave Robin alone?*

She had stumbled and paused for breath, realizing that she had wandered in circles and that she was at a familiar point on the riverbank which she had avoided for sixteen years. On the heels of this realization she became aware that for only the second time in memory, the winds were wholly stilled.

Her eyes, swollen with crying, ached as she tried to pierce the gloom of the mist, lilac-tinted with the approaching sunrise, which hung around the water. Through the dispersing mist she made out, dimly, the form of a man.

He was tall, and his pale skin shone with misty white colors. Helen sat frozen, her mouth open, and for the space of several seconds he looked down at her without moving. His eyes, dark splashes in the pale face, had an air of infinite sadness and compassion, and she thought his lips moved in speech, but she heard only a thin familiar rustle of wind.

Behind him, mere flickers, she seemed to make out the ghosts of other faces, tips of fingers of invisible hands, eyes, the outline of a woman's breast, the curve of a child's foot. For a minute, in Helen's weary numbed state, all her defenses went down and she thought: *Then I'm not mad and it wasn't a dream and Robin isn't Reynolds' son at all. His father was this— one of these—and they've been watching me and Robin, Robin has seen them, he doesn't know he's one of them, but they know. They know and I've kept Robin from them all these sixteen years.*

The man took two steps toward her, the translucent body shifting to a dozen colors before her blurred eyes. His face had a curious familiarity—*familiarity*—and in a sudden spasm of terror Helen thought, "I'm going mad, it's Robin, *it's Robin!*"

His hand was actually outstretched to touch her when her scream cut icy lashes through the forest, stirring wild echoes in the wind-voices, and she whirled and ran blindly toward the treacherous, crumbling bank. Behind her came steps, a voice, a cry—Robin, the strange dryad-man, she could not guess. The horror of incest, the son the father the lover suddenly melting into one, overwhelmed her reeling brain and she fled insanely to the brink. She felt a masculine hand actually gripping her shoulder, she might have been pulled back even then, but she twisted free blindly, shrieking, "No, Robin, no, no—" and flung herself down the steep bank, to slip and hurl downward and whirl around in the raging current to spinning oblivion and death . . .

Many years later, Merrihew, grown old in the Space Service, falsified a log entry to send his ship for a little while into the orbit of the tiny green planet he had named Robin's World. The old buildings had fallen into rotted timbers, and Merrihew quartered the little world for two months from pole to pole but found nothing. Nothing but shadows and whispers and the unending voices of the wind. Finally, he lifted his ship and went away.

(1959)

The Wild One

This is a story that they tell on the solitary farms on the borders of the Catskill mountains, where I grew up. It is a mistake to think that country is settled and modern, just because the big highways stretch from city to city, and the factories hold out clean jobs that pay better than the scratch-the-soil farming on shale rock. For between every farm is a stretch of woodland, and every farm has its own woods, and by night there are deer and rabbits and even wolves and the big lynxes that prowl south of Canada in a hungry season. And every now and again, to some lonely farm-girl who roams the edges and center of the deep woods by night, a child will be born like Helma Lassiter . . .

Roger Lassiter lifted his hands abruptly from the keys of the piano, and stared across the room at his sobbing young wife.

"Helma, dear!" he said contritely, "If I'd known—I didn't hear you come in, dear. Please forgive me?"

"Of course!" Helma wiped away her tears, and her strange, hesitant smile flickered for an instant on the wet face, "If I'd known you wanted to play, I wouldn't have come back so early." She crossed the room, and Roger held out his arms to stop her as she passed and hold her, for a moment, close to him. "Did you and Nell Connor have a good time?"

She dropped her eyes. "I didn't go to see Nell, Roger, it was too lovely in the woods. And—and there'll be a full moon tonight. . . ."

He slid his arm around the girl's waist. "You're the

wildest child of nature I ever knew," he murmured, halfway between exasperation and indulgence, and from the piano bench he twisted to look out the window at the deep stretch of dark woodland, oaks and maple and birch, that surrounded their house; then he turned back to rest his eyes on Helma.

She was good to look at; a tawny blonde girl, slight, delicately but strongly made, with creamy skin and dark-gray eyes that lightened to amber or an odd gold-flecked green when she was angry or excited, and so incredibly supple that he often wondered if she had been a ballet dancer. He did not know what she had been; she never talked about her childhood, and he knew only that she had run away from a farm in the Adirondacks when she was only fourteen years old. She had been twenty-three when they met, a chance acquaintance, almost a pick-up, at the swimming pool in Albany. Roger, escorting a pair of frisky nephews, had been attracted, then charmed, by her unbelievable grace in the water, her swift clean beauty; a seal-woman of the legends could have shown herself no more at home in the sea. He had been shocked at the change which had come over her when she had run back to the dressing-rooms and reappeared in a cheap skirt and blouse, her hair brushed down and her legs encased in lumpy socks and shoes. It was as if rust had suddenly covered a bright coin. But he had not been able to forget the laughing, glowing nymph of the pool. And he had never forgotten. It had not taken him long to discover how she revived in the woods, in the country. After their marriage, they had built this small house at the edge of the forest; a necessity, not a luxury, for Helma drooped and wilted in an apartment. They had built the house with their own hands, camping in the woods while it rose from the foundations, sleeping at night in a tent; and day by day a visible radiance had crept over Helma until she seemed alive with an inner, glowing beauty. Still, on the first night they had slept in their new home, she had murmured "I think I liked the tent better!" Even now, for choice, she slept on the open porch when she could.

He smiled now into her half-closed eyes and murmured what he had said many times, "I think you're half wood-cat, Helma!"

"Oh, I am," she returned, as always, "I am. Didn't you know?"

"And say, I used to have a dog who howled just like that when I played the piano. It's not what you'd call a compliment to my playing!"

She colored . . . even after four years of marriage, she was very sensitive about this. "I can't help it," she whispered for the hundredth time, "It hurts my ears so much—"

He patted her shoulder gently. "Well, never mind, honey, I try not to play when you're around," he told her, "but seriously, I'm beginning to wonder if you ought to go so far into the woods alone. Bob Connor told me he's heard wolves, and the other day he shot a lynx. Perhaps it's all right in broad daylight, but I wish you'd stay out of the woods at night, Helma."

He was not a countryman by habit; born and reared in cities, it had thrown him into a panic, the first time that he had waked in the night and found himself alone in bed. He had hunted the house through and found it empty; in a growing apprehension, mounting to absolute terror, he had searched the woods with a lantern, shouting, panicked, until he had finally found Helma, snuggled into a hollow of summer grass, sleeping, a rabbit bolting from her side as he came near.

After a few months he had come to take it for granted; Helma was almost physically incapable of staying out of the woods when they were so near, night or day. Sometimes Roger wondered if he had been wise to bring her so far from the cities and the plowed farms on the highways; she might have been unhappy, but she might have been less wild.

He murmured, "Perhaps if we had a child—"

He had spoken almost under his breath, but her body stiffened in the curve of his arm and she pulled away from him. "Roger," she murmured, "You know I can't—"

He said, low-voiced, "We haven't talked much about this, because it always makes you so unhappy. Now I think we must. How do you *know* you can't have children? Perhaps we could see Doctor Clemons when we go into town this Saturday. Perhaps—"

Helma jerked away from him furiously, taut, her head flung back, even the short sleek tawny hair seeming electric and alive, and her eyes flared green. The small blunt hands were flexed into claws. "I won't!" she spat at him, "I won't be mauled about and stared at by some doctor. . . ."

"Helma! Roger's sharp voice cut through her hysteria; she relaxed a little, but went on in a low angry voice, "I've never told you much about me, have I? I know that. I can't have your child, such a child as I could have, you wouldn't want, I—" She slumped down on a corner of the divan and buried her face in her arms despondently. After a long time she raised her face. "Would it make you so happy if I had a baby, Roger?" she asked pitifully.

The man could not bear it. He stood up and went to her, seating himself on the divan at her side and pulling the blonde head down on his shoulder. "Not if you don't want to, Helma," he said, in a gentle voice, "Maybe you're right, maybe—"

Her wide eyes burned tearlessly in the twilight. "You think I'm wild, you think I'm a crazy woman who might be normal if I had a baby to tie me down a little bit. You want me to be like your friends' wives, like Nell Connor, sleep in my bed nights and never step out further than the chickenhouse!" Her voice fell steadily, accusing. She pushed him away from her, stood up and backed away toward the door, a low menace, not quite a word, in her throat. Before her green glare his own eyes fell. "Well, damn it, Helma," he muttered, "I'd appreciate it if you'd try, at least, to act like a normal adult human being! There are times when you're like a wild animal!"

"I am," she said huskily, and swiftly turned and went out of the room. Half rising, the man saw through the window the quick bound with which she crossed the porch and lawn, watched her bend, with that amazing suppleness, and unfasten first one sandal, then the other. She kicked her feet free and ran toward the back gate; with a single lissome movement she was up and over it, and Roger saw the pale gold of her hair and the green-and-brown plaid of her housedress melt into the forest like a shadow, and there was a tight breathlessness in his throat as he watched her slide away and vanish in the leaves.

But she was back before morning, slipping silently, barefoot, through the doors, and sliding into bed beside him, as noiselessly as a cat. Roger, who had not closed his eyes all night, felt her presence and moved toward her, but she shoved him away. Roger shrugged and sighed; he was used to this, too. Helma could be as violent and passionate as a young lioness when aroused, but she was curiously cold at other times, and would push or cuff him away if he touched her when she was not in the mood. Roger had reflected that civilized man alone, of all animals, is not cyclic in desire, and that Helma's odd wildness was probably nothing more than a reversion to an earlier, possibly a cleaner day. Since in spite of occasional exasperations, Roger loved his wife devotedly, he respected her moods; it was as well that he did, for once, in the first year of their marriage—before he had learned how deep this was ingrained into Helma's whole nature—he had been less tolerant, and had once—only once—attempted to take her by force. There was still a tiny white line across his cheek where her wild hands had raked bone-deep. She had sobbed frenzied apologies afterward, but Roger had never risked it again. All women, he knew, were periodic to some extent; and it was true that she was altogether satisfying when her nature allowed her to be compliant.

In the days and weeks that followed, Helma was unusually quiet, subdued and docile. Summer lazed to a close; the crisp leaves of September drifted from helpless branches and the twanging winds of autumn played mournful threnodies in the deserted woods. Helma haunted the leaf-deep paths by day, but not once did she run off by night, and Roger Lassiter began to wonder if she was actually settling down. Surely it was time, after four years of marriage, that Helma should take on a look of sleekness and content, and for her body to soften a little from its hard angularity. She worked around the house happily—it was always neat and clean, but now it positively shone with soap and wax and polished floors, and Helma herself seemed as smooth and clean as a well-kept cat. Even her quick dancing walk seemed, although just as graceful, a trifle firmer and more subdued. And sometimes in the evenings when Roger returned home . . . he worked days, in a chemical factory . . . he would hear Helma singing, a curious contralto croon, almost toneless, but rising and falling in smooth, well-defined rhythmic cadences that were sweetly resonant.

She never told him, in so many words, that she was pregnant. Roger, although he guessed it as early as September, kept aloof from asking, thinking that perhaps she wanted to tell him herself, when she chose; but she never did, and finally he asked her only "When?"

"Early in the spring," she said, and her greeny eyes glanced, half-sorrowful, at his glad face. He told her gently, "You see, you were wrong, Helma. Aren't you happy about this?"

She did not answer, but put down her book and came to curl up on the rug at his feet, putting her head of thick short straight hair into his lap. He stroked it without speaking, and she shut her eyes, leaning against his knee. After a time she began the odd rough contralto crooning, and he smiled. "What kind of witch-chant is that, Helma? I never heard you sing before. I didn't know you knew one note from another."

"I don't," her smile was a gamin, enigmatic thing.

"I don't know, I remember hearing my mother sing like this when I was very small."

"What was your mother like?" he asked, and Helma laughed softly. "Like me."

"I'd like to have seen that! What was your father like?"

She shrugged. "I don't know. Perhaps—someone like you. Perhaps he was—different. Perhaps I never had a father, I can't remember."

Roger persisted "Did your mother never tell you?"

Helma suddenly drew her head away from her husband's stroking hands, looking up at him slantwise through her hair. "You would have called my mother mad," she said evenly, "She said my father was a lynx—a wildcat she called it."

Roger abruptly shivered as if a freezing wind had blown out the cozy fire. "Don't talk rubbish, Helma."

She shrugged. "You asked me. It's what my mother used to say. She was mad, madder than I am. She lived on a farm away up in the mountains, with only her grandfather and a little sister. She used to listen to hunters' stories about men and women who turned into wolves and wildcats when the moon was full, and ran in the woods at night. I've heard old men howl like the gray timber-wolf, when the moon lit up the snow like daylight, and seen them slink through the shadows with red eyes. . . ."

"Hell! You're morbid tonight!"

"No. Why? When I was a little girl I used to run around the hunters' huts. I could walk along a path and a wildcat would walk along the limb of a tree right over me and never even snarl, and I could pick up rabbits with my bare hands. I still can." Her smile was frankly malicious now. "You don't *believe* those old stories, do you? Till she died, my mother used to run out in the woods every full moon. *She* said my father was a lynx, I didn't. Do you believe I'll turn into a wildcat some night and rip out your throat? A silver bullet isn't any good, you know. That's just an old wife's tale. Just an iron knife, a knife of cold iron will kill a turnskin animal. That's what they say. Iron, or lead. Are you afraid of me?" She laughed, and Roger felt his goosefleshed arms stiffen and crawl. "For Godsake, cut it out!" he almost shouted.

She had stiffened and pulled away.

"I'm sorry. You asked me."

Roger Lassiter dreamed that night of wandering in black leafless woods, while green cat-eyes, disturbingly like Helma's, watched him from low branches; she came in before dawn, her dress torn, a bloodstain on one foot, shivering with cold, and lay huddled in warmed blankets, sobbing, while a dismayed and horrified Roger washed her thorn-lacerated legs, forced brandy between her blue lips, and for the first time in their married life laid down the law.

"This damned monkey business has *got to stop*, Helma. I thought that now, with the baby coming, you'd show some sense. Now, listen. You're going to a doctor, today, if you have to be carried. You're going to stay in the house, nights, if I have to lock you in. I know women act funny when they're pregnant, but you act clean crazy, and it's got to stop." For the first time her tears and pleas had no effect on him; he spooned hot milk between her chattering teeth, and continued, thin-lipped, "One more trick like this—just one, Helma—and we move back to Albany, at least till after the baby comes. Helma, if I have to have you examined by a psychiatrist, maybe—" he could not, although he wanted to, form the threat he had intended. Helma suffered enough in a house. Her acute claustrophobia would certainly kill her in a hospital.

But the threats he had already made had been effective enough to terrify Helma into submission. She saw the doctor, as he stipulated, and reacted quite normally when he assured her that he believed she would have twins. As the winter settled in in earnest, the house took on the air of tranquil peace which only the happily pregnant woman knows how to create around the home she has made. As in everything else, Helma was almost animal in this; Roger had never known a woman to seem so healthy, so casual. The wives of his friends fretted and were ungainly and unlovely and given to whims and complaints, and for the first time Roger could favorably compare his wife's docility with theirs.

The winter sneaked by on quiet-running feet. Snow came heavy that year, but the roads were kept plowed, and Roger managed to get back and forth every day. If Helma sometimes walked in the woods during the daytime, Roger did not know it, and she never left the house by night. The season was cruelly cold; now and then they could stand at the window and see a deer, made bold by the severity of the season, step out of the forest to the garden gate; and at night wolves howled in the darkness and now and then they heard the fierce snarl of a lynx, far away across the branch. Roger frowned and talked of getting a rifle, but Helma protested, "Wolves are cowards. They never attack anything bigger than a rabbit. And a lynx never bothered anybody who wasn't pokin' around him."

In February Bob Connor shot a lynx, less than a mile from the Lassiter house, and brought it over his shoulder to the door, thumping gaily till they came to look.

"I shot this big fellow down by the rocks on your creek, Roger. Listen, I've been making my kids stay right in the back yard, and if I were you, I wouldn't go in the woods at night, or let your wife. There are a lot of these cats around," he continued, dumping the stiff corpse on the step to ease his shoulder, "And they can be nasty customers—God, Helma, what's the matter! Rog—lookout—" he warned, just in time for Roger to catch Helma as she slumped in a dead faint.

When she had been carried into the bedroom and revived, and had apologized shakily for being such a fool, Bob, out of earshot, had blamed himself severely.

"I'm sorry, Roger. I guess maybe the blood made her fainty-like. Nell hates seeing dead things. I knowed she was in the family way, too, and I ought to had more sense than barge in like that with an old dead wildcat!"

"I don't think that was it," Roger said, baffled, "Helma's never been squeamish about blood."

"She's a bit odd about wild things, though, ain't she?" Bob asked in a tone discreetly lowered, and Roger, distracted, confessed that she was. He watched Bob go down the road, feeling something like despair, realizing that Bob Connor would certainly add his bit to the stories—already far too prevalent—of Helma Lassiter's "Queerness." But he had not the heart to reprimand or question Helma, nor to repeat Bob Connor's final words, said in that tactfully-dropped voice, "I wouldn't let her run off into the woods thataway, Roger. I go out a lot, shooting these cats, and wolves—bounty on wolves, you know. I try to be careful, and God! I'd hate to shoot somebody!"

After that day Helma grew even quieter, more subdued, losing even the spasmodic impulse to wander in the woods even in broad daylight. Somewhat alarmed, Roger found himself circuitously urging Helma into the garden, at least out of doors, out of the house which she now haunted, sleeping a great deal by day, but rising at night to prowl sleeplessly with her soft pacing movements through all the rooms. When Roger anxiously questioned her, she answered evasively: she was too tired to go far from the house, and the baby's movements in her body were most troublesome at night, and made her restless. She was heavy now, and her face was fuller, giving the wide-set cheekbones under her thick, tawny level brows a curiously unfathomable, animal, enigmatic look. She spoke little, but she seemed happy and tranquil, apart from her restlessness. Roger believed that Helma was trying consciously to wean herself from her wild ways and that she was silently suffering the torture of claustrophobia, for there seemed a curious disturbed look behind the green eyes, when she thought no one was watching her. Roger knew his young wife to be a strong-willed girl, and believed that she could discipline herself unsparingly.

In March came raging winds and a blizzard that swept down from the Adirondacks in a sort of apocalyptic violence, locking both Lassiters in the house for days. Then, overnight, the snow began to melt; the back of the winter was broken, the creeks overflowed with cool melting rains, and a strange moist green appeared through the soaked dead brownness of the grass. Crows and bluejays racketed in new-plowed fields, and a sweet chirping came from the trees at the edge of the woods. Sometimes now on the damp evenings, when light lingered at sundown, Helma would drag her distorted body to the forest gate and lean there, her face poignant with such longing that Roger, watching, felt a hurting pain and pity seeing his wild thing straining so hard at the leash of love he had finally girded about her heart. The gate was never locked, but Helma never touched her fingers to the light latch. Roger was just as well pleased, for now in the warm nights they often heard the snarl and spit of the big wildcats, and in these spring days he knew, the females would be defending their young. Nor did Roger fail to wonder if Helma would likewise be violent in defence of her child.

He had assumed that when the time came for her confinement he would drive her to the hospital in Albany. She did not say that she approved this arrangement, but on the other hand, she made no protest, and Roger took it for granted.

One evening in late March, while they sat at supper, Helma said quietly "You better drive to Albany and get some coffee, Roger. I used the last for breakfast this morning, and there's none for tomorrow's breakfast."

Like many pliant and easygoing men, Roger was crotchety in small and unimportant trifles, and he scolded Helma with as much severity as he ever used to her; why hadn't she told him at breakfast? She just looked back at him with her closed and heavy face.

"You better go now, or the stores are all going to be closed before you get there."

She was walking around the room restlessly, now and again stopping to pick up some small object and examine it meticulously, handle it with a curious, fidgety stroking movement of her small, rather stubby fingers, then put it impatiently down and resume her feline prowling, "But do you mind if I don't ride along? I'll stay here and go—go to bed. I'm awful tired."

Roger protested. "I don't like to leave you alone, specially at night. Suppose the baby started to come?"

"Well, you'll be back in an hour," Helma said reasonably.

"For heaven's sake, sit down, you'll drive me crazy, *pacing* like that—" Roger snapped at her, "Are you going to start your fool tricks again?"

"Oh, Roger, please," she started to sob, "I don't think I could stand it, being bounced around, until I *have* to!"

The man felt like a brute. Why, he wondered, should he get in a dither, because a girl in the last month of pregnancy didn't want to take a twenty-mile ride in an old car, over the worst roads in New York State? He shrugged and went to the closet for his coat.

"All right, honey," he said tenderly. "Would you like me to get Mrs. Connor to come and sit with you while I'm gone?"

Helma said in a tone of intense disgust, "Look. I'm twenty-seven years old."

Roger hugged her. "Oh, all right, all right. I'll be back in an hour." He went to the garage to back out the car, but on another thought, ran back up the steps.

"Helma?"

"Yes? I thought you'd gone!"

"You *sure* you don't want to ride along, or come and stay to Nell Connor's place while I'm gone? I can pick you up on the way back."

Helma's clear laugh raised staccato echoes in the unlighted porch. "Who's pregnant, you or me? Go along with you, or you'll have to drive all over town to find a store open!"

The muddy roads were now nearly clean of snow, and Roger made good time on the way to Albany. On the edge of town he found a small all-night grocery and decided to go in there, and turn back at once, instead of driving to the uptown chain-store where they usually traded. He bought the coffee and hurried out to the car again, forgetting his change, and only realizing when half-way home again that it had been a five-dollar bill.

It was already dark. Roger, his headlights sweeping a beam across the dark edges of the woods, pictured Helma, curled up kitten-fashion under quilts, but somehow the mental picture held no conviction nor comfort, and he pressed down the accelerator to the floorboard. If a state trooper caught up with him, he'd tell the truth. His wife was pregnant and he didn't like to leave her alone after dark. If it came to that, he'd rather pay a fine than leave her alone any longer.

The house was dark. Only the reflection of his headlights made ghosts on the unlighted window, and then Roger Lassiter saw that the garden gate swung open on its hinges, and that Helma's brown oxfords and crumpled dirty socks lay in the mud beside the open gate.

At that sight Roger Lassiter's terror jumped up from behind the wall of consciousness, and caught him by the throat. One last wild hope still beat with the thudding of his pulse; Helma might have felt her labor imminent and run to Connor's—the path through the woods was shorter than the road. Like a crazy man he jumped into the auto and sent it careening wildly down the mud road. Before it had fully come to a stop before the Connor farmhouse, he flung the door open and pelted toward the kitchen door entrance.

Through the lighted window a Connor child saw him coming, and flung the door open.

"Mommy, here's Mister Lassiter!"

Nell Connor's horsy kind face peered over her child's head. "Roger, come in! What's wrong?"

The man stood blinking numbly in the light. "Is Helma here?"

"*Helma?* Why, no, Roger! I saw you drive by, earlier, and thought perhaps her time had come and you was takin' her to the hospital!"

"She's gone," Roger said numbly, "She's gone. I drove to Albany to get a pound of coffee, and she said she was too tired to come along. And when I come back she's just gone! Where's Bob?"

"He went out to hunt lynxes, he said it was full moon and the big cats would prowl all night—oh, my God, Roger!" Nell Connor's pleasant florid face was drained of color, "S'pose Helma's in the woods!" She lowered her voice, glancing at the children, "Bob told me last year that she run off in the woods sometimes, and he said he was scared to hunt. But this winter he's figured that with the baby coming, she'd stay right close to the house." She was reaching for a man's mackinaw that hung behind the stove, as she spoke. "Molly," she said to the oldest girl, "You put Kenneth and Edna to bed, now. Miz. Lassiter's lost in the woods, and I'm going to help Mister Lassiter look for her. Donny, you get a lantern and come along. An' Molly, after you get the kids to bed, you make up lots of hot coffee, mind, and you put a couple of hot-water bottles in my bed and put on both teakettles to boil." She explained in an undertone, "If the baby started to come, Helma's kind of nervous, she might get scared to death and just run off and get lost trying to come down here, poor thing. If she did, and the baby started to come, we'll bring her back here. I've had five, I reckon I could kind of look after her."

"You're so good—" Roger faltered.

"Oh, shucks, what's neighbors for? I s'pect Helma'd worry 'bout me, if I got lost." She beckoned to her oldest boy, and took the lantern from his hand.

"We'll go down the path, Donnie. You take the flashlight, and go down the back pasture, 'hind the barn. Keep yelling for your Dad, now. And if you find Miz. Lassiter, you yell like crazy and keep on hollering till we hear you, and then come back and tell Molly to come an' help you get her in the house. Hurry up, now."

Never afterward in his life could Roger remember anything of the next few hours except plodding through moonlit darkness, with the lantern bobbing dully in his hand and Nell Connor's staunch and confident voice growing gradually tired and afraid. They shouted "Hel-ma! Hel-ma! Hel-ma!" until their lips were cracked with cold and their throats hoarse, stopping to listen for answering shouts, and Mrs. Connor faltered, "I dunno how Helma could come so far, being big like she was!" They trembled when they heard an animal snarl in the woods; and once Nell Connor—steady, nerve-less Nell, a farm woman all her life, fifty years old—screamed aloud as she saw green eyes and ears laid flat, peering down from a low branch. But worse than this were the times when they heard the distant *crack!* of a rifle and knew that Bob Connor had shot. Behind Roger's burning eyes was the picture of Helma lying still and stiff beside the path somewhere, shot by accident, or, overcome by travail, lying somewhere in agony, unable to come to them, too far away to hear their shouts and calls, or—worse—hearing, and too weak to answer. Roger wandered into a dark nightmare, which suddenly dissolved around him as a shout sounded in his ears; his heart stopped and began painfully to beat again, for it seemed that he had heard Helma cry out—Helma, screaming, not far away—

He caught at Nell's arm.

"Did you hear that?"

"I heard a catbird or something—" she said doubtfully.

"It's Helma! Oh, come on!"

"Roger!" She gripped and held him fast, "I didn't hear anything. Go easy, now. Hark, I heard something—steps—I think it's Bob." She raised her voice, shouting "Bob! Hel-ma! Helma—!"

Out of the night came the harsh snapping CRACK!

of rifle fire, close at hand; two shots in rapid succession, then a crashing in the thickets, and Bob Connor lumbered out of the brushwood.

"Nell! Roger! For God's sake, what's the matter! You look like—has something happened to Helma?"

"She's gone—"

"Christ!" said Bob Connor simply. "How long you been hunting her?"

"All night. Bob, I just heard her scream! She's back in there—" Roger gabbled like a madman, "I heard her, and something else—like a baby crying—"

"Easy, easy, Roger!" Bob Connor, his big face compassionate, caught his arm, "I shot a 'cat. A big female, just had cubs. I couldn't leave the little things to die without their mom, so I shot 'em, too."

"It's Helma! Helma's back in there, dying! Let me go, damn it, let me go—" He twisted away from Bob's restraining hands and ran toward the thicket. The Connors followed, breaking into a run after him, catching up as he stopped over the body of the dead lynx.

It was a large female, not yet stiff, tawny gold in color, with strange eyes, and the limp newborn cubs were still wet with slime, unlicked. Roger stood a moment, numbly, over the big graceful still body; then slumped. Bob Connor stepped to put an arm about his shoulders and held him up.

"Come on, Roger. Come on, come on back to the house, you're worn out. Come on. Don't worry. We'll find Helma. When we get back to the house, you have some coffee, and you look like you could use a shot of whisky. Come on. You're beat right out, man." While he talked, he was urging Roger's limp steps toward the path, "The minute we get to the house," he said soothingly, "I'll get right in the car and go get the state troopers. They'll look all over. Maybe she wandered across to one of the other farms. They'll find her, Roger. Come on."

Roger jerked up his head and looked into Bob Connor's eyes with the blank stare of a man who has been hit and does not know it yet.

"It's no use, Bob. Helma's dead. I know she's dead."

He dropped his head then and began to cry harshly. Over his head, Bob and Nell Connor exchanged grave, sympathetic glances. "He's worn right out. Come on, Roger, Lean on me. Come on, now, fellow. . . ."

And where I grew up, they end the story there, because Helma Lassiter never came back. All the farm folks wonder, sometimes, whatever happened to the poor crazy girl.

I used to ride my bike past the Lassiter house that summer and see Mister Lassiter just sitting on his back porch, day after day, just looking off into the woods. The lawn went to rack and ruin, and the rabbits used to hop right up into the garden where he was sitting. And my Daddy never would let me go into the woods looking for nuts again, unless he could go with me with a gun.

(1960)

Treason of the Blood

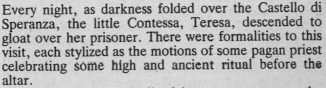

Every night, as darkness folded over the Castello di Speranza, the little Contessa, Teresa, descended to gloat over her prisoner. There were formalities to this visit, each stylized as the motions of some pagan priest celebrating some high and ancient ritual before the altar.

First she dismissed all of her servants, even the deaf-mute Rondo who obeyed her as a trained dog. Then, each night bruising her frail hands anew on the steel, she drew the bolts of her chamber and fastened the locks of each casement. If some mythical observer could have hidden behind the arras he would have seen a strange thing; into each metal bolt, roughly and painfully scratched by hands unused to such labor, the sign of the cross had been inscribed.

Then she knelt for a moment before the oaken prie-dieu, clasping her fingers about her beads; mere habit now, for she had long ceased to pray. The mirror at the far end of the chamber gave back her reflection dimly, a shadow pattern in black and white; the black coils of her hair netted with thin lace, the close black of a mourning gown crossed by the clasped fingers of white hands on ivory beads, her face—drawn to the whiteness of bone, of alabaster—brushed with black silken brows.

A face made for softness and for love, but hard now and cruel, the eyes level with hate, the soft mouth drawn to a thin white line. A saint, transformed by the double lashes of grief and sworn revenge into a fiend from the pit.

Rising and laying aside her beads, the Contessa lifted the lid of a carven chest, and took a three-thonged whip of braided leather. At the end of each thong, bits of razor-steel had been fixed; the leather was blackened and the bits of steel dulled with a dull brownish-red stain. She touched her fingertips to the steel and drew them back quickly; the sharp steel had drawn her blood.

She shrugged, disregarding the pain. In the leather grip of the quirt, crudely cut by an inexpert knife, was again the sign of the cross.

There was no answering creak as she drew back the bolt of the secret panel. This door was kept oiled and in perfect repair. A taper held high in one hand, she descended the stairs as noiselessly as her own shadow, her trailing skirts sweeping aside fresh cobwebs and sending small spiders scurrying into the cracks of the stone.

The brackish smell of stagnant underground pools came up to meet her. There had been a time when her delicate nostrils had shuddered at this smell, but that time was long past. She herself hardly realized how much she had changed from the young girl, afraid of every shadow, her frail fingers bleeding from the struggle with the then-rusted bolt, who had first come down these steps in despair and terror.

She paused and sighed. "Why do I come?" she asked almost aloud, and like an echo cast back from the dank depths there was a whisper and a sigh, "Come."

Two turns of the winding stair and she came into an arched corridor, lighted with dim moonlight filtering down long shafts built centuries ago. The passageway was lined with remnants of a grimmer day; the rusted bars of a pulley still suggesting the strappado, a criss-cross of bars like a hard couch, the grim green-bronze stare of an Iron Maiden. The Contessa barely gazed at these things which once had made her shudder; now they seemed familiar friends. She toyed, indeed, with a moment's thought—*they could be put in order*—before she turned the final twist in the passage, where a steel grating reared from stone floor to arched ceiling. Taking the great key from the chatelaine at her belt, the Contessa unlocked the grating and passed through.

"Good evening, Contessa," said the man chained to the wall.

The Contessa bowed her head. "And to you a good evening, messire, she said in her melodious voice, whose modulation was so deep a habit that even the transformation of maiden to fiend could not alter it.

She surveyed the man before her; his arms encased in cuffs of iron secured to the wall by long chains that passed through a ringbolt there. His legs too were locked in anklets of steel joined by a chain. A tattered white shirt and dark-stained leather riding breeches were all his clothing, yet, as he bowed, his fair hair caught the gleam of the taper and the dancing shadow, on the stone wall seemed to reflect wide wings.

The woman, standing carefully beyond the furthest reach of the chain, let her eyes linger on the features, thin, sharp and subtly sensual. As he raised his head again, his eyes, blazing with some strange spark, crossed hers. He shuddered as if with some terrible pain.

The long look was almost like a lover's glance. Again the Contessa was shaken by the curious beauty of the chained man. Beauty? A strange word, yet beauty it was, the beauty of some restless caged eagle, beating its wings with the fierce despair and agony of its inhuman hunger. But his glance fell first, though when he spoke his voice held a lilting mockery.

"You are beautiful this evening, madonna," he said, "I regret that I may not kiss your hand."

A spasm of indefinable emotion seemed to convulse her face. "So," she said abruptly, "kiss if you will," and extended her slender fingers, bruised and bleeding, to him. It was a mocking gesture, but he seized her hand in his and bent low over it, touching his lips to the hand. Then, abruptly, he struggled as if sudden madness possessed him, his chained hands crushing over her wrist, bringing them up avidly to his lips.

With a single swift gesture she brought up the whip and, wrenching her other hand free, lashed out with a single brutal blow. He flinched momentarily and in that instant she was beyond his reach again, her eyes flaming.

"I had forgotten," she taunted, "it is full moon and you—hunger!"

He stood slumped in his chains, not deigning to answer her mockery. At last he said, quietly, "Aye, full moon again. Are not your dreams evil, madonna?"

She shuddered as if to ward off the memory, but said, "I count myself lucky if you can do no more harm than this—to send me evil dreams!" A spasm of disgust twisted her mouth. Suddenly she stepped back and caught up the whip again.

"Angelo, Count Fioresi," she cried in a ringing voice, "You have fed on your last victim—*vampire!*"

She laughed aloud.

"Three months have I kept you in chains and watched your strength diminish and your evil hunger grow!"

Suddenly he strained wildly against the chains, but the spasm was feeble and soon he fell back exhausted, leaning against the wall and sagging.

"Once you could have burst those chains," she said, smiling in cruel triumph, "had I not carved the cross into each bracelet! Now even ordinary chains would hold you, I think!"

He propped himself up on his hands.

"Madonna," he said in a low voice, "my life is at your mercy; you might end it at your pleasure. None could blame you, if you sought my death. But why do you find pleasure in tormenting me?"

"Need you ask?" she cried in a high anguished voice—the last remnant of the young girl she had been three scant months ago. "You, who came to this castle as my suitor, beguiling my father by posing as the grandson of his oldest friend? How often he spoke of you, saying he felt, when he was in your company, that the friend of his youth had returned from the dead? He did not know how true he spoke!"

The Count shook his head.

"No," he said wearily. "If you must tell again that old sad tale, tell it truly. That is but old wives telling, that such as I return from death. We do not die, but live many times the span of mortal men, unless accident cuts off our life—or, or, we are barred too long from our other source of life."

Her convulsed face seemed to waver in the dim light.

"Be it so then. Your old friend, my father, sickened and died, then Rico my brother, of a wasting sickness. Last of all Cassilda, the sister who had mothered me when I was left motherless, was laid in unhallowed Earth—still you sought to wed me."

"Madonna, you call me a fiend—"

"Can you deny it?" she cried. "Can you claim to be man, you who have touched neither food nor drink in these months since I brought you here?"

"I have admitted I am not a man of your sort," he said, his head bowed. "My race is far older than yours, Madonna, perhaps made before your own God gave dominion to your kind. Like some beasts, we live—when we have passed youth—only by the blood of living things. Till my thirtieth year, I thought myself as other men. Yet I did not kill your kin, Contessa. And if I had; if I had? Your eldest brother Stefano was slain in a duel with the lord of Monteno, yet Monteno's kin are honored guests here in Castello di Speranzo. I did not know—" He seemed suddenly to writhe in pain—"I did not know, death was already in your kinfolk when I came here."

"You lie!" she cried out, and the lash whistled in the air as it caught the man across face and chest. He cried out hoarsely and the fiend smile crossed the girl's face.

"It gives me joy to know that you can suffer!" she cried. "Suffer as I suffered!"

The whiplash had drawn blood; she looked at the crimson drops with a strange gloating smile.

"Have a care, Lady," said Angelo, Count Fioresi,

softly. "I sought the blood of men so that I might not die; you have come to seek it for pleasure."

She raised the whip again, then lowered it.

"Why can I not seek your death?" she cried. "Why did I not kill you then? What can I not rid God's sweet earth of such a thing as you?"

"And why are your dreams so evil?" he asked softly, "and why was it that once you loved me, Madonna? Your God has forbidden revenge to his faithful. Why could you not slay me, and leave me to his vengeance and hell—or to his mercy?"

She turned suddenly and fled down the passage and up the winding stairs. Her footsteps made crisp echoes in the night. And Angelo, Count Fioresi, man, monster, vampire, whatever he was, dropped his face into his hands and wept.

The Contessa flung her windows wide, shivering as the night wind blew the dungeon stench from her gown; she would have knelt, but the words of the vampire burned in her heart; God has forbidden revenge.

What have I become? she asked herself, almost in wonder. She lay down in her great bed, but she feared to sleep, so great was the encompassing horror of the dreams that visited her. It was some evil spell of the vampire she held chained, she told herself; yet so great was the terror at the nights of full moon that she dared not close her eyes. She lay there recalling how she had first trapped the evil thing in man's form which lay now in her dungeon.

When first he came to them he had been ever at hand. She thought it was Cassilda's hand he sought, for her sister was both older and more beautiful; yet he showed to Cassilda only a curious courteous kindliness. It was the kindliness which she could not now reconcile with the horrors. When her father, then her brother had died, she had wept, "I am ill-fated; you cannot want me now." He had smiled and said, "Perhaps, when you are my wife, evil fortune will weary of following you."

But it seemed as if some evil spell lay on them all in those days, for there were deaths all through the village, as if some mysterious sickness plagued them. At last even Cassilda died, though the castle's priest, Father Milo, hid away her body from Teresa.

Angelo had come to her that day where she wept near the chapel—aye, she now, recalled, he had never stopped within the chapel doors here—his fair and beautiful face wrung with what had seemed to be honest compasion. Was it truly hell-black hypocrisy?

"Teresa, Teresa, I cannot bear to see you so alone!"

Now she wondered; what, indeed, would have happened, had she succumbed to his pleas? Could he indeed have come within the chapel? Her cross-signs had held him fast; could he have wedded her indeed?

Would, she not, indeed, have accomplished her purpose by binding him fast in Sacrament. . . ?

Father Milo, drawn and quivering with his own terror, had drawn her into the chapel that night, and signed her with the cross, then bidden her sit on his bench while he stood before her, his face taut with pain and horror. At first she had hardly listened to his rambling tale of strange deaths in the village, the marks found on the throat of her father and brother, the hint of some more dreadful horror surrounding Cassilda's death. Only slowly and incredulously did she realize what he was telling her—that these deaths were the work of a vampire!

"But this is only wicked superstition," she cried in protest, and he shook his head.

"No, it is the devil's work, done by one in league with that same devil!" Father Milo replied, his face drawn and white. Slowly, word by word, he had convinced her. Even then she had never more than half believed the dreadful tales he had told—that the Count had been seen to fly in the form of a bat from the windows of the old tower, that a holy woman of the village had smelled graveclothes and the musk of the coffin when he passed by; but when at last she believed, she had knelt before the priest, a passion of rage and terror surging up in her heart.

"What can be done?" and Father Milo answered slowly:

"The creature must die."

"Death alone would not serve!" she cried out in anguish, her face as white as her mourning veil. "I remember—I remember the night before she died, Cassilda came to my bedside and wept; and I—I did not know, why!"

Father Milo laid his hand on her head. "Bear what I must tell you now, with courage, my daughter. Cassilda died by her own hand, for fear of that same fate."

Teresa cried out in pain. "Then death alone cannot serve this monster! He must suffer—suffer as I and mine have suffered!"

"Revenge belongs to God alone," the priest rebuked. "I know not for certain, but I have heard that these monstrous creatures of the devil—cannot truly die, but live on in their coffins, rising to seek the blood of living things. Daughter, I must travel to Rome, and seek dispensation to deal with this—this thing, so that we may be rid of him forever."

"You must go tonight."

"But first we must make all secure," replied the priest, "So that he cannot harm you nor destroy you as he has done to your kin. Be watchful, but show no change in your manner, so that he will not suspect we know him for what he is. Then, when I return, we can destroy him and send him into true death back to his coffin for God in his infinite mercy to punish or pardon."

Teresa covered her face with her hands. "A thing from the grave and I had loved him!" she whispered. "God's mercy? I would see him burn forever in hell!"

The priest crossed himself, shaking his head sadly. "It grieves me that you speak such evil words," he said in rebuke. "Can you set limits on the mercy of God?"

"For that devil, yes!"

"Yet a great saint said once to Satan's self, daughter: 'to thee also I may promise God's mercy, when thou prayest for it.' Think you, Teresa; the Count Fioresi is a valiant soldier and a gallant courtier. He has borne this devil's curse many years, and for him this must be true hell, cast out of God's sight. Can you deny that the merciful God might one day pardon him?"

"If I thought this," she cried out passionately, "then would I find a way to keep him ever from that pardon—to make him live and suffer as me and mine!"

The priest had answered simply, "You are overwrought, and small wonder. Pray God to forgive your thoughtless words." He gave her his hand to rise. "I must go tonight; come now to your room, where we must make all safe."

His hands then had cut the sign of the cross into each door and window, and he had sprinkled them with holy water. He had left the main door for last, but as he turned to it Teresa felt a sudden, stifling terror. Even to save herself from death she could not endure to be shut in by spells, even holy spells.

"This I will seal myself with my crucifix when I am within," she said, and as she spoke, her plan leaped full-formed into her heart.

"Perhaps it is better so," he said thoughtfully. He drew from his robes a small vial. "Give him this in his wine," he said, "and God forgive us, daughter, but at least it will send him to the first death. When I return from Rome we will deal with the vampire, with stake and fire." Reverently he gave her a rosary. "This was blessed by a great Saint and is an heirloom of my family. It will keep him from rising from the dead until I come again."

He laid his hand on her head in blessing. "And mark," he added severely, "forget these wicked thoughts of revenge! I command you, on peril of your soul's health, pray for the soul of this lost sheep of God; pray for the soul of Angelo Fioresi."

But the words had fallen on a hard heart. She bowed her head, but cried out inside, "Never!"

With her own hands she prepared food and drink for the first stage of the priest's journey; but as she bade him farewell and his palfrey ambled away, she had turned away with the first cruel smile, crushing the little vial in her hand. "But you will not return," she murmured, "and vengeance will be *mine!*"

Then, turning from the door, she met the smiling eyes of Count Angelo, and forced herself to smile and give him her hand to kiss.

"Why has the priest left us?"

"To secure permission for our marriage," she replied steadily.

"Then we are alone here?" he drew her close, smiling. "May his journey be swift!"

But a curious frown had touched his forehead, and Teresa quailed and shrank from his kiss. "Not now!"

She lay awake that night, feeling like the chained goat staked out to draw the prowling mountain lion, the pale light from the open door lying across her face, waiting for the step and shadow, as of black wings across her door. She clasped the cross in terror, thinking; it is true, then, that the vampire moves like cat or ghost on noiseless feet.

Slowly the shadow bent till the full lips touched her throat, then, as if she feigned waking, she murmured, "Angelo?"

"Love—"

"Wait," she whispered, clutching the cross in her hand, "the door is ajar."

"Surely not," he whispered, turning, but with a scurry of steps she reached it, slammed it to, and jammed the bolt together with the crucifix. "Now," she cried, white as her nightgown, "let me see if you can leave as you came, Angelo, Count Fioresi—fiend, monster, murderer—vampire!" She rushed at him, holding the light aloft. He whirled like a beast at the death, making a dash at the sealed windows, the other door, in vain.

She said in a voice that shook, "I never more than half believed, till now. It seemed a monstrous lie, but true, then!"

The Count stretched his hands toward her and she raised the cross to ward him away, but although she had expected him to rush at her, bent on murder, he did not stir. "Teresa," he implored, "it is not what you think. I beg—I implore you, hear me before it is too late."

But in her wrath and fury she would not listen. She caught up the whip and rushed at him, raining blows on his face and shoulders. He cried out and with one swift movement wrenched the lash from her hands and cast it on the carpet.

"Have a care, lady," he said in a low, voice, "I know many things you know not. And I tell you, Teresa, at this moment you stand in peril more deadly than mine. Will you hear me—hear me but a moment, for the sake of the father who lies dead?"

Hear *you*, monster, murderer, grave-ghoul?" she cried, and a bleak smile crossed his face.

"The old tale that I rise from a coffin of death? No, Lady, I have never known death, yet. Nor do I want to die, yet. But if you kill me now, you pass into peril, so hear me first."

He strode toward her again, as if he would seize her and compel her to listen, but she snatched up the crucifix from the prie-dieu and held it before her. He flinched away and she gloated, "So that much superstition is true?" He cowered, his lifted arm covering his face.

"True in part, Teresa; I cannot harm you while you bear that symbol of your faith, that sign that you are under God's protection. Yet for the last time I beg you—"

"Would you beguile me with words?" she cried. Crucifix in hand, she raised the whip and brought it down across his cowering form. He retreated a step and she followed, the lash rising and falling. "So you can bleed and suffer?" she cried in triumph.

"Even as yourself," he muttered, and slumped to his knees. Warding herself with the cross, Teresa wielded the lash, savoring each dull crack and the thin lines of blood that gradually crisscrossed his body. At last she stood gasping above him; he lay senseless and bloody at her feet. With wary glances, fearing his faint was feigned, Teresa ran to the chest and dragged the heavy chains thence. Her own frail fingers had scratched the cross in each bracelet with her diamond ring. Then she summoned Rondo, the deaf-mute, and with his help she dragged the Count down the long stairs and, shivering, locked the chains to the dungeon wall. Then, sick with horror and replete with the satisfaction of her first plan of revenge, she fell almost senseless on her bed.

"Throw the windows wide," she motioned to Rondo, "I am fainting!"

When he had left she slept, but her dreams were evil. She seemed to rise and pass like a silent wraith from the castle, and confused horrors of blood and dying faces wandered in her mind. She woke to discover that she had walked in her sleep and lay half-in, half-out of the leaded casements.

Has he bewitched me? she wondered, as she fell across her bed in the growing daylight and slept.

She woke at dusk and descended, shuddering, into the crypt; but her fear was somehow soothed by seeing her enemy in chains. There she began the custom of descending each evening into the crypt . . .

As the days passed this began to absorb her more and more, so that she lived only for the moments when she came before the chained man, looked into his fierce eyes like a caged falcon, and when his pleas grew too disturbing, silenced them with the cruel lash into which she had now cut the cross so that he could not wrench it away.

The evil dreams still tormented her. The spell seemed to seize all the castle, for some of her servants fled, and others came to her with a tale of deaths in the village, but she brushed them aside like buzzing flies.

The maker of deaths is safely chained below, she thought; they cannot now ascribe them to supernatural visits, nor lay all deaths to such a cause! She was impatient and cruel with them, longing only for the moment when she would descend to gloat over her prisoner, then return to sleep the sleep of dead exhaustion.

The people of the village murmured because Father Milo did not return, and sent old women to her to beg that she should find another priest. "Would you command me?" she shouted, pacing the floor, and when the delegation had fled, she stared at herself in horror in the glass; they will think I am mad!

So three moons waxed and waned, bringing little change. Then came a night when Angelo barely stirred when she spoke to him, but lay seemingly senseless in the straw and chains.

At last he opened his eyes and murmured, "Gloat your fill at my despair, madonna. The end comes. But I see you passing further and further into peril. For your own sake I beg you; end this."

"Why," she mocked, "the devil was sick, the devil a monk would be! Shall I set you as priest in Father Milo's chapel?"

"I am no monster of cruelty," he said, "though I cannot blame you for thinking me so. Yet, Teresa, I am safely chained here. Why, then, the deaths of your people?"

She shrugged callously. "Such folk are always dying. Am I responsible for them, bodies or souls?"

The chained creature gave her a curious calculating look. "Once you would not have spoken so. Once you were gentle and pious."

"And if I am a fiend from hell, who but yourself made me so?"

Almost he laughed. "No, no, you have guarded yourself from me, but have you not made yourself a fiend?"

"Silence," she shrieked. "Silence!" She brought down

the whip full across his face, and, with a terrible cry he fell, blood breaking from his broken lips.

She let the whip fall, and knelt beside him. "He spoke truly; the end is near," she thought. "Here let him lie forever."

The crucifix she still wore swayed back and forth, casting a strange shadow on her prisoner, and a random thought touched her:

I have had my revenge. It is not too late to put aside my hate and do as Father Milo bid me; put an end to his sufferings and convey him to God's mercy. I need but strike him through the heart. He has said that he cannot rise from the dead. Even so I can pray for him the prayers for the dead, doing penance. Then will I, too, return to God's mercy. And Angelo—Angelo will pass to the dust he should long have been, and his soul settle for his crimes before God.

She' had the strange sense that the dungeon was crowded with watching, waiting spirits; it was as if she stood at some crossroads waiting for a victim to be hanged or pardoned, and the victim was herself. She could cast aside hate, and seek mercy, or—

Her lips curled in a smile of terrible cruelty. Never, never could she forego the pleasure she had found in this! No, let him suffer, let him suffer forever! Who had need of God's forgiveness? There were many outside God's domain!

"So it is too late," he said. She shrank back, but moving inexorably he sat up, gripped her roughly and burst the chains from his hands, then from his ankles.

Teresa shrieked aloud, cowering back and starting to her feet. She tripped over the fallen lash and fell to the stones and Angelo, rising, strode to her and stood over her.

"I would have saved you," he said at last. "Think, Teresa, of your evil dreams. Had they not begun before ever I came to Castello Speranza? Long years ago, one of the women of the Fioresi married into the Speranza clan; and I knew that one at least of your kin would be—of the full blood of my folk. Had it been

Rico, I would have taken him as esquire in my service, to guard and protect him. I—I would have saved you," he said almost inaudibly, "guarded you as a thing more precious than my life. I watched over you, kept you safe, guarded you in innocence of what you were, though I came too late to save your father—"

She shrieked in horror as the words filtered through her brain, but he went on remorselessly.

"When Rico met his death, I could bear it no longer, and in desperation, seeking only to guard you, I made it known to Cassilda. I—I did not know she would slay herself with the horror. I thought only that together we might guard you, till I could bring you safely to knowledge of what you were. You could have come to accept it—not as a thing of terror, but simply another kind of life; a different nature living harmlessly by its own laws. No, I did not slay your kin," he said. "I have lived so for two hundred years. Since the first year when I first learned what I was, no man has— died from my touch; I know how to—take life—and harm them no more than a leech's blood-letting. I am neither evil nor cruel, madonna, because I live as I must."

He bent over her. She recoiled, mad with fear, and thrust the crucifix at him.

"No," he said gently, taking her shoulders in his hands, "it will not protect you now."

He went on, almost sadly:

"I was reared to fear it; it was instilled into my inmost heart and brain, that I might never touch one who called sincerely on God's mercy. While you were still ignorant of what you were, Teresa, while you were sincerely pious in your faith, I could not pass through the symbol of your sincere belief. And the cross which you carved on my chains, thinking when you did so that you would protect others from my evil was a barrier to me. But now you have grown evil. You have rejected the teachings of your faith. You cannot call now upon your God for protection. The cross is now, to you, only an empty symbol, and it will not hold me."

He ripped the crucifix from her throat, gazed on it sadly and laid it aside.

"Perhaps I never had a soul," he said wearily, "but you, Teresa, cast yours away. You are too much monster even to live among my people."

The last thing the Contessa ever saw was his face, torn with pain, descending into a crimson blur into which she fell like death.

Hours later villagers gathered to watch the Castello di Speranza crash down in flames, and none marked the quiet, scarred man who rode silently into the forest, bowed as if in long agony, crouched in his saddle with grief and pain. He never looked back at the rising flame, but rode with head bowed over the neck of his horse and muttered again and again, "Teresa! Teresa! Teresa!"

(1962)

The Day of the Butterflies

Diana was a city girl, had always been a city girl and liked it that way.

She came through the revolving doors at half-past-five, pulling kid gloves over her hands. The soft kid insulated her hands from the rough touch of wall and door, as her stilt heels tapping in bright rhythm insulated her feet from the hard and filthy concrete pavement. Her eyes burned with the smog, but to her senses it was fresh air, a normal sunshiny day in the city. She bought a paper from a street vendor without looking at him or it, and turned for the brisk three block walk to the subway which was her daily constitutional.

And then—what happened exactly? She never knew. There was a tiny queer lurch as if the sidewalk had shifted very slightly either this way or that, and . . .

. . . the sun was golden and honeywarm and the green light filtered through a soft leaf canopy, lying like silk on her bare shoulders. Soft-scented wind rustled grass and caressed her bare feet, and suddenly she was dancing, a joyous ecstatic whirl of dance, in a cloud of crimson and yellow butterflies, circling like sparks around the tossing strands of her hair. She flung out her hands to trap them, pressed cold turgid grass blades underfoot, the chilly scent of hyacinths refreshed her nose, and as the butterflies flowed away from her fingertips she was . . .

. . . slipping down the first step of the subway, so

violently that she turned her foot over hard and had to grab at the railing. A fat garlic-smelling woman shoved by, muttering "Whynya look whereya going?" Diana shut her eyes, opened them again with a sort of shudder. The sooty light of the subway struck her with almost a physical pain; it's very strange, she thought with confused detachment, that I never realized before quite how *ugly* a subway staircase is, how grimy and dark . . . and then the jolt, delayed, hit her.

My goodness, she thought, there must be something wrong with my mind! Because I was *there*, for just a minute, *dancing!* I didn't just smell it, or feel it, or see it, I smelled it *and* felt it *and* saw it, and tasted it and walked on it and touched it! It was a hallucination, of course. A thought pinked her cheek with tingles, did I really *dance* here on Lexington Avenue? Automatically she thrust her token into the subway turnstile.

A golden butterfly fluttered from her hand.

Diana let the man behind shove her through the turnstile. She looked up, dazed, as the brilliant flicker of gold danced up through the noisy dismal stench and was gone. A tiny child squealed, "Oh, lookit the butterfly!" but none of the grim faces pouring through the maw of the subway station faltered or looked up.

Diana wedged herself into the train and grabbed, dazed, at a strap. The rattle and jolt under her feet was acutely painful, though she had never noticed it before. Her toes wriggled, craving the cold of grass; she breathed, trying to recapture hyacinth and choked on garlic, sweaty bodies fetid with chemical deodorants, hairspray, cheap perfume and soot.

But what happened? She thought wildly that she wasn't the kind of person things like that ever happened to! No, I dreamed it, butterfly and all, or there's something wrong with my eyes.

And so, as a child of the twentieth century, who never had believed anything she could not see, and in these days of TV and camera dynamation and special effects, only about half of what she did see, she managed to close her mind against this incredible opening of the door.

Until the next time.

The next time she was in the hurly burly of Penn Station, midmorning of a busy Saturday. Bodies pushed, shouted, stared anxiously at some destination known only to themselves. The public address system made cryptic noises distorted into improbable sounds. Diana hurried along, her gloved hands resting firmly on Pete's serge arm, her heels racing to keep pace with his stride. It was not that they were in any particular hurry, but all the surroundings screamed at them to hurryhurryhurry, and obediently they hurryhurried.

It was as rapid as a thought, the fading of the thick noisy air, the descent of silence . . . except for the gently rustling wind in the long dry grass at her feet. She was running, dancing in a whirl of jeweled butterflies, tossing her arms in wild abandon, the play of chilly winds against her bare legs and feet . . .

. . . she was *not*. The air was thick and harsh in her lungs, and she literally gasped at the impact of noise in the moment before she felt Pete stop in his tracks and watch her with a frown.

"Something the matter, Di?"

She felt like saying "Yes, everything. This horrible place, I've just realized just how horrible it is . . ." but she didn't. That would be to give reality, to give preference even to that . . . that dream or hallucination or whatever it was. She moved her feet inside the tight shoes, sighing a little.

"No, nothing. I felt—it's a little hot and stuffy in here and I felt a little absent-minded."

Absent-minded is right. My body was here—or Pete would have noticed—but my mind went off on a leave of absence, heaven know's *where* my mind was. She asked, "Why did you ask, Pete? What did I do?"

"Well, you sort of stopped in your tracks, and I couldn't see what you were looking at," said Pete the practical, "and you sort of lurched a little like you turned your ankle. You all right?"

"Of course," she said, responding to the tenderness in his voice. Oh, she loved him, he wasn't just another date, he was the right one, the one she wanted to spend her life with, and yet, was anything *here* ever really right, after all?

No, thinking like that gave all this reality . . . that hallucination . . .

"Got something on your foot? Chewing gum, dog mess?"

"No," said Diana, scraped her foot backward and it was true. Who would see or believe a crushed blade of grass here in the noise of Penn Station?

"Then let's hurry and get our train," he urged.

"Is there really any hurry?" she asked in sudden rebellion, "except, maybe, to hurry up and get out of this ugly filthy station? Did you ever stop and think how *ugly* most of the city is?"

"Wouldn't live anywhere else," Pete said promptly, "and neither would you! Or are you getting homesick for the cornfed hills of Iowa or something like that?"

"Pete, you nut, you know I was born in Queens!" It isn't even nostalgia for some faraway and lovely childhood! But what is it, then? How can I be—homesick? —for something I never saw, never even *dreamed?* Maybe I've just had a little too much of a good thing. Surely the city is a good thing, everything man ever wanted is here, culture, progress, companionship, even beauty, and Pete. . . .

"Pete," she said, "do we have to finish this shopping right now?"

"No, certainly not. You're the one who was in a hurry to pick out towels and skillets and things and put them away for the day when we find that apartment and get that license. But what shall we do instead, then?"

And all too accurately she foresaw the astonishment in his face when she said, "Let's go walk in the park— under the trees—and look at some flowers." But she knew he would say yes, and he did. It wasn't much. But it helped. A little.

And now she never knew, when she blinked her eyes, whether she would open them to the noise and roar of the city—or to the green and dancing world of the butterfly glade. In some part of herself she *knew* it was hallucination, aberration of eyes and mind, but . . . why did she, now and then, find herself clasping a butterfly, a flower, a blade of grass? But she did not deceive herself about why she put off, again and again, her promised visit to a doctor—or an optician—or a psychiatrist. Next time, she told herself, next time for sure. But she knew why it was always next time and never this.

If it's a hallucination a doctor would make it go away.

And I don't want it to go away!

She flattered herself that no one knew, and yet one day she emerged from a maenad dance to the sound of distant Pan pipes, her disheveled hair hot and sweaty on her bare neck—and then with the shock and jerk, feeling the pins taut in the French knot at her neck, her hands just touching the keys of her office Selectric, and the girl at the next desk staring.

"What's *with* you, Diana? I've spoken to you three times."

She raised her hands from the keyboard, unwilling to let it go this time, aware that she had lost the thread of the document she was copying. ". . . comprising that particular tract of land being the Western half of a section beginning at the point of intersection between the Northern line of 48th Street and the Eastern Line of Raymond Street, formerly called Beaver Street, as said streets are shown on the map and hereinafter referred to as Lots 13, 14 and 15 of . . ."

What absolute, utter rubbish! she thought, cradling in her hand the cool softness of the tiny blue blossom, her fingers cherishing the tiny petals. She concealed it inside her palm from the other girl's eyes and knew that her voice sounded strange as she said, "I'm sorry, Jessie. A—a kind of daydream, I guess."

"It must have been a real doozy," Jessie said, "you looked all sort of soft and radiant. Who was the guy? Michael Sarrazin, or somebody? Or just Pete? If he turns you on *that* much, you're one lucky woman!"

Diana laughed softly. "If it was anybody, it would be Pete. No, I just—" she found the words hard to form, "I was daydreaming about a—a wood. A kind of grove full of flowers and butterflies."

She had expected a flippant comment from the other woman, but it did not come. Instead Jessie's round face took on a remembering look. "Funny. That sounds like what I did the other day. I went to see my Aunt Marge in Staten Island, and I took the ferryboat, and I thought, all of a sudden, that I was running on a beach picking up shells. It seemed so *real*. I could hear the gulls, and smell the salt, and I even thought there was sand under my feet—*bare* feet, that is. Only the only beach I ever been to is Coney Island, you know, so it wasn't that, this was a beach like in the movies, you know." She laughed, embarrassed. "Funny thing happened later."

"Yes?" Diana felt a choking lump in her throat and her upper arms prickled goose flesh.

"You won't believe me," Jessie said, "but when I got home, I took off my shoes—I always take my shoes off first thing when I get home, and—"

"Yes?"

"You won't believe it. But there was sand in my shoes."

"Sand?"

"Sand. White sand. Like it was all over my *rug*."

"You're right," Diana said, "I won't believe it."

If I did, what else would I have to believe?

She might have written it off as frustration—for she was very much a child of the Freudian age, and repressions and frustrations were as much a part of her vocabulary as computers and typewriters, but there was nothing either of repression or frustration in the surroundings next time, for she and Pete were curled up together on the big sofa in her apartment, the lights were low and the music soft, but Pete was quiet, abstracted; she thought for a moment he had dropped off to sleep, and moved ever so gently to extricate her arm, but he murmured, not opening his eyes, "Golly, that wood smoke smells great—" and the implication electrified her, so that she jerked upright as if an electric current had jolted them apart.

"Pete—*you too?*"

He sat up, with the look she knew had been so often on her own face, but to his murmured disclaimer she charged, "Where were you this time? Pete, it's happened to me too, only with me it's a wood, a wood with butterflies and grass . . . Pete, what's happening to people? I thought it was only me, but a girl in my office . . . and now you . . ."

"Here, here, hold on!" His hands seized, calmed her. "But it's happened to me—oh, maybe a dozen times; suddenly I'm *somewhere else*, I know it's a dream, but it smells so damned real . . ." He looked thoughtful. "What's real anyhow? Maybe this is only *one* reality, or maybe our reality has something wrong with it. *Look* at us . . . all packed together like in a hive . . . fine for bees, sure, but people? Is this the way a million years of Nature evolved man to live?"

Diana felt curious choked excitement; but felt compelled to cling to logic. "And you a city boy? You always said the city was the end result of man's progress, social evolution—"

"I said too many damnfool things. Yeah, end result, all right. *Dead* end."

"Oh, yes," she sighed, "I hate it so now. Maybe I've always hated it and didn't know."

"And maybe there's nothing . . . nothing abnormal about this daydream, or hallucination, or whatever it is. Maybe it's just our subconscious minds warning us that we've had enough city, that we've got to get out if we want to stay sane."

"Maybe," she said, unconvinced, and shifted weight as he changed position, bending to retrieve what fell from his lap.

It was a tiny brown-scented pinecone, no longer than her thumbnail. She held it out to him, her throat tight with excitement.

"Pete—what's *real*?

Pete turned the small cone tenderly between his fingers. He said at last, "Suppose—suppose experiences are only a form of *agreements*? Even the scientists are saying, now, that space and matter, and above all, time, are not what the material physicists have always thought. Did you ever hear that all the solid matter in a planet the size of our Earth could be compressed into a sphere the size of a tennis ball—that all the rest of it is the space between the atoms and the electrons and their nuclei? Maybe we only see the material universe *this* way—" he gestured at the room around them, "because this is the way we *learned* to see it. And now humanity is so overcrowded and our senses so bombarded with stimuli that the—the texture of the *agreements* is breaking down, and those little spaces between the electrons are changing to conform to a new set of agreements? So that we find that ice isn't necessarily cold, and fire doesn't *necessarily* burn, and the chemical elements of smog might be butterflies in the oxygen—"

"But what would *make* that set of—of agreements break down, Pete?"

"God knows," he said slowly, and she knew he was not swearing. "Sensory deprivation can drive a man's sense receptors to pick up very funny things—five hours in a deprivation tank, they found out, was the most a man could take without going raving mad. Maybe sensory overload could do the same thing. Maybe—"

But she did not hear the rest, for the world dissolved in a green swirl, and she ran, dancing, through the green glade. Only this time Pete was there, too . . .

From that day she began to look for signs. Her boss

paused at her desk to ask for a legal document she was typing, but before Diana could pull it out of her type-writer he cocked his head to one side and she heard, briefly, the twittering of a distant bird, and he shivered a little, snapped, "I'll talk to you later about it," and she saw him, dazedly, heading downstairs for a drink. In a sudden rainstorm she managed to be first in the crush for a taxi—and a soft, curling green oakleaf lay on the seat.

Is it happening everywhere, then? And does every-body it happens to, think he or she is the only one?

She found herself scanning newspapers for strange happenings, felt a curiously confirmatory thrill the night a news correspondent, straight from wherever the "front" was this year, came on the air, sounding dazed, with a story he tried to refer to, flippantly, as "the gremlins getting out of hand again." It seemed that eight Army tanks had vanished without trace, before the eyes of an entire regiment. Sabotage was suggested, but then who had bothered to plant half a dozen beds of tulips in their place? A practical joke of enormous proportions?

But Diana was beyond surprise. Her own hands were filled with flowers she had gathered . . . some-where. . . .

It made the cover of *Time,* next week, when after a lengthy manhunt, a criminal serving a sentence for armed robbery was found only a mile from the prison. Questioned, he said, "I just got into a mood where I forgot the prison was there, and walked out," while the guards on the walls swore repeatedly—and lie detectors confirmed—that no one had gone in or out, not even the usual laundry truck. And the man might have rifled a supermarket—only there weren't any in the locality—for his arms were filled with exotic tropical fruits.

All Pete said to this, when the story was shown to him, was "The fabric of *this* reality is getting thinner and thinner. I bet a day will come when every morning more of the cells in that prison will be empty, and they'll never find most of the ones who walk out. After all, *their* reality is a lot more unbearable than most."

He frowned, staring into space. She thought he had gone away again, but he only mused, "It's getting pretty thin. I wonder how long it will last, and where it will rip all the way across?"

She clung to him in terror. "Oh, Pete, I don't want to lose you! Suppose it does—tear all the way across— and we lose each other, or one of us can't get back?"

"Hey, hey, hey!" he held her, comfortingly. "I've got a feeling that whatever it is between you and me, it's part of a reality that's maybe realer than this. We might have to find each other again, but if what we have is real, it'll last through whatever form reality takes." He looked somewhat abashed as he added, "I know it sounds corny in this day and age, but I love you, Diana, and if love isn't real, I don't know what is."

She was hardly surprised when, though his arms were still around her, she felt the cool grass beneath them, saw the green light through the trees. She whispered, against the singing winds, "Let's never go back!"

But they did.

But the fabric thinned for Diana daily. Shopping in the East Village for beads to back up an advertising display, she was struck by the look of blank-faced ecstasy, the impression of being *elsewhere,* on the soft preoccupied faces of bearded boys and long-haired barefoot girls. *They can't all be on drugs,* she thought.

This is something else. And I think I know what.

A delicate wispy girl, in a long faded dress, her hair waistlength, looked up at Diana; and Diana was conscious of her own elaborately twisted hair, her heels forced high on fashionable platforms, her legs itchingly imprisoned in nylon; thought wistfully of green forest light and gleaming butterflies, bare feet racing through the glades . . . *no. No. I'm here in the city, and I have to live with it. They seem to be living elsewhere. . . .*

The hippie girl smiled gently up at Diana and gave

her a flower. Diana would have sworn she had not been carrying flowers. She whispered, "You *know*, don't you? Do your thing while you can, if it's really your thing. It won't be long." And in her eyes Diana saw strange skies reflected, heard the distant roll of breakers and a faraway cry of gulls from . . . somewhere? Jessie's beach? She murmured, "I know where *you* are."

The sound of breakers died. "Oh, no," the girl said sadly, "but you know where *we* ought to be. It won't be long now, though. They're trying to pave it all over, you know. Make it into one big parking lot. But it won't work. Even if they covered over the whole planet with concrete, one day it would just *happen*. The Great God Pan would step down off that statue in Central Park—the *real* one—and stamp his hoof down through the concrete, and then . . . then violets would spring up through the dead land. . . ."

Her voice trailed into silence; she smiled and wandered away, her bare feet treading the filthy pavement as if she already wandered on the prophesied violets. Diana wanted to run after her, into that place where she so obviously spent so much of her time now, but she forced her feet on her own errand. She and the girl were in different layers of time, almost in different layers of space, and only by some curious magic had they come within speaking distance; like passing ships drifting through fog just within hail, or two falling leaves just touching as they fell from separate trees. She saw the street through a blur of tears, and for the first time tried, deliberately, to breach the veil, to reach for that other world which broke through into this so unpredictably, and never when you wanted it. . . .

Even as a city girl, Diana had never liked Wall Street. At high noon it is chaos, noise and robotlike humans all alike and all perpetually rushing nowhere; a human ant hill populated by mimic creatures, in suits and ties of a pattern so rigid that they seem to have grown on the semihuman forms. The rush and pandemonium assaulted her senses so violently that she stopped dead, letting the insectlike mimics—surely they could *not* be human—divide their flow around her, as if she were a rock in their stream.

Ugliness! Noise everywhere! Horror! She thought wildly, this world is *wrong*, a huge cosmic mistake, a planetary practical joke! If everyone who *knew*, everyone who's seen the *real* world, would somehow just say *NO* to all this, would just reach out all together, say, *This is too much, we don't, we won't, we can't stand* . . . then maybe those ugly skyscrapers would just dissolve, violets spring up. . . .

Oh, *listen*, she implored, her whole body and mind and senses all one strained hunger, *listen!* If they'd only stop and see all this the way it *really* is, see what's happening to people who think it's real and think they have to live in it!

Time and space are only this way because we have made them this way, and we've made them all wrong! Let's start all over again and do it right this time!

She never knew how long she stood there, because for her the accidents of time and space had stopped. She only knew that everything she was and ever had been had poured itself into the one, anguished, passionate plea, *listen!* And then she became aware that hers was only one voice in a vast, swelling choral song. As perception slowly came back to her overloaded senses, she saw first one, then another and another of the rigidly suited forms stop, fling away umbrella and briefcase, then split like an insect shedding his chitinous shell and burst into humanity again. The veil of illusion shredded from top to bottom; skyscrapers thinned to transparency, melted and vanished, and the great, towering, *real* trees could be seen through their wavering outlines. Through the dead and splitting concrete, a shy blade of grass poked up its head, wavered slightly, then erupted in a joyous riot of green, swiftly blotting out the concrete.

Great green lawns expanded from horizon to horizon, as the sky quickly cleared to a delicious blue.

Silence descended, threaded with tracery of birdsong; one lonely, bewildered taxi horn lingered, questioning and frantic, before it died away forever; in the canyons of Manhattan, the *real* Manhattan breaking through, men and women ran naked on the grass, flowers in their hands and garlands in their hair, as the jeweled butterflies flashed upward, flaming and gleaming in the sun.

Diana, sobbing with joy, ran into the throng; knowing that Pete was there somewhere, and Jessie, and the hippie girl, and children and prisoners and everyone for whom illusion had vanished. She ran on, shedding butterflies at every step, and wondered, once and never again, if the other world, the one that wasn't real, was still there for *anybody*. But she didn't really care . . . it wasn't there for *her* anymore, and Pete was waiting for her here. She knew she would find him, and of course she did.

(1976)

Hero's Moon

"That could be him now," Feniston said.

Young Rawlins bent to examine the whirling flickers on the radar screen, trying to distinguish any clear pattern in the "snow" and chaos of interference. "Yeah," he said at last, "or it could be another sunspot. I'm betting on the sunspot."

It was so quiet in the bubble-dome that the scrape of their shoes on the floor, the very brush of Feniston's starched tunic against his chair, sounded loud. That; and the soft mechanical beeping, burping, clicking, rattling and plinking of instruments; the background rattle and sputter of static from the screens and relays. But they lived with that, and they never heard it. Only some abrupt change, or the cessation of those mechanical tickings and pipings, would have been audible to them. They would have heard it instantly if one of those ticks, tocks, peeps, beeps or clucks had *not* sounded at its appointed split second. But not while each one sounded in its mechanical perfection.

Feniston was a neat straight man of fifty, his whole personality as combed and brushed and starched as his uniform, but the starch was beginning to show a pattern of thin fine cracks from tension and weariness. He didn't answer Rawlins, watching the younger man with an odd sense of detachment, as if neither of them were quite real any more. *Psych Section would tell me it's just fatigue. I'm not so sure.*

The events of the last few days, it seemed to Feniston, had worn a little of the new off the Rawlins kid. Rawlins still had his Earthside tan, and nothing could affect the bounce in his step, but he moved with a kind of hesitation that had never been there before, and there was something new in his eyes. Not fear, not yet. But *something*.

And above their heads was a narrow, smoked-glass horizon, and outside all hell was raging.

There is no air on Charmides, and therefore no rain, no wind, no thunder. From time to time a small vibration beat up through the soles of their shoes, or there would be the tiniest possible brightening of the light in the dome. Otherwise, only the insane racing and flickering of their dials and screens, the epileptic jerking of the indicators, back and forth without any pattern, told them that there was a wild hell of electric storm raging outside. The fierce glare and the eternal, unstirring dust were unchanged. Earthmen think of storms in terms of roaring wind, noise, visual and sonic battering. *So it's hard to think of it as a storm. But there's nothing else to call it.* And that quiet hell outside had damped out the fragile electrical impulses which held relays together and had turned the bubble-dome, which was Relay Station Twelve, into a private universe no wider than a tomb.

And it is a tomb. . . .

There was a third man in the tomb, but he didn't count. Dead men don't, and Rubichek was very, very dead indeed. He was draped with a sheet because he hadn't been much to look at even when he was alive; and after a four-hundred-pound rock had smashed down on his spacesuit, he was a lot less to look at. Even though he hadn't been alive when the rock smashed on him. He'd been fried alive first, when the insulation failed in his stormsuit.

Feniston turned his back on the draped and sheeted form and began to walk around the dome, pausing to make brief notations on a clipboard in his hand. Rawlins watched him with barely concealed rage, as he patiently worked his way around the perimeter, and finally exploded.

"Reading - on - this - instrument - made - impossible - by electrical - interference. Reading - on - this - instrument - made - impossible - by - electrical—good God, sir, how many times in the last three days have you written that all down word for word? How many times have you made me write it all down, every twenty minutes? Every instrument, day or night, every twenty minutes—damn it, Feniston, *why!*

"Rule book," Feniston said, knowing it would trigger an outburst, and it did. Rawlins swung around and told him in a loud voice what he could do with his censored, deleted and otherwise qualified rule book. Feniston listened, concealing a dismayed amusement at the kid's command of obscenities. *They've got some new expressions Earthside. I always thought cussing was unoriginal.* Rawlins finished by demanding: "Isn't there any paragraph something, section umpty-ump, rule whatsit, that tells you what to do with a dead man when you can't even get through to report his *corpse?*"

"As a matter of fact," Feniston said, putting the clipboard back into its cubbyhole, "there is. Section Nine-four Alpha. You preserve said corpse with all due attention to decency and the religious preferences of deceased as far as said preferences are known to you, unless such preservation shall endanger health, safety or morale, in which case the senior officer present shall at his personal discretion bury, burn or otherwise dispose of said corpse without further—"

"Oh, damnation!" shouted Rawlins, "you've got an answer for everything, every goddamn thing, and all the time Rubichek lying *dead,* just because of you and your forever-be-damned rule book—"

Feniston sighed, picked up pen and clipboard and returned to the meaningless task of checking his instruments. He thought, *poor Rubichek,* but it was an impersonal sadness. Neither of them had known the dead man more than a few hours; when the storm broke he'd been outside, servicing the air mechanism on his regular monthly rounds. Feniston was a little worried about the air system. Rubichek hadn't finished the servicing when he ran into trouble. And there were all those other Relay Stations he hadn't gotten to yet this month. *He'll never get to them, now. Poor Rubichek.*

And poor Rawlins. Poor Tommy. Like all the other bright-eyed kids, when they first got to the Alpha Centaurus system, all full of big-eyed wonder about their life-time dream, and to run into something like this, his first assignment.

And the kid had been so excited, under a veneer of grown-up calm, about his first station in the Service. Feniston's bleak, disciplined face went gentle. *Like Mike.* Feniston and his son had discussed their plans, on his last furlough, two years ago. Mike had already wanted the Space Service himself. But his eyes weren't quite good enough. Good enough had to be just a little better than perfect, and Mike's eyes weren't, not quite. *So he followed the old man into Comm Section. And he's coming out this month on the* Astraea. *He won't be the first of the second-generation men in the Service. Not quite. But there aren't so many, at that.*

He let Rawlins pace the floor, though it got on his nerves. *There's a time to be tough with kids, and a time to let them think they're getting away with something.* Rawlins' outburst hadn't been exactly the way for a first-year man to talk to his senior, and discipline in the Section was not quite military, but close enough; on a planet like Charmides it had to be. So most of the time when Rawlins did it, Feniston slapped him down hard, the way he'd have done with Mike when his son was younger. But today, knowing that in some indefinable way the outburst had done them both good, he let Rawlins pace and snort for a while, then called a halt to it as naturally as he could.

"It's getting pretty bright in here. Want to adjust the darkeners?"

Rawlins went to manipulate the controls that adjusted the thickness and darkness of the opaque fluid between the two layers of the bubble-dome, shutting out the glare of midday. At the height of noon which lasted for thirteen and a half hours, Earth reckoning—

the smoked glass and dark fluid would be reinforced by steel louvers, encasing the dome like an insect's carapace.

He's still mad. But not too mad to do what he's told. He knows my report this time will make or break him in Comm. So he's learning—slow, but he's learning—to keep his temper. And that's as it should be. You can't make it in the Section without control. Whether it makes sense by Earth standards or not.

"It's mealtime, Tom, but I want to get on the panel—it might clear for a minute, and I might be able to patch a message around by Seventeen and Four. Want to fix us something? Let's have some of the chocolate for a change, and break out some of that canned jam." It was a time, he knew, for small, morale-building luxuries. "I'm sick of that instant lye the Rations Board calls coffee."

Rawlins grinned. "You mean to tell me that after thirty years you can still tell what ration coffee tastes like?"

Later he took the panel so that Feniston could eat. The older man noticed that his face changed when he straddled the monitor bench, became grave, intent, *responsible*. The older man, spooning peach jam on a biscuit, watched him with genuine affection. *He'll make a good relay man, someday.*

"I'll eat as fast as I can, Tom, and get back on the board."

"Take your time," Rawlins did not take his eyes off the monitor. "No sense getting ulcers; you're hard enough to live with, as it is."

Feniston chuckled. "Hardly have time to get an ulcer now."

"Will you be sorry to retire, sir? Get back Earthside?"

"How do I know, yet? Thirty years is a long time."

"You ought to have had a comfortable desk job, ten years ago, sir. Earthside, or at least Port Major."

Feniston set his cup down with a bang. "You think that's what I wanted? Sure, I could have had a desk job, or retired five years ago with full pension, but they're still short of qualified men, and they were glad I didn't start squawking to retire. And I went into debt to get Mike into technical school so he'd be ready for the Service." His thoughts ran a familiar channel. "I'll retire when he can come out and replace me. You know it's this month—"

"You told me," Rawlins reminded him, laughing, "half a dozen times. I'll be glad when that son of yours *does* get here."

Feniston laughed with him and spooned up the last of the jam. "I'll take the board now; you'd better get some sleep before it's time to go on shift again."

Rawlins had slept and returned, and the darkeners had been twice adjusted against the brightening day, when Rawlins at the monitor roused Feniston from a brief doze on the lounge in the dome.

"I think this is really it. Come and see, sir."

Feniston came barefoot across the cold tiles and blinked at the screen. "Something out there, yes," he said at last. "Try it on visual."

Rawlins turned the knobs; blurred geometrical patterns chased one another across the TV monitor and cleared for a second into the litter of dust, rubble and rocks that was Outside. Then it dissolved into racing waveforms.

"Can't tell anything from that."

"But I know I picked up something that doesn't belong there," Rawlins argued, "just this side of that pointed rock you always use for your sightings. Watch when it clears." They bent side by side in front of the screen, Rawlins fiddling with dials; then the TV screen cleared for an instant. It dissolved three seconds later, but Feniston's trained eyes had seen.

"Looks like a Twelve Bug, Tom."

Rawlins let out an explosive sigh. "Thank God!"

"So glad to have company? Even a Special Agent come trouble-shooting?"

"Sir, after the last few watches, with Rubichek there, I'd be glad to see a cop come to arrest me for his murder." Rawlins bit off the word and looked away from Feniston. "When will he get here?"

"No telling, in that thing." The Twelve Bug—Surface Individual Transit, Model Twelve-B in the Service manuals—was little more than a spacesuit equipped with caterpillar treads and a motor; they crawled along, powered by cheap unprocessed crudes, residues from the mines all over the planet. "In good weather, twenty minutes."

But it was two hours before the little bubble-shaped vehicle crawled into the airlock and signaled. Since the lights downstairs were not working—the emergency generator covered only the minimum services without which no human could survive an instant on Charmides—Feniston went down with a handlamp. Through the thick glass of the decompression chamber, Feniston saw a tentacled monster emerge from the Twelve Bug and move toward the door. Heavy, overbalanced, it raised one arm, encased in the tool-tipped pressure gloves, to unfasten clamps and grommets; then a reassuringly human head emerged from the monster, a head with close-clipped graying hair, features lined by years of hard living, hard thinking, hard discipline. He handed the huge Dayside helmet to Rawlins, who had come down the hatch after Feniston.

"Jesus, what a trip!" He shook his head inside the collar of the suit, easing cramped muscles. "Lucky I had my Dayside helmet in the Bug, or my eyes would have been fried. When I started, I expected to get here before Centaurus was over the horizon. It's hell out there, did you know?"

"Glad you're safe, sir," Feniston said curtly. "My name is Feniston, senior in Relay Twelve Station—"

"Look, let me get the hell out of this straight jacket before you start spouting the formalities, do you mind?"

"As you wish," Feniston said stiffly. "Rawlins will help you out of your suit. One of us should be on the panel." He disappeared up the metal stairway; the stranger raised his eyes, but didn't comment. A chip still on his shoulder, Rawlins demanded, "What possessed you to leave Port Major on a day like this, sir?"

The man gave him a single clinical glance. "I didn't. I left before the storm hit Port Major."

"But—good God, sir, that means you've been seventy hours and a bit, on a five-hour run!"

"Right. And a Twelve Bug feels like a coffin from the inside. I'd appreciate a basin of water, a soft place to sit down, and something to eat beside Basic Nute pills."

Rawlins helped ease the man out of his spacesuit. "Make yourself at home, sir. My quarters are right through there. No showers since the main generator went off, but there's *some* hot water, and I'll fix you some food."

"Thanks." Out of his suit he was a tall, thin man of forty, in sweat-stained and filthy fatigues. "I'm Special Agent Martell—Paul Martell, rank of major. And I'll take you up on all of that as soon as I finish checkover. Do you suppose your hospitality could run to a suit of clean clothes?" He started, with dragging movements, on the mandatory checkout for leaving a spacesuit—on an airless world like Charmides you never knew when you might have to jump right back into it. So you serviced it immediately, dumping disinfectant into body-waste units, checking air-hoses, wiping rubber grommets with preservative. But Rawlins saw that the man could barely stand. "Go in and get cleaned up, Major," he said roughly. "I'll service the damn thing. Help yourself to anything that fits."

An hour later, bathed, shaved and dressed in some off-duty clothes of Rawlins', Major Martell lay stretched out on the sofa in the main dome, finishing his coffee.

"Before we get started, sir, what's the news from Port Major? We've been cut off for days," Feniston said. The major shook his head. "Not much. Remember, I've been on the road for days myself. Oh, the *Astraea* landed with a new load fresh from Earthside—greenest bunch of scared kids I ever saw. A bogey came within a few hundred feet of holing their shuttle, but before I left they were all on their feet and piling into Orientation One. By now, they're probably all on their way to their first stations—unless the storm hit Port Major before then."

Feniston did not even try to conceal his excitement. "Was my son among them? Michael Feniston, Junior?"

"Sorry, I just saw them in a clump. I didn't see any name labels. Is that your son?" He took the photocube from Feniston's desk and studied it a moment, then shook his head, frowning in a good-natured effort to remember. "Sorry. I seem to remember half a dozen of those lanky, dark-haired kids; I suppose he could have been there, but I couldn't say for sure." Feniston set down the cube. "Tough luck, this storm cutting you off just when he's coming in. Even if he tried to call you from Central, he'd have found that all the relays out this way have been cut off by the storm. Now you probably won't hear anything till he's settled down at his first station."

"Well, that's the way the breaks run," Feniston said, trying to conceal his disappointment. "Well, Major, I expect you want to make out your report on the accident."

It didn't take long. When Martell had finished, he put the sheet back over Rubichek, with impersonal sadness. "Poor devil. By the way, I checked with Records before I left Port Major. He never did fill out a Form A-14. So there's no need to wait for transshipment space; we can go ahead and dispose of the body. I suppose your units will handle it here?"

"Oh, sure. Even without the main generator working." Feniston saw Rawlins flinch. "What's the matter, kid? Seem cold-blooded?"

"I thought at least he'd be shipped back to Port Major for burial!"

"Not unless his family had requested it in advance, or he had. Like I said, I checked. That's a damn silly law anyhow," Martell said, "using valuable cargo space on dead bodies that belong in the disposal units. Sop to public relations, that's all," Martell said. Feniston looked at him in agreement. After the unspoken condemnation that had blown like a stream of canned air, cold and sour, from Rawlins' direction for the last few days, it was good to have Martell's support. He saw the muscles move in Rawlins' throat, but the kid only cast a murderous glare at Feniston and bent to his work.

Disposal was a messy but, fortunately, a brief affair. Afterward they had supper in the dome, Feniston interrupting himself every few minutes to check the instruments. Rawlins ate little; Feniston, watching him with pity, wished there was something he could say.

Martell finally pushed back his chair, sighing. "I've made a pig of myself. You fellows in the domes live pretty well, don't you? Oh well, something pleasant against that beautiful trip I've got ahead of me. I wonder if I have time for a couple of hours sleep before I hit the road back? They say you can sleep in a Twelve Bug, but I wonder if the guy who put that in the manual had ever been in one?"

"Got my doubts about it." Feniston pulled down the clipboard and started on his rounds again. Rawlins sneered. "Sacred ritual under way again. You could write it without moving from your chair—nothing's working yet, and you know it."

"Can't tell till you try." Feniston moved a useless dial. "Major, why not stay till the storm clears? Start now, and you'll be three days on the road again; wait till it clears, and you can make it in five hours."

Rawlins' mouth twisted. "Wouldn't that be against your precious rule book?"

Feniston started to answer, but Martell, with one swift movement, rose and stood looking down at Rawlins. "All right, mister, out with it. What's that chip on your shoulder? You've been dying to say something ever since I got here. Say it, or shut up!"

Rawlins shot to his feet. He swung from Feniston to Martell, with a trapped, desperate earnestness. "Damn it, we could have *saved* what's-his-name, Rubichek,

that poor bastard we just cut up and put down the
unit," he blurted. "We could have saved him, and we
didn't! Feniston might just as well have killed him!
The way I see it, Feniston murdered him!"

The dome was silent. Feniston heard, for the first
time in years, the futile cricket chirps, bleeps, poops,
ticks and tocks of his instruments. "Tom, I went all
over that—"

"Wait." Martell held up his hand. "Let the kid have
his say.

"Look, Major, I know I could have reached him. It
was just a question of rigging a couple of tackles—
we've got the equipment downstairs. Then we could
have switched off the surface wiring for a few minutes
and gone out in suits. Sir, I was on the tumbling team
in college, I'm damn near a professional acrobat, even
in a suit; I know I could have reached him. Feniston
wouldn't have had to risk his precious neck—"

"It wasn't the risk, dammit—"

"Let the kid finish, Feniston."

"Since we'd both have been outside in suits, we
could have cut out the gears in the air system and
brought him up through the baffle. We would have
had a fighting chance to get him up inside, and everything switched on again, before there was a direct
hit—"

Martell held up his hand. "Spare me the details," he
said. "I'm neither an electrician or a mechanic, and
certainly no acrobat. I'll willingly concede that a proper
rescue team could have reached the poor devil somehow. But you've said enough to convince me there
was no negligence on your senior's part. Feniston,
didn't you tell him why it wasn't possible to tamper
with the dome mechanisms that way? And—how long
have you been in Service, Rawlins? Surely you know
the first rule is that both members must never be
outside the dome at the same time—"

"*Oh,* the rules and regulations were coming out of
his ears," Rawlins said passionately, "but I thought all

rules were off when there was a life at stake! And there was, here! Rubichek died because Feniston couldn't let go of his damn rule book for ten lousy minutes. . . ."

Martell's mouth was set. Feniston started to speak, but Martell gestured him to silence. "And suppose you'd been killed too," he said, "and Feniston was left alone here with two dead bodies to put into the disposal instead of one?"

"But I *wouldn't* have been killed—" Rawlins swallowed hard. His voice stopped working. Feniston put a hand on his shoulder, but Rawlins shook it off. "I suppose if I'd been out there, you'd have let me lie there and fry?"

"I hope to God that decision never comes up," Feniston said steadily.

"But you would?"

"I'd have to. I'd hate it, but I'd have to." Feniston bit his lip. "You're not Earthside now, or in a nice safe dome on Mars. When you're out here, the first thing you learn is to live by the rule book. Or you don't live long enough to learn anything else." He turned away and went to the instrument panel, not looking back.

"Okay, dammit, so you'd let me lie there and fry! But suppose it was somebody you cared about! Your son, maybe? How'd you stick to your precious damn rule book then?"

Feniston did not turn round. He said, "They wouldn't let Mike and me *work* in the same dome. Just for that reason. There's just so much human nature can take."

Martell said, half aloud, "The Bronson kids. It was my first year out here."

Feniston nodded, not turning, remembering, trying not to remember. He said, "Yeah, I was on the wire that night. I was a junior then at Seventeen."

God, yes, the Bronsons. Dave and—what was his name, the little red-headed kid? Toby, that was it. Dave and Toby. Brothers. Not wanting to, his mind insisted on playing the tape again, obsessively; now he had started. The Bronsons had somehow, no one knew how they'd wangled it—*Section Twenty-two wasn't on the books then*—gotten assigned together to a dome. Feniston had been working the interdome relay the night Toby had gone out in his suit and somehow, God knows how, slid down a pile of rocks and broken his hip and—they found out later—his back. *He lay out there and screamed for hours. God knows why he never lost consciousness. Begging, pleading. Then he got delirious and started talking to Dave over his suitcom like they were little kids back home. Every dome down the line heard it. Hours. Days. Rescue One made it about an hour after Toby stopped talking. And about ten minutes after Dave blew his brains out.*

The dome had been darkened to maximum now, and the steel louvers closed, turtleshell, over the relay station. Martell went to look over Feniston's shoulder at one of the TV monitors.

"Looks like it might be easing up, now."

"Not really," said Feniston, looking at the newly cleared screen. "It clears up for a minute or two at a time, then starts again; there's a regular pulse to it. You can see Outside, if you want to, though."

"*I* don't guess the scenery's much to look at," Martell said, with a wry grin. "I think I'll get that sleep—"

"God almighty!" Rawlins jerked as if he had been stung, and pointed. "Feniston, look—by the big rock out there! I guess I must be coming unstuck, thinking everything in the screen is electrical interference! Do you see it?"

"I thought I did. Let me try to clear it up again—" for the maddening swirls had covered the monitor once again. Martell had dropped right out of their consciousness. Again they were a team, operating together at peak. "I think I've got it—I can't make it out. I thought it was a pile of rocks. Has there been another rockslide out there?"

"Maybe I'm crazy, sir, but I thought it looked like a crawler." They were kneeling side by side on the bench, systematically trying the TV monitors and the outside radar. "Look, that blip—try the signal channels, one by one, will you?"

Confusing sounds crackled and blipped in random, infuriating patterns. It was Rawlins who flipped the switch that made him jerk back his hand as if it had shocked him; through the random static a loud, frantic blasting, a scream, shattered the silence in the dome. Feniston knew that Rawlins' horrified face only reflected his own. He wet his lips. "God help us," he muttered.

"What is it, Mr. Feniston?" Martell's voice intruded on their consciousness, and Feniston said, "Rescue One Alert; Extreme Distress Signal, from the crawler out there. Loud and clear."

"Whatever's out there is in trouble, then?"

"Anything out there is in trouble by definition, Major, but that signal means extra-special trouble." Feniston was frantically trying the visuals again. "No damn good. Pull the louvers—put on your Dayside glasses first, dammit! Major, get your Dayside glasses on, or—with respect, sir—leave the dome. Get downstairs."

Moving fast, Rawlins obeyed, while the major, whipping on his Dayside glasses, squeezed his eyes against the hellish brightness.

"By the big peak—my God," Rawlins almost whispered. "Look at *that!*"

Across the glaring, unstirring dust of Charmides, they could see now; a metal craft lay tilted sidewise, tractor treads up-ended, like some monster insect spilled helplessly on its back. Feniston sucked in his breath.

"God, those poor devils!"

The fierce sheet-lightning, never slackening, came and went with a searing glare. Feniston, his eyes watering, pushed the button that closed the steel louvers, feeling the comparative darkness with relief. He went to the transmitter and, without much hope, started sending. Voice reception would be drowned by static; this was the archaic dot-dash, electrical-pulse language, kept for just such emergencies. Static would probably drown it out too, but he had to try.

"Relay Station Twelve calling, crawler, calling crawler—come in, crawler. . . ." He sent the message again and again, his nerves screaming with the relentless, automatic shrilling of the Extreme Distress Signal, which, preset, would keep blasting on all frequencies until someone answered it. It was a long time before the static gave them a returning trickle of weak dashes and dots. "Relay . . . need assistance . . . crawler Fourteen-oh-nine, down in sector . . . need assist. . . ."

"Crawler, we have your position, we can see you from the Relay Station. Can you make the dome? Have you spacesuits and ground equipment?" He waited, endlessly, for an answer that did not come. Rawlins fiddled with the receivers and managed to lower the Extreme Distress blast to an endurable ear level, making the joke all the new men thought was funny, about an extremely distressing signal. "Dammit, why don't they answer?"

"They may be answering, and the static cut out their answer," Feniston said. "Or, of course, there may not be anyone alive in there—or anyone in a condition to answer." Feniston went to the relief map of the surrounding terrain and marked the crawler's position in erasable crayon. "Those crawlers don't just turn over. Probably the cliff above the road crumbled, and everybody inside is smashed to hell."

"Then who answered your signal?" Martell asked, but it needed no answer. The answerer might now be unconscious or dead inside the smashed crawler, or think himself safer inside an insulated crawler than he would be trying to make it to the dome in an ordinary spacesuit. Feniston was trying bands again, hopelessly, one by one. Abruptly, like a special miracle, the static momentarily quieted, and from one band came the first human voice the men in the Relay Station had heard in days.

"This is Rescue One. Rescue One. This is a special

emergency band; state the nature of your emergency or get off this frequency at once."

"Rescue One, this is Relay Station Twelve. There is a downed crawler directly visible from relay windows, emitting Extreme Distress Signal. Inhabitants do not reply to call." Feniston went on, quickly reporting position, time and local conditions before the worsening storm should cut him off again. The voice at Rescue One said, "No crawler is scheduled to be within two kilometers of Relay Twelve, but someone may have been navigating on instruments that went out in the storm. We'll investigate when we can."

"How long?"

"No promises; we're snowed under here, and we have emergencies calling for help, men we know are alive. If you get any acknowledgment from them again, call us with the data. Otherwise, we'll assume they're dead or dying and leave them till we have the live ones rescued. Now get off this band, Relay Twelve, we're swamped. Rescue One, out."

Feniston watched young Rawlins pacing the floor, staring at the steel shutters. "Can't we do anything?"

"The young hero, raring to go again?" Martell frowned at Feniston. "Are you game for an extra hour on shift, Feniston? If you can run things awhile, I'll take Rawlins and go out. Maybe we can find out, at least, if there's anyone alive in there and get Rescue One to put them on a priority."

Feniston consulted the chronometer. "Oh, sure," he said, "I can work straight through Tom's shift, if I have to; mark it down as Emergency Status. Go ahead."

He heard them go clanging down the metal stairway and felt, suddenly, very old and tired. *They didn't even consider me for the rescue work. Oh, sure, it makes sense to pick the younger man.*

But it would have felt good, rules or no, to do the human thing for once. To get out there, all of us, leave the station to look after itself and fight the black glare for those men's lives. . . .

And they didn't even ask me. . . .

Time crawled by grimly, stretching minutes until they felt like quarter hours, and hours into days. Now and then Feniston put on dayside glasses and drew the shutters back, scanning the burning rocks for some sign of the two suited figures. Once he saw them, crawling slowly between two great rocks, then lost them again in the shadows.

He followed them a little while longer through the confused, flickering shadows of the TV monitor, then lost them once and for all. Time crawled on, stretched out and finally lost meaning and merged into eternity. Hours later, when the steel shutters had been drawn back and the dark fluid adjusted to opaque the dome, he heard a noise downstairs at the airlock, then dragging, uneven steps from the hatchway. Rawlins, filthy and exhausted, hauled Martell into the dome.

"No good," muttered Martell, and slumped; Feniston sprang to help him into a chair, and he lay there collapsed, not moving. Rawlins, too, looked dead beat.

"Hell out there . . . ," Martell whispered, "almost got fried by—close hits. Got within half a kilometer and I—slid. Pulled muscle—back. Hadn't been for the kid—still be lying out there."

Rawlins straddled a chair, his head slumped on the back. "Crawler's turned over—door jammed shut, need a torch to burn them out—I heard them hammering inside—alive, all right—later I'll take a torch and go back—"

Martell pulled himself painfully upright. A kind of respect was mingled with his annoyance. "You don't give up easy, do you?"

"Not with lives at stake. Hell, no, sir! You want to sit and watch them die?"

Martell groaned and lay back. "In my case it's academic; until that ligament in my back heals up, I'm not going anywhere. I'm going to catch hell from Central. A few hundred feet more, and you'd have had to leave me out there." He smiled grimly. "Feniston, the damn-fool kid half carried me in. Rawlins, I'm sorry, it was a good try, but there's nothing more we can do. We'll call in and tell Rescue One that they're alive in there and that we've done all we can."

Before Rawlins could muster the confused words that were gathering, Feniston explained it again, gently. "Tom, we don't have rescue facilities here. We've got to leave them for Rescue One. I know how you feel—"

"The hell you do!" Rawlins had gone white under the dirt on his face. "You don't know a goddamn thing but your stinking rule book!"

"Look," Martell said, "in the long run, regulations cover situations with the greatest good for the greatest number—and the least danger. Charmides is short of qualified men, but it's better for two men to die waiting for Rescue One to get around to them than for a well-meaning amateur to take a hand and have *three* corpses to bury."

The color had returned to Rawlins' face in irregular patches, and white showed all around the pupils of his eyes. "You damned—monsters," he all but screamed. "You stinking, inhuman—"

Feniston knew the kid was hysterical, but he, too, had had all he could take.

"That's enough, mister. Get down to your quarters and get some sleep. You go on shift again in two hours. Damn it, that's an order. *Move!*"

Rawlins didn't move. Feniston, thought, almost incredulous, *he's going to cry.* But he didn't. Finally he turned on his heel, and his feet clanged on the metal stairway.

Poor, damned fool of a kid. . . .

Martell said it aloud. "Poor kid. Damn-fool kid."

Feniston covered his face with his hands. He finally said, mastering the curious pain, "He'll get over it."

"Yeah, I know. Someday he'll be just like all the rest of us, learn to line it up like double-entry bookkeeping. With reason, logic and good sense on one side, and common humanity on the other. And he'll even sleep nights after he learns it."

Feniston didn't look around at him. He only said,

"There's some codeine in the medix box. I'd better get you some for your back, Major."

Martell dozed feverishly on the sofa; Feniston wearily went through the rounds at his panel. He was ready to drop; he had worked sixteen hours straight. At the end of the two hours' grace he had given Rawlins, he buzzed Rawlins' quarters, thinking longingly of a shave, some hot soup, and a good long sleep. *Yeah, I'm getting old. Where the hell is Rawlins?*

There was no answering buzz from below; Feniston swore, and Martell opened his eyes, started to sit up, winced and didn't. "Where's the kid? Still playing Achilles-sulking-in-his-tent?"

"Probably dead asleep," Feniston said slowly, "but this buzzer would wake up the Sphinx. Maybe it's gone out of service. With the main generator out, nothing works right." He was beginning to worry. In the Service, quarters had doors. On an airless world where you lived in domes, privacy meant sanity. But the doors had no locks. So if your junior went stir-crazy and tried to suicide, he couldn't lock himself in to finish the job . . . he hit the buzzer hard and repeatedly, swore, clanged down the metal ladder and banged, hard, on Rawlins' door. "Rawlins! Hey—Tom, damn it, you're on-shift! Get the hell up here!"

He thrust open the door. The bed was dented, not slept in. Feniston retraced his steps, an awful suspicion growing on him.

His own quarters were bare and shipshape; the tiny galley empty and clean. Finally there was nowhere else to look, and Feniston's steps dragged as he turned toward the airlock room.

Empty, but the light glowed on the panel.

WHEN THIS LIGHT IS ON
SOMEONE IS *OUT*.
DO NOT FASTEN DOOR
FROM INSIDE.

And Rawlins' spacesuit was gone.

*　　*　　*

He didn't have to tell Martell what had happened. The major swore, unprintably. Feniston slumped.

"What could I have done? Short of putting him under arrest in advance?"

"I know, damn it," Martell muttered. "I couldn't be too rough on him. Damn kid saved my life."

"Well, it's out of our hands now." Feniston, shaking with fatigue, dropped on the bench. His body felt as if it was permanently molded to it. He pulled down the log and wrote down the time, adding: "Unable to assign panel to second officer account—" His hand-writing, he noticed with the glassy clarity of a brain fatigued almost to breaking point, had gone illegible. He braced his hand and printed in block capitals: RAWLINS AWOL.

Martell said, "Feniston, you've been working six-teen hours straight. You'll keel over. Can I take the panel?"

"Good of you, sir. But—against regulations to let an outsider on the panel. I'll get some wakers from the medix box." He went and swallowed the drug, waiting for the burst of energy. *This is against regs too, except in emergencies. Well, we've got one hell of an emergency.*

I had such hopes for the kid. As if he was filling in for Mike. And for his own sake, too. For the time when I wasn't around any more.

Martell muttered, when he came back, "I wonder if he realized we'll have to send Rescue One after him too?"

"I don't know what he thinks. Or *if* he thinks." Feniston hit the button. Miraculously, there was a clear channel. For once, Feniston wished there hadn't been. But he knew what he had to do, and he did it. His voice faltered a little as he reported Rawlins AWOL. *It's just fatigue,* he told himself. But he knew it wasn't.

Time wasn't time any more. Martell dozed, pain and codeine winning out over anxiety. Feniston stayed

awake, half sick with the reaction from the wakers in
his system, mingled with anger. Once he tried to pick
up Rawlins on the TV monitor, but the bubble-dome's
own revolving shadow cut off the light. Radar picked
up a small, just-moving fleck that was about the right
size for a man in a spacesuit. As the hours crawled by,
Feniston's anger mingled with fear. Against his own
will, something of the rage, the determination of Rawlins' fight with death got through to the older man.

He felt an atavistic, almost savage approval as that
little fleck crawled buglike across the screen. Every
inch was a half mile nearer, across the crackling hell
out there. A hazard surmounted. A margin of safety
gained. It was a purely human reaction, logic aside,
and Feniston didn't try to fight it. And as the little
fleck neared the dome again on the return journey, for
the first time in his thirty years Feniston forgot his
panel checks. The last hundred feet were the worst.
Feniston had exhausted his supply of desperation. He
breathed with the flicker of light that was Rawlins on
the radar. *Easy now . . . watch the rocks out there . . .
if this was a house you'd be on the front lawn . . . he's
going to make it back, by God he's going to make it. . . .*

Roughly he went and shook Martell awake. "Open
the shutters! Can you get him on visual?"

Martell hobbled to the control, groping for his Dayside glasses. "Can't see—oh, God, look what that
crazy kid did! He took my Twelve Bug—wouldn't hold
all of them, so he's adapted the crawler panel—they're
riding on top of it! Rawlins and—one, two—three of
the men from the crawler! On one damn Twelve Bug!"

*Another charge against him, Unlawful use and
adaptation. . . .*

"He's rigged a lightning deflector—yes, damn it, I
know as well as you do . . . Feniston, my God, look at
that crazy kid—"

"Told you he was a clever youngster," Feniston
growled. But he didn't come and look. He didn't look
at all.

*　　*　　*

And then it was over. Quietly, like an anticlimax, Feniston heard the airlock open, the hiss of the decompression room, and four men struggled up the steps into the dome. Rawlins and another man were carrying a third between them; the fourth man was limping, but he was on his feet. Feniston turned from the panel.

"Well, Tom!" It was welcome, grateful prayer of thanks, and unutterable weariness, all in one.

Rawlins smiled. His clothes clung like wet wash to his body. He wiped his face with a dripping sleeve and said blissfully, "I made it, sir."

The third man straightened. "Maydon, sir. I thought we'd had it for sure. He almost killed himself getting us out." He gestured to the man Rawlins had helped to carry, now lying inert on the sofa. "I thought sure the kid here wasn't going to make it, but now I guess he's got a chance."

Feniston said briefly, "I guess we can look after you all here until the men from Rescue One make it. Do any of you have a cert to fix a generator?"

"Yeah, me," Maydon said, staring at Rawlins. "You mean *you're* not from Rescue One? Man, I want to shake your hand!"

Rawlins gleamed at Feniston as Maydon wrung his hand. "I told you I could do it, sir! Regulations be damned! I *told* you—"

Maydon stopped dead. He dropped Rawlins' hand and stared, saying slowly, "Hey, you mean—"

"Later, Maydon," Feniston said. "Go below, Rawlins."

"You damn old sourpuss," Rawlins burst out, *"All right*—so raise hell, raise hell because I walked all over your precious rule book. I saved three men's lives. Can't you get that through your damned thick head. I saved *three lives!* And will you have a look at this other kid here before he dies on us? Or is that against the rule book too?"

Feniston bent over the wounded man.

And froze there. *It's just an insane, obscene nightmare. And now, at last, after all this, I can wake up—*

But he didn't. Gripped by nightmare, paralyzed, Feniston saw the wounded man's face. Crushed and dirty and bloody, eyes closed in weakness and exhaustion, Feniston saw the face of his son Mike.

"No," Feniston said, thickly, *"No!* Oh, God, *Mike!"*

Rawlins was so near collapse himself that he absorbed the shock without surprise. ". . . glad," he mumbled, "heard nothing out of you for a month but Mike . . . maybe take the curse off . . . have a heart. . . ."

Mike Feniston opened his eyes. To an impersonal watcher—if there were any—he would have been only a nice-looking kid of twenty or so, who should never have been brought all these millions of miles from Earth to be smashed and left to fry inside a broken crawler in the hell of Charmides. He looked at his father without curiosity, as if the last hours had held so many shocks that nothing could ever surprise him again.

"I made it, Dad," he whispered through bleeding lips, "only I goofed. Guess you won't be very proud of me, goofing up the works first thing. . . ." he whispered, and died.

Rawlins' tears rolled down, unashamed, and fell on Mike's face. "God! I'm so sorry, sir, so sorry—I did my best—I'd have risked my life twice over—"

"You did just exactly that, didn't you?" Feniston let go of Mike's hand. It was cold, now, and limp. "Quite the hero."

"I was glad to do it, sir." Rawlins, for all his filth stood there, somehow shining. "I like to think anyone in the Service would have done the same thing."

He means it. Feniston thought. And realized for the first time how the old cliches could seem, somehow, new and meaningful, with bright new sharp edges on them. He breathed deep, feeling the hurt down where pain still had meaning, knowing that his next words would sear away that shining thing in the boy forever. He had never hated anything so much in his life.

"Major Martell, I request that you place Rawlins under arrest. Reasons: general lack of discipline, insubordination, direct defiance of an order, and unlawfully modifying equipment outside the regular field of his duty." His mouth was dry, empty of words. Martell's face was compassionate, but Feniston, floundering in his own pain, saw only Rawlins. The shine had gone out of the young hero's face; now he was just a beaten, exhausted kid.

"I—I—did I hear you right? Arrest? For saving a—for saving three lives?"

Martell rapped, "For risking your own life, almost making it four deaths, and unauthorized use of a Surface Transit Twelve-B. You were dumb and lucky, Rawlins. But out here you don't gamble on dumb luck, or heroics! Nobody gets a second chance out here, and you had yours!"

"I—" Rawlins looked around for something, someone, but there was only Martell, like a judgment of God. Feniston knew he would never forget that despairing sweep of Rawlins' head around the dome, as if appealing to a higher court for justice, before Martell took him by the arm, not unkindly.

"Better get below, mister. You'll be going back to Port Major with me—and probably out on the *Astraea*, return trip to Earth."

Rawlins stumbled on the metal rung. "Okay," he muttered, and Feniston knew that the whole dead load of fatigue was finally caving in on the kid, crushing him at last. "Okay. All right if I get a little—little sleep first? I'm *dead*."

And as he stumbled down the stairs, Feniston heard the sobs break out, thick, exhausted sobs of a hero beaten down to a whipped kid who still couldn't figure out what had hit him—and probably never would.

Blind with pain, Feniston turned to Maydon. "You're certified. You take the panel. Emergency," he muttered. He felt his face crumple as he looked down into the face of his dead son. Like Rawlins' dream, his own life had crumbled into the dust and rubble of that quiet hell that was Charmides. He pulled a blanket over Mike's face.

And they won't even let me stay here to die. . . .

Mechanically, under the dimming glare, he adjusted the darkeners; the black sky of Charmides opened up, endless as space itself, over his head. He looked over his son's body into the blackness, but he didn't see it.

"I had two sons, really," he said in a hoarse, old man's voice, to no one in particular, "and today I lost them both."

He put his arm over his eyes. He would be very glad to get back to Earth.

(1976)

The Engine

I am hating the Engine.

Yes of course I know that it is the miracle of our century, that no man, and especially no woman, now suffers from deprivation as they have done from the dawn of history. It certainly was a barbarian thing, to leave the satisfaction of an instinct so vital to the chance clumsiness of mutual attraction or purely subjective emotions, or to deny it, perhaps, to those who need it most. The Engine takes care of all that. It reliably monitors all the reflexes, even to the reddening of the earlobes and the painless contractions of the womb, so that nothing is left to chance.

A half-hour treatment on the Engine twice a month and all that tension and neurosis is ended forever. The neo-Reichians proved, a long time ago, how valuable it was, but not until the genius who invented the Engine could we free ourselves from the kind of deprivation that led not only to neurotic behavior and hysteria but to physical pathologies such as cancer and social pathologies such as war.

But I am still hating the Engine.

It is not painful this time, it has not been painful since I was twelve or so. The Med says my responses are boringly normal. Yet I wonder if all women feel, as I do, the numb terror and humiliation when feet are locked up into the stirrups and the sensors snake down to attach themselves to the areas richest in nerve endings.

I go to the trouble of reading the little booklet the Meds will give you, if you ask, about understanding the Engine, even though my Med warns against it: "Don't intellectualize," he tells me; "simply give yourself up to the physical experience. It is completely programmed and monitors all your responses. You don't need to know how or why it works. Simply give yourself up to it. It is more beneficial that way."

Yet I read the book, finding to my chagrin that it only gives diagrams of nerve-fiber bundles and anatomical drawings that I find too grotesque to look at. I was hoping for something to explain the resentment, the hatred, the wrath, but nothing of that sort, just stories of all the ailments women had had before this century, ailments directly traceable to the lack of the Engine.

I am angriest when I have to take the main appliance in my hands and insert it myself. Of course now I am sticky with my own secretions and the mechanical lubricant that the sensors supply in precisely optimum amounts, compensating for lack or oversupply. I hate the smell of the mechanical lubricant, the smooth soft slickness between my fingers. Loathsome, like some animal. Yet once I program for mechanical entry I cannot endure watching the slow, seeking approach, the numb nuzzling, the sudden hard shock so that I hear myself screaming like the women in the other cubicles. Then the worst is over. I try to relax and let the Engine monitor the responses I cannot control or resist. Even that I resent, resent the way it takes control of consciousness, so that I writhe, I gasp, cry out, scream like the other women I can faintly hear, until the moment when even sound blacks out. I am boringly normal, the Med declares. I have had preorgasmic treatment only once or twice since I was fourteen. And only two or three times do I attempt to resist the Engine, experiment with inhibiting response, and the Med says most adolescents do that once or twice too, simply a way of experimenting, testing their own responses. After all, they remind me, it does not matter, the sensors are programmed to occasional resistance, they can monitor it in skin tension and internal pulses, and they are programmed to linger as long as needed on manipulations of nerve-rich areas, which finally diminish even the most determined resistance.

And after this the responses and detensioning are so powerful that one is lassitudinous and weak, too weak to walk, and I find it worse humiliation to be helped gently out of the cubicle by a Med and given stimulants in view of the waiting line of women outside the cubicles, twelve-year-olds frightened or grinning in bravado before their early treatments, married women coming in for detension monitoring weekly, menopausal spinsters for the more frequent treatment, which prevents the physical and nervous degeneration that used to set in at that time.

Once I apply for exemption. Sometimes women are exempt because of low vitality or ill health, and I wonder if my hatred of the Engine betrays some such unsuspected condition, when I am perfectly well aware of how beneficial the treatments are. I take all the tests, watch them checking my psych profile, actually monitoring, live rather than by sensor, one or two treatments. I am so nervous at the thought of the living monitor behind the controls that I resist the Engine and have to be given reprogramming for resistance and preorgasmic treatment for the first time since I was fourteen. But they say that is normal too under the circumstances. The Meds are kind, as all androids are always kind. But afterward they show me the spiked curve of those boringly normal responses, and then show me the flattened ones of women who have legitimate exemptions, who cannot respond even after manual programming and preorgasmic treament. Such women comprise three point two in a thousand, they tell me, and most of them are heart cases or chronic low thyroids or severe mental retardates. I don't mention hate. What is the point of mentioning a purely subjective reality?

Lorn is deviling me again to marry him. I remember that marriage is a legal exemption. It might be worth trying. We apply for marriage permits, have our psych profiles checked and our legal status reregistered, apply for joint housing. I go in for my marriage exemption and am warned to come in every seven days for detension monitoring. I am told, to my shocked amazement, that I am always free to request extra sessions up to the legal maximum of three times a week. Again I wonder if I am unique, the only woman to feel this resistance and hatred. But I cling to the notion that I need never go on the Engine again, if detensioning is complete, while the marriage endures.

Lorn is very much in love. I try to match his eagerness. He is sweet, companionable. The Engine, I know, has made marriage less risky; no man now needs to marry for the detensioning and physical relief which the Engine can legally give him. I am shown drawings of the male models so that we will know about one another's experience. I am also told that now there is less pressure on a man's virility, since the Engine is always there to supplement detensioning to the exact level necessary. The men's model is even more grotesque, round and neutral, pouched, plastic pink and obscenely soft. It has fewer auxiliary sensors because the male erogenous zones are more narrowly located.

We are together. For a moment I wonder if I can respond to him as readily as the computer-controlled sensors do, but he seems content. I am startled to see that men, too, cry out and writhe in the grip of the reflexes. The smell is subtly different from the mechanical lubricant, but Lorn tells me that is imagination, the chemical composition is precisely equivalent, and synthetic hormones are exact equivalents. I feel very tender. I am surprised and excited when he does not discover the richest nerve endings as the sensors do, but the very excitement makes me respond. I am ashamed to cry out as I do in the cubicle, but I find myself weeping, and he is dismayed. I tell him truthfully that it is from happiness. I love him. Lorn is my freedom.

I go for detension monitoring. The Med says it is not quite complete, and recommends—it is not compulsory—a treatment; I refuse, and he prescribes a relaxation exercise. It is better with Lorn the next time, even though I am troubled. If detension is not complete they will put me on the Engine again. I cry, I beg him for some of the nerve touches which the computer has discovered are my most responsive. He does his best, and this time I am sure it is complete.

I am completely happy. I go to work; Lorn and I sleep together, eat together, experiment with manual cooking—Lorn thinks it is not sanitary, but I tell him that for thousands of years humanity lived on such foods and substances. They have a subtle, different flavor, not quite like synthetics. He says that is my imagination too. For the first time since I was twelve years old, I go from week to week without thought of the upcoming Engine appointment. I am happy.

Yet the weekly detension monitorings frighten me, too. I am always recommended for relaxation therapy, even though they do not demand Engine treatment. I grow more and more worried, find myself begging Lorn to help me. It must succeed! It must!

A week comes when the detension monitoring ends in the Red Zone. They send me into the line for the cubicle. I cry all the time my feet are locked into the stirrups. I scream, I resist the machine, I resist so long that I am finally given override programming and come out weak, unable to walk. I cry all the time the Meds are giving me stimulants; I stop only when they tell me I must have successful detension monitoring before I go home, and crying like this will inhibit the monitoring and give false responses. Again I cry, on the way home, and Lorn is desperate; I cry, I accuse him, I tell him that it is his fault that he could not give me the detensioning I need so desperately. We make it up in one another's arms, but I am too limp to respond after the long purgatory of the cubicle. He grows angry, then is frightened when I cannot stop crying. He wants to call a Med. I beg him not to, stifle my sobs. I fall asleep hating him, wanting to die, but he is contrite, begs me for forgiveness, says we will try again.

We are gentle with one another now, and courteous. We try to relax with one another, and my next two detension monitorings come clear. The Med has told me that there are many early problems of adjustment. Maybe the worst is over. I touch Lorn gently, marveling at his soft liveness. I love him. I rest in his arms, happy.

Later he asks me for something I find myself unable to do. Surely there are no nerve endings *there!* But he pleads until I try. I am sickened, I retch, I rush away to vomit. He is angry at first, then contrite. But he asks again and again. Finally, when I refuse, he tells me angrily that if I refuse him he will go to the Engine, that the Engine's sensors have determined his needs and this is not unreasonable. I scream at him to go to the Engine and be damned. He stares at me in shock, and we end in one another's arms.

I think he is punishing me for my refusal. Four nights he lies silent beside me, without a touch. At first I am stubborn, I say nothing. On the fourth night I begin to worry. My detension monitoring is tomorrow, and I will surely end in the Red Zone again. I tell him, and he takes me gently in his arms, but nothing happens. I am sure he has been going to the Engine for what he asked me and I refused.

We cannot go on like this! I am frantic, knowing I am tense and will surely fail my monitoring. I want to shriek insults at him. This once I message the center, giving them my ident, saying I have a chill and must skip the monitoring this week. They accept the excuse so easily I am elated. I will use it as often as I can.

Time passes and so far I am free of the Engine, but Lorn is going, I am sure, for legal supplementation. Since our psych profiles were matched for complementary needs, I am afraid that the supplementation will lessen his energy, leaving him less able to give me the detensioning I need. I grow more and more frightened. It is humiliating to go for detension monitoring when I know it is programmed on my card that my husband has applied for legal supplementation for need.

I beg him to work a little more on the nerve fibers always programmed for my major needs. He refuses. Finally he lashes out at me, "Detension monitoring, detension monitoring, it is all you ever think about! I can never simply enjoy being with you any more!"

I flare at him, "Why do you think I married you? You were the only legal exemption I could get!"

Ice cold, we stare at one another. His voice is cold. "Do you want a divorce?"

I shrug. "Why bother? This is a comfortable apartment. We can get in another bed if you would rather."

I do not bother to go for detension monitoring the next day. I am humiliated, but I fill out a card for legal supplementation. I program it for mechanical entry. I will resist, I will fight, they will give me preorgasmic treatment, I will come out too weak to walk, enjoy the stimulants, let them send me home in a public conveyance. I will not worry about Lorn. He is entitled to legal supplementation from the Engine.

(1977)

The Secret of the Blue Star

On a night in Sanctuary, when the streets bore a false glamour in the silver glow of full moon, so that every ruin seemed an enchanted tower and every dark street and square an island of mystery, the mercenary-magician Lythande sallied forth to seek adventure.

Lythande had but recently returned—if the mysterious comings and goings of a magician can be called by so prosaic a name—from guarding a caravan across the Grey Wastes to Twand. Somewhere in the Wastes, a gaggle of desert rats—two-legged rats with poisoned steel teeth—had set upon the caravan, not knowing it was guarded by magic, and had found themselves fighting skeletons that howled and fought with eyes of flame; and at their center a tall magician with a blue star between blazing eyes, a star that shot lightnings of a cold and paralyzing flame. So the desert rats ran, and never stopped running until they reached Aurvesh, and the tales they told did Lythande no harm except in the ears of the pious.

And so there was gold in the pockets of the long, dark magician's robe, or perhaps concealed in whatever dwelling sheltered Lythande.

For at the end, the caravan master had been almost more afraid of Lythande than he was of the bandits, a situation which added to the generosity with which he rewarded the magician. According to custom, Lythande neither smiled nor frowned, but remarked, days later, to Myrtis, the proprietor of the Aphrodisia House in the Street of Red Lanterns, that sorcery, while a useful skill and filled with many aesthetic delights for the contemplation of the philosopher, in itself put no beans on the table.

A curious remark, that, Myrtis pondered, putting away the ounce of gold Lythande had bestowed upon her in consideration of a secret which lay many years behind them both. Curious that Lythande should speak of beans on the table, when no one but herself had ever seen a bit of food or a drop of drink pass the magician's lips since the blue star had adorned that high and narrow brow. Nor had any woman in the Quarter ever been able to boast that a great magician had paid for her favors, or been able to imagine how such a magician behaved in that situation when all men were alike reduced to flesh and blood.

Perhaps Myrtis could have told if she would; some of her girls thought so, when, as sometimes happened, Lythande came to the Aphrodisia House and was closeted long with its owner; even, on rare intervals, for an entire night. It was said, of Lythande, that the Aphrodisia House itself had been the magician's gift to Myrtis, after a famous adventure still whispered in the bazaar, involving an evil wizard, two horse-traders, a caravan master, and a few assorted toughs who had prided themselves upon never giving gold for any woman and thought it funny to cheat an honest working woman. None of them had ever showed their faces—what was left of them—in Sanctuary again, and Myrtis boasted that she need never again sweat to earn her living, and never again entertain a man, but would claim her madam's privilege of a solitary bed.

And then, too, the girls thought, a magician of Lythande's stature could have claimed the most beautiful women from Sanctuary to the mountains beyond Ilsig; not courtesans alone, but princesses and noblewomen and priestesses would have been for Lythande's taking. Myrtis had doubtless been beautiful in her youth, and certainly she boasted enough of the princes and wizards and travelers who had paid great sums for her love. She was beautiful still (and of course there were those who said that Lythande did not pay *her*, but that, on the contrary, Myrtis paid the magician great sums to maintain her aging beauty with strong magic) but her hair had gone gray and she no longer troubled to dye it with henna or goldenwash from Tyris-beyond-the-sea.

But if Myrtis were not the woman who knew how Lythande behaved in that most elemental of situations, then there was no woman in Sanctuary who could say. Rumor said also that Lythande called up female demons from the Grey Wastes, to couple in lechery, and certainly Lythande was neither the first nor the last magician of whom that could be said.

But on this night Lythande sought neither food nor drink nor the delights of amorous entertainment; although Lythande was a great frequenter of taverns, no man had ever yet seen a drop of ale or mead or fire-drink pass the barrier of the magician's lips. Lythande walked along the far edge of the bazaar, skirting the old rim of the governor's palace, keeping to the shadows in defiance of footpads and cutpurses, out of that love for shadows which made the folk of the city say that Lythande could appear and disappear into thin air.

Tall and thin, Lythande, above the height of a tall man, lean to emaciation, with the blue star-shaped tattoo of the Magician-Adept above thin, arching eyebrows; wearing a long, hooded robe which melted into the shadows. Clean-shaven, the face of Lythande, or beardless—none had come close enough, in living memory, to say whether this was the whim of an effeminate or the hairlessness of a freak. The hair beneath the hood was as long and luxuriant as a woman's, but graying, as no woman in this city of harlots would have allowed it to do.

Striding quickly along a shadowed wall, Lythande stepped through an open door, over which the sandal of Thufir, god of pilgrims, had been nailed up for luck; but the footsteps were so soft, and the hooded robe blended so well into the shadows, that eyewitnesses would later swear, truthfully, that they had seen

Lythande appear from the air, protected by sorceries, or by a cloak of invisibility.

Around the hearthfire, a group of men were banging their mugs noisily to the sound of a rowdy drinking-song, strummed on a worn and tinny lute—Lythande knew it belonged to the tavern-keeper, and could be borrowed—by a young man, dressed in fragments of foppish finery, torn and slashed by the chances of the road. He was sitting lazily, with one knee crossed over the other; and when the rowdy song died away, the young man drifted into another, a quiet love-song from another time and another country. Lythande had known the song, more years ago than bore remembering, and in those days Lythande the magician had borne another name and had known little of sorcery. When the song died, Lythande had stepped from the shadows, visible, and the firelight glinted on the blue star, mocking at the center of the high forehead.

There was a little muttering in the tavern, but they were not unaccustomed to Lythande's invisible comings and goings. The young man raised eyes which were surprisingly blue beneath the black hair elaborately curled above his brow. He was slender and agile, and Lythande marked the rapier at his side, which looked well handled, and the amulet, in the form of a coiled snake, at his throat. The young man said, "Who are you, who has the habit of coming and going into thin air like that?"

"One who compliments your skill at song." Lythande flung a coin to the tapster's boy. "Will you drink?"

"A minstrel never refuses such an invitation. Singing is dry work." But when the drink was brought, he said, "Not drinking with me, then?"

"No man has ever seen Lythande eat or drink," muttered one of the men in the circle round them.

"Why, then, I hold that unfriendly," cried the young minstrel. "A friendly drink between comrades shared is one thing; but I am no servant to sing for pay or to drink except as a friendly gesture!"

Lythande shrugged, and the blue star above the

high brow began to shimmer and give forth blue light. The onlookers slowly edged backward, for when a wizard who wore the blue star was angered, bystanders did well to be out of the way. The minstrel set down the lute, so it would be well out of range if he must leap to his feet. Lythande knew, by the excruciating slowness of his movements and great care, that he had already shared a good many drinks with chance-met comrades. But the minstrel's hand did not go to his swordhilt but instead closed like a fist over the amulet in the form of a snake.

"You are like no man I have ever met before," he observed mildly, and Lythande, feeling inside the little ripple, nerve-long, that told a magician he was in the presence of spellcasting, hazarded quickly that the amulet was one of those which would not protect its master unless the wearer first stated a set number of truths—usually three or five—about the owner's attacker or foe. Wary, but amused, Lythande said, "A true word. Nor am I like any man you will ever meet, live you never so long, minstrel."

The minstrel saw, beyond the angry blue glare of the star, a curl of friendly mockery in Lythande's mouth. He said, letting the amulet go, "And I wish you no ill; and you wish me none, and those are true sayings, too, wizard, hey? And there's an end of that. But although perhaps you are like to no other, you are not the only wizard I have seen in Sanctuary who bears a blue star about his forehead."

Now the blue star blazed rage, but not for the minstrel. They both knew it. The crowd around them had all mysteriously discovered that they had business elsewhere. The minstrel looked at the empty benches.

"I must go elsewhere to sing for my supper, it seems."

"I meant you no offense when I refused to share a drink," said Lythande. "A magician's vow is not as lightly overset as a lute. Yet I may guest-gift you with dinner and drink in plenty without loss of dignity, and in return ask a service of a friend, may I not?"

"Such is the custom of my country. Cappen Varra thanks you, magician."

"Tapster! Your best dinner for my guest, and all he can drink tonight!"

"For such liberal guesting I'll not haggle about the service," Cappen Varra said, and set to the smoking dishes brought before him. As he ate, Lythande drew from the folds of his robe a small pouch containing a quantity of sweet-smelling herbs, rolled them into a blue-gray leaf, and touched his ring to spark the roll alight. He drew on the smoke, which drifted up sweet and grayish.

"As for the service, it is nothing so great; tell me all you know of this other wizard who wears the blue star. I know of none other of my order south of Azehur, and I would be certain you did not see me, nor my wraith."

Cappen Varra sucked at a marrow-bone and wiped his fingers fastidiously on the tray-cloth beneath the meats. He bit into a ginger-fruit before replying.

"Not you, wizard, nor your fetch or doppelganger; this one had shoulders brawnier by half, and he wore no sword, but two daggers cross-girt astride his hips. His beard was black; and his left hand missing three fingers."

"Ils of the Thousand Eyes! Rabben the Half-handed, here in Sanctuary! Where did you see him, minstrel?"

"I saw him crossing the bazaar; but he bought nothing that I saw. And I saw him in the Street of Red Lanterns, talking to a woman. What service am I to do for you, magician?"

"You have done it." Lythande gave silver to the tavernkeeper—so much that the surly man bade Shalpa's cloak cover him as he went—and laid another coin, gold this time, beside the borrowed lute.

"Redeem your harp; that one will do your voice no boon." But when the minstrel raised his head in thanks, the magician had gone unseen into the shadows.

Pocketing the gold, the minstrel asked, "How did he know that? And how did he go out?"

"Shalpa the swift alone knows," the tapster said. "Flew out by the smoke-hole in the chimney, for all I ken! That one needs not the night-dark cloak of Shalpa to cover him, for he has one of his own. He paid for your drinks, good sir; what will you have?" And Cappen Varra proceeded to get very drunk, that being the wisest thing to do when one becomes entangled unawares in the private affairs of a wizard.

Outside in the street, Lythande paused to consider. Rabben the Half-handed was no friend; yet there was no reason his presence in Sanctuary must deal with Lythande, or personal revenge. If it were business concerned with the Order of the Blue Star, if Lythande must lend Rabben aid, or the Half-handed had been sent to summon all the members of the Order, the star they both wore would have given warning.

Yet it would do no harm to make certain. Walking swiftly, the magician had reached a line of old stables behind the governor's palace. There was silence and secrecy for magic. Lythande stepped into one of the little side alleys, drawing up the magician's cloak until no light remained, slowly withdrawing farther and farther into the silence until nothing remained anywhere in the world—anywhere in the universe but the light of the blue star ever glowing in front. Lythande remembered how it had been set there, and at what cost—the price an Adept paid for power.

The blue glow gathered, fulminated in many-colored patterns, pulsing and glowing, until Lythande stood *within* the light; and there, in the Place That Is Not, seated upon a throne carved apparently from Sapphire, was the Master of the Star.

"Greetings to you, fellow star, star-born, *shyryu.*" The terms of endearment could mean fellow, companion, brother, sister, beloved, equal, pilgrim; its literal meaning was *sharer of starlight.* "What brings you into the Pilgrim Place this night from afar?"

"The need for knowledge, star-sharer. Have you sent one to seek me out in Sanctuary?"

"Not so, *shyryu*. All is well in the Temple of the Starsharers; you have not yet been summoned; the hour is not yet come."

For every Adept of the Blue Star knows; it is one of the prices of power. At the world's end, when all the doings of mankind and mortals are done, the last to fall under the assault of Chaos will be the Temple of the Star; and then, in the Place That Is Not, the Master of the Star will summon all of the Pilgrim Adepts from the farthest corners of the world, to fight with all their magic against Chaos; but until that day, they have such freedom as will best strengthen their powers. The Master of the Star repeated, reassuringly, "The hour has not come. You are free to walk as you will in the world."

The blue glow faded, and Lythande stood shivering. So Rabben had not been sent in that final summoning. Yet the end and Chaos might well be at hand for Lythande before the hour appointed, if Rabben the Half-handed had his way.

It was a fair test of strength, ordained by our masters. Rabben should bear me no ill-will. . . . Rabben's presence in Sanctuary need not have to do with Lythande. He might be here upon his lawful occasions—if anything of Rabben's could be said to be lawful; for it was only upon the last day of all that the Pilgrim Adepts were pledged to fight upon the side of Law against Chaos. And Rabben had not chosen to do so before then.

Caution would be needed, and yet Lythande knew that Rabben was near. . . .

South and east of the governor's palace, there is a little triangular park, across from the Street of Temples. By day the graveled walks and turns of shrubbery are given over to predicants and priests who find not enough worship or offerings for their liking; by night the place is the haunt of women who worship no goddess except She of the filled purse and the empty womb. And for both reasons the place is called, in irony, the Promise of Heaven; in Sanctuary, as elsewhere, it is well known that those who promise do not always perform.

Lythande, who frequented neither women nor priests as a usual thing, did not often walk here. The park seemed deserted; the evil winds had begun to blow, whipping bushes and shrubbery into the shapes of strange beasts performing unnatural acts; and moaning weirdly around the walls and eaves of the Temples across the street, the wind that was said in Sanctuary to be the moaning of Azyuna in Vashanka's bed. Lythande moved swiftly, skirting the darkness of the paths. And then a woman's scream rent the air.

From the shadows Lythande could see the frail form of a young girl in a torn and ragged dress; she was barefoot and her ear was bleeding where one jeweled earring had been torn from the lobe. She was struggling in the iron grip of a huge burly black-bearded man, and the first thing Lythande saw was the hand gripped around the girl's thin, bony wrist, dragging her; two fingers missing and the other cut away to the first joint. Only then—when it was no longer needed—did Lythande see the blue star between the black bristling brows, the cat-yellow eyes of Rabben the Half-handed!

Lythande knew him of old, from the Temple of the Star. Even then Rabben had been a vicious man, his lecheries notorious. Why, Lythande wondered, had the Masters not demanded that he renounce them as the price of his power? Lythande's lips tightened in a mirthless grimace; so notorious had been Rabben's lecheries that if he renounced them, everyone would know the Secret of his Power.

For the powers of an Adept of the Blue Star depended upon a secret. As in the old legend of the giant who kept his heart in a secret place outside his body, and with it his immortality, so the Adept of the Blue Star poured all his psychic force into a single Secret; and the one who discovered the Secret would acquire all of that Adept's power. So Rabben's Secret

must be something else . . . Lythande did not specu-
late on it.

The girl cried out pitifully as Rabben jerked at her
wrist; as the burly magician's star began to glow, she
thrust her free hand over her eyes to shield them from
it. Without fully intending to intervene, Lythande
stepped from the shadows, and the rich voice that had
made the prentice-magicians in the outer court of the
Blue Star call Lythande "minstrel" rather than "magician," rang out:

"By Shipri the All-Mother, release that woman!"

Rabben whirled. "By the nine-hundred-and-ninety-
ninth eye of Ils! Lythande!"

"Are there not enough women in the Street of Red
Lanterns, that you must mishandle girl-children in the
Street of Temples?" For Lythande could see how young
she was, the thin arms and childish legs and ankles,
the breasts not yet full-formed beneath the dirty, torn
tunic.

Rabben turned on Lythande and sneered, "You
were always squeamish, *shyryu*. No woman walks here
unless she is for sale. Do you want her for yourself?
Have you tired of your fat madame in the Aphrodisia
House?"

"You will not take her name into your mouth,
shyryu!"

"So tender for the honor of a harlot?"

Lythande ignored that. "Let that girl go, or stand to
my challenge."

Rabben's star shot lightning; he shoved the girl to
one side. She fell nerveless to the pavement and lay
without moving. "She'll stay there until we've done.
Did you think she could run away while we fought?
Come to think of it, I never did see you with a woman,
Lythande—is that your Secret, Lythande, that you've
no use for women?"

Lythande maintained an impassive face; but whatever came, Rabben must not be allowed to pursue *that*
line. "You may couple like an animal in the streets of

Sanctuary, Rabben, but I do not. Will you yield her up, or fight?"

"Perhaps I should yield her to you; this is unheard of, that Lythande should fight in the streets over a woman! You see, I know your habits well, Lythande!"

Damnation of Vashanka! Now indeed I shall have to fight for the girl!

Lythande's rapier snicked from its scabbard and thrust at Rabben as if of its own will.

"Ha! Do you think Rabben fights street-brawls with the sword like any mercenary?" Lythande's sword-tip exploded in the blue star-glow, and became a shimmering snake, twisting back on itself to climb past the hilt, fangs dripping venom as it sought to coil around Lythande's fist. Lythande's own star blazed. The sword was metal again but twisted and useless, in the shape of the snake it had been, coiling back toward the scabbard. Enraged, Lythande jerked free of the twisted metal, sent a spitting rain of fire in Rabben's direction. Quickly the huge Adept covered himself in fog, and the fire-spray extinguished itself. Somewhere outside consciousness Lythande was aware of a crowd gathering; not twice in a lifetime did two Adepts of the Blue Star battle by sorcery in the streets of Sanctuary. The blaze of the stars, blazing from each magician's brow, raged lightnings in the square.

On a howling wind came little torches ravening, that flickered and whipped at Lythande; they touched the tall form of the magician and vanished. Then a wild whirlwind sent trees lashing, leaves swirling bare from branches, and battered Rabben to his knees. Lythande was bored; this must be finished quickly. Not one of the goggling onlookers in the crowd knew afterward what had been done, but Rabben bent, slowly, slowly, forced inch by inch down and down, to his knees, to all fours, prone, pressing and grinding his face farther and farther into the dust, rocking back and forth, pressing harder and harder into the sand. . . .

Lythande turned and lifted the girl. She stared in

disbelief at the burly sorcerer grinding his black beard frantically into the dirt.

"What did you—"

"Never mind—let's get out of here. The spell will not hold him long, and when he wakes from it he will be angry." Neutral mockery edged Lythande's voice, and the girl could see it, too. Rabben with beard and eyes and blue star covered with the dirt and dust—

She scurried along in the wake of the magician's robe; when they were well away from the Promise of Heaven, Lythande halted, so abruptly that the girl stumbled.

"Who are you, girl?"

"My name is Bercy. And yours?"

"A magician's name is not lightly given. In Sanctuary they call me Lythande." Looking down at the girl, the magician noted, with a pang, that beneath the dirt and dishevelment she was very beautiful and very young. "You can go, Bercy. He will not touch you again; I have bested him fairly upon challenge."

She flung herself on to Lythande's shoulder, clinging. "Don't send me away!" she begged, clutching, eyes filled with adoration. Lythande scowled.

Predictable, of course, Bercy believed, and who in Sanctuary would have disbelieved, that the duel had been fought for the girl as prize, and she was ready to give herself to the winner. Lythande made a gesture of protest.

"No—"

The girl narrowed her eyes in pity. "Is it then with you as Rabben said—that your secret is that you have been deprived of manhood?" But beyond the pity was a delicious flicker of amusement—what a tidbit of gossip! A juicy bit for the Streets of Women.

"Silence!" Lythande's glance was imperative. "Come."

She followed along the twisting streets that led into the Street of Red Lanterns. Lythande strode with confidence, now, past the House of Mermaids, where, it was said, delights as exotic as the name promised were to be found; past the House of Whips, shunned by all except those who refused to go elsewhere; and at last, beneath the face of the Green Lady as she was worshiped far away and beyond Ranke, the Aphrodisia House.

Bercy looked around, eyes wide, at the pillared lobby, the brilliance of a hundred lanterns, the exquisitely dressed women lounging on cushions till they were summoned. They were finely dressed and bejeweled—Myrtis knew her trade, and how to present her wares—and Lythande guessed that the ragged Bercy's glance was one of envy; she had probably sold herself in the bazaars for a few coppers or for a loaf of bread, since she was old enough. Yet somehow, like flowers covering a dungheap, she had kept an exquisite fresh beauty, all gold and white, flowerlike. Even ragged and half-starved, she touched Lythande's heart.

"Bercy, have you eaten today?"

"No, master."

Lythande summoned the huge eunuch Jiro, whose business it was to conduct the favored customers to the chambers of their chosen women, and throw out the drunks and abusive customers into the street. He came—huge-bellied, naked except for a skimpy loincloth and a dozen rings in his ear—he had once had a lover who was an earring-seller and had used him to display her wares.

"How may we serve the magician Lythande?"

The women on the couches and cushions were twittering at one another in surprise and dismay, and Lythande could almost hear their thoughts;

None of us has been able to attract or seduce the great magician, and this ragged street wench has caught his eyes? And, being women, Lythande knew they could see the unclouded beauty that shone through the girl's rags.

"Is Madame Myrtis available, Jiro?"

"She's sleeping, O great wizard, but for you she's given orders she's to be waked at any hour. Is this—" no one alive can be quite so supercilious as the chief eunuch of a fashionable brothel—"*yours*, Lythande, or a gift for my madame?"

"Both, perhaps. Give her something to eat and find her a place to spend the night."

"And a bath, magician? She has fleas enough to louse a floorful of cushions!"

"A bath, certainly, and a bath-woman with scents and oils," Lythande said, "and something in the nature of a whole garment."

"Leave it to me," said Jiro expansively, and Bercy looked at Lythande in dread, but went when the magician gestured to her to go. As Jiro took her away, Lythande saw Myrtis standing in the doorway; a heavy woman, no longer young, but with the frozen beauty of a spell. Through the perfect spelled features, her eyes were warm and welcoming as she smiled at Lythande.

"My dear, I had not expected to see you. Is that yours?" She moved her head toward the door through which Jiro had conducted the frightened Bercy. "She'll probably run away, you know, once you take your eyes off her."

"I wish I thought so, Myrtis. But no such luck, I fear."

"You had better tell me the whole story," Myrtis said, and listened to Lythande's brief, succinct account of the affair.

"And if you laugh, Myrtis, I take back my spell and leave your gray hairs and wrinkles open to the mockery of everyone in Sanctuary!"

But Myrtis had known Lythande too long to take that threat very seriously. "So the maiden you rescued is all maddened with desire for the love of Lythande!" She chuckled. "It is like an old ballad, indeed!"

"But what am I to do, Myrtis? By the paps of Shipri the All-mother, this is a dilemma!"

"Take her into your confidence and tell her why your love cannot be hers," Myrtis said.

Lythande frowned. "You hold my Secret, since I

had no choice; you knew me before I was made magician, or bore the Blue Star—"

"And before I was a harlot," Myrtis agreed.

"But if I make this girl feel like a fool for loving me, she will hate me as much as she loves; and I cannot confide in anyone I cannot trust with my life and my power. All I have is yours, Myrtis, because of that past we shared. And that includes my power, if you ever should need it. But I cannot entrust it to this girl."

"Still she owes you something, for delivering her out of the hands of Rabben."

Lythande said, "I will think about it; and now make haste to bring me food, for I am hungry and athirst." Taken to a private room, Lythande ate and drank, served by Myrtis' own hands. And Myrtis said, "I could never have sworn your vow—to eat and drink in the sight of no man!"

"If you sought the power of a magician, you would keep it well enough," said Lythande. "I am seldom tempted now to break it; I fear only lest I break it unawares; I cannot drink in a tavern lest among the women there might be some one of those strange men who find diversion in putting on the garments of a female; even here I will not eat or drink among your women, for that reason. All power depends on the vows and the secret."

"Then I cannot aid you," Myrtis said, "but you are not bound to speak truth to her; tell her you have vowed to live without women."

"I may do that," Lythande said, and finished the food, scowling.

Later Bercy was brought in, wide-eyed, enthralled by her fine gown and her freshly washed hair, softly curling about her pink-and-white face and the sweet scent of bath oils and perfumes that hung about her.

"The girls here wear such pretty clothes, and one of them told me they could eat twice a day if they wished! Am I pretty enough, do you think, that Madame Myrtis would have me here?"

"If that is what you wish. You are more than beautiful."

Bercy said boldly, "I would rather belong to *you*, magician," and flung herself again on Lythande, her hands clutching and clinging, dragging the lean face down to hers. Lythande, who rarely touched anything living, held her gently, trying not to reveal consternation.

"Bercy, child, this is only a fancy. It will pass."

"No," she wept. "I love you, I want only you!"

And then, unmistakably, along the magician's nerves, Lythande felt that little ripple, that warning thrill of tension which said: *spellcasting is in use.* Not against Lythande. That could have been countered. But somewhere within the room.

Here, in the Aphrodisia House? Myrtis, Lythande knew, could be trusted with life, reputation, fortune, the magical power of the Blue Star itself; she had been tested before this. Had she altered enough to turn betrayer, it would have been apparent in her aura when Lythande came near.

That left only the girl, who was clinging and whimpering; "I will die if you do not love me! I will die! Tell me it is not true, Lythande, that you are unable to love! Tell me it is an evil lie that magicians are emasculated, incapable of loving woman . . ."

"That is certainly an evil lie," Lythande agreed gravely. "I give you my solemn assurance that I have never been emasculated." But Lythande's nerves tingled as the words were spoken. A magician might lie, and most of them did. Lythande would lie as readily as any other, in a good cause. But the law of the Blue Star was this: when questioned directly on a matter bearing directly on the Secret, the Adept might not tell a direct lie. And Bercy, unknowing, was only one question away from the fatal one hiding the Secret.

With a mighty effort, Lythande's magic wrenched at the very fabric of Time itself; the girl stood motionless, aware of no lapse, as Lythande stepped away far enough to read her aura. And yes, there within the traces of that vibrating field, was the shadow of the Blue Star. Rabben's; overpowering her will.

Rabben. Rabben the Half-handed, who had set his will on the girl, who had staged and contrived the whole thing, including the encounter where the girl had needed rescue; put the girl under a spell to attract and bespell Lythande.

The law of the Blue Star forbade one Adept of the Star to kill another; for all would be needed to fight side by side, on the last day, against Chaos. Yet if one Adept could prise forth the secret of another's power . . . then the powerless one was not needed against Chaos and could be killed.

What could be done now? Kill the girl? Rabben would take that, too, as an answer: Bercy had been so bespelled as to be irresistible to any man; if Lythande sent her away untouched, Rabben would know that Lythande's secret lay in that area and would never rest in his attempts to uncover it. For if Lythande was untouched by this sex-spell to make Bercy irresistible, then Lythande was a eunuch, or a homosexual, or . . . sweating, Lythande dared not even think beyond that. The Secret was safe only if never questioned. It would not be read in the aura; but one simple question, and all was ended.

I should kill her, Lythande thought. *For now I am fighting, not for my magic alone, but for my secret and for my life. For surely, with my power gone, Rabben would lose no time in making an end of me, in revenge for the loss of half a hand.*

The girl was still motionless, entranced. How easily she could be killed! Then Lythande recalled an old fairy-tale, which might be used to save the Secret of the Star.

The light flickered as Time returned to the chamber. Bercy was still clinging and weeping, unaware of the lapse; Lythande had resolved what to do, and the girl felt Lythande's arms enfolding her, and the magician's kiss on her welcoming mouth.

"You must love me or I shall die!" Bercy wept.

Lythande said, "You shall be mine." The soft neutral voice was very gentle. "But even a magician is vulnerable in love, and I must protect myself. A place shall be made ready for us without light or sound save for what I provide with my magic; and you must swear that you will not seek to see or to touch me except by that magical light. Will you swear it by the All-Mother, Bercy? For if you swear this, I shall love you as no woman has ever been loved before."

Trembling, she whispered, "I swear." And Lythande's heart went out in pity, for Rabben had used her ruthlessly; so that she burned alive with her unslaked and bewitched love for the magician, that she was all caught up in her passion for Lythande. Painfully, Lythande thought; *if she had only loved me, without the spell; then I could have loved. . . .*

Would that I could trust her with my secret! But she is only Rabben's tool; her love for me is his doing, and none of her own will . . . and not real . . . And so everything which would pass between them now must be only a drama staged for Rabben.

"I shall make all ready for you with my magic."

Lythande went and confided to Myrtis what was needed; the woman began to laugh, but a single glance at Lythande's bleak face stopped her cold. She had known Lythande since long before the blue star was set between those eyes; and she kept the Secret for love of Lythande. It wrung her heart to see one she loved in the grip of such suffering. So she said, "All will be prepared. Shall I give her a drug in her wine, to weaken her will, that you may the more readily throw a glamour upon her?"

Lythande's voice held a terrible bitterness. "Rabben has done that already for us, when he put a spell upon her to love me."

"You would have it otherwise?" Myrtis asked, hesitating.

"All the gods of Sanctuary—they laugh at me! All-Mother, help me! But I would have it otherwise; I could love her, if she were not Rabben's tool."

When all was prepared, Lythande entered the darkened room. There was no light but the light of the Blue Star. The girl lay on a bed, stretching up her arms to the magician with exalted abandon.

"Come to me, come to me, my love!"

"Soon," said Lythande, sitting beside her, stroking her hair with a tenderness even Myrtis would never have guessed. "I will sing to you a love-song of my people, far away."

She writhed in erotic ecstasy. "All you do is good to me, my love, my magician!"

Lythande felt the blankness of utter despair. She was beautiful, and she was in love. She lay in a bed spread for the two of them, and they were separated by the breadth of the world. The magician could not endure it.

Lythande sang, in that rich and beautiful voice; a voice lovelier than any spell;

Half the night is spent; and the crown of moonlight
Fades, and now the crown of the stars is paling;
Yields the sky reluctant to coming morning;
Still I lie lonely.

Lythande could see tears on Bercy's cheeks.

I will love you as no woman has ever been loved.

Between the girl on the bed, and the motionless form of the magician, as the magician's robe fell heavily to the floor, a wraith-form grew, the very wraith and fetch, at first, of Lythande, tall and lean, with blazing eyes and a star between its brows and a body white and unscarred; the form of the magician, but this one triumphant in virility, advancing on the motionless woman, waiting. Her mind fluttered away in arousal, was caught, captured, bespelled. Lythande let her see the image for a moment; she could not see the true Lythande behind; then, as her eyes closed in ecstatic awareness of the touch, Lythande smoothed light fingers over her closed eyes.

"See—what I bid you to see!

"Hear—what I bid you hear!

"Feel—only what I bid you feel, Bercy!"

And now she was wholly under the spell of the wraith. Unmoving, stony-eyed, Lythande watched as her lips closed on emptiness and she kissed invisible lips; and moment by moment Lythande knew what touched her, what caressed her. Rapt and ravished by illusion, that brought her again and again to the heights of ecstasy, till she cried out in abandonment. Only to Lythande that cry was bitter; for she cried out not to Lythande but to the man-wraith who possessed her.

At last she lay all but unconscious, satiated; and Lythande watched in agony. When she opened her eyes again, Lythande was looking down at her, sorrowfully.

Bercy stretched up languid arms. "Truly, my beloved, you have loved me as no woman has ever been loved before."

For the first and last time, Lythande bent over her and pressed her lips in a long, infinitely tender kiss. "Sleep, my darling."

And as she sank into ecstatic, exhausted sleep, Lythande wept.

Long before she woke, Lythande stood, girt for travel, in the little room belonging to Myrtis.

"The spell will hold. She will make all haste to carry her tale to Rabben—the tale of Lythande, the incomparable lover! Of Lythande, of untiring virility, who can love a maiden into exhaustion!" The rich voice of Lythande was harsh with bitterness.

"And long before you return to Sanctuary, once freed of the spell, she will have forgotten you in many other lovers," Myrtis agreed. "It is better and safer that it should be so."

"True." But Lythande's voice broke. "Take care of her, Myrtis. Be kind to her."

"I swear it, Lythande."

"If only she could have loved *me*"—the magician broke and sobbed again for a moment; Myrtis looked away, wrung with pain, knowing not what comfort to offer.

"If only she could have loved me as I am, freed of Rabben's spell! Loved me without pretense! But I feared I could not master the spell Rabben had put on her . . . nor trust her not to betray me, knowing . . .

Myrtis put her plump arms around Lythande, tenderly.

"Do you regret?"

The question was ambiguous. It might have meant: *Do you regret that you did not kill the girl?* Or even: *Do you regret your oath and the secret you must bear to the last day?* Lythande chose to answer the last.

"Regret? How can I regret? One day I shall fight against Chaos with all of my order; even at the side of Rabben, if he lives unmurdered as long as that. And that alone must justify my existence and my Secret. But now I must leave Sanctuary, and who knows when the chances of the world will bring me this way again? Kiss me farewell, my sister."

Myrtis stood on tiptoe. Her lips met the lips of the magician.

"Until we meet again, Lythande. May She attend and guard you forever. Farewell, my beloved, my sister."

Then, the magician Lythande girded on her sword, and went silently and by unseen ways out of the city of Sanctuary, just as the dawn was breaking. And on her forehead the glow of the Blue Star was dimmed by the rising sun. Never once did she look back.

(1979)

To Keep the Oath

The red light lingered on the hills; two of the four small moons were in the sky, green Idriel near to setting, and the tiny crescent of Mormallor, ivory-pale, near the zenith. The night would be dark. Kindra n'ha Mhari did not, at first, see anything strange about the little town. She was too grateful to have reached it before sunset—shelter against the rainswept chill of a Darkovan night, a bed to sleep in after four days of traveling, a cup of wine before she slept.

But slowly she began to realize that there was something wrong. Normally, at this hour, the women would be going back and forth in the streets, gossiping with neighbors, marketing for the evening meal, while their children played and squabbled in the street. But tonight there was not a single woman in the street, nor a single child.

What was wrong? Frowning, she rode along the main street toward the inn. She was hungry and weary.

She had left Dalereuth many days before with a companion, bound for Neskaya Guild-house. But unknown to either of them, her companion had been pregnant; she had fallen sick of a fever, and in Thendara Guild-house she had miscarried and still lay there, very ill. Kindra had gone alone to Neskaya; but she had turned aside three days' ride to carry a message to the sick woman's oath-mother. She had found her in a village in the hills, working to help a group of women set up a small dairy.

Kindra was not afraid of traveling alone; she had journeyed in these hills at all seasons and in all weathers. But her provisions were beginning to run low. Fortunately, the innkeeper was an old acquaintance; she had little money with her, because her journey had been so unexpectedly prolonged, but old Jorik would feed her and her horse, give her a bed for the night, and trust her to send money to pay for it—knowing that if she did not, or could not, her Guild-house would pay, for the honor of the Guild.

The man who took her horse in the stable had known her for many years, too. He scowled as she alighted. "I don't know where we shall stable your horse, and that's certain, *mestra,* with all these strange horses here . . . Will she share a box stall without kicking, do you suppose? Or shall I tie her loose at the end?" Kindra noticed that the stable was crammed with horses, two dozen of them and more. Instead of a lonely village inn, it looked like Neskaya on market-day!

"Did you meet with any riders on the road, *mestra?*"

"No, none," Kindra said, frowning a little. "All the horses in the Kilghard Hills seem to be here in your stable—what is it, a royal visit? What is the matter with you? You keep looking over your shoulder as if you expect to find your master there with a stick to beat you—where is old Jorik, why is he not here to greet his guests?"

"Why, *mestra,* old Jorik's dead," the old man said, "and Dame Janella is trying to manage the inn alone with young Annelys and Marga."
Dead? Gods preserve us," Kindra said. "What happened?"

"It was those bandits, *mestra,* Scarface's gang; they came here and cut Jorik down with his apron still on," said the old groom. "Made havoc in the town, broke all the ale-pots, and when the menfolk drove 'em off with pitchforks, they swore they'd be back and fire the town! So Dame Janella and the elders put the cap round and raised copper to hire Brydar of Fen Hills and all his men to come and defend us when they come back; and here Brydar's men have been ever since, *mestra,* quarrelling and drinking and casting eyes on the women until the townfolk are ready to say the remedy's worse than the sickness! But go in, go in, *mestra*, Janella's ready to welcome you."

Plump Janella looked paler and thinner than Kindra had ever seen her. She greeted Kindra with unaccustomed warmth. Under ordinary conditions, she was cold to Kindra, as befitted a respectable wife in the presence of a member of the Amazon Guild; now, Kindra supposed, she was learning that an innkeeper could not afford to alienate a customer. Jorik, Kindra knew, had not approved of the Free Amazons either; but he had learned from experience that they were quiet guests who kept to themselves, caused no trouble, did not get drunk and break bar-stools and ale-pots, and paid their reckoning promptly. A *guests's reputation*, Kindra thought wryly, *does not tarnish the color of his money*.

"You have heard, good *mestra?* Those wicked men, Scarface's fellows, they cut my good man down, and for nothing—just because he flung an ale-pot at one of them who laid rough hands on my little girl, and Annelys not fifteen yet! Monsters!"

"And they killed him? Shocking!" Kindra murmured, but her pity was for the girl. All her life, young Annelys must remember that her father had been killed in defending her, because she could not defend herself. Like all the women of the Guild, Kindra was sworn to defend herself, to turn to no man for protection. She had been a member of the Guild for half her lifetime; it seemed shocking to her that a man should die defending a girl from advances she should have known how to ward off herself.

"Ah, you don't know what it's like, *mestra*, being alone without the goodman. Living alone as you do, you can't imagine!"

"Well, you have daughters to help you," Kindra said, and Janella shook her head and mourned. "But they can't come out among all those rough men, they are only little girls!"

"It will do them good to learn something of the

world and its ways," Kindra said, but the woman sighed. "I wouldn't like them to learn too much of that."

"Then, I suppose, you must get you another husband," Kindra said, knowing that there was simply no way she and Janella could communicate. "But indeed I am sorry for your grief. Jorik was a good man."

"You can't imagine how good, *mestra,*" Janella said plaintively. "You women of the Guild, you call yourselves free women, only it seems to me I have always been free, until now, when I must watch myself night and day, lest someone get the wrong idea about a woman alone. Only the other day, one of Brydar's men said to me—and that's another thing, these men of Brydar's. Eating us out of house and home, and just look, *mestra,* no room in the stable for the horses of our paying customers, with half the village keeping their horses here against bandits, and those hired swords drinking up my good old man's beer day after day—" Abruptly she recalled her duties as landlord. "But come into the common-room, *mestra,* warm yourself, and I'll bring you some supper; we have a roast haunch of *chervine.* Or would you fancy something lighter, rabbithorn stewed with mushrooms, perhaps? We're crowded, yes, but there's the little room at the head of the stairs, you can have that to yourself, a room fit for a fine lady, indeed Lady Hastur slept here in that very bed, a few years gone. Lilla! Lilla! Where's that simpleminded wench gone? When I took her in, her mother told me she was lack-witted, but she has wits enough to hang about talking to that young hired sword, Zandru scratch them all! Lilla! Hurry now, show the good woman her room, fetch her wash-water, see to her saddlebags!"

Later, Kindra went down to the common-room. Like all Guild-women, she had learned to be discreet when traveling alone; a solitary woman was prey to questions, at least, so they usually journeyed in pairs. This subjected them to raised eyebrows and occasional dirty speculations, but warded off the less palatable ap-

proaches to which a lone woman traveling on Darkover was subject. Of course, any woman of the Guild
could protect herself if it went past rude words, but
that could cause trouble for all the Guild. It was better
to conduct oneself in a way that minimized the possi-
bility of trouble. So Kindra sat alone in a tiny corner
near the fireplace, kept her hood drawn around her
face—she was neither young nor particularly pretty—
sipped her wine and warmed her feet, and did nothing
to attract anyone's attention. It occurred to her that at
this moment she, who called herself a Free Amazon,
was considerably less constrained than Janella's young
daughters, going back and forth, protected by their
family's roof and their mother's presence.

She finished her meal—she had chosen the stewed
rabbithorn—and called for a second glass of wine, too
weary to climb the stairs to her chamber and too tired
to sleep if she did.

Some of Brydar's hired swords were sitting around a
long table at the other end of the room, drinking and
playing dice. They were a mixed crew; Kindra knew
none of them, but she had met Brydar himself a few
times, and had even hired out with him, once, to
guard a merchant caravan across the desert to the Dry
Towns. She nodded courteously to him, and he sa-
luted her, but paid her no further attention; he knew
her well enough to know that she would not welcome
even polite conversation when she was in a roomful of
strangers.

One of the younger mercenaries, a young man, tall,
beardless and weedy, ginger hair cut close to his head,
rose and came toward her. Kindra braced herself for
the inevitable. If she had been with two or three other
Guild-women, she would have welcomed harmless companionship, a drink together and talk about the chances
of the road, but a lone Amazon simply did *not* drink
with men in public taverns, and, damn it, Brydar knew
it as well as she did.

One of the older mercenaries must have been having some fun with the green boy, needling him to

prove his manhood by approaching the Amazon, amusing themselves by enjoying the rebuff he'd inevitably get.

One of the men looked up and made a remark Kindra didn't hear. The boy snarled something, a hand to his dagger. "Watch yourself, you—!" He spoke a foulness. Then he came to Kindra's table and said, in a soft, husky voice, "A good evening to you, honorable mistress."

Startled at the courteous phrase, but still wary, Kindra said, "And to you, young sir."

"May I offer you a tankard of wine?"

"I have had enough to drink," Kindra said, "but I thank you for the kind offer." Something faintly out of key, almost effeminate, in the youth's bearing, alerted her; his proposition, then, would not be the usual thing. Most people knew that Free Amazons took lovers if and when they chose, and all too many men interpreted that to mean that any Amazon could be had, at any time. Kindra was an expert at turning covert advances aside without ever letting it come to question or refusal; with ruder approaches, she managed with scant courtesy. But that wasn't what this youngster wanted; she knew when a man was looking at her with desire, whether he put it into words or not, and although there was certainly interest in this young man's face, it wasn't sexual interest! What did he want with her, then?

"May I—may I sit here and talk to you for a moment, honorable dame?"

Rudeness she could have managed. This excessive courtesy was a puzzle. Were they simply making game of a womanhater, wagering he would not have the courage to talk to her? She said neutrally, "This is a public room; the chairs are not mine. Sit where you like."

Ill at ease, the boy took a seat. He was young indeed. He was still beardless, but his hands were callused and hard, and there was a long-healed scar on one cheek; he was not as young as she thought.

"You are a Free Amazon, *mestra?*" He used the common, and rather offensive, term; but she did not hold it against him. Many knew no other name.

"I am," she said, "but we would rather say: I am of the oath-bound—" The word she used was *Comhi-Letzis*—"A Renunciate of the Sisterhood of Freed Women."

"May I ask—without giving offense—why the name Renunciate, *mestra?*"

Actually, Kindra welcomed a chance to explain. "Because, sir, in return for our freedom as women of the Guild, we swear an oath renouncing those privileges that we might have by choosing to belong to some man. If we renounce the disabilities of being property and chattel, we must renounce, also, whatever benefits there may be; so that no man can accuse us of trying to have the best of both choices."

He said gravely, "That seems to me an honorable choice. I have never yet met a—a—a—Renunciate. Tell me, *mestra*—" His voice suddenly cracked high. "I suppose you know the slanders that are spoken of you—tell me, how does any woman have the courage to join the Guild, knowing what will be said of her?"

"I suppose," Kindra said quietly, "for some women, a time comes when they think that there are worse things than being the subject of public slanders. It was so with me."

He thought that over for a moment, frowning. "I have never seen a Free—er—a Renunciate traveling alone before. Do you not usually travel in pairs, honorable dame?"

"True. But need knows no mistress," Kindra said, and explained that her companion had fallen sick in Thendara.

"And you came so far to bear a message? Is she your *bredhis?*" the boy asked, using the polite word for a woman's freemate or female lover; and because it was the polite word he used, not the gutter one, Kindra did not take offense. "No, only a comrade."

"I—I would not have dared speak if there had been two of you—"

Kindra laughed. "Why not? Even in twos or threes, we are not dogs to bite strangers."

The boy stared at his boots. "I have cause to fear—women—" he said, almost inaudibly. "But you seemed kind. And I suppose, *mestra,* that whenever you come into these hills, where life is so hard for women, you are always seeking out wives and daughters who are discontented at home, to recruit them for your Guild?"

Would that we might! Kindra thought, with all the old bitterness; but she shook her head. "Our charter forbids it," she said. "It is the law that a woman must seek us out herself, and formally petition to be allowed to join us. I am not even allowed to tell women of the advantages of the Guild, when they ask. I may only tell them of the things they must renounce, by oath." She tightened her lips and added, "If we were to do as you say, to seek out discontented wives and daughters and lure them away to the Guild, the men would not let any Guild-house stand in the Domains, but would burn our houses about our ears." It was the old injustice; the women of Darkover had won this concession, the charter of the Guild, but so hedged about with restrictions that many women never saw or spoke with a Guild-sister.

"I suppose," she said, "that they have found out that we are not whores, so they insist that we are all lovers of women, intent on stealing out their wives and daughters. We must be, it seems, one evil thing or the other."

"Are there no lovers of women among you, then?"

Kindra shrugged. "Certainly," she said. "You must know that there are some women who would rather die than marry; and even with all the restrictions and rununciations of the oath, it seems a preferable alternative. But I assure you we are not all so. We are free women—free to be thus or otherwise, at our own will." After a moment's thought she added carefully,

"And if you have a sister you may tell her so from me."

The young man started, and Kindra bit her lip; again she had let her guard down, picking up hunches so clearly formed that sometimes her companions accused her of having a little of the telepathic gift of the higher castes; *laran*. Kindra, who was, as far as she knew, all commoner and without either noble blood or telepathic gift, usually kept herself barricaded; but she had picked up a random thought, a bitter thought from somewhere, *My sister would not believe . . .* a thought quickly vanished, so quickly that Kindra wondered if she had imagined the whole thing.

The young face across the table twisted into bitter lines.

"There is none, now, I may call my sister."

"I am sorry," Kindra said, puzzled. "To be alone, that is a sorrowful thing. May I ask your name?"

The boy hesitated again, and Kindra knew, with that odd intuition, that the real name had almost escaped the taut lips; but he bit it back.

"Brydar's men call me Marco. Don't ask my lineage; there is none who will claim kin to me now— thanks to those foul bandits under Scarface." He twisted his mouth and spat. "Why do you think I am in this company? For the few coppers these village folk can pay? No, *mestra*. I too am oath-bound. To revenge."

Kindra left the common-room early, but she could not sleep for a long time. Something in the young man's voice, his words, had plucked a resonating string in her own mind and memory. Why had he questioned her so insistently? Had he a sister or kinswoman, perhaps, who had spoken of becoming a Renunciate? Or was he, an obvious effeminate, jealous of her because she could escape the role ordained by society for her sex and he could not? Did he fantasy, perhaps, some such escape from the demands made upon men? Surely not; there were simpler lives for men than that of a hired sword! And men had a choice of what lives they would live—more choice, anyhow, than most women. Kindra had chosen to become a Renunciate, making herself an outcaste among most people in the Domains. Even the innkeeper only tolerated her, because she was a regular customer and paid well, but he would have equally tolerated a prostitute or a traveling juggler, and would have had fewer prejudices against either.

Was the youth, she wondered, one of the rumored spies sent out by *cortes*, the governing body in Thendara, to trap Renunciates who broke the terms of their charter by proselytizing and attempting to recruit women into the Guild? If so, at least she had resisted the temptation. She had not even said, though tempted, that if Janella were a Renunciate she would have felt competent to run the inn by herself, with the help of her daughters.

A few times, in the history of the Guild, men had even tried to infiltrate them in disguise. Unmasked, they had met with summary justice, but it had happened and might happen again. At that, she thought, he might be convincing enough in women's clothes; but not with the scar on his face, or those callused hands. Then she laughed in the dark, feeling the calluses on her own fingers. Well, if he was fool enough to try it, so much the worse for him. Laughing, she fell asleep.

Hours later she woke to the sound of hoofbeats, the clash of steel, yells and cries outside. Somewhere women were shrieking. Kindra flung on her outer clothes and ran downstairs. Brydar was standing in the courtyard, bellowing orders. Over the wall of the courtyard she could see a sky reddened with flames. Scarface and his bandit crew were loose in the town, it seemed.

"Go, Renwal," Brydar ordered. "Slip behind their rearguard and set their horses loose, stampede them, so they must stand to fight, not strike and flee again! And since all the good horses are stabled here, one of you must stay and guard them lest they strike here for ours . . . the rest of you come with me, and have your swords at the ready—"

Janella was huddled beneath the overhanging roof of an outbuilding, her daughters and serving women like roosting hens around her. "Will you leave us all here unguarded, when we have housed you all for seven days and never a penny in pay? Scarface and his men are sure to strike here for the horses, and we are unprotected, at their mercy—"

Brydar gestured to the boy Marco. "You. Stay and guard horses and women—"

The boy snarled, "No! I joined your crew on the pledge that I should face Scarface, steel in hand! It is an affair of honor—do you think I need your dirty coppers?"

Beyond the wall all was shrieking confusion. "I have no time to bandy words," Brydar said quickly. "Kindra—this is no quarrel of yours, but you know me a man of my word; stay here and guard the horses and these women, and I will make it worth your while!"

"At the mercy of a woman? A woman to guard us? Why not set a mouse to guard a lion!" Janella's shrewish cry cut him off. The boy Marco urged, eyes blazing, "Whatever I have been promised for this foray is yours, *mestra*, if you free me to meet my sworn foe!"

"Go; I'll look after them," Kindra said. It was unlikely Scarface would get this far, but it was really no affair of hers; normally she fought beside the men, and would have been angry at being left in a post of safety. But Janella's cry had put her on her mettle. Marco caught up his sword and hurried to the gate, Brydar following him. Kindra watched them go, her mind on her own early battles. Some turn of gesture, of phrase, had alerted her. *The boy Marco is noble,* she thought. *Perhaps even Comyn, some bastard of a great lord, perhaps even a Hastur. I don't know what he's doing with Brydar's men, but he's no ordinary hired sword!*

Janella's wailing brought her back to her duty. "Oh!

339

Oh! Horrible," she howled. "Left here with only a woman to look after us . . ."

Kindra said tersely, "Come on!" She gestured. "Help me close that gate!"

"I don't take orders from one of you shameless women in breeches—"

"Let the damned gate stay open, then," Kindra said, right out of patience. "Let Scarface walk in without any trouble. Do you want me to go and invite him, or shall we send one of your daughters?"

"Mother!" remonstrated a girl of fifteen, breaking away from Janella's hand. "That is no way to speak— Lilla, Marga, help the good *mestra* shove this gate shut!" She came and joined Kindra, helping to thrust the heavy wooden gate tightly into place, pull down the heavy crossbeam. The women were wailing in dismay; Kindra singled out one of them, a young girl about six or seven moons along in pregnancy, who was huddled in a blanket over her nightgear.

"You," she said, "take all the babies and the little children upstairs into the strongest chamber, bolt the doors and don't open them unless you hear my voice or Janella's." The woman did not move, still sobbing, and Kindra said sharply, "Hurry! Don't stand there like a rabbithorn frozen in the snow! Damn you, *move,* or I'll slap you senseless!" She made a menacing gesture and the woman started, then began to hurry the children up the stairs; she picked up one of the littlest ones, hurried the others along with frightened, clucking noises.

Kindra surveyed the rest of the frightened women. Janella was hopeless. She was fat and short of breath, and she was staring resentfully at Kindra, furious that she had been left in charge of their defense. Furthermore, she was trembling on the edge of a panic that would infect everyone; but if she had something to do, she might calm down. "Janella, go into the kitchen and make up some hot wine punch," she said. "The men will want it when they come back, and they'll deserve it, too. Then start hunting out some linen for bandages, in case anyone's hurt. Don't worry," she added, "they won't get to you while we're here. And take that one with you," she added, pointing to the terrified simpleton Lilla, who was clinging to Janella's skirt, round-eyed with terror, whimpering. "She'll only be in our way.

When Janella had gone, grumbling, the lackwit at her heels, Kindra looked around at the sturdy young women who remained.

"Come, all of you, into the stables, and pile heavy bales of hay around the horses, so they can't drive the horses over them or stampede them out. No, leave the lantern there; if Scarface and his men break through, we'll set a couple of bales afire; that will frighten the horses and they might well kick a bandit or two to death. Even so, the women can escape while they round up the horses; contrary to what you may have heard, most bandits look first for horses and rich plunder, and women are not the first item on their list. And none of you have jewels or rich garments they would seek to strip from you." Kindra herself knew that any man who laid his hand on her, intending rape, would quickly regret it; and if she was overpowered by numbers, she had been taught ways in which she could survive the experience undestroyed; but these women had had no such teaching. It was not right to blame them for their fears.

I could teach them this. But the laws of our charter prevent me and I am bound by oath to obey those laws; laws made, not by our own Guild-mothers, but by men who fear what we might have to say to their women!

Well, perhaps at least they will find it a matter for pride that they can defend their home against invaders! Kindra went to lend her own wiry strength to the task of piling up the heavy bales around the horses; the women worked, forgetting their fears in hard effort. But one grumbled, just loud enough for Kindra to hear, "It's all very well for *her!* She was trained as a warrior and she's used to this kind of work! I'm not!"

It was no time to debate Guild-house ethics; Kindra

only asked mildly, "Are you proud of the fact that you have not been taught to defend yourself, child?" But the girl did not answer, sullenly hauling at her heavy hay-bale.

It was not difficult for Kindra to follow her thought; if it had not been for Brydar, each man of the town could have protected each one his own women! Kindra thought, in utter disgust, that this was the sort of thinking that laid villages in flames, year after year, because no man owed loyalty to another or would protect any household but his own! It had taken a threat like Scarface to get these village men organized enough to buy the services of a few hired swords, and now their women were grumbling because their men could not stand, each at his own door, protecting his own woman and hearth!

Once the horses had been barricaded, the women clustered together nervously in the courtyard. Even Janella came to the kitchen door to watch. Kindra went to the barred gate, her knife loose in its scabbard. The other girls and women stood under the roof of the kitchen, but one young girl, the same who had helped Kindra to shut the gate, bent and tucked her skirt resolutely up to her knees, then went and brought back a big wood-chopping hatchet and stood with it in her hand, taking up a place at the gate beside Kindra.

"Annelys!" Janella called. "Come back here! By me!"

The girl cast a look of contempt at her mother and said, "If any bandit climbs these walls, he will not get his hands on me, or on my little sister, without facing cold steel. It's not a sword, but I think even in a girl's hands, this blade would change his mind in a hurry!" She glanced defiantly at Kindra and said, "I am ashamed for all of you, that you would let one lone woman protect us! Even a rabbithorn doe protects her kits!"

Kindra gave the girl a companionable grin. "If you have half as much skill with that thing as you have guts, little sister, I would rather have you at my back than any man. Hold the axe with your hands close together, if the time comes to use it, and don't try anything fancy, just take a good hard chop at his legs, just like you were cutting down a tree. The thing is, he won't be expecting it, see?"

The night dragged on. The women huddled on hay-bales and boxes, listening with apprehension and occasional sobs and tears as they heard the clash of swords, cries and shouts. Only Annelys stood grimly beside Kindra, clutching her axe. After an hour or so, Kindra said, settling herself down on a hay-bale, "You needn't clutch it like that, you'll only weary yourself for an attack. Lean it against the bale, so you can snatch it up when the need comes."

Annelys asked in an undertone, "How did you know so well what to do? Are all the Free Amazons—you call them something else, don't you—how do the Guild-women learn? Are they all fighting women and hired swords?"

"No, no, not even many of us," Kindra said. "It is only that I have not many other talents; I cannot weave or embroider very well, and my skill at gardening is only good in the summertime. My own oath-mother is a midwife, that is our most respected trade; even those who despise the Renunciates confess that we can often save babies alive when the village healer-women fail. She would have taught me her profession; but I had no talent for that, either, and I am squeamish about the sight of blood—" She looked down suddenly at her long knife, remembering her many battles, and laughed; and Annelys laughed with her, a strange sound against the frightened moaning of the other women.

"*You* are afraid of the sight of blood?"

"It's different," Kindra said. "I can't stand suffering when I can't do anything about it, and if a babe is born easily they seldom send for the midwife; we come only when matters are desperate. I would rather fight with men, or beasts, than for the life of a helpless woman or baby . . ."

"I think I would too," said Annelys, and Kindra

thought: *Now, if I were not bound by the laws of the Guild, I could tell her what we are. And this one would be a credit to the Sisterhood . . .*

But her oath held her silent. She sighed and looked at Annelys, frustrated.

She was beginning to think the precautions had been useless, that Scarface's men would never come here at all, when there was a shriek from one of the women, and Kindra saw the tassel of a coarse knitted cap come up over the wall; then two men appeared on top of the wall, knives gripped in their teeth to free their hands for climbing.

"So here's where they've hidden it all, women, horses, all of it—" growled one. "You go for the horses, I'll take care of—oh, you would," he shouted as Kindra ran at him with her knife drawn. He was taller than Kindra; as they fought, she could only defend herself, backing step by step toward the stables. Where were the men? Why had the bandits been able to get this far? Were they the last defense of the town? Behind her, out of the corner of her eye she saw the other bandit coming up with his sword; she circled, backing carefully so she could face them both.

Then there was a shriek from Annelys, the axe flashed once, and the second bandit fell, howling, his leg spouting blood. Kindra's opponent faltered at the sound; Kindra brought up her knife and ran him through the shoulder, snatching up his knife as it fell from his limp hand. He fell backward, and she leaped on top of him.

"Annelys!" she shouted. "You women! Bring thongs, rope, anything to tie him up—there may be others—"

Janella came with a clothesline and stood by as Kindra tied the man, then, stepping back, looked at the bandit, lying in a pool of his own blood. His leg was nearly severed at the knee. He was still breathing, but he was too far gone even to moan and while the women stood and looked at him, he died. Janella stared at Annelys in horror, as if her young daughter had suddenly sprouted another head.

"You killed him," she breathed. "You chopped his leg off!"

"Would you rather he had chopped off mine, mother?" Annelys asked, and bent to look at the other bandit. "He is only stabbed through the shoulder, he'll live to be hanged!"

Breathing hard, Kindra straightened, giving the clothesline a final tug. She looked at Annelys and said, "You saved my life, little sister."

The girl smiled up at her, excited, her hair coming down and tumbling into her eyes. There was a cold sleet beginning to fall in the courtyard; their faces were wet. Annelys suddenly flung her arms around Kindra, and the older woman hugged her, disregarding the mother's troubled face.

"One of our own could not have done better. My thanks, little one!" Damn it, the girl had *earned* her thanks and approval, and if Janella stared at them as if Kindra were a wicked seducer of young women, then so much the worse for Janella! She let the girl's arm stay around her shoulders as she said, "Listen; I think that is the men coming back."

And in a minute they heard Brydar's hail, and they struggled to raise the great crossbeam of the gate. His men drove before them more than a dozen good horses, and Brydar laughed, saying, "Scarface's men will have no more use for them; so we're well paid! I see you women got the last of them?" He looked down at the bandit lying in his gore, at the other, tied with Janella's clothesline. "Good work, *mestra,* I'll see you have a share in the booty!"

"The girl helped," Kindra said. "I'd have been dead without her."

"One of them killed my father," the girl said fiercely, "so I have paid my just debt, that is all!" She turned to Janella and ordered, "Mother, bring our defenders some of that wine punch, at once!"

Brydar's men sat all over the common-room, drinking the hot wine gratefully. Brydar set down the tankard and rubbed his hands over his eyes with a tired

"Whoosh!" He said, "Some of my men are hurt, dame Janella; have any of your women skill with leech-craft? We will need bandages, and perhaps some salves and herbs. I—" He broke off as one of the men beckoned him urgently from the door, and he went at a run.

Annelys brought Kindra a tankard and put it shyly into her hand. Kindra sipped; it was not the wine-punch Janella had made, but a clear, fine, golden wine from the mountains. Kindra sipped it slowly, knowing the girl had been telling her something. She sat across from Kindra, taking a sip now and then of the hot wine in her own tankard. They were both reluctant to part.

Damn that fool law that says I cannot tell her of the Sisterhood! She is too good for this place and for that fool mother of hers; the idiot Lilla is more what her mother needs to help run the inn, and I suppose Janella will marry her off to some yokel at once, just to have help in running this place! Honor demanded she keep silent. Yet, watching Annelys, thinking of the life the girl would lead here, she wondered, troubled, what kind of honor it was, to require that she leave a girl like this in a place like this.

Yet she supposed it was a wise law; anyway, it had been made by wiser heads than hers. She supposed, otherwise, young girls, glamored for the moment with the thought of a life of excitement and adventure, might follow the Sisterhood without being fully aware of the hardships and the renunciations that awaited them. The name Renunciate was not lightly given; it was not an easy life. And considering the way Annelys was looking at her, Annelys might follow her simply out of hero-worship. That wouldn't do. She sighed, and said, "Well, the excitement is over for tonight, I suppose. I must be away to my bed; I have a long way to ride tomorrow. Listen to that racket! I didn't know any of Brydar's men were seriously hurt—"

"It sounds more like a quarrel than men in pain,"

Annelys said, listening to the shouts and protests. "Are they quarrelling over the spoils?"

Abruptly the door was thrust open and Brydar of Fen Hills came into the room. "*Mestra,* forgive me, you are wearied—"

"Enough," she said, "but after all this hullabaloo I am not like to sleep much; what can I do for you?"

"I beg you—will you come? It is the boy—young Marco; he is hurt, badly hurt, but he will not let us tend his wounds until he has spoken with you. He says he has an urgent message, very urgent, which he must give before he dies. . . ."

"Avarra's mercy," Kindra said, shocked. "Is he dying, then?"

"I cannot tell, he will not let us near enough to dress his wound. If he would be reasonable and let us care for him—but he is bleeding like a slaughtered *chervine,* and he has threatened to slit the throat of any man who touches him. We tried to hold him down and tend him willy-nilly, but it made his wounds bleed so sore as he struggled that we dared not wait—will you come, *mestra?*"

Kindra looked at him with question—she had not thought he would humor any man of his band so. Brydar said defensively, "The lad is nothing to me; not foster-brother, kinsman, nor even friend. But he fought at my side, and he is brave; it was he who killed Scarface in single combat. And may have had his death from it."

"Why should he want to speak to me?"

"He says, *mestra,* that it is a matter concerning his sister. And he begs you in the name of Avarra the pitiful that you will come. And he is young enough, almost, to be your son."

"So," Kindra said at last. She had not seen her own son since he was eight days old; and he would, she thought, be too young to bear a sword. "I cannot refuse anyone who begs me in the name of the Goddess," she said, and rose, frowning; young Marco had said he had no sister. No; he had said that there was none, now, that he could call sister. Which might be a different thing.

On the stairs she heard the voice of one of Brydar's men, expostulating, "Lad, we won't hurt ye, but if we don't get to that wound and tend to it, you could die, do ye hear?"

"Get away from me!" The young voice cracked. "I swear by Zandu's hells, and, by the spilt tripes of Scarface out there dead, I'll shove this knife into the throat of the first man who touches me!"

Inside, by torchlight, Kindra saw Marco half-sitting, half-lying on a straw pallet; he had a dagger in his hand, holding them away with it; but he was pale as death, and there was icy sweat on his forehead. The straw pallet was slowly reddening with a pool of blood. Kindra knew enough of wounds to know that the human body could lose more blood than most people thought possible without serious danger; but to any ordinary person it looked most alarming.

Marco saw Kindra and gasped, "*Mestra,* I beg you—I must speak with you alone—"

"That's no way to speak to a comrade, lad," said one of the mercenaries, kneeling behind him, as Kindra knelt beside the pallet. The wound was high on the leg, near the groin; the leather breeches had broken the blow somewhat, or the boy would have met the same fate as the man Annelys had struck with the axe.

"You little fool," Kindra said. "I can't do half as much for you as your friend can."

Marco's eyes closed for a moment, from pain or weakness. Kindra thought he had lost consciousness, and gestured to the man behind him. "Quick, now, while he is unconscious—" she said swiftly, but the tortured eyes flicked open.

"Would you betray me, too?" He gestured with the dagger, but so feebly that Kindra was shocked. There was certainly no time to be lost. The best thing was to humor him.

"Go," she said, "I'll reason with him, and if he won't listen, well, he is old enough to take the consequences of his folly." Her mouth twisted as the men went away. "I hope what you have to tell me is worth risking your life for, you lackwitted simpleton!"

But a great and terrifying suspicion was born in her as she knelt on the bloody pallet. "You fool, do you know this is likely to be your deathwound? I have small skill at leechcraft; your comrades could do better for you."

"It is sure to be my death unless you help me," said the hoarse, weakening voice. "None of these men is comrade enough that I could trust him . . . *mestra*, help me, I beg you, in the name of the merciful Avarra—I am a woman."

Kindra drew a sharp breath. She had begun to suspect—and it was true, then. "And none of Brydar's men knows—"

"None. I have dwelt among them for half a year, and I do not think any man of them suspects—and I fear women even more. But you, you I felt I might trust—"

"I swear it," Kindra said hastily. "I am oath-bound never to refuse aid to any woman who asks me in the name of the Goddess. But let me help you now, my poor girl, and pray Avarra you have not delayed too long!"

"Even if it was so—" the strange girl whispered—"I would rather die as a woman, than—disgraced and exposed. I have known so much disgrace—"

"Hush! Hush, child!" But she fell back against the pallet; she had really fainted, this time, at last; and Kindra cut away the leather breeches, looking at the serious cut that sliced through the top of the thigh and into the pubic mound. It had bled heavily, but was not, Kindra thought, fatal. She picked up one of the clean towels the men had left, pressed heavily against the wound; when it slowed to an ooze, she frowned, thinking it should be stitched. She hesitated to do it—she had little skill at such things, and she was sure the man from Brydar's band could do it more tidily and sure-handed; but she knew that was exactly what the young woman had feared, to be handled and exposed by men. Kindra thought: *If it could be done before she recovers consciousness, she need not know . . .* But she had promised the girl, and she would keep her promise. The girl did not stir as she stepped out into the hall.

Brydar came halfway up the stairs. "How goes it?"

"Send young Annelys to me," Kindra said. "Tell her to bring linen thread and a needle; and linen for bandages, and hot water and soap." Annelys had courage and strength; what was more, she was sure that if Kindra asked her to keep a secret, Annelys would do so, instead of gossiping about it.

Brydar said, in an undertone that did not carry a yard past Kindra's ear, "It's a woman—isn't it?"

Kindra demanded, with a frown. "Were you listening?"

"Listening, hell! I've got the brains I was born with, and I was remembering a couple of other little things. Can you think of any other reason a member of my band wouldn't let us get his britches off? Whoever she is, she's got guts enough for two!"

Kindra shook her head in dismay. Then all the girl's suffering was useless, scandal and disgrace there would be in any case. "Brydar, you pledged this would be worth my while. Do you owe me, or not?"

"I owe you," Brydar said.

"Then swear by your sword that you will never open your mouth about this, and I am paid. Fair enough?"

Brydar grinned. "I won't cheat you out of your pay for that," he said. "You think I want it to get round these hills that Brydar of Fen Hills can't tell the men from the ladies? Young Marco rode with my band for half a year and proved himself the man. If his foster-sister or kinswoman or cousin or what you will chooses to nurse him herself, and take him home with her afterward, what's it to any of my men? Damned if I want my crew thinking some girl killed Scarface right under my nose!" He put his hand to sword-hilt. "Zandru take this hand with the palsy if I say any word about this. I'll send Annelys to you," he promised, and went.

Kindra returned to the girl's side. She was still unconscious; when Annelys came in, Kindra said curtly, "Hold the lamp there; I want to get this stitched before she recovers consciousness. And try not to get squeamish or faint; I want to get it done quick enough so we don't have to hold her down while we do it."

Annelys gulped at the sight of the girl and the gaping wound, which had begun to bleed again. "A woman! Blessed Evanda! Kindra, is she one of your Sisterhood? Did you know?"

"No, to both questions. Here, hold the light—"

"No," said Annelys. "I have done this many times; I have steady hands for this. Once when my brother cut his thigh chopping wood, I sewed it up, and I have helped the midwife, too. You hold the light."

Relieved, Kindra surrendered the needle. Annelys began her work as skillfully as if she were embroidering a cushion; halfway through the business, the girl regained consciousness; she gave a faint cry of fright, but Kindra spoke to her, and she quieted and lay still, her teeth clamped in her lip, clinging to Kindra's hand. Halfway through, she moistened her lip and whispered, "Is she one of you, *mestra?*"

"No. No more than yourself, child. But she is a friend. And she will not gossip about you, I know it," Kindra said confidently.

When Annelys had finished, she fetched a glass of wine for the woman, and held her head while she drank it. Some color came back into the pale cheeks, and she was breathing more easily. Annelys brought one of her own nightgowns and said, "You will be more comfortable in this, I think. I wish we could carry you to my bed, but I don't think you should be moved yet. Kindra, help me to lift her." With a pillow and a couple of clean sheets she set about making the woman comfortable on the straw pallet.

The stranger made a faint sound of protest as they began to undress her, but was too weak to protest effectively. Kindra stared in shock as the undertunic came off. She would never have believed that any woman over fourteen could successfully pose as a man among men; yet this woman had done it, and now she saw how. The revealed form was flat, spare, breastless; the shoulders had the hardened musculature of any swordsman. There was more hair on the arms than most women would have tolerated without removing it somehow, with bleach or wax. Annelys stared in amazement, and the woman, seeing that shocked look, hid her face in the pillow. Kindra said sharply, "There is no need to stare. She is *emmasca*, that is all; haven't you ever seen one before?" The neutering operation was illegal all over Darkover, and dangerous; and in this woman it must have been done before, or shortly after puberty. She was filled with questions, but courtesy forbade any of them.

"But—but—" Annelys whispered. "Was she born so or made so? It is unlawful—who would dare—"

"Made so," the girl said, her face still hidden in the pillow. "Had I been born so, I would have had nothing to fear . . . and I chose this so that I might have nothing more to fear!"

She tightened her mouth as they lifted and turned her; Annelys gasped aloud at the shocking scars, like the marks of whips, across the woman's back; but she said nothing, only pulled the merciful concealment of her own nightgown over the frightful revelation of those scars. Gently, she washed the woman's face and hands with soapy water. The ginger-pale hair was dark with sweat, but at the roots Kindra saw something else, the hair was beginning to grow in fire-red there.

Comyn. The telepath caste, red-haired . . . this woman was a noblewoman, born to rule in the Domains of Darkover!

In the name of all the Gods, Kindra wondered, who can she be, what has come to her? How came she here in this disguise, even her hair bleached so none can guess at her lineage? And who has mishandled her so? She must have been beaten like an animal . . .

And then, shocked, she heard the words forming in her mind, not knowing how.

Scarface, said the voice in her mind. *But now I am avenged. Even if it means my death . . .*

She was frightened; never had she so clearly perceived; her rudimentary telepath gift had always, before, been a matter of quick intuition, hunch, lucky guess. She whispered aloud, in horror and dismay, "By the Goddess! Child, who are you?"

The pale face contorted in a grimace which Kindra recognized, in dismay, was intended for a smile. "I am—no one," she said. "I had thought myself the daughter of Alaric Lindir. Have you heard the tale?"

Alaric Lindir. The Lindir family were a proud and wealthy family, distantly akin to the Aillard family of the Comyn. Too highly born, in fact, for Kindra to claim acquaintance with any of that kin; they were of the ancient blood of the Hastur-kin.

"Yes, they are a proud people," whispered the woman. "My mother's name was Kyria, and she was a younger sister to Dom Lewis Ardais—not the Ardais Lord, but his younger brother. But still, she was highborn enough that when she proved to be with child by one of the Hastur lords of Thendara, she was hurried away and married in haste to Alaric Lindir. And my father—he that I had always believed my father—he was proud of his red-haired daughter; all during my childhood I heard how proud he was of me, for I would marry into Comyn, or go to one of the Towers and become a great and powerful sorceress or Keeper. And then—then came Scarface and his crew, and they sacked the castle, and carried away some of the women, just as an afterthought, and by the time Scarface discovered who he had as his latest captive—well, the damage was done, but still he sent to my father for ransom. And my father, that selfsame Dom Alaric who had not enough proud words for his red-haired beauty who should further his ambition by a proud marriage into the Comyn, my father—" She choked, then spat the words out. "He sent word that if Scarface could guarantee me—untouched—then he would ransom me at a great price; but if not, then he would pay nothing. For if I was—was spoilt, ravaged—then I was no use to him, and Scarface might hang me or give me to one of his men, as he saw fit."

"Holy Bearer of Burdens!" Annelys whispered. "And this man had reared you as his own child?"

"Yes—and I had thought he loved me," she said, her face twisting. Kindra closed her eyes in horror, seeing all too clearly the man who had welcomed his wife's bastard—but only while she could further his ambition.

Annelys' eyes were filled with tears. "How dreadful! Oh, how could any man—"

"I have come to believe any man would do so," the girl said, "for Scarface was so angry at my father's refusal that he gave me to one of his men to be a plaything, and you can see how he used me. *That* one I killed while he lay sleeping one night, when at last he had come to believe me beaten into submission—and so made my escape, and back to my mother, and she welcomed me with tears and with pity, but I could see in her mind that her greatest fear, now, was that I should shame her by bearing the child of Scarface's bastard; she feared that my father would say to her, *like mother, like daughter,* and my disgrace would revive the old story of her own. And I could not forgive my mother—that she should continue to love and to live with that man who had rejected me and given me over to such a fate. And so I made my way to a *leronis,* who took pity on me—or perhaps she, too, wanted only to be certain I would not disgrace my Comyn blood by becoming a whore or a bandit's drab—and she made me *emmasca,* as you see. And I took service with Brydar's men, and so I won my revenge—"

Annelys was weeping; but the girl lay with a face like stone. Her very calm was more terrible than hysteria; she had gone beyond tears, into a place where grief and satisfaction were all one, and that one wore the face of death.

Kindra said softly, "You are safe now; none will harm you. But you must not talk any more; you are weary, and weakened with loss of blood. Come, drink the rest of this wine and sleep, my girl." She supported the girl's head while she finished the wine, filled with horror. And yet, through the horror, was admiration. Broken, beaten, ravaged, and then rejected, this girl had won free of her captors by killing one of them; and then she had survived the further rejection of her family, to plot her revenge, and to carry it out, as a noble might do.

And the proud Comyn rejected this woman? She has the courage of any two of their menfolk! It is this kind of pride and folly that will one day bring the reign of the Comyn crashing down into ruin! And she shuddered with a strange premonitory fear, seeing with her wakening telepathic gift a flashing picture of flames over the Hellers, strange sky-ships, alien men walking the streets of Thendara clad in black leather . . .

The woman's eyes closed, her hands tightening on Kindra's. "Well, I have had my revenge," she whispered again, "and so I can die. And with my last breath I will bless you, that I die as a woman, and not in this hated disguise, among men . . ."

"But you are not going to die," Kindra said. "You will live, child."

"No." Her face was set stubbornly in lines of refusal, closed and barriered. "What does life hold for a woman friendless and without kin? I could endure to live alone and secret, among men, disguised, while I nursed the thought of my revenge to strengthen me for the—the daily pretense. But I hate men, I loathe the way they speak of women among themselves, I would rather die than go back to Brydar's band, or live further among men."

Annelys said softly, "But now you are revenged, now you can live as a woman again."

Again the nameless woman shook her head. "Live as a woman, subject to men like my father? Go back and beg shelter from my mother, who might give me bread in secret so I would not disgrace them further by dying across her doorstep, and keep me hidden away, to drudge among them hidden, sew or spin, when I have ridden free with a mercenary band? Or shall I live as a lone woman, at the mercy of men? I would rather face the mercy of the blizzard and the banshee!" Her hand closed on Kindra's. "No," she said, "I would rather die."

Kindra drew the girl into her arms, holding her against her breast. "Hush, my poor girl, hush, you are over-wrought, you must not talk like that. When you have slept you will not feel this way," she soothed, but she felt the depth of despair in the woman in her arms, and her rage overflowed.

The laws of her Guild forbade her to speak of the Sisterhood, to tell this girl that she could live free, protected by the Guild Charter, never again to be at the mercy of any man. The laws of the Guild, which she might not break, the oath she must keep. And yet on a deeper level, was it not breaking the oath to withhold from this woman, who had risked so much and who had appealed to her in the name of her Goddess, the knowledge that might give her the will to live?

Whatever I do, I am forsworn; either I break my oath by refusing this girl my help, or I break it by speaking when I am forbidden by the law to speak.

The law! The law made by men, which still hemmed her in on every side, though she had cast off the ordinary laws by which men forced women to live! And she was doubly damned if she spoke of the Guild before Annelys, though Annelys had fought at her side. The just law of the Hellers would protect Annelys from this knowledge; it would make trouble for the Sisterhood if Kindra should lure away a daughter of a respectable innkeeper, whose mother needed her, and needed the help her husband would bring to the running of her inn!

Against her breast, the nameless girl had closed her eyes. Kindra caught the faint thread of her thoughts;

she knew that the telepath caste could will themselves to die . . . as this girl had willed herself to live, despite everything that had happened, until she had had her cherished revenge.

Let me sleep so . . . and I can believe myself in my mother's arms, in the days when I was still her child and this horror had not touched me . . . Let me sleep so and never wake . . .

Already she was drifting away, and for a moment, in despair, Kindra was tempted to let her die. *The law forbids me to speak.* And if she should speak, then Annelys, already struck with hero-worship of Kindra, already rebelling against a woman's lot, having tasted the pride of defending herself, Annelys would follow her, too. Kindra knew it, with a strange, premonitory shiver.

She let the rage in her have its way and overflow. She shook the nameless woman awake, knowing that already she was willing herself to death.

"Listen to me! Listen! You must not die," she said angrily. "Not when you have suffered so much! That is a coward's way, and you have proven again and again that you are no coward!"

"Oh, but I am a coward," the woman said. "I am too much a coward to live in the only way a woman like me can live—through the charity of women such as my mother—or the mercy of men like my father, or like Scarface! I dreamed that when I had my revenge, I could find some other way. But there is no other way."

And Kindra's rage and resolution overflowed. She looked despairing over the nameless woman's head, into Annelys' frightened eyes. She swallowed, knowing the seriousness of the step she was about to take.

"There—there might be another way," she said, still temporizing. "You—I do not even know your name, what is your name?"

"I am nameless," the woman said, her face like stone. "I swore I would never again speak the name given me by the father and the mother who rejected me. If I had lived, I would have taken another name. Call me what pleases you."

And with a great surge of wrath, Kindra made up her mind. She drew the girl against her.

"I will call you Camilla," she said, "for from this day forth, I swear it, I shall be mother and sister to you, as was the blessed Cassilda to Camilla; this I swear. Camilla, you shall not die," she said, pulling the girl upright. Then, with a deep resolute breath, clasping Camilla's hand in one of hers, and stretching the other to Annelys, she began.

"My little sisters, let me tell you of the Sisterhood of Free Women, which men call Free Amazons. Let me tell you of the ways of the Renunciates, the Oathbound, the *Comhi-Letzii* . . ."

(1979)

Elbow Room

Sometimes I feel the need to go to confession on my way to work.

It's quiet at firstdawn, with Aleph Prime not above the horizon yet; there's always some cognitive dissonance because, with the antigravs turned up high enough for comfort, you feel that the "days" ought to reflect a planet of human mass, not a mini-planetoid space station. So at firstdawn you're set for an ordinary-sized day; twenty hours, or twenty-three, or something your circadian rhythms could compromise with. Thus when Prime sets again for firstdark you aren't prepared for it. With your mind, maybe, but not down where you need it, in your guts. By thirddawn you're gearing up for a whole day on Checkout Station again, and you can cope with thirddark and fifthdark and by twelfthdark you're ready to put on your sleep mask and draw the curtains and shut it all out again till firstdawn next day.

But at firstdawn you get that illusion, and I always enjoy it for a little while. It's like being really alone on a silent world, a real world. And even before I came here to Checkout I was always a loner, preferring my own company to anyone else's.

That's the kind they always pick for the Vortex stations, like Checkout. There isn't much company there. And we learn to give each other elbow room.

You'd think, with only five of us here—or is it only four; I've never been quite sure, for reasons I'll go into later—we'd do a lot of socializing. You'd think we would huddle together against the enormous agoraphobia of space. I really don't know why we don't. I guess, though, the kind of person who could really enjoy living on Checkout—and I do—would have to be a loner. And I go squirrelly when there are too many other people around.

Of course, I know I couldn't really live here alone, as much as I'd like to. They tried that, early in the days of the Vortex stations, sending one man or woman out alone. One after another, with monotonous regularity, they suicided. Then they tried sending well-adjusted couples, small groups, sociable types who would huddle together and socialize, and they all went nuts and did one another in. I know why, of course; they saw too much of each other, and began to rely on one another for their sanity and self-validation. And of course that solution didn't work. You have to be the kind of person who can be wholly self-reliant.

So now they do it this way. I always know I'm not alone. But I never have to *see* too much of the other people here; I never have to see them unless I *want* to. I don't know how much socializing the others do, but I suspect they're as much loners as I am. I don't really care, as long as they don't intrude on *my* privacy and as long as they take orders the way they're supposed to. I love them all, of course, all four or maybe five of them. They told me, back at Psych Conditioning, that this would happen. But I don't remember how it happened, whether it just happened or whether they *made* it happen. I don't ask too many questions. I'm glad that I love them; I'd hate to think that some Psych-tech *made* me love them! Because they're sweet, dear, wonderful, lovable people. All of them.

As long as I don't have to see them very often.

Because I'm the boss. I'm in control. It's *my* Station! Slight tendencies toward megalomania, they called it in Psych. It's good for a Station Programmer to have these mild megalomanic tendencies, they explained it all to me. If they put humble self-effacing types out here, they'd start thinking of themselves as wee little fleabites upon the vast face of the Universe, and sooner or later they'd be found with their throats cut, because they couldn't believe they were big enough to be in control of anything on the cosmic scale of the Vortex.

Lonely, yes. But I like it that way. I like being boss out here. And I like the way they've provided for my needs. I think I have the best chef in the galaxy. She cooks all my favorite foods—I suppose Psych gave her my profile. I wonder sometimes if the other people at the station have to eat what I like, or if they get to order their own favorites. I don't really care, as long as I get to order what I like. And then I have my own personal librarian, with all the music of the galaxy at her fingertips, the best sound-equipment known, state-of-the-art stuff I'd never be able to afford in any comparable job back Earthside. And my own gardener, and a technician to do the work I can't handle. And even my own personal priest. Can you imagine that? Sending a priest all the way out here, just to minister to my spiritual needs! Well, at least to a congregation of four. Or five.

Or is it six? I keep thinking I've forgotten somebody.

Firstdawn is rapidly giving way to firstnoon when I leave the garden and kneel in the little confessional booth. I whisper "Bless me, Father, for I have sinned."

"Bless you, my child." Father Nicholas is there, although his Mass must be long over. I sometimes wonder if this doesn't violate the sanctity of the confessional, that he cannot help knowing which of his congregation is kneeling there; I am the only one who ever gets up before seconddawn. And I don't really know whether I have sinned or not. How could I sin against God or my fellow man, when I am thousands of millions of miles away from all but five or six of them? And I so seldom see the others, I have no chance to sin with them or against them. Maybe I only need to hear his voice; a human voice, a light, not particularly masculine voice. Deeper than mine, though *different* from mine. That's the important thing; to hear a voice which *isn't* mine.

"Father, I have entertained doubts about the nature of God."

"Continue, my child."

"When I was out in the Wheel the other day, watching the Vortex, I found myself wondering if the Vortex was God. After all, God is unknowable, and the Vortex is so totally alien from human experience. Isn't this the closest thing that the human race has ever found, to the traditional view of God? Something totally beyond matter, energy, space or time?"

There is a moment of silence. Have I shocked the priest? But after a long time his soft voice comes quietly into the little confessional. Outside the light is already dimming toward firstdark.

"There is no harm in regarding the Vortex as a symbol of God's relationship to man, my child. After all, the Vortexes are perhaps the most glorious of God's works. It is written in scripture that the Heavens declare the glory of God, and the firmament proclaims the wonder of His work."

"But does this mean, then, that God is distant, incapable of loving mankind? I can't imagine the Vortex loving anyone or being conscious of anyone. Not even me."

"Is that a defect in God, or a defect in your own imagination, my child, in ascribing limits to God's power?"

I persist. "But does it matter if I say my prayers to the Vortex, and worship it?"

Behind the screen I hear a soft laugh. "God will hear your prayers wherever you say them, dear child, and whenever you find anything worthy of worship and admiration you are worshiping God, by whatever name you choose to call it. Is there anything else, my child?"

"I have been guilty of uncharitable thoughts about my cook, Father. Last night she didn't fix my dinner till late, and I wanted to tear her eyes out!"

"Did you harm her, child?"

"No. I just yelled through the screen that she was a

lazy, selfish, stupid bitch. I wanted to go out and hit her, but I didn't."

"Then you exercised commendable self-restraint, did you not? What did she answer?"

"She didn't answer at all. And that made me madder than ever."

"You should love your neighbor—and I mean your chef, too—as yourself, child," he reproves, and I say, hanging my head, "I'm not loving myself very much these days, maybe that's the trouble."

Mind, now, I'm not sure there really is a Father Nicholas behind that screen. Maybe it's a relay system which puts me into touch with a priest Earthside. Or maybe Father Nicholas is only a special voice program on the main computer, which is why I sometimes ask the craziest questions, and play a game with myself to see how long it takes "Father Nicholas" to find the right program for an answer. As I said, it seems crazy to send a priest out here for five people. Or is it six?

But then, why not? We people at the Vortex stations keep the whole galaxy running. Nothing is too good for us, so why not my personal priest?

"Tell me what is troubling you, my child."

Always *my child*. Never by name. Does he even know it? He must. After all, I am in charge here; Checkout Programmer. The boss. Or is this just the manners of the confessional, a subtle way of reemphasizing that all of us are the same to him, equal in his sight and in the sight of God? I don't know if I like that. It's disquieting. Perhaps my chef runs to him and tells tales of me, how I shrieked foul names at her, and abused her through the kitchen hatch! I cover my face with my hands and sob, hearing him make soothing sounds.

I envy that priest, secure behind his curtain. Listening to the human faults of others, having none of his own. I almost became a priest myself. I tell him so.

"I know that, child, you told me. But I'm not clear in my mind why you chose not to be ordained."

I'm not clear either, and I tell him so, trying to

remember. If I had been a man I would surely have gone through with it, but it is still not entirely easy to be ordained, for a woman, and the thought of seminary, with ninety or a hundred other priestlings and priestlets herded all together, even then the thought made me uneasy. I couldn't have endured the fight for a woman to be ordained. "I'm not a fighter, Father."

But I am disquieted when he agrees with me. "No. If you were, you wouldn't be out here, would you?" Again I feel uneasy; am I just running away? I choose to live here on the ragged rim of the Universe, tending the Vortex, literally at the back end of Beyond. I pour all this uncertainty out to him, knowing he will reassure me, understand me as always.

But his reassuring noises are too soothing, too calming, humoring me. Damn it, is there anyone *there* behind that curtain? I want to tear it down, to see the priest's face, his human face, or else to be sure that it is only a bland computer console programmed to reassure and thus to mock me. My hand already extended, I draw it back. I don't really want to know. Let them laugh at me, if there is really a *they,* a priest Earthside listening over this unthinkable extension of the kilometers and the megakilometers, let them laugh. They deserve it, if they are really such clever programmers, making it possible for me to draw endless sympathy and reassurance from the sound of an alien voice.

Whatever we do, we do to make it possible for you to live and keep your sanity . . . "I think, Father, that I am—am a little lonely. The dreams are building up again."

"Perfectly natural," he says soothingly, and I know that he will arrange one of Julian's rare visits. Even now I hang my head, blush, cannot face him, but it is less embarrassing this way than if I had to take the initiative alone, unaided. It's part of being the kind of loner I am, that I could never endure it, to call Julian direct, have to take—perhaps—a rebuff or a downright rejection. Well, I never claimed to be a well-adjusted personality. A well-adjusted personality could not survive out here, at the rim of nowhere. Back on Earthside I probably wouldn't even *have* a love life, I avoid people too much. But here they provide for all my needs. All. Even this one, which, left to myself, I would probably neglect.

Ego te absolvo.

I kneel briefly to say my penance, knowing that the ritual is foolish. Comforting; but foolish. He reminds me to turn on the monitor in my room and he will say Mass for me tomorrow. And again I am certain that there is nobody there, that it is a program in the computer; is there any other reason we do not all assemble for Christian fellowship? Or do we all share this inability to tolerate one another's company?

But I feel soothed and comforted as I go down between the automatic sprinklers through the little patch of garden tended so carefully by my own gardener. I catch a glimpse, a shimmer in the air, of someone in the garden, turned away like a distant reflection, but no one is supposed to be here at this hour and I quickly look away.

Still it is comforting not to be alone and I call out a cheery good-morning to the invisible image, wondering, with a strange little cramp of excitement low in my body; *is it Julian?* I see him so briefly, so seldom, except in the half-darkness of my room on those rare occasions he comes to me. I'm not even sure what he does here. We don't talk about his work. We have better things to do. Thinking of that makes me tremble, squeeze my legs tight, thinking that it may not be long till I see him again. But I have a day's work to do, and with seconddawn brightening the sky, glinting on reflections from which I glance away . . . *you never look in mirrors* . . . I climb up into the seat that will take me up to the Wheel, out by the Vortex.

There is an exhilaration to that, shooting up toward the strange seething no-color of it. There is a ship already waiting. Waiting for *me,* for the Vortex to open. All that power and burning and fusion and raw energy, all waiting for *me,* and I enjoy my daily dose of megalomania as I push the speech button.

"Checkout speaking. Register your name and business."

It is always a shock to hear a voice from outside, a really strange voice. But I register the captain's voice, the name and registry number so that later they can match programs with Checkin, my opposite number on the far side of the Vortex—in a manner of speaking. Where the Vortex is concerned, of course, Near and Far, or Here and There, or Before and After, have no more meaning than—oh, than I and Thou. In one of the mirrors on the wheel I catch a glimpse of my technician, waiting, and I sit back and listen as she rattles off the coordinates in a sharp staccato. She and I have nothing to say to each other. I don't really think that girl is interested in anything except mathematics. I drift, watching myself in the mirror, listening to the ship's captain arguing with the technician, and I am irritated. How dare he argue, her conduct reflects on me and I am enraged by any hint of rudeness to my staff. So I speak the code which starts the Vortex into its strange nonspace whorl, the colors and swirls.

This could all be done by computers, of course.

I am here, almost literally, to push a button by hand if one gets stuck. From the earliest days of telemetered equipment, machinery has tended to go flukey and sometimes jam; and during the two hundred years that the Vortex stations have been in operation, they've found out that it's easier and cheaper to maintain the stations with their little crews of agoraphobic and solitary loners. They even provide us with chefs and gardeners and all our mental and spiritual comforts. We humans are just software which doesn't—all things considered—get out of order quite as often as the elaborate self-maintaining machineries do. Furthermore, we can be serviced more cheaply when we *do* get out of order. So we're there to make sure that if any of the buttons stick, we can unstick them before they cost the

Galaxy more than the whole operating costs of Checkout for the next fifty years.

I watch the Vortex swirl, and my knowledge and judgment tell me the same thing as do my instruments. "Whenever you're ready," I say, receive their acknowledgment, and then the strange metal shape of the ship swirls with the Vortex, becomes nonshape, I almost see it vanish into amorphous nothingness, to come out—or so the theory is—at Checkin Station, several hundred light-years away. Do these ships go anywhere at all, I wonder? Do they ever return? They vanish when I push those buttons, and they never come back. Am I sending them into oblivion, or to their proper prearranged destination? I don't know. And, if the truth be told, I don't really care. For all the difference it makes to me they could be going into another dimension, or to the theological Hell.

But I like it out here on the Wheel. There is *real* solitude up here. Down there on Checkout there is solitude with other people around, though I seldom see them. I realize I am still twitching from a brief encounter with the gardener this morning. Don't they know, these people, that they aren't supposed to be around when I am walking in the gardens? But even that brief surge of adrenaline has been good for me, I suppose. Do they arrange for me to get a glimpse of one of my fellow humans only when I *need* that kind of stirring up?

Back at Checkout—there will not be another ship today—I walk again through the garden, putter a little, cherish with my eyes the choice melon I am growing under glass, warn the gardener through the intercom not to touch it until I myself order it served up for my supper. I remember the satisfaction of the cargo ship waiting, metal tentacles silent against the black of space, waiting. Waiting for me, waiting for my good pleasure, gatekeeper to the Void, Cerberus at a new, kind of hell.

Rank has its privileges. While I am in the garden none of the others come near; but I am a little fatigued, I leave the garden to the others and go to my room for deep meditation. I can sense them all around me, the gardener working with the plants like an extension of my own consciousness, I sit like a small spider at the center of a web and watch the others working as I sit back to meditate. My mind floats free, my alpha rhythms take over, I disappear . . .

Later, waiting for my supper, I wonder what kind of woman would become chef on a Checkout station. I *can* cook, I *have* done my own cooking, I am a damn good cook, but I wouldn't have taken a job like that. Is she completely without ambition? I don't see her very often. We wouldn't have much in common; what could I possibly have to say to a woman like that? Waiting, floating, spider in my web, I find I can imagine her going carefully through the motions and little soothing rituals, chopping fresh vegetables I fingered in the garden this morning, heating the trays, all the little soothing mindless things. But to spend her life like that? The woman must be a fool.

I come out of the meditative state to find my supper waiting for me. I call my thanks to her, eat. The food is good, it is always good, but the dishes are too hot, somehow I have burned my hand on them. But it doesn't matter, I have something more to look forward to, tonight. I delay, savoring the knowledge, listening to one of my operatic tapes, lost in a vague romantic reverie. Tonight, Julian is coming.

I wonder sometimes why we are not allowed to see one another more often. Surely, if he cares for me as much as he says, it would be proper to see each other casually now and then, to talk about our work. But I am sure Psych is right, that it is better for us not to see each other too often. On Earth, if we grew tired of one another, we could each find someone else. But here there *is* no one else—for either of us. A phrase floats through my mind from nowhere, *chains of mnemonic suggestion,* as I set the controls which will allow him to come, silent and alone, into my room after I have gone to bed.

*   *   *

He has come and gone.

I do not know why the rules are as they are. Perhaps to keep us from quarreling, to avoid the tragedies of the early days of the Vortex stations. Perhaps, simply, to avoid our growing bored with each other. As if I could ever be bored with Julian! To me, he is perfect, even his name. Julian has always seemed to me the most perfect name for a man, and Julian, *my* Julian, my lover, the perfect man to match the perfect name. So why is it we are not allowed to meet more often? Why can we meet like this, only in the silent dark?

Langorous, satisfied, exhausted, I muse drowsily, wondering if it is some obscure mystery of my inner Psych-profile, that one of us subconsciously desires the old myth of Pysche, who could retain her lover Eros only as long as she never saw his face? I see him only for a moment in the mirror, misty, never clearly perceived, over my shoulder; but I know he is handsome.

I am so sensitive to Julian's moods that I think sometimes I am developing special senses for my love; becoming a telepath, but only for him. When our bodies join it seems often as if I were one in mind with him, touching him, how else could I be so aware of his emotions, so completely secure of his tenderness and his concern? How else could he know so perfectly all my body's obscurer desires, when I myself can hardly bring myself to speak them, when I would be afraid or ashamed to voice them aloud? But he knows, he always knows, leaving me satisficd, worn, spent. I wish, with a longing so intense it is pain, that the regulations by which we live would let him lie here in my arms for the rest of the night, that I could feel myself held close and cherished, comforted against this vast, eternal loneliness; that he could cuddle me in his arms, that we could meet sometimes for a drink or share our dinner. Why not?

A terrible thought comes to me. They give me everything else. My own cook. My own gardener. My technician. My personal priest.

My very own male whore.

I cannot believe it. No, no. No. I do not believe it. Julian loves me, and I love him. Anyhow, it would not suit the Puritan consciences of our legislators. No, I can't see it; how would they justify it on the requisition forms? *Whore, male, one, Checkout Programmer, for the use of.* No, such a thing couldn't happen. Surely they just hired some male technician, determined by Psych-profile to have the maximum sexual compatibility with myself. That's bad enough, heaven knows.

Now an even more frightening thought surges up into my conscious mind. Can it be possible—oh, God, no!—that Julian, *my* Julian, is an android?

They have designed some of them, I know, with extremely sophisticated sex programs. I have seen them advertised in those catalogs we used to giggle over when we were little girls. I am sick with fear and dread at the thought that during those conditioning trances which I have been conditioned to forget, I gave up all that data about my secret dreams and desires and sexual fantasies, so that they might program them all into the computer of an android, and what emerged was . . . Julian.

Is he a multipurpose android, perhaps, then? Hardware, no more, both useful and economical; perhaps that gardener I see dimly sometimes, like a hologram, in the distance. He could, of course, be the gardener, though in the brief glimpses of the gardener I had the impression the gardener was a woman. Who can tell, with these coveralls we all wear, uniform, unisex? And it would look better on the congressional requisitions: *Android, one, multiprogrammed. Checkout Station, for the maintenance of.* And a special sexual program would only be a memo in the files of Psych. Nothing to embarrass anyone—anyone but me, that is, and I am not supposed to know. Just another piece of Station hardware. For maintenance of the Station. And of the Station Programmer. Hardware. Yes, very. Oh, God!

I have no time now for worrying about Julian, or

what he is, or about my own dissatisfactions and fears. I cannot take any of these disquieting thoughts to that computerized priest, if he is indeed only a sophisticated computer, a mechanical priest-psychiatrist! Is he another android, perhaps? Or is he indeed the same android with still another program? Priest and male whore at the flip of a switch? Am I alone here with a multipurpose android serving all my functions? No time for that. A ship is out there, waiting for me; and my instruments tell me, as I ride out to the Wheel, even before I get the message; that ship is in trouble.

Perhaps all the signs, all my fears that I am going mad, are simply signs of developing telepathic potential; I never believed that I was even potentially an esper, yet somehow I am aware of nearly everything my technician said to the ship's captain. I did not understand it all, of course, I have no technical skill at all. My skills are all executive. I can barely manage to make my little pocket calculator figure out the tariffs for the ships I send into the Vortex; I joked with Central that they should allow me a bookkeeper, but they are too stingy. But even though I did not understand all of what the technician said, when I read the report she left for me, I know that if the ship went into the Vortex in this state, it might never emerge; worse, it might create spatial anomalies to disturb the fields for other ships and put the Vortex very badly out of commission. So I know that they dare not pass through that gate; I cannot follow the precise mathematics of the switch, though, and I feel like a fool. When I was in preparatory school I tested higher in all the groups, including mathematical ability. But I ended up with no technical skill. How, I wonder, did that happen?

Later I have leisure to visit the captain by screen. He is a big man, youthful, soft-spoken, his smile strangely stirring. And he asks me a strange question.

"You are the Programmer? Are you people a clone?"

"Why, no, nothing like that," I say to him, and ask why.

"The technician—she's very like you. Oh, of course,

you are nothing alike otherwise, she's all business—a shame, in a lovely young woman! I could hardly get her to say a pleasant word to me!"

I tell him that I am an only child. Only children are best for work like this; the necessary isolation from peer groups. A child reared in a puppy-pack, under peer pressure from siblings and agemates, becomes other-directed; dependent upon the opinions and the approval of others, without the inner resources to tolerate the solitude which is the breath of life to me. I am even a little offended. "I can't see the slightest resemblance between us," I tell him, and he shakes his head and says diplomatically that perhaps it is a similarity of height and coloring which misled him.

"Anyway, I didn't like her much, she flayed me with her tongue, kept strictly to business—you'd think it was my *fault* the ship was out of commission! You're much, *much* pleasanter than she is!"

And that is as it should be, I am the one with leisure for reflection and conversation; it wouldn't be right for my technician to waste her time talking! So we talk, we even flirt a little. I am aware of it; I pose and preen a little for him, letting the animal woman surface from all the other faces I wear, and finally I agree to the hazardous step, to visit him on his ship.

So strange, so strange to think of being with one who is not carefully Psych-profiled to be agreeable to me. There is nothing in the regulations against it, of course, perhaps they believe our love of solitude will keep us away as it has always done before, for me. Even a little welcome, alien. But when I am actually through the airlock I am shocked into silence by the strange faces, the alien smells, the different body-chemistry of strange male life. They say that men give off hormones, analogous to pheromones in the lower kingdoms, which they cannot smell on one another; which only a woman is chemically able to smell. I believe, it, it is true, the ship reeks of maleness. Ushered into a room where I may strip my suit I avoid the mirror. *Never look into a mirror, unless . . . unless*

. . . why would Psych have imprinted that prohibition on me? I need to see that my hair is tidy, my coverall free of grease. Defiantly I look into it anyway, my head swims and I look away in haste.

Fear, fear of what I may see, my face dissolving, identity lost . . . stranger, not myself, unknown. . . .

A drink in my hand, flattery and compliments; I find I am hungry for this after long isolation. Of course I am selfish and vain, it is a professional necessity, like my little touch of daily megalomania. I accept this, and revel in seeing others, interacting with strange faces—*really* strange, not programmed to my personal needs and wishes. Yes, I know I need to be alone, I remember all the reasons, but I know also, too well, the terrible face of loneliness. All my carefully chosen companions are so dovetailed to my personality that talking to them is like . . . *like talking to myself, like looking in a mirror . . .*

Two drinks help me unwind, relax. I know all the dangers of alcohol, but tonight I am defiant; we are off duty, both the captain and myself, we need not guard ourselves. Before too long I find the captain's hands on me, touching me, rousing me in a way Julian has not done since his first visits. I give myself over to his kisses, and when he asks the inevitable question I brace myself for a moment, then shrug and ask myself *Why not?* His touch on me is welcome, I brush aside thoughts of Julian, even Julian has been too carefully adjusted, dovetailed, programmed to my own personality; perhaps even a little abrasiveness helps to alter the far-too-even tenor of the days, to create something of the necessary *otherness* of lovemaking. That is what I have missed, the otherness; Julian being too carefully selected and Psych-profiled to me.

If a love-partner is too similar to the self there is not the needed, satisfying *merging*. Even the amoeba which splits itself, infinitely reduplicating perfect analogies of its own personality and awareness, feels now and then the need to merge, to exchange its very protoplasm and cell-stuff with the *other;* too much of even the most necessary similarity is deadly, and makes of love-making only a more elaborate and ritualized masturbation. It is good to be touched by *another*.

Together, then, into his room. And our bodies merge abruptly into an unlovely struggle at the height of which he blurts out, as if in shock, "But you couldn't *possibly* be that inexperienced . . ." and then, seeing and sensing my shock, he is all gentleness again, apologetic, saying he had forgotten how young I was. I am confused and distressed; *I* inexperienced? Now I am on my mettle, to prove myself equal to passion, sophisticated and knowledgeable, tolerating discomfort and strangeness, to think longingly of Julian. It serves me right, to be unfaithful to him, Psych was right, Julian is exactly what I need; I know, even while the captain and I are lying close, afterward, all tenderness, that I will not do this again. The regulations are wise. Back to the Station, back to my quarters, blur the experience all away in sleep, all of it . . . *awkwardness, struggle that felt like rape* . . . no, I will not do this again, I know now why it is forbidden. I do not think I will confess it even to the priest, I have done penance enough. Seal it all away in some inaccessible part of my mind, the bruising and humiliation of the memory.

Flotsam in my mind from the vast amnesia of the training program, as I seek to forget, that conditioning they will never let us remember; that I am suitable for this work because I dissociate with abnormal rapidity. . . .

And next morning at firstdawn I go up even before breakfast to the Wheel, their repairs are made and they do not want to lose time. The captain wants to speak with me, but I let him speak with the technician while I watch out of sight. I do not want to look into his face again; I never want to see again in any face that mixture of tenderness, pity—contempt.

I am glad to see their ship dissolve into the vast nonshape of the Vortex. I do not care if their repairs have been made properly or if they lose themselves somewhere inside the Vortex and never return. Watching their shape vanish I see a face dissolving in a mirror and I am agitated and frightened, frightened . . . they are not part of my world, I have seen them go, I have perhaps destroyed them. I think of how easy it would have been, how glad I would have been if my technician had given them the wrong program and they had vanished into the Vortex and come out . . . nowhere. As I have destroyed everything not the self.

Julian has been destroyed for me too. . . .

Maybe there is nothing out there, no ship, no Vortex, nothing. Everything comes into the human mind through the filters of self, my priest created to absolve a self which is not there, or is it the priest who is not there at all? Maybe there is nothing out there, maybe I created it all out of my own inner needs, priest, ship, Station, Vortex, perhaps I am still lying in the conditioning trances down there on Earth, fantasizing people who would help me to survive the terrors of loneliness, perhaps these people whom I see, but never clearly, are all androids, or fantasies born of my own madness and my inner needs . . . a random phrase floats again through my mind, *always the danger of solipsism, in the dissociator, the feeling that only the self exists . . . eternal preoccupation with internal states is morbid and we take advantage . . .*

Was there ever a ship out there? Did my mind create it to break the vast monotony of solitude, the loneliness I find I cannot endure, did I even fantasize the captain's gross body lying on my own?

Or is it Julian that I created, my own hands on my body, fantasy . . . a half-lighted image in a mirror . . .

The terrible solitude, the solitude I need and yet cannot endure, the solitude that is madness. And yet I need the solitude, so that I will not kill them all, I could murder them as all the earlier Vortex stations murdered one another, or is it only suicide when there is nothing but myself?

Is the whole cosmos out there—stars, galaxies, Vortex—only an emanation of my own brain? If so, then I can unmake it with a thought as I made it. I can snatch up my cook's kitchen knife and plunge it into my throat and all the stars will go away and all the universes. What am I doing in the kitchen . . . the cook's knife in my hand . . . here where I never go? She will be angry; I am supposed to give her the same privacy I yield to myself, I call out an apology and leave. Or is that pointless, am I crying out apology or abuse to myself? I have had no breakfast, at this hour, near thirddawn, the cook always prepares, I always prepare breakfast, I meditate while breakfast is prepared and served to me on my tray, facing the mirror from which I emerge . . . I am the other, the one with leisure for meditation and reflection—the executive, creative, I am God creating all these universes inside and outside of my mind . . . dizzied, I catch at the mirror, the knife slips, my face dissolves, my hand bleeds and all the universes wobble and spin on their cosmic axes, the face in the mirror commands in the voice of Father Nicholas, "Go, my child, and meditate."

"No! No!" I refuse to be tranquilized again, to be deceived . . .

"Command over-ride!" A voice I do not remember. "Go and meditate, meditate . . ." *meditate, meditate. . .*

Like the tolling of a great bell, commanding, rising out of the deeps, the voice of God. I meditate, seeing my face dissolve and change. . . .

No wonder I can read the technician's mind, I am the technician . . .

There is no one here. There has never been anyone here.

Only myself, and I am all, I am the God, the maker and unmaker of all the universes, I am Brahma, I am the Cosmos and the Vortex, I am the slow unraveling. . .
. . . unraveling of the mind . . .

I stumble to the chapel, images dissolving in my mind like the cook's face with the knife, into the confessional, the confessional I have always known is empty, sob out a prayer to the empty shrine. *Oh, God, if there is a God, let there be a God, let there be somebody there . . . or is God too only an emanation of my mind . . .*

And the slow dissolve into the mirror, the priest's voice saying soothing things which I do not really hear, the mirror as my mind dissolves, the priest's voice soothing and calm, my own voice weeping, pleading, sobbing, begging . . .

But his words mean nothing, a fragment of my own disintegration, I want to die, I want to die, I am dying, gone, nowhere . . .

The phenomenon of selective attention, what used to be called hypnosis, a self-induced dissociation or fugue state, dissociational hysteria sometimes regarded as multiple personality when the fragmented self-organized chains of memory and personality sets organize themselves into different consciousness. There is always the danger of solipsism, but the personality defends itself with enormously complex coping mechanisms. For instance, although we knew she had briefly attended a seminary, we had not expected the priest. . . .

"Ego te absolvo. Make a good act of contrition, my child."

I murmur the foolish, comforting, ritual words. He says, gently, "Go and meditate, child, you will feel better."

He is right. He is always right. I think sometimes that Father Nicholas is my conscience. That, of course, is the function of a priest. I meditate. All the terrors dissolve while I sit quietly in meditation, spinning the threads of this web where I sit, happy at the center, conscious of all the others moving around me. I must be developing esper powers, there is no other explanation, for while I sit quietly here meditating in the chapel the soothing vibrations of the garden come up through my fingers while my gardener works quietly, detached and calm, in my garden, growing delicious things for my supper. I love them all, all my friends around me here, they are all so kind to me, protecting my precious solitude, my privacy. I cannot cook the lovely things he grows, so I sit in my cherished solitude while my cook creates all manner of delicious things for my supper. How kind she is to me, a sweet woman really, though I know that I would have nothing to say to a woman like that. I waken out of meditation to see supper in my tray. How quickly the day has gone, seventhdawn brightening into seventhnoon, and darkness will be upon all of us again soon. How good it is, how sweet and fresh the food from my own garden; I call my thanks to her, this cook who spends all her time thinking up delightful things for me to eat. She must have esper powers too, my prize melon is on my tray, she knew exactly what I wanted after such a day as this.

"Good-night, dear cook, thank you, God bless you, goodnight."

She does not answer, I know she will not answer, she knows her place, but I know she hears and is pleased at my praise.

"Sleep well, my dear, good-night."

As I go to my room through the dimming of eighthdark, it crosses my mind that sometimes I am a little lonely here. But I am doing important work, and after all, the Psych people knew what they were doing. They knew that I need elbow room.

(1980)

Blood Will Tell

Dio Ridenow saw them first in the lobby of the luxury
hotel serving humans, and humanoids, on the pleasure
world of Vainwal. They were tall, sturdy men, but it
was the blaze of red hair on the elder of them that
drew her eyes. Comyn red. He was past fifty and
walked with a limp, stiff-kneed; his back was bent.
Behind him walked a young man in nondescript clothing,
tall, dark-haired and black-browed, sullen with steel-
gray eyes. Somehow he had the look of deformity, of
suffering, which she associated with lifetime cripples,
hunchbacks; yet he had no visible defect except a few
half-healed scars along one cheek. The scars drew, up
one corner of his mouth into a permanent sneer, and
Dio turned her eyes away with a faint sense of revulsion. Why would a Comyn lord have such a person in
his entourage? Some hanger-on, poor relation?

For it was obvious that the man was a Comyn lord.
There were redheads in the galaxy, on other worlds,
but the facial stamp, the features of the Comyn, were
unmistakable, combined with that hair; flame-red,
dusted with gray now, but still—Comyn. And what
was he doing here? For that matter, who was he,
anyhow? It was rare to find Darkovans anywhere except on their home world. The girl smiled and thought
to herself that she, too, might have been asked that
question, for she was Darkovan and far from home.
Her brothers came here because, basically, neither
was interested in political intrigue; but they had had to
defend and justify their absence often enough.

The Comyn lord moved slowly across the hall; limping, but with a kind of arrogance that drew all eyes, though he did nothing unusual. Dio framed it to herself, in an unfocused way: he moved as if he should have been preceded by his own drone-pipers and wearing high boots and a swirling cape—not the drab featureless Terran clothing he actually wore.

And having identified his Terran dress she suddenly knew who he was. One Comyn lord, and only one as far as anyone knew, had actually married, legally and with full ceremony, a Terran woman. He had managed to outface the scandal, which in any case had been before Dio was born; Dio had not seen him more than twice in her life, but now she knew who he was; Kennard Lanart-Alton, Lord Armida, self-exiled lord of the Alton Domain. And now she knew who the young man with the sullen eyes must be; this was his half-caste son, Lewis, who had been horribly injured during a rebellion back in the Hellers—Dio took no particular interest in such things and didn't know the details, she had still been playing with dolls when it all happened. But she knew Lew's foster sister, Linnell Aillard, who had a sister who was Keeper in Arilinn; and Linnell had told her of Lord Kennard's son Lewis and that her foster father had taken Lew to Terra in the hope that they could help him.

The two Comyn were standing beside the central computer of the main hotel desk; Kennard was giving some quietly definite order about their luggage to the human servants who were one of the luxury touches of the hotel, of the pleasure world. Dio herself had been brought up on a world where human servants were commonplace and could accept it without embarrassment, but many people could not overcome their shyness or dismay at being waited on by people rather than servomechs or robots. Dio's poise about such things had given her status among the other young women of Vainwal, many of them new-rich people who flocked to the pleasure worlds, knowing nothing of the refinements or niceties of good living, unable to accept luxury as if they had been brought up to it. Blood, Dio thought watching the exactly right way Kennard spoke to the servants, would always tell.

The younger man turned; Dio could see now that one hand was kept concealed in a fold of his coat, and that he moved awkwardly, struggling to handle some piece of their equipment which he did not want touched by anyone else. Kennard spoke to him in a low voice, but Dio could hear the impatient tone of the words, and the young man scowled, a black and angry scowl which made Dio shudder. Suddenly she realized she did not want to see any more of that young man. But from where she stood she could not cross the lobby without crossing their path.

She felt like lowering her head and pretending they were not there at all. After all, one of the delights of pleasure worlds such as Vainwal was to be anonymous, free of the restrictions of class or caste on one's home world. She would not recognize them, give them the privacy she wanted for herself. But as she crossed their path the young man made a clumsy movement; he did not see Dio, and banged full into her. Whatever piece of luggage he was carrying slid out of his awkward one-handed gripp and slid to the floor with a metallic clatter. He flung an angry word at her and stooped to retrieve it. It was long, narrow, closely wrapped; it might have held a pair of dueling swords, prized possessions never trusted to anyone else to handle. Dio automatically stepped back, but the young man could not get his hand on it, it slithered away, and she bent to reach for it and hand it to him.

"Don't touch that!" he said angrily. His voice was harsh, raw, and grating; he actually reached out and shoved her away from it and she saw the folded empty sleeve at the end of his arm. She stared, open-mouthed with indignation; she had only been trying to help!

"Lew!" Kennard Alton's voice was sharp with reproof; the young man scowled and muttered something like an apology, turning away and scrambling the wrapped dueling swords, or whatever they were, awkwardly into his arms, turning ungraciously to conceal the folded sleeve. Suddenly Dio felt herself shudder, a deep shudder that went all the way to the bone. But why should it affect her so? She had seen wounded men before; surely a missing hand was hardly reason to go about as this one did, with a continual outraged, defensive scowl, a black refusal to meet the eyes of another human being!

With a small shrug she turned away from him. There was no reason to waste thought or courtesy on this graceless fellow whose manners were as ugly as his face! Kennard was asking, "But you are a country-women, *vai domna?* I did not know there were Darkovans on Vainwal."

She dropped him a curtsy. "I am Diotima Ridenow of Serrais, my lord, and I am here with my brothers Lerrys and Geremy, by leave of my brother and my lord."

"I had believed you were destined for the Tower, mistress Dio."

She shook her head and knew the swift color was rising in her face. "It was so ordained when I was a child; I—I was invited to do so. But in the end I chose otherwise."

"Well, well, it is not a vocation for everyone," Kennard said genially, and she contrasted the charm of the father with the sneering scowl of the son, who stood frowning, without the most elementary formal phrases of courtesy! Was it his Terran blood which had robbed him of any vestige of his father's charm: In the name of the Blessed Cassilda, couldn't he even *look* at her? It was the scar tissue at the corner of his mouth which had drawn his face into a sneer; but he had taken it into his very soul, it seemed.

"So Lerrys and Geremy are here? Are they in the hotel?"

"We have a suite here, on the ninetieth floor," Dio said, "but they are in the amphitheater, watching a competition in null-gravity dancing. Lerrys is an amateur of the sport, but he was eliminated early in the competition, when he twisted a muscle in his knee and the medics would not allow him to continue."

Kennard bowed. "Convey them both my compliments," he said, "and my invitation, lady, for the three of you to be my guests tomorrow night, when the finalists perform in the amphitheater here."

"I am sure they will be charmed," Dio said, and took her leave.

She heard the rest of the story that evening from her brothers.

"Lew? That was the traitor," Geremy said. "Went to Aldaran as his father's envoy and sold Kennard out, to join up with those pirates and bandits at Aldaran. His mother's people, after all, and believe me, Aldaran blood isn't to be trusted. They had some kind of super-matrix back there, and young Aldaran was experimenting with it. Burned down half of Caer Donn when the thing got out of hand. I heard Lew switched sides again, joining up with one of those hill-woman bitches, one of Aldaran's bastard daughters, I heard, and sold out Aldaran like he sold out the rest of us; and got his hand burned off. Serves him right, too. But I guess Kennard couldn't admit what a mistake he'd made, after all he went through to get Lew declared his heir. Did they manage to regenerate his hands?" Geremy wriggled the three fingers lost in a duel, years ago, and regenerated, regrown good as new by Empire medics. "No? Maybe old Kennard thought he ought to have something to remember his treachery by."

"No," Lerrys said, "you have it wrong way round, Geremy. Lew's not a bad chap. He did his damnedest, so I heard, to control the fire-image when it got out of hand; and the girl died. I heard he'd married her. One of the monitors of Arilinn told me how hard they worked to save her, and to save Lew's hand; but the girl was too far gone, and Lew—" He shrugged. "Zandru's hells, what a thing to face! Lew was one of the most powerful telepaths they ever had at Arilinn, I heard; but I knew him best in the cadets. Quiet fellow, standoffish if anything; but he had to put up with a lot of trouble from people who felt he had no right to be there, and I think it warped him. Good enough in his own way, though. I liked him, though he was touchy as the devil, and like a monk in some ways." He grinned. "He had so little to do with women that I made the mistake of thinking he was one of my kind, and made him a certain proposal. Oh, he didn't *say* much. But I never asked him *that* again!" Lerrys chuckled. "I'll wager he didn't give you a kind word, either? That's a new thing for you, isn't it, little sister, to meet a man who's not at your feet within a few minutes?" Teasing, he chucked her under the chin.

Dio said pettishly, "I didn't like him. I hope he stays far away from me!"

"Oh, you could do worse," Geremy mused. "After all, he *is* Heir to Alton; and Kennard's old and lame and probably not long for this life. How would you like to be Lady of Alton, sister?"

"No." Lerrys put a protective arm around her. "We can do better than that for Dio. Council will never accept him, after that Sharra business. Ken forced them to accept Lew, but they never accepted his other son, though young Marius is worth two of Lew; and once Kennard's gone, they'll look elsewhere for someone to inherit the Domain of Alton. No, Dio—" Gently, he turned her around to look at him. "I know, there aren't many young men of your caste here, and Lew's Darkovan, and, I suppose, handsome as women think of these things. But stay away from him. Be polite, but keep your distance. I like him, in a way, but he's trouble."

"You needn't worry about that," Dio said. "I can't stand the sight of him."

Yet, inside where it hurt, she felt a pained wonder. She thought of the unknown girl Lew had married, who had died to save them all from the unknown menace of the fire-Goddess. So it had been Lew who

raised the fires, then, and suffered in order to quench
them again? She felt herself shiver in dread and terror.
What must his memories be like, what nightmares
must he live, night and day! Perhaps it was no wonder
that he walked apart, scowling, and could give no one
a kind word or a smile!

Around the ring of the null-gravity field, small
crystalline tables were suspended in midair; their seats
apparently hanging from jeweled chains of stars. Actually, they were all surrounded by energy-nets, so that
even if a diner fell out of his chair (and where the wine
and spirits flowed so freely, some of them did) he
would not fall; but the illusion was breathtaking, bringing a momentary look of wonder and interest even to
Lew's closed face.

Kennard Alton was a generous and gracious host;
he had commanded seats at the very edge of the
gravity ring, and sent for the finest of wines and delicacies; they sat suspended over the starry gulf, watching the gravity-free dancers whirling and spinning across
the void below them, soaring like birds in free flight.
Dio sat at Kennard's right hand, across from Lew,
who, after that first flash of reaction to the illusion of
far space, sat silent, motionless, his scarred and frowning face oblivious; past them galaxies flamed and flowed
and the dancers, half-naked in spangles and loose veils,
flew like exotic birds, soaring on the star-streams. His
right hand—evidently artificial and motionless—lay on
the table, unstirring, encased in a black glove. That
unmoving hand made Dio uncomfortable; the empty
sleeve had seemed somehow more honest.

Only Lerrys was really at ease, greeting Lew with a
touch of real cordiality; but Lew replied only in mono-
syllables, and even Lerrys finally tired of trying to
force conversation, and bent over the gulf of dancers,
studying the finalists with unfeigned envy, comment-
ing on the skills, or lack of them, of the performers.
Dio knew he wished he was among them.

When the winners had been chosen and the prizes

awarded, the gravity was turned on, and the tables drifted in spiral orbits, down to the floor. Music began to play, and dancers moved onto the ballroom surface, glittering and transparent, as if they danced on the same gulf where the gravity-dancers had whirled in free-soaring flight. Lew murmured something about leaving, but Kennard called for more drinks, and under the confusion Dio heard him sharply reprimanding Lew; all she heard was, " Damn it, you can't hide forever!"

Lerrys rose and slipped away; a little later they saw him moving onto the dance floor with an exquisite woman whom they recognized as one of the dance performers, in starry blue now covered with drifts of silvery gauze.

"How well he dances," Kennard said genially. "A pity he had to withdraw from the competition, though it hardly seems fitting to a Comyn lord—"

"Comyn means nothing here," Geremy laughed, "and that is why we come here, to do things unbefitting Comyn dignity on our own world! Come, wasn't that why *you* came here, kinsman, for adventures which might be unseemly or worse in the Domains?"

Dio was watching the dancers, envious. Perhaps Lerrys would come back and dance with her. But she saw that the woman dancer, perhaps recognizing him as the finalist who had had to withdraw, perhaps simply impressed by his dancing, had carried him off to talk to the other finalists, and now Lerrys was talking intimately with a young, handsome lad, his red head bent close to the boy's. The dancer was clad only in nets of gilt thread and the barest possible gilt patches for decency; his hair was dyed a striking blue. It was doubtful, now, that he remembered that there were such creatures as women in existence, far less sisters.

Kennard, watching the direction of her glance, said, "I have not been able to dance for many years, Lady Dio, or I would give myself the pleasure; I can see you are longing to be with the dancers. And it is small pleasure to a young maiden to dance with her brothers, as I have heard my foster sisters and now my foster daughters complain. But you are too young to dance in such a public place as this except with kinsmen—"

Dio tossed her head, setting her fair curls flying. She said, "I do as I please, Lord Alton, here on Vainwal!" Then, seized by some imp of boredom or mischief, she turned to the scowling Lew. "Will you dance with me, cousin?"

He raised his head and glared at her; Dio quailed, wishing she had not started this. This was no one to flirt with, to exchange light pleasantries! He gave her a glance of pure hate; but even so, he was shoving back his chair.

"As you wish, cousin. If you will do me the kindness." His harsh voice was amiable, even friendly—if you did not see the look deep in his eyes. It hardened Dio's resolve. Damn him, this was arrogance! He was not the only crippled man in the universe, nor on this planet, nor even in the room—his own father could hardly put one foot before the other, and made no bones about saying so!

He held out his good arm to her. "You will have to forgive me if I step on your feet. I have not danced in many years. It is not a skill much valued on Terra, and my years there were spent mostly in different hospitals."

He did not step on her feet, though. He moved as lightly as a drift of wind, and after a very little time, Dio gave herself up to the music and the pure enjoyment of the dance. They were well-matched, and after a few minutes of moving together in the perfect matching of the rhythm—she knew she was dancing with a Darkovan, nowhere else in the civilized Empire did any people place so much emphasis on dancing as did the Darkovan culture—she raised her eyes and smiled at him, lowering mental barriers in a way any Comyn would have known to be an invitation for the telepathic touch of their caste.

For the barest instant, his eyes met hers, and she sensed him reach out to her, as if by instinct, attuned to the sympathy between their moving bodies; then the barriers slammed down between them, hard, leaving her breathless with the shock of the rebuff. It took all her self-control not to cry out with the pain of that rebuff, but she would not give him the satisfaction of knowing he had hurt her; she simply smiled and went on dancing at the ordinary level, enjoying the movement, the sense of being perfectly in tune with his steps.

But, inside, she was dazed and bewildered. What had she done to merit such a rebuff? Nothing, certainly; her gesture had been bold, indeed, but not indecently so. He was, after all, a man of her own caste, a telepath and a kinsman. So, since she had done nothing to deserve it, it must have been made in response to his own inner turmoil, and had nothing to do with her at all.

So, she went on smiling, and when the dance slowed to a softer, more romantic movement, and the dancers around them were moving closer, cheek against cheek, almost embracing, she moved instinctively toward him. For an instant he went stiff and she wondered if he would violently reject the physical touch, too; but she moved instinctively toward him, and after a moment his arm tightened around her. Through the very touch, though his mental defenses were locked tight, she sensed the starved hunger in him. How long had it been, she wondered, since he had touched a woman? Far too long, she was sure of that. The telepath Comyn, particularly the Alton and Ridenow, were well-known for their fastidiousness in such matters; they were hypersensitive, much too aware of the random or casual touch. Not many of the Comyn were capable of tolerating casual love affairs.

The dance slowed, the lights dimming, and she sensed that all around them couples were moving into one another's arms. A miasma of sensuality seemed to lie over the whole room, almost visible. Lew held her tight against him, bending his head, and she raised her face to him, again inviting the touch he had rebuffed.

He did not lower his mental barriers, but their lips touched, and Dio felt a slow, drowsy excitement climbing in her and they kissed. When they drew apart his lips smiled, but there was still a great sadness behind his eyes.

He looked around the great room filled with dancing couples, many now entwined in close embrace. "This—this is decadent," he said.

She smiled, snuggling closer to him. "Surely no more than midsummer-festival in the streets of Thendara. I am not too young to know what goes on when the moons have set."

His harsh voice sounded gentler than usual. "Your brothers would call me out and challenge me to a duel."

She lifted her chin angrily. "We are not in the Kilghard Hills! Lew Alton, I do not allow any other person, even a brother, to tell me what I may or may not do! If my brothers disapprove of my conduct, they may come to me for an accounting of it, not to you!"

He laughed, and with his good hand touched the feathery edges of her short fair hair. It was, she thought, a beautiful hand, sensitive and strong without being over-delicate. "So you have cut your hair and taken on the independence of a Free Amazon? Have you taken their oath too, cousin?"

"No," she said, snuggling close to him again. "I am too fond of men ever to do that." When he smiled, she thought he was very handsome; even the scar that drew his lip tight only gave his smile a little more irony and warmth.

They danced together much of the evening, and before they parted, agreed to meet the next day for a hunt in the great hunting preserves of Vainwal. When they said goodnight, Kennard was smiling benevolently, but Geremy was sullen and brooding, and when the three of them were alone in their luxurious suite, he demanded wrathfully, "Why did you do that? I told you, stay away from Lew! We don't really want an entanglement with that branch of the Altons!"

"How dare you try and tell me who I can dance with? Or, if I choose, who I can make love with? I don't censure your choice of entertainers and singing-women and whores, do I?"

"You are a lady of the Comyn. When you behave so blatantly—"

"Hold your tongue!" Dio flared at him, "You are insulting! I dance one evening with a man of my own caste, because my brothers left me no one else to dance with, and you already have me bedded down with him! Geremy, I will tell you once again, I do what I wish, and neither you nor any other man can stop me!"

"Lerrys," Geremy appealed, "can you reason with her?"

But Lerrys stood regarding his sister with admiration. "That's the spirit, Dio. What is the good of being in an alien world in a civilized Empire if you keep the provincial spirit and customs of your backwater? Do what you wish, Dio. Geremy, let her alone!"

Geremy shook his head, laughing. "You two! Always one in mind, as if you had been born twins!"

"Certainly," Lerrys said. "Why, do you think, am I a lover of men? Because, to my ill-fortune, the only woman I have ever known with a man's spirit and a man's strength is my own sister." He kissed her, laughing. "Enjoy yourself, *breda*, but don't get hurt. He may have been in a romantic mood tonight, but he could be savage, I suspect."

"No." Suddenly Geremy was sober. "This is no joke. I don't want you to see him again, Diotima. One evening, perhaps to do courtesy to our kinsman; I grant you that, and I am sorry if I implied there was more than courtesy. But no more, Dio, not again. There are enough men on this world, to dance with, flirt with, hunt with—yes, damn it, and bed down with if that should be your will! But let Kennard Alton's damned half-caste bastard alone—do you hear? I tell you, if you disobey me, I shall make you both regret it."

"Now," said Lerrys, still laughing, as Dio tossed her head in defiance, "You have made it sure that she will see him again, Geremy; you have all but spread the bridal bed for them! Don't you know that no man can forbid Dio to do anything?"

In the hunting preserve the next day, they chose horses, and the great hawks not unlike the *verrin* hawks of the Kilghard Hills. Lew was smiling and good-natured, but she sensed that he was just a little shocked, too, at her riding breeches and boots. "So you are the Amazon you said you were not, after all?" he teased, and she smiled back into his eyes and said, "No; I told you why I could never be an Amazon, and the more I see of you, the more certain I am of that."

He was a good rider, although the lifeless artificial hand seemed to be very much in his way, and she wondered if he could not, after all, have managed better one-handed. She would have thought that even a metal hook would have been better, if they could not, for some reason, regrow the hand. But perhaps he was too proud for that, or feared she would think it ugly. He carried the hawk on a special saddle-block, as women did, rather than holding it on his wrist as most Darkovan men chose to do, and when she looked at it he colored and turned angrily away, swearing under his breath. Again Dio thought, with that sudden anger which he seemed able to rouse in her so swiftly, *Why is he so sensitive and self-indulgent about it? What arrogance! Does he think I really care whether he has two hands, or one, or three?*

The hunting preserve had been carefully landscaped and terraformed to beautiful and varied scenery, low hills which did not strain the horses, smooth plains, a variety of wildlife, colorful vegetation from a dozen worlds. But as they rode she heard him sigh a little. He said, just loud enough for her to hear, "It is beautiful here. But I wish I were in the Domains. The sun here is—is wrong, somehow.

"Are you homesick, Lew?" she asked.

He tightened his mouth. "Yes. Sometimes," he said, but he had slammed down his defenses again, and Dio turned back to attend to the hawk on her saddle.

The preserve was stocked with a variety of game, large and small; after a time they let their hawks loose: Dio watched in delight as hers soared high, wheeled in midair and set off on long strong wings after a flight of small white birds, directly overhead. Lew's hawk came after, swiftly stooping, striking at one of the small birds, seizing it in midair. The white bird struggled pitifully, with a long eerie scream. Dio had hunted with hawks all her life, and watched with interest, but as drops of blood fell from the dying bird, spattering them, she realized that Lew's face was drawn with horror; he looked paralyzed.

"Lew, what is the matter?"

He said, his voice strained and hoarse, "That sound—I cannot bear it—" and flung up his two arms over his eyes, the black-gloved artificial hand striking his forehead hard and awkwardly; searing, he wrenched it off his wrist and flung it to the ground under his horse's hooves.

"No, it's not pretty," he mocked, in a rage, "like blood, and death, and the screams of dying things! If you take pleasure in them, so much the worse for you, lady! Take pleasure, then, in this!" He held up the hideously scarred bare stump, shaking it in fury at her; then he wheeled his horse, jerking at the reins with his good hand, and riding off as if all the devils in all the hells were chasing him.

Dio stared in dismay; then, forgetting the hawks, set after him at a breakneck gallop. After a time they came abreast; he was fighting the reins with his one hand, struggling to rein in the mount; but as she watched in horror, he lost control and was tossed out of his saddle, coming heavily to the ground to lie there senseless and stunned.

Dio slid from her horse and knelt at his side. He had been knocked unconscious, but while she was trying to decide if she should go bring help, he opened his eyes and looked at her without recognition.

"It's all right," she said, "the horse threw you. Can you sit up?"

"Yes, of course." He sat up awkwardly, as if the stump pained him, wincing; then saw it, colored and tried to thrust it quickly into a fold of his riding cloak, out of sight.

"It's all right, Lew, you don't have to hide. . . ."

He turned his face away from her, and the taut scar tissue drew up his mouth as if he were ready to cry. "Oh, God, I'm sorry, I didn't mean . . ."

"What was it, Lew? Why did you lose your temper like that?"

Dazed, he shook his head. "I—I cannot bear the sight of blood, now, or the thought of some small helpless thing dying for my pleasure," he said, and his voice sounded exhausted. "I heard the little white bird crying, and I saw the blood, and I remembered—Oh God, I remembered—Dio, go away, don't, don't, in the name of the merciful Evanda, Dio, don't—" His face twisted again and he was weeping, his face ugly and crumpled, turning away so that she would not see, trying to choke back the hoarse painful sobs. "I have seen . . . too much pain . . . Dio, don't . . . ."

She put out her arms, folded him in them, drawing him against her breast. He resisted, for a moment, frantically, then let the woman draw him close. She was crying, too.

"I never thought," she whispered. "Death in hunting, I am so used to it, it never seemed quite real to me. Lew, what was it, who died, what happened, what did it make you remember?"

"She was my wife," he said hoarsely, "my wife, bearing our child. And she died, died horribly in Sharra's fires—Dio, don't touch me, somehow I hurt everyone I touch, go away before I hurt you too—I don't want you to be hurt."

She said, "It's too late for that," and he raised his one hand to her face, touching her eyes. She felt him slam down his defenses again, but this time she knew it was not the rebuff she feared, only the defense of a man unimaginably hurt, a man who could endure no more.

"Were you hurt?" he said, his hand lingering on her wet eyes, on her cheeks. "There is blood on your face."

"It's the bird's blood. It's on you too," she said, and wiped it away. He took her hand in his and pressed the fingertips to his lips. Somehow, the gesture made her want to cry again, and she asked, "Were you hurt when you fell?"

"Not much." He sat up, testing his muscles. They taught me, in the Empire hospital on Terra, how to fall without hurting myself, when I was . . . before this healed." Uneasily, he moved the stump. "I can't get used to the damned hand, though. I can do better one-handed."

"Why do you wear it, then? Do you think I would care?"

His face was bleak. "Father would care. He thinks when I wear the empty sleeve I am making a show of my lameness. He hates his own so much. I would rather not—not flaunt mine at him."

Dio thought swiftly, then decided what she could say. "It seems to me that you are a grown man, and need not consult your father about your own arm and hand."

He sighed, nodded. "But he has been so good to me, never reproached me for these years of exile, and the way in which his own plans had been brought to nothing. I do not want to distress him." He rose, went to collect the grotesque, lifeless thing in its black glove. He put it away in the saddlebag, and fumbled one-handed to pin the sleeve over the stump. She started, matter-of-factly, to offer help, then decided it was too soon for that. He looked into the sky and said, "I suppose the hawks are gone beyond recall and we will be charged for losing them."

"No." She blew the silver whistle around her neck. "They are birds with brains modified, so they cannot choose but come to the whistle . . . see?" She pointed as they spiraled down and landed, standing patiently on the saddle blocks, awaiting their hoods. "Their instinct for freedom has been burnt out."

"They are like some men I know" said Lew, slipping the hood on his hawk. But neither of them moved to mount. Dio hesitated, then decided he had probably had enough of politely averted eyes and pretenses of courteous unawareness. "Do you need help to mount? Can I help you, or shall I fetch someone who can?"

"Thank you, but I can manage, though it looks awkward." Again, suddenly he smiled, and his ugly scarred face seemed handsome again to her. "How did you know it would do me good to hear that said?"

"I have always been very strong. But I think if I were hurt I would not want people to pretend everything was exactly the same and perfectly normal. Please don't ever pretend with me, Lew." And then she asked, "I have wanted to know. Don't tell me if you don't want to, I'm not trying to pry. But—Geremy lost three fingers in a duel. The Terran medics re-grew them, just as they were before. Why did they not do that with your hand?"

"They—tried," he said. "Twice. Then I could—could bear no more. Somehow, the pattern of the cells—you are not a matrix technician, are you? I wonder if you can understand . . . the pattern of the cells, the—the knowledge in the cells, which makes a hand a hand, and not a finger or an eye or a bird's wing, had been damaged beyond renewing, and what grew on my wrist was—was a horror. I—when I woke from the drugs, just once, and saw, I—I screamed my throat raw; my voice will never be right again, either; for half a year I could only whisper. I was not myself for—for years. I can live with it, now, because I must. I can face the knowledge that I am—am maimed. What I cannot face," he said with sudden violence, "is my father's pretense that I am—am whole!"

Dio felt sudden violent anger. So even the father could not face the reality of what had happened to his son! Could not even face the son's need to face what had happened to him. She said, voice low, "Don't ever think you have to pretend to me, Lew Alton."

He seized her in a rough grip, dragged her close. It was hardly an embrace. He said, in that hoarse voice, "Girl, do you know what you are saying? You can't know!"

She said, shaking, "If you can endure what you have endured, I can bear to know what it is that you have had to suffer. Lew, let me prove that to you!"

In the back of her mind she wondered, *why am I doing this?* But she knew that when they had come into each other's arms on the dancing floor, last night, even behind the barriers of Lew's locked defenses, their bodies had somehow made a pact. Barricade themselves from one another as they would, something in each of them had reached out to the other and accepted what the other was, wholly and forever.

She raised her face to him. His arms went around her in grateful surprise, and he murmured, still holding back, "But you are so young, *chiya,* you can't know . . . I should be horsewhipped for this, but it has been so long, so long . . ." and she knew he was not speaking of the obvious. She felt herself dissolve in total awareness of him, the receding barriers, the memory of pain and horror, the starved sexuality, the ordeals which had gone on beyond human endurance; the black and encompassing horror of guilt, of a loved one dead, self-knowledge, blame, mutilation, guilt at living on when the beloved was dead. . . .

In a desperate, hungering endurance, she clasped him closer, knowing it was this for which he had longed most, someone who could touch him without pretense, accept his suffering, love him nevertheless. For an instant she saw herself reflected in his mind, not recognizing, glowing with tenderness, warm, woman, and for a moment loved herself for what she had become to him; then the contact broke and receded like a tide, leaving her awed, shaken, leaving tears and tenderness that could never grow less. Only then did he kiss her; and as she laughed and accepted the kiss she said in a whisper, "Geremy was right."

"What, Dio?"

"Nothing," she said, light-hearted with relief. "Come, love, the hawks are restless and we must get them back to their mews. We will have our fee refunded because we have claimed no kill, but I for one have had full value for my hunt. I have captured what I most wanted."

"And what is that?" he asked, teasing, but she knew he did not need an answer. He was not touching her now, as they mounted, but she knew that somehow they were still touching, still embraced.

He flung up his empty sleeve in a laughing gesture. "Come on," he called, "we may as well have a ride, at least! Which of us will be first at the stables?"

And he was off, Dio after him, laughing. She knew as well as he how this day would end. And it was only the beginning of a long season on Vainwal.

It would be a beautiful summer.

(1980)

DAW

DAW PRESENTS THESE BESTSELLERS BY
MARION ZIMMER BRADLEY

THE DARKOVER NOVELS

The Founding

☐ DARKOVER LANDFALL   UE2234—$3.95

The Ages of Chaos

☐ HAWKMISTRESS!   UE2239—$3.95
☐ STORMQUEEN!   UE2092—$3.95

The Hundred Kingdoms

☐ TWO TO CONQUER   UE2174—$3.50

The Renunciates (Free Amazons)

☐ THE SHATTERED CHAIN   UE1961—$3.50
☐ THENDARA HOUSE   UE2240—$3.95
☐ CITY OF SORCERY   UE2122—$3.95

Against the Terrans: The First Age

☐ THE SPELL SWORD   UE2091—$2.50
☐ THE FORBIDDEN TOWER   UE2235—$3.95

Against the Terrans: The Second Age

☐ THE HERITAGE OF HASTUR   UE2079—$3.95
☐ SHARRA'S EXILE   UE1988—$3.95

THE DARKOVER ANTHOLOGIES
with The Friends of Darkover

☐ THE KEEPER'S PRICE   UE2236—$3.95
☐ SWORD OF CHAOS   UE2172—$3.50
☐ FREE AMAZONS OF DARKOVER   UE2096—$3.50
☐ THE OTHER SIDE OF THE MIRROR   UE2185—$3.50
☐ RED SUN OF DARKOVER   UE2230—$3.95

DAW

DAW PRESENTS THESE BESTSELLERS BY
MARION ZIMMER BRADLEY

NON-DARKOVER NOVELS

- ☐ **HUNTERS OF THE RED MOON**   (UE1968—$2.95)
- ☐ **THE SURVIVORS**   (UE1861—$2.95)
  (With Paul Edwin Zimmer)
- ☐ **WARRIOR WOMAN**   (UE2253—$3.50)

NON-DARKOVER ANTHOLOGIES

- ☐ **GREYHAVEN**   (UE1985—$2.75)
- ☐ **SWORD AND SORCERESS**   (UE1928—$2.95)
- ☐ **SWORD AND SORCERESS II**   (UE2041—$2.95)
- ☐ **SWORD AND SORCERESS III**   (UE2141—$3.50)
- ☐ **SWORD AND SORCERESS IV**   (UE2210—$3.50)
- ☐ **SWORD AND SORCERESS V**
  (August 1988)   (UE2288—$3.50)

COLLECTIONS

- ☐ **LYTHANDE** (with Vonda N. McIntyre)   (UE2154—$3.50)
- ☐ **THE BEST OF MARION ZIMMER BRADLEY** (edited
  by Martin H. Greenberg, April 1988)   (UE2268—$3.95)

NEW AMERICAN LIBRARY
P.O. Box 999, Bergenfield, New Jersey 07621

Please send me the DAW BOOKS I have checked above. I am enclosing $_____
(check or money order—no currency or C.O.D.'s). Please include the list price plus
$1.00 per order to cover handling costs. Prices and numbers are subject to change
without notice.

Name _____

Address _____

City _____ State _____ Zip _____
Please allow 4-6 weeks for delivery.

DAW
A GALAXY OF SCIENCE FICTION STARS